DESIRE'S EMBRACE

Alexandria could feel the iron grip of his hands on her shoulders even through the thickness of the coat she wore. He dragged her against him without ceremony and began kissing her—her ears, her cheeks, her eyes, and finally, just as she thought she would go mad with impatience, her mouth.

"I've been starved for this," Rhys rasped. "For you . . ." As they sank onto the blanket, he said, "Lord, we can't do this—it's too cold. Alex, we've got to stop."

All the while his hands were slipping beneath her coat, stroking her shoulde___ _____ ____ heavy wool garment back___ _____ _____ from the cumbersome _____ _____ his neck, drawing him ___ _____ _____ _ish kisses.

"No, don't s___ _____ _____ l the cold at all."

And it was t___ _____ ____ hands were arousing the most w_____ warmth within her, dispelling the chill of the October day. Each place he touched her seemed to glow with a slowly spreading fire. . . .

Northern Fire, Northern Star

SCOTNEY ST. JAMES

ZEBRA BOOKS
KENSINGTON PUBLISHING CORP.

ZEBRA BOOKS

are published by

Kensington Publishing Corp.
475 Park Avenue South
New York, NY 10016

First printing: September, 1990

Printed in the United States of America

This book is dedicated to my parents, Edward ("Buck") and Frances Faulkner, with my love, respect, and gratitude. They have given me membership in a wonderful and unique family, unqualified love and encouragement, a penchant for laughter and adventure, and a lifetime of special memories. There is no way to thank them enough. . . .

L.V.

Chapter One

"Blast my hairy hide! The brides are here at last! Ya-hoo!"
The jubilant shout echoed through the fort to be met by a rousing masculine cheer.

Rhys Morgan was sprawled in a chair, deep in conversation with another man, when he heard the news. A backwoodsman stuck his head around the corner, smiling broadly.

"The women are here, Rhys. The sentry saw 'em coming up the river."

Morgan immediately sprang to his feet. "Go round up the men," he ordered. "I'll get down to the docks to meet the brigade."

"Remember," the man warned, "I already spoke for the redhead."

When he had gone, Rhys turned to Dr. McLoughlin. "Coming with me?"

"You bet. I wouldn't miss it for anything. You

7

know, this is a hell of a time for the brides to arrive. The fort is full of males who haven't seen a white woman in years."

"Exactly why my men are here to meet them. We didn't pay their passage from Montreal just to have them stolen from under our noses."

"Well, considering the circumstances, you'd better get on with the weddings as soon as possible. A ship-load of gold couldn't have stirred more interest—or envy. To tell the truth, I'm anxious to meet these intrepid females myself."

Rhys suddenly grinned. "I have a feeling it would take a rare breed of woman to willingly leave the city behind to travel into the wilderness. I'll wager the chaperons had their hands full."

"Chaperons, eh?"

"Yes, a missionary and his wife. And, of course, the doctor recruited for the settlement."

McLoughlin chuckled. "Your brides-to-be just spent four months in the company of missionaries? That will hardly prepare them for this place."

"I know. But maybe the good doctor had a chance to forewarn them about Rendezvous."

"And they may not find it so shocking. After all, they did agree to come out here to marry men they've never seen, so they can't be too timid."

"Well, whether they're timid or bold will be the worry of their husbands-to-be. My only responsibility is to get them to Sabaskong Falls and to provide for their medical needs."

"Aye, the services of a doctor will be indispensable in about nine months, I suspect."

Rhys Morgan sighed. "No doubt. Lord, I tried to

talk the men out of this, but they'd have it no other way."

"Not everyone is as cynical about marriage as you are, Rhys."

"No, and it's a damned shame. But once I knew their minds were made up, I quit arguing. Though I did insist they hire a doctor. God knows I didn't want to find myself delivering their babies!"

"You've hardly the patience to be a midwife," agreed McLoughlin. As they walked, he brought up another question. "How did you manage to acquire this much-needed doctor?"

"I directed a message to my attorney in Montreal last fall, asking him to attend to the details. He sent a reply with the first brigades that came through here this spring, saying he'd found women willing to make the journey but the only doctor who expressed interest was an elderly fellow. It wasn't what we'd hoped for, but we had no choice. Doctors who will undertake risks are scarce these days." Morgan cast a sideways glance at his friend. "You ought to know, since you've turned down similar jobs yourself."

McLoughlin's laugh boomed. "I have no appetite for starting a new practice in an isolated place. You'll do much better with some crusty old sawbones who'll grouch and grumble and intimidate everyone with his years of experience."

"Think so?" Rhys gave a halfhearted smile. "Well, that's probably what we'll get if he wasn't too ancient or feeble to survive the trip out."

As they approached the waterfront, a wave of giggles swept through a cluster of Indian girls when they caught sight of Morgan and several of them boldly called out his name: "Reese! Re-eese!" He ignored them, his long swinging steps taking him onto the wharf where two men with broad grins were helping the newcomers ashore. The ladies stood huddled together, looking shy and uncertain. Besides the missionaries who had acted as chaperons, there were eight women and two children.

Rhys addressed the elderly gentleman clad in black. "Reverend Rosswell? Welcome to Fort Kaministiquia." He extended his hand. "I'm Rhys Morgan, the . . . uh, spokesman for the men from Sabaskong Falls."

"How do you do?" returned the reverend. "This is my wife, Ellie. And these are the ladies bound for your little settlement."

One or two of the women nodded and smiled, but for the most part the new arrivals were staring at the scene around them with what appeared to be a mixture of fear and disbelief.

The last passenger to alight from the canoes, Alexandria MacKenzie shifted the heavy, hinged basket she carried but did not release her firm grip on its handle. Gray eyes wide with excitement, she gazed at the colorful mass of people swarming down the hill toward the wharf to meet the canoe brigade that had just landed.

Men in buckskins hastened through the log gates of the fort to join the voyageurs and Indians who poured from the tents and tepees along the riverbank. Mixed among them like brilliant flowers were the young Chippewa girls wearing red dresses and chattering in a strange combination of Indian, French, and broken English. A group of nearly naked children scampered through the crowd, followed by a pack of barking dogs.

Neither Alexandria nor any of the other women had ever witnessed such a sight. After four months of travel through quiet northern lakes flanked by endless forests, the noise and confusion were daunting, to say the least. With a quick glance at her companions, Alexandria realized she was the only one looking upon the situation with interest or excitement. Judging from their tense, unsmiling faces, there was not a shred of anticipation left among the eight of them. Even the children, huddled behind their mother's skirts, seemed fearful. Because the others were so obviously doubting their decision to make this trip, Alex feared it must be some serious flaw in her nature that caused her to feel such an exhilarating sense of adventure. Behind her, the canoemen began unloading trunks and boxes, and, with a distracted air, she turned to direct them.

"Please be careful with that one," she said. "The contents are extremely fragile."

"We remember, *mademoiselle*." Baptiste, a young French-Canadian voyageur, grinned. "You have announced this fact every day of our journey."

"Oh . . . sorry."

When she looked back at the women, her eyes were unexpectedly drawn to the commanding figure of the man talking to them. Though he was surrounded by half a dozen others, there was something about him — the way he moved with easy self-assurance, perhaps — that marked him as someone to be reckoned with.

He was dressed as a backwoodsman, in buckskins, the fringed shirt accentuating the breadth of chest and shoulder, the trousers clinging to narrow hips and long legs. His knee-high moccasins were beaded and

11

fringed in the Indian style.

He had a chiseled, hollow-cheeked face, decidedly handsome but not soft in any way. His head was bared to the July sun, displaying thick black hair shagging just over his collar, with wings of obviously premature silver sweeping backward at each temple. He wore a full, black moustache that framed, but did not conceal, a firm and unyielding mouth.

As she came closer, Alexandria thought he looked much younger. Younger but no less formidable.

"Did you have a good trip, Reverend?" the man in buckskins was asking.

His voice was quiet, deep, with a gravelly texture that sent a tiny chill up the back of Alexandria's neck. She found it strange that an apparently well-educated man would seem so at home in such crude surroundings. It made her curious about him, and suddenly she found herself wondering which of the women he had selected as his wife.

"Yes, it was a pleasant enough journey. And I'm relieved that your prospective brides have all arrived safe and sound."

"You had a couple of extra passengers, I see," Morgan commented, grinning at the small children clinging to their mother's skirts. "We weren't prepared for them, but there's no harm done, I suppose."

The woman heaved an audible sigh of relief as she realized he intended to be good-natured about the unexpected appearance of her offspring.

Morgan's blue-gray eyes continued to scan the silent group; then he nodded in satisfaction. "Welcome to the wilderness, ladies."

There was a brief murmur of voices, which swiftly

faded away.

As if sensing their apprehension, Morgan spoke more kindly. "I know you must be tired, so my men and I will escort you to your quarters. You can rest before the get-acquainted dinner this evening."

"Uh, Mr. Morgan." The black-coated minister spoke hesitantly, nervously clearing his throat. "About our other passenger. . . ."

Morgan turned back to the man, fixing him with a frown. "Lord, yes, the doctor . . . has something happened to him?"

Reverend Rosswell's bony Adam's apple bobbed fitfully above his limp white collar. "Oh, no, nothing has happened. It's just that . . . well, I feel I should mention one small thing that may . . . uh, surprise you somewhat."

A grim expression settled on Rhys's face. "Maybe you'd better tell me what it is you're talking about."

Alexandria deemed it time to step forward. "How do you do, Mr. Morgan?" she said. "I'm Alexandria MacKenzie . . . please call me Alex. I'm the new doctor."

Rhys Morgan stared at her with a steely glint in his eye. "This had better, by God, be a joke."

"Oh, it's no joke," affirmed the reverend. "I knew you wouldn't be at all pleased."

"To say I am displeased is an incredible understatement, Reverend."

Rhys observed the slight figure dressed in a drab brown dress and sunbonnet with something akin to disgust. Hell, she didn't look strong enough to empty a bedpan, let alone perform the duties of a midwife. How could she have the effrontery to claim she was a

13

a doctor?

"Women are not doctors," he said flatly.

"I am," Alexandria replied, untying the ribbons of her bonnet and pulling it off her head. She looked serene, as if completely unaware of the outrageousness of the statement she had just made.

"Impossible."

"I assure you, it's not."

"Do you have any written substantiation of your claim?" he demanded. "Papers from the university, for instance?"

"I think you will find my credentials adequate," she said with dignity. "I served an apprenticeship with my grandfather, a well-known physician in Montreal. Actually, he . . ."

As the river breeze lifted strands of her long hair and flung them across her face, the man's eyes narrowed in speculation and she realized he was no longer listening. She watched, fascinated, as his blue-gray eyes began to change, to assume the green hue of the trees lining the bank of the river — to glow with a new, intense expression.

Rhys Morgan found himself distracted by the beauty that had been revealed by the removal of her sunbonnet. Vaguely aware that her very appearance had brought a hush to the waiting crowd, he let his gaze move over her with slow deliberation. The points of light created by sunshine striking the mass of red-gold hair spilling down her back were dazzling, surrounding her head in a glorious aura. Expressive rain gray eyes dominated a perfectly shaped face, made exotic by high, sculptured cheekbones and a generous, sensual mouth — a face that was saved from haughti-

14

ness by a sprinkle of faint freckles across a straight nose. Despite himself, Morgan found he was appreciating her feminine grace, and that fact irritated him more than ever.

"What in God's name possessed Tuttle to hire a woman? Did you somehow misrepresent yourself?"

All the way from Montreal, Alexandria had rehearsed several blatant falsehoods. Now, in the face of Morgan's anger, she decided the simple truth would serve her best. "In the beginning, it was my grandfather whom Mr. Tuttle employed. But you see, he . . . he passed away last January." For an instant, the girl bowed her head, as though still unused to the painful reality. Then, squaring her shoulders, she went on. "After a great deal of thought, I decided not to notify the attorney but to take Grandfather's place myself."

"However," Rhys said coldly, "that was not your decision to make."

"You wanted a doctor," she pointed out, "and Mr. Tuttle had already mentioned there were no other applicants. Besides, my qualifications are excellent."

"Tell me this, did you ever meet with Tuttle?" Rhys's tone was sharply suspicious.

"Not until the morning of departure," Alexandria answered.

"And did he fail to notice you were a female?"

"Well . . . no."

"Actually, Mr. Tuttle seemed very taken aback by Miss MacKenzie's appearance," interjected Rosswell, "but, by then, it was a bit late to remedy the situation."

"And if I know Tuttle he probably thought it a

15

damned funny joke." Morgan uttered an expletive that was short and vehement, causing Mrs. Rosswell to gasp in shock.

"Please, Mr. Morgan," admonished the minister. "There is no need for profanity. I believe we need to find someplace more private to discuss this matter. . . ."

"Oh, yes," agreed Morgan, "you can be sure we'll discuss it. We'll discuss my intention to send Miss Alexandria MacKenzie right back to Montreal with the first brigade that leaves this fort."

"You can't do that," Alex cried. "I have been promised employment as a doctor . . . and I won't go back to the city."

"Your grandfather was promised the job," he stated. "Since you are here under false pretenses, we don't have to honor the contract."

"If you'd only permit me to explain," she said, "I am certain I can convince you of my capabilities."

"Frankly, Miss MacKenzie, I'm not the least bit interested in your . . . capabilities. Sabaskong Falls needs a doctor with a certain amount of brawn and brains. Your lack of brawn is apparent, and as for brains . . . well, at this moment I think it might be wisest if I refrain from comment."

Alexandria felt a tide of choking anger rising within her. "I have encountered such ignorant prejudice in the city," she spat out, "but I thought it would be different here. I expected that people would be judged by their merit, not by their gender."

Dr. McLoughlin, who had been watching the encounter with amused interest, now spoke up. "I think it might be to your benefit to avoid a hasty decision in the matter, Rhys. After all, you do need a doctor in your settlement—where are you going to find a replacement at this late date? Maybe you owe the lady the opportunity to explain herself."

"Yes," Alex chimed in, "I would like to set matters straight."

"The time for that was before the canoes left Montreal. Oh, all right." Morgan sighed. "We can talk about it—but don't expect me to change my mind." He turned his back on her and gestured to one of the men standing behind him, a burly, dark-haired fellow. "Ladies, this is John Hay, Sabaskong's blacksmith. He will lead you to the rooms that have been prepared for your stay here at Kaministiquia."

Rhys Morgan spoke to the rest of his men concerning the transportation of trunks and luggage into the fort.

Then, shouldering one of the wooden chests himself, he strode away without another glance in Alexandria's direction.

She watched him go, aware of the stubborn set of his jaw but equally aware of her own determination to continue with her plan to become the first female doctor in the wilderness. She sighed wearily. Or anywhere else that she knew of. For the thousandth time in her young life, she wished nature had simplified things by allowing her to be born a man.

Baptiste unloaded a battered black leather case onto the dock, and Alex hurried over to retrieve it. Sadly, she recalled the many times she had seen her grandfather carrying the satchel. But, she reminded herself, that was in the past. Now the bag was hers and she rarely let it out of her sight, for it contained some of

17

her most important medical supplies.

She had just started down the wharf when a bearded man stepped in front of her, blocking her way. "Well, well," he said in a raspy voice. "I do believe you're the prettiest little sawbones I ever saw. You can cure my itch any time you're ready."

Repelled by the rank odor of his unwashed body and greasy clothing, Alex quickly moved away, shifting the basket she still held before her in instinctive protection. "Get out of my way," she ordered in a calm voice.

Sensing her revulsion, the man laughed harshly and took a long drink from the tin cup he carried. The smell of strong spirits wafted toward her.

"Hell, you're a damned partic'lar female, considerin' you and them others came all this way alone with those Frenchies. Looks to me like you could at least be civil."

He reached out, but she dodged his gnarled hand and turned her back, directing a polite farewell to the voyageurs unloading the canoes.

Rhys Morgan had watched the entire exchange from the gates of the fort. When he saw the man make a grab for Alexandria, he assumed it was going to be up to him to rescue her and unshouldered the chest he carried, dumping it onto the sand. He had already started toward them when he realized the girl had somehow thwarted the drunk's advances, leaving him standing to one side, a stupid expression on his whiskery face. For an instant, Morgan feared the expression on his own face was just as dumbfounded.

Unconcerned by the incident, Alexandria picked up the leather satchel and started down the dock, moving slowly beneath its weight and that of the basket she also carried. She came to an abrupt halt before Rhys Morgan, who was still staring at her.

"Why didn't you go with the others?" he questioned. "Lingering on the docks while men like that are around can be dangerous."

"You needn't worry about me. I can take care of myself."

"Good Lord, woman," he snapped, "you must be insane to think you can take care of yourself out here! This is wilderness—Indian country. You should have stayed in your parlor in Montreal."

She bristled instantly. "You needn't shout."

"I'm not shouting," he shouted.

At that moment there was a faint scratching from inside the basket Alex held and the hinged top lifted slightly. Setting down the black leather case, she raised the lid at one end to reveal two softly furred ears and a pair of inquisitive sea green eyes.

"It's all right, Nasturtium," Alexandria murmured, stroking the animal's head. "Don't be afraid."

Morgan almost choked. "What the . . . ?"

At the sound of his voice, the animal hissed angrily.

Alex gently closed the lid and cast a disdainful glance at the man. "Your loud tone frightened her."

Rhys looked incredulous. "Was that a cat?"

"Yes," she replied defensively.

"My God, it's worse than I thought," he said aloud. "Tuttle must be getting feebleminded. What other reason could he have for sending you out here?"

"He sent a doctor as you requested," she said stubbornly.

"He sent me a deluded, illogical woman with . . .

19

with a damn-fool cat!"

Alexandria drew herself up to her full height, which was only average at best. "What is bothering you, Mr. Morgan? Are you afraid to give me a chance?"

"A chance to maim or poison my men or the women who came all this way to marry them? You're damned right I'm afraid to give you that chance."

"I resent your unreasonable attitude."

"Be that as it may, I don't have the time to argue the point now. The others are waiting."

"But we will talk about this later?" she persisted. "You promised."

"God help me, I did," he conceded.

He turned and walked off the dock, stopping to hoist the chest to his shoulder a second time. A mutinous look on her face, Alexandria followed him, refusing to acknowledge the fact that he might truly intend to send her back to Montreal. She was so engrossed in thought, she failed to notice the drunken man until he was again standing in her way.

"Ain't you goin' to talk to me, missy?" he snarled. "Maybe you think you're too good?"

"Not at all, Mr. . . . ? What *is* your name?"

"Webster," he grunted.

"You, Mr. Webster, are in a sad state of inebriation," Alex pointed out.

"Huh?"

"And I should think you would realize I have no desire to converse with you in your present condition."

"A little kiss might help my present condition." He leered, grasping her forearm.

"Oh, for heaven's sake," Alex cried, at the end of her patience. Was every man she met in Upper Canada going to be crude, lecherous, or arrogant? In a moment of frustration, she abandoned the manners instilled by her grandmother and resorted to a more primitive measure she had learned from her grandfather.

Hearing Alexandria's outraged exclamation, Morgan paused to look back. He was just in time to see her deliver a well-aimed blow to Webster's groin with a gingham-clad knee. The bearded man gave a shrill cry of pain and, clutching himself, crumpled to the sand. Alexandria tightened her grip on the hinged basket and the doctor's bag, and, nose in the air, marched on down the path to enter the fort.

As she passed him by, Rhys heard her clearly say, "It seems here in the wilderness a man won't take a lady seriously until she has his full attention. One simply has to appeal to the part of him that serves as a brain."

Rhys Morgan watched her go, a look of amazement playing over his features. Despite her own usage of a masculine nickname, she was most certainly dangerously feminine. And in his experience that always meant trouble. He wished he could shrug off the sudden feeling that, somehow, the majority of the trouble was going to fall squarely upon his shoulders.

Chapter Two

Fort Kaministiquia was located on a bend of the Kaministiquia River, just a half-mile from where it emptied into Lake Superior's Thunder Bay, so named for the ferocious storms that besieged it during the summer months.

At first sight, there was little doubt the fort was as defensible as man could make it. Even in the year 1804, when Indian attacks were no longer such a serious threat, the North West Company could not allow its major fur trade depot to be vulnerable. Not only was amity between the traders and Indian tribes uncertain, as always, but the escalation of the Nor'westers' competition with the men of the rival Hudson Bay Company posed an ever-increasing possibility of outright warfare. Thus, the fort was surrounded by high palisades, its bastions and watchtowers lined with gleaming cannons. Flying overhead, as if to symbolize the strength behind the North West Company was the red and white banner of Saint George, patron saint of

England, the mother country.

As Alexandria stepped past the crude log buildings on either side of the gateway into Fort Kaministiquia, her first view of the post's interior was a surprise. More than anything else, it resembled a rural village. Warehouses, shops, and the houses providing living quarters were staggered around a grassy square. Straight ahead was the Mess Hall, an inelegant name for the two-storied structure with a veranda extending along the front. This, Rhys Morgan informed them, was where they would be staying until time to depart for Sabaskong Falls.

A group of North West Company officials was standing on the front steps to greet them. Alexandria failed to hear a single word of the welcoming speech made by the proprietor, as the Nor'westers called the fort commander, for she was casting curious glances about the square.

Though it might have the look of a country village, on this day in mid July, it was caught in the grip of chaotic excitement. Crowded with people and ringing with noise, Fort Kaministiquia was filled with an almost tangible feeling of celebration, for the Rendezvous was at its height.

Rendezvous! Alex had heard about it all her life — the very word made her shiver in delicious apprehension, made her heart beat a little faster. What must the Rendezvous mean to the men who had survived the long, lonely winters of the Indian country? Men who had gone seven ice-bound months without news from home or the conveniences of civilization. Men anxious for the burn of corn liquor in their throats, for the feel of a woman in their arms. Lusty, brawling men, so she'd heard, who lived for this one month each year when they left behind their usual grueling existence to feast and fight—boasting and swaggering their way through the fort, drinking up any profits they might have made, and more likely than not, before the Rendezvous was over, signing on for another year or two of life in the wilderness.

Alexandria's grandfather had explained to her that the Rendezvous had been created for a very serious purpose: getting the valuable beaver pelts out of the scattered wilderness outposts and getting supplies back in. Because Canada was locked in the grip of winter for most of the year, there wasn't enough time for the men from the far northwest to take the furs accumulated during the trapping season all the way to Montreal, a distance of three thousand miles in some cases.

Therefore, as soon as the ice went off the northern lakes, brigades of canoes set out from the various posts, loaded with prime pelts and crews eager for a taste of civilization. At the same time, canoes carrying trade goods left from Montreal. The brigades met at the Kaministiquia depot, a midway point where the cargoes were exchanged and the voyageurs allowed a few weeks of rest and revelry, while the Nor'wester agents and partners conducted the more serious business of the company.

When that business had been transacted, the festivities were terminated with a ceremonial ball, after which the fleets of canoes once again departed—those from Montreal carrying the precious loads of furs back to the merchants awaiting them, those from the north country returning to the interior with supplies necessary for surviving yet another long, hard winter.

"Miss MacKenzie," called an irritated Rhys M
gan. "These gentlemen would like to meet you."

"Oh, sorry to have kept you waiting."

Alex scurried forward to join the knot of people
standing in front of the officers' quarters. She was very
much aware of the eyes fixed upon her — the officers'
interested and frankly admiring, Rhys Morgan's undeniably disapproving.

"This is Alexandria MacKenzie," muttered Rhys.
"She's a midwife."

"Doctor," she corrected placidly.

"Alexandria," said Reverend Rosswell quickly, "the
proprietor's name is Kenneth MacKenzie. Is there any
chance the two of you are related?"

"I really couldn't say," Alex answered. "I'm afraid my
parents died when I was very young and I've met only
a few of my kin."

"MacKenzie is a common surname here," stated the
proprietor, "especially since the North West Company
was originally begun by Scottish merchants and traders. But even if we can't prove familial ties, I would be
honored to claim kinship to such a charming lady." He
took her hand and bowed low over it. Out of the corner of her eye, Alexandria could see Rhys Morgan
shift his stance impatiently.

"Can we go inside now?" he asked, his tone stopping
just short of rudeness. "These ladies would like some
time to rest before dinner tonight."

"By all means," Kenneth MacKenzie responded,
taking the basket from Alexandria and offering her his
arm. Morgan stared in disbelief as the hinged lid
raised enough for the cat to poke her head over the
side, purr loudly and rub her whiskered face against

25

MacKenzie's wrist as though they were old friends.

As he led the way through the mess hall, MacKenzie explained, "Even though much of the construction here at the fort is as yet unfinished, you will find this building in excellent condition. Indeed, we are rather proud of its elegance."

Alex glanced around the large dining hall, and though she knew little about the usual accommodations at fur-trade forts, she realized this room was probably luxurious by comparison. The cream-colored walls were hung with portraits of distinguished company officials, draperies of the Nor'westers' blue and green tartan hung at the row of long windows, and the large sideboards along one wall were lined with china bearing the North West Company's insignia. The tables and benches looked comfortable, if somewhat roughly fashioned.

"We will gather here for supper tonight," MacKenzie continued as they crossed the planked floor. "In the meantime, these two bedrooms will be at your disposal."

He guided them to rooms just off the dining area. Opening the door to one, he said, "Reverend, you and your lovely wife will be here, and the ladies can share the officers' dormitory adjacent."

The women were herded into the long room, where they stood clustered together as the voyageurs and Morgan's men unloaded their trunks and belongings. The walls had been freshly whitewashed, and each of the narrow beds lining them was covered with a new woven coverlet. There was a fireplace at one end, and the two windows at the other overlooked the kitchen garden.

Kenneth MacKenzie and Rhys Morgan made a point of staying by the door until the last curious man had exited the bedroom.

"Rest well, ladies," Morgan said. "And in a few hours I guarantee you'll get an introduction to the men you came all this way to meet."

"For those of you who would like a bath, I'll send some of the native girls in with hot water," promised the proprietor, and on that note he stepped into the hall and firmly shut the door behind him.

"I've never seen quieter women," he commented with a wry grin.

"Yeah," grunted Rhys. "Why do I have the feeling it's too good to last?"

As soon as the door closed, pandemonium set in. Finally free of the reticence that had held them in check, the Montreal women burst into simultaneous chatter.

"Oh, Lordy me! Have you ever seen so many men?" squealed a plump blonde with a pretty, doll-like face.

"Now, Birdie," cautioned the older Cordelia, "don't get your bloomers in a flap. You're already promised to one of those men — best keep your eyes from straying too soon."

"I can look, can't I?" sniffed Birdie.

"There are some fine specimens, I'll agree." Lily, the youngest female in the group, laughed. "But I've already spied the man I hope is mine. I think I'm in love with him, so it's going to be mighty inconvenient if I'm contracted to marry someone else."

"Oh, for mercy's sake," scolded Alexandria. "I was

27

worried because the lot of you were so quiet. Now I see I had good reason to worry—did the sun this morning addle your wits?"

"I tell you," insisted Birdie, "it was the sight of all those men."

"Did you notice that they looked at us like . . . like ravenous hounds?" asked Mellicent, a beanpole of a woman known for her gloomy imagination. "It's frightening to know we are the bones that are going to be tossed to the starving pack."

"You weren't so frightened when you signed on back in Montreal," Cordelia pointed out.

"But it's different now that we're actually here," responded Christiana, whose usually lovely face seemed pale and tense. "This place terrifies me."

"You're just tired, Christy," soothed Alexandria. "Come lie down for a while. You'll feel better after you've slept a bit."

A redheaded woman sank down onto one of the beds, pulling her two children close against her. The older, a boy, was looking around the room with interest, but the little girl clutched a rag doll and nodded sleepily.

"It was a relief when Mr. Morgan didn't make a fuss about Tobias and Annie," the redhead said. "I was so worried."

"The man obviously has a fondness for bairns," observed Aberdeen, a plain, outspoken Scotswoman. " 'Tis only female doctors he doesna like."

"Yes, he certainly seemed angry with you, Alex," said Lily. "And that's too bad, because he is most assuredly a handsome man."

"Which of you is contracted to Rhys Morgan?"

Birdie suddenly asked, her round dark eyes bright with curiosity. "I can't recall anyone mentioning his name."

"A man like that probably has a wife already," interjected Mellicent. "Let's face it, he'd hardly have need to buy a wife."

"They didn't buy us," protested Lily.

"What else would you call it?" Cordelia put her hands on her narrow hips and looked stern. "They paid our passage out here, so we're indebted to them."

"Mr. Tuttle said no one would be forced to go through with marriage," Lily reminded her, "if they discover they are in . . . in . . ."

"Incompatible," supplied Alexandria.

"Yes, that's the word."

"Just supposin' you were to back out, miss," snapped Cordelia. "What would happen then? You'd find yourself without protection in a fort filled with love-starved men."

"A maiden's dream," teased Birdie.

"Not this maiden." Claire, the redhead, shuddered. "Just give me a decent man who will make a living for me and my young ones."

"Did you recognize your fiancé?" Mellicent asked. "I just hope he's as tolerant as Mr. Morgan."

"Tolerant?" snorted Aberdeen.

Claire shook her head. "His name is Gideon Marsh and he's a carpenter. That's all I know about him."

"I'm sure it will work out for the best," Alex said. "Who could help but love Toby and Annie? They're wonderful children."

"And, if he is at the fort," added Birdie, "he's probably already seen them. He'll have plenty of time to get used to the idea before the two of you meet officially."

"Or time to hie out without us," murmured Claire, rubbing her cheek against her daughter's soft chestnut curls.

"Now, ye quit thinkin' like that," chided Aberdeen. "Things will be fine."

"The real problem is Alexandria." The thin, homely girl named Judith spoke up for the first time. The others were used to her taciturn ways; they also knew that when she did speak out, she usually had something of value to say. "If Mr. Morgan remains true to his word and sends her back to Montreal, we are going to be living in a wilderness outpost with no medical help at all. I believe we must do what we can to prevent that."

"I won't go back," declared Alex.

"But, child," said Aberdeen, laying a hand on Alexandria's shoulder, "what will ye do? He's a mighty stubborn man."

"And I'm a mighty stubborn woman. I'll think of something." She set the basket she carried on the bed beside her and opened the lid, lifting the gray tabby cat into her arms. She scratched the animal's head thoughtfully. "After all Mr. Rhys Morgan is merely a man. If I apply myself, I know I can come up with some way to get around him."

"Ye canna become a laddie," chuckled Aberdeen. "It seems to me that'd be the only way to please him."

"I know. Like all men, he doesn't think I can perform the duties of a physician because I'm a woman. But I will devise some means of proving to him that I am as capable of being a good doctor as any male."

"And we'll be right behind you, Alex," promised

Claire. "As far as I'm concerned, you showed your mettle on the trip out here."

"Thank you . . . that means a great deal to me."

"Momma, how can Alex have mettle?" Annie asked, stifling a huge yawn. "Isn't that what knives and guns are made from?"

"There's some as would say the lass is just as deadly." Aberdeen laughed and winked broadly.

Alexandria favored her friend with a severe look, then turned to Claire with a smile. "Why don't I help you with the children's baths? And then we'll see if there's anything in the kitchen for an early supper for them."

"Alex, I don't know what we would do without you," sighed Claire.

The room was filled with a chorus of agreement.

Rhys Morgan glanced about the crowded dining hall with annoyance. As expected, the women were creating quite a stir!

In a fort where the only civilized females ever seen were the proper middle-aged wives of the company agents who occasionally passed through, the appearance of these ladylike creatures would have been cause for celebration had they all been as plain and dull witted as spruce hens.

As it was, they had provided an unparalleled diversion at the usually staid and uneventful evening meal. The eyes of every male in the room were fixed on the nine women with hungry fascination. It had been a long time since many of them had seen shining blond curls, blue eyes, or lace-trimmed calico gowns. The

31

murmur of soft, feminine voices was totally entrancing by comparison to the harsh jabber of the Indian girls. Even when the meal of baked ham and wild rice was finished, and all but the prospective bridegrooms were ushered outside, the men of the fort crowded onto the veranda to peer through the windows, watching the proceedings with interest and great envy.

Silence fell over the room as the handful of men and women found themselves alone . . . and suddenly self-conscious. After a few desperate glances at the Rosswells and Doc McLoughlin, Rhys Morgan got to his feet.

"I . . . uh, well, since I've been elected spokesman for the men of Sabaskong Falls, I guess it's up to me to get the introductions underway." He ran a hand through his thick dark hair, indicating he was not completely comfortable with the task. "As you ladies know, we sent letters to Lawyer Tuttle describing each of the men who desired . . . er, wanted a wife. Those of you who responded were matched with them according to age and so forth. Since you should already know the name of the man you are here to meet, the best way to begin would probably be for the ladies to come forward one by one."

The silence deepened as the women, seated on one side of the room, stared at the men, seated on the other. The twenty feet of floor space between them might just as well have been a mile. Rhys Morgan coughed nervously and shuffled his feet. What in the hell was he supposed to do now?

There was a loud scraping sound as one of the women finally pushed the bench on which she was sitting away from the table and got to her feet.

"Well, my name's Birdie and I came all the way from Montreal to get a man," said the short, round blonde. "I'll be switched if I'm going to be bashful. John Hay, where are you?"

The laughter that greeted her bold remarks eased the tension in the hall immensely. John Hay, the blacksmith, got to his feet, a broad smile on his face. Birdie, skirts swinging, crossed the floor to stand in front of him, her head barely reaching the middle of his chest. He nodded in approval and kept smiling.

"Hope you'll be a hearty eater because I love to cook," Birdie said, "and I don't tolerate a finicky man."

John Hay nodded again, his smile inching wider.

"Birdie," Rhys said gently, "John can't speak. He was once captured by Indians and they cut out his tongue."

"Oh! How awful," exclaimed Birdie, looking shocked. Then her face cleared. "Everything else works, doesn't it?" she asked.

Hay nodded emphatically, and amid the general laughter, Birdie took the blacksmith's beefy hand. "Good. As for the other . . . well, I do enjoy talking, and this way, I'll get to do it for both of us!"

John Hay slipped an arm about the woman's waist and led her away to a corner where they sat, she chattering and he nodding contentedly.

"Who would like to be next?" asked Rhys.

When none of the women volunteered, Alexandria stood up. "We'll be here all night at this rate," she said. "Why don't I simply read off the names the ladies have and you can introduce the men?"

"Fair enough."

"All right gentlemen," she said in a clear voice.

"This is Cordelia—she came here to marry a man named Malachi Harper."

A tall rawboned farmer rose to meet the equally tall, thin woman. The two stared intently at each other for a few seconds, then abruptly looked away. Silently they crossed the room and sank onto a bench, sitting side by side but not exchanging a single word.

"Christiana has contracted to marry Joseph Patterson," announced Alexandria, clutching the woman's arm as though afraid she might flee.

"I'm sorry, ma'am," said Rhys, "but Joe isn't here. We cast lots to see who had to stay back at the Falls to help my partner tend the livestock and Joe lost. I'm afraid you'll have to wait a while longer to meet him."

There was no denying the look of relief that crossed Christiana's pale features. "Why, I don't mind at all," she murmured, the fact more than evident in the lightness of her tone. "And since my presence isn't really needed here, Alex, I believe I'll go back to the room. I still feel quite tired."

"All right." Alexandria watched her go, a worried frown creasing her forehead. "Let's see, Lily . . . want to go next?"

The pretty young girl looked both eager and apprehensive. But as soon as she saw the man she had agreed to marry, apprehension faded.

"It's him!" she whispered. "He's the one I told you about."

Pacer was one of the most handsome men Alexandria had ever seen in her life. A half-Chippewa, half-French trapper, the young man towered over every other male in the room except Rhys Morgan. His blue-black hair fell to his shoulders, matching the

34

darkness of his eyes. Smooth bronze skin covered hawklike features; his expression was proud and aloof. When he came forward to claim his bride-to-be, he moved with the graceful insolence of a big mountain cat. His lean hand caressed the golden hair that rippled down Lily's slender back, and a slow, possessive smile signaled his satisfaction with their bargain.

Alex heaved a sigh. She sensed that at least these two would find a successful means of communication.

Aberdeen did not fare so well. Her man, Waldo Anderson, was also a trapper, but there any resemblance to Pacer ended. Waldo was small and wiry, dressed in buckskins that had seen far better days. Wispy white hair was matted to a freckled scalp and his face, one jaw distorted by a wad of chewing tobacco, was covered with white stubble. When he opened his mouth to speak to Aberdeen, his voice was a trifle high-pitched and his choice of a greeting was regrettable.

"Well, lookit this. Yer a spindly bag of bones, ain't ya?"

Aberdeen was, of course, offended. She drew herself up, brown eyes blazing, and replied, "Ye, sir, are no' a pretty sight yerself. Dinna think I'll be wantin' to wed the likes o' ye, ye skellie-eyed scunner!"

Waldo turned to Alexandria. "Is she speakin' English?"

Alex was both amused and dismayed. She had hoped for someone a bit more presentable for her friend. "Well yes, she is English mixed with Scots, actually."

"What did she say?" he asked, his suspicious gaze flitting back to Aberdeen.

"Why, I believe she took offense at your . . . your

35

calling her a bag of bones. She was only answering in kind."

"She called me a name, didn't she? There ain't nuthin' kind about that."

"Waldo . . ."

"I want to know what she said," he insisted.

"All right, she said she is unwilling to marry a squint-eyed . . ." She cast a helpless look at Morgan, who was watching, a wide grin curving his lips. "This part is a little more difficult to explain. Uh, she referred to you as a disgusting . . . and nauseating person."

"She called me that?"

"I did, ye great gowk," snapped Aberdeen.

Waldo beamed. "You must be one smart female to use words like that. Yessir, Miss Aberdeen, I think me and you is gonna hit it off jist fine."

"Is he speaking English?" Aberdeen asked Alexandria, her voice as cold as a winter night on Hudson Bay.

"Aberdeen, be nice," Alex pleaded.

"He called me a bag o' bones! I won't stay around and be insulted—and I won't marry such a puir excuse for a man." With that the Scotswoman turned and left the room, head held high.

"But I like nice trim females," Waldo shouted after her. "What's she so all-fired mad about?"

"Perhaps she will be in better spirits tomorrow," Alex said lamely. The trapper was clearly at a loss as to what he had done wrong, and Alexandria reflected that he might not be hardy enough to survive the courtship of Aberdeen McPhie.

Things went more smoothly as the plain, pious Judith was introduced to Hardesty Ames, a farmer whose small herd of dairy cows supplied Sabaskong with milk and cream. Though the pair was too reserved to speak much in front of the others, they were at least cordial.

The gloomy Mellicent was matched up with a most unlikely partner, and Alex was thankful when she voiced no objection. Albert Braunswager was a chubby, red-faced man with a booming laugh and a reputation as a good storyteller and fiddler of some renown. Apparently, Mellicent was more kindly disposed toward the idea of matrimony than Aberdeen, for she took Albert's arm and allowed him to lead her to a quiet corner where they might get better acquainted.

"You're the last one, Claire," Alexandria said in relief. "What was the name you held?"

"Gideon Marsh," Claire answered.

The nice-looking young man who had apprised Rhys of the women's arrival earlier in the day stepped forward, a pleased smile on his face.

Claire shook his hand, but her face was grave. "I am afraid I wasn't completely honest when I signed up for this trip," she said in a rush. "You knew I had been widowed, but . . . I failed to mention that I have two small children. So, I will understand if you should wish to—"

"Claire," Gideon said, still holding her hand, "I saw them this afternoon. They're fine-looking youngsters. If you'll have me, I'd be proud to welcome both you and them into my home."

His kindness brought a quick blur of tears to her eyes. "But are you sure? I mean . . ."

"I like children. Besides," he added with a wicked grin, "I've always had a hankering for a redheaded woman — and you've got just about the prettiest hair I ever saw."

Claire's hand flew to the coil of auburn hair at the nape of her neck, and she looked astonished. Could a man like Gideon Marsh actually ask so little of life? The open honesty of his face reassured her, and she smiled in return.

Gideon tucked her hand in the crook of his arm and, with a wink over his shoulder at Rhys guided her away. "I told you it was going to be worth the wait, didn't I?"

"Well," Rhys said, turning to Alexandria, "what do you think? Is this matchmaking business going to be successful or not?"

"I'm not entirely certain yet," she replied, "although several of the couples seem well pleased."

"But then, there are those like Aberdeen and Waldo. Not much hope there."

"You might be surprised," Alex commented. "Waldo could put her into a better mood if he would shave and bathe."

"As I said, there's not much hope there."

"What do you mean?"

"Look at it from his point of view. Would a woman be worth all that much trouble?"

"You have a rather cynical view of women, Mr. Morgan. And, I suspect, of marriage as well. Is that why you didn't send for a bride yourself?"

"How do you know I'm not already married?"

"I don't of course." She scanned the room, pleased to see that most of the couples were now talking to each other. "But you don't have the demeanor of a married man."

"That's because I'm not."

"And why is that, may I ask?" For the first time, she turned to look directly into his eyes. Tonight they were as dark as ebony.

"A wife is the last thing in the world that I would want, Miss MacKenzie. As you surmised, I don't believe in marriage."

Well, Alexandria thought wryly, for the first time we have finally agreed on something.

Chapter Three

Alexandria stood in the dining hall the next morning, looking out through the long windows at the bustling fort beyond. How she longed to be a part of the noise and confusion! But that wish was rendered impossible by the harsh edict issued by Rhys Morgan: no woman was to venture forth without a male escort.

Nothing about the scene framed by the window looked all that threatening, but Alexandria curbed her impulse to step out into it, knowing she dare not risk Morgan's wrath another time. At least, not this soon.

Once I get settled at Sabaskong Falls, she told herself grimly, I can defy the man at every turn . . . for the time being, I have to behave.

But it irked her all the same. Right out there within a few acres was more drama and excitement than she had seen in all her twenty-four years of life. She was impatient to be a part of it, to start knowing the wilderness to which she was now committed.

Most of the other women had already left the dormitory, accompanied by their intended husbands. In the next several days, they would have an opportunity to get acquainted before the weddings, which were scheduled for the night before departure from Fort Kaministiquia.

In all honesty, the only thing Alex envied the women was their freedom to wander through the compound instead of being cooped up as she was. Otherwise, there was nothing about their situation she felt she could deal with. In her opinion, they had a courage she lacked. They had left behind homes and families, and were seeking new lives for a variety of reasons. But in so doing, they were placing themselves in the controlling hands of men they did not know—men whose touch they would have to tolerate, whose children they would have to bear. And in the event the marriages proved unsuccessful or the life too difficult, the ice and snow would hold them prisoners for endless months before they could even think of escape. Alex shuddered. She never wanted to be caught in such a trap. She'd rather face broken limbs or raging fevers any day.

The front doors banged noisily, interrupting her thoughts, and she glanced up to see Waldo Anderson, the trapper who had so angered Aberdeen. He looked no less disreputable—in fact, his appearance had been worsened by the addition of a hat made from the skin of a skunk. The mound of black and white fur perched jauntily above the man's wizened face, the bushy tail hanging over his collar in back. As he approached Alexandria, she noticed with dismay that the pungency usually associated with that particular animal still clung to the pelt.

41

"Mornin', Miss Alex," Waldo said with a smile. "I've come to see if Aberdeen would care to take a stroll around the fort."

"Well . . ." Alexandria faltered. "Isn't that . . . nice." She had her doubts about Aberdeen's reaction to the suggestion.

"She up yet? I didn't see her at breakfast."

Knowing the woman had purposely refused to leave the bedroom because she had no desire to encounter Waldo, Alex had no hope she would accept his invitation. If only he hadn't gotten off to such a horrible start with Aberdeen . . .

"I believe she's awake, but I'll make certain if you'd like."

"I'd be obliged."

Alexandria had just started across the floor when the bedroom door opened to reveal the Scotswoman. Dressed in a dark cotton gown, her black hair twisted into a severe knot above her narrow forehead, she looked dour and forbidding. When she caught sight of Waldo Anderson, she came to an abrupt halt.

"What are ye doing here?" she demanded.

The little trapper beamed, whipping the skunkskin hat off. Wispy white hair formed a messy halo around his head.

"Good mornin', Miss Aberdeen. You want to see the fort?"

She looked down her long nose at him. "With ye, ye mean?"

"Yep."

"I'd rather drap deid," she said flatly. "I'll no be seen with a mon wearin' his moolie brother atop his heid. 'Tis puttin' him in a kist and buryin' him, ye should be."

Waldo turned to Alex, looking puzzled.

"I think she means your hat," Alexandria said softly, feeling pity for him. Whenever Aberdeen dredged up as many Scots words as she did with Waldo, the prospects for a happy outcome were small, indeed.

"I put on my fanciest one," the trapper said proudly. "Does she like it?"

"Waldo," Alex began, "perhaps you should—"

"Gae wi' haste to Auld Nick," finished Aberdeen, marching back into the bedchamber and slamming the door behind her.

"I guess the old biddy didn't want to go walking," remarked Waldo, clapping his hat back on his head. "What did she say?"

"I . . . well . . ."

"Don't spare me, gal. I can take it. If I'm to marry that scrawny crow I need to learn to understand her."

"I don't know why she is being so rude," faltered Alex. "She usually isn't."

"Like ya said, I got off to a bad start. Now tell me, what did she say?"

Alex drew a deep breath. "She said that she'd rather drop dead than go with you. She also suggested that you could go to the devil . . . with haste."

"And my hat? What'd she say about it?"

"That she wouldn't be seen with a man wearing his own . . . moldy brother on his head." Alexandria's voice grew fainter. "She said you should put it in a coffin and bury it. . . ."

To her surprise, Waldo chuckled. "Criminy, she's a game one," he said in admiration. "The best of the whole lot."

"Do you really think so?"

"I do. I'm goin' to enjoy marryin' that skinny sour-puss."

"Don't get too hopeful, Waldo. About marrying Aberdeen, that is. Somehow I can't foresee things working out between the two of you."

"You jist watch, little gal," he said with a wink. "She'll come around. She's too blessed smart not to know a good man when she sees one."

His confidence seemed ill placed, but Alex didn't want to dwell on the hopelessness of his cause. Instead, she decided on tact and changed the subject.

"Would you mind escorting me to Dr. McLoughlin's office?" she asked. "I need to talk to him, but I can't go out alone."

"Why, it'd be a pleasure, Miss Alex."

When they stepped outside the mess hall, Alex discovered the morning was something of a rarity for the north country—hot and sunny, with no wind. She lifted her face to the sunshine and inhaled the various odors in the air. She caught the scent of sun-baked grass, a faint fishy tang from the river, the resinous smell of fresh lumber, and the more earthy aromas of a barnyard. And all of these, Alex acknowledged with a grin, were underlined by the definite smell of skunk from Waldo's primitive headpiece.

The doctor's office was located just to the east of the main gate. When McLoughlin answered the knock on his door, Waldo doffed his hat, made his farewells, and left Alexandria in the doctor's care.

"I hope you're not too busy to spare me a few minutes," she began. "I need to talk with you."

"I'm never too busy for a pretty lady," stated

McLoughlin. "Especially one who proclaims such love for my own profession. In fact, I'd welcome the chance to show off my new apothecary."

He led the way to a small, square room attached to his office and living quarters.

"How I envy you such a wonderful place to work," Alex exclaimed, gazing raptly about. The wide floorboards were clean and bare, the only furniture a narrow cot covered with a white sheet and cupboards for the storage of surgical tools and equipment. Bottles, tins, and jars lined the wooden shelves built along two walls.

"Opium, arsenic, prussic acid . . . strychnine," she murmured, reading a few of the labels aloud. "Your apothecary is well stocked. Hyssop, coltsfoot—juniper. I see you also favor the use of herbs. So did my grandfather, and you should see the plants I gathered and dried on the way from Montreal!" She turned to the physician, her eyes sparkling. "Grandfather theorized that the Greeks and Egyptians had the purest knowledge of healing. What do you think?"

"I'd have to agree. In my practice, I use methods that had their origins in early history nearly every day."

"Oh, I wish Grandfather could be here! I'm sure you and he would have been great friends."

"It sounds very likely. He must have been an inspiration to you, Alex."

"I guess that's rather apparent," she said with a smile.

"Yes—why else would someone like you aspire to medicine? It's a baffling and bloody business at best."

"I know. But I watched Grandfather use his skills to

help and heal so many people that it just seemed natural for me to want to follow the example he set."

"Still, it's an unusual ambition for a woman."

She frowned. "Please don't tell me an intelligent man like yourself labors under the misconception that a woman is unfit to be a doctor."

"No, no," McLoughlin said hastily. "I'm only saying that it's a rare woman who would have the desire for such a career."

"And you have no reservations about their capabilities?"

"I hadn't thought much about it, but . . . no, I don't believe I do."

"Good. I would hate to think every man in this fort was as hardheaded and narrow-minded as Rhys Morgan. His attitude is archaic, to say the least."

"Alexandria, you must understand that Rhys is . . . well, he has . . ."

"A highly developed regard for his own opinion?" she queried mockingly.

"That's not exactly what I had in mind."

"Perhaps you were going to mention his inflated arrogance? Indeed, it does rival that of any man I've ever met. It must be so difficult for all you mere mortals who have to dwell in the presence of such a god-like being."

"Would that I had a thunderbolt or two at hand right now," drawled a gravel-edged voice behind her. "I'd aim them right at your haughty little backside."

Alexandria whirled about, her face growing pale as she found herself staring at the very object of her insults.

Rhys Morgan loomed in the doorway, filling it com-

46

pletely with his rangy, buckskin clad body. His face was noticeably devoid of any sign of humor.

Alex darted a quick glance at Dr. McLoughlin; as she suspected, he was highly amused by her blunder. Well, it wasn't the first time her impulsive nature had gotten her into trouble. And though it irked her, she realized she was going to have to extricate herself as gracefully as possible, even if it meant groveling before the tall tyrant.

Tall tyrant? she thought, a smile flitting across her face. Well, it was a fairly accurate description of the man. The way he strutted around the fort, he must consider himself in full command. Rather like the—she gave her imagination full rein—king of Kaministiquia. Or, perhaps, the baron of the backwoods. It was all she could do to keep from laughing aloud. No, she had it—lord of the lakes, that's what he was.

"I'm glad you find the situation so entertaining," said Rhys Morgan dryly.

Chagrined at her silly flights of fancy, Alex sternly told herself that a bit of groveling was definitely going to be necessary now.

"Oh, but I don't . . . truly." She composed her face. "I must beg your pardon, Mr. Morgan. There is simply no excuse for my rudeness."

He crossed his arms over his chest and leaned against the doorframe, a dubious expression masking his features. "No need to overdo it."

"What?"

"You can't really believe I didn't see through such a flimsy apology?"

"Why, you . . . ! I didn't have to apologize at all. The things I said were the truth."

47

"If you think about it again, you'll remember that you do need to apologize," he informed her, a wicked glint in his eyes. "Or have you forgotten that you need to stay on my good side?"

"Because of the matter of employment?" she asked faintly.

He nodded.

She sighed. "Yes, you are absolutely right. I . . . I do beg your pardon, most humbly. Will you please forgive my ill-bred remarks?"

He fairly smirked. "With pleasure."

She looked relieved. "Does this mean you are withdrawing your objection to my being hired as a doctor?"

"No, not at all."

"What?" Her voice rose angrily.

"I haven't changed my mind in any way. You are not suited to be a doctor—"

"That's ridiculous! I am a doctor, whether you think I'm suited or not. I have passed every exam—"

"Did you attend a university?"

"You are quite aware that a woman would not be allowed to attend medical classes."

"Then how can you insist you have adequate education?" he insisted.

"My grandfather was a marvelous teacher. And even you would have to admit a privately tutored pupil is bound to learn more than one attending public classes. I learned by working at his side, by observing, and by assisting."

"Miss MacKenzie, I'm sure your grandfather was a remarkable man, but just because he let you play at being a doctor doesn't mean everyone else will."

48

Her gray eyes smoldered as she took a step toward him, chin rising and fists clenching at her sides. "I did not play at being a doctor," she said slowly, emphasizing each word. "I've spent hundreds of hours studying and learning everything any other physician would have to know. The only reason I don't have a license is because I am a woman!"

"Of course," he said triumphantly. "The same reason you will never be employed as a doctor at the Falls."

"But why? What possible difference could my gender make?"

"Look, woman," he growled, suddenly impatient with the entire matter, "I don't deny that you are probably very efficient when it comes to bathing fevered brows or administering headache powders. You may even be able to numb a toothache. But have you ever tried to put back together a man who's been mauled by a bear? How do you plan to hold a screaming woodsman down long enough to amputate the leg he crushed while felling timber?"

"But—"

"Ever seen a trapper whose hand has been mutilated by one of his own traps?" he asked fiercely. "Or a voyageur who got into a drunken fight where someone tried to cut out his bowels?"

"Mr. Morgan—"

"What will you do when smallpox breaks out among the Indians again, killing three of every four in the tribe? You'd be responsible for the settlement. How are you going to protect your friends and neighbors from the disease?"

"Rhys," interrupted McLoughlin. "Aren't you being a bit harsh?"

"No," he snapped. "She needs to know this isn't some goddamned tea party. Back in the city, a few bandages and a pretty smile might have sufficed, but it's different here. It takes strength and courage and a hell of a lot of grit just to survive." He leveled a burning look at the astonished Alex. "I'd be the first to admit you have a real pretty smile, Miss MacKenzie, but it's not enough. Not nearly." He offered a bleak shrug. "Go on home to Montreal," he said softly. He turned and strode across the room and out the door without looking back.

Alexandria turned to Dr. McLoughlin with a stricken look. "No," she cried, "I can't go back! I won't. Blast him, why does he have to be so mean?"

"Alex, he thinks he's acting in your best interest. It isn't anything against you personally. He just happens to be of the opinion that women are too frail to adjust to the hard life out here. In many cases, he's right, you know."

"But I'm not frail," she persisted. "I'm healthy and strong. And well trained. I know what to do in a crisis. How can I make him realize that? Can't you please talk to him?"

McLoughlin shook his head. "I'll try, but if Rhys doesn't want to listen, it'll be like shouting into a cave. Pretty soon the echo of my own voice will deafen me!" He gave a small chuckle. "Don't look so forlorn, girl. There's plenty of work to be done right here during Rendezvous. Why don't you lend a hand with my practice? And maybe Rhys will observe for himself what you can do."

"Do you really mean that? Oh, Doc, thank you so much. I'd be honored to assist you."

50

At that moment the very walls of the apothecary seemed to vibrate with the shouts that rippled through the fort. "Brigade! Brigade's coming!"

"What's happening?" Alex asked, seeing the doctor's sudden delight.

"It's the brigade from Athabasca, I suspect. They should've been here two weeks ago. Want to walk down to the docks with me?"

"I'd love to!"

As they hurried along through the gathering crowd, Alex felt herself being caught up in the excitement of the arrival. Holding her skirts in her hands, she was nearly flying by the time they reached the front gates. Walking in front of her, McLoughlin effectively cleared the way through the press of bodies, finding a spot with an unimpeded view of the river.

Looking about her, Alex saw several of her friends, each with a protective escort. Some of them, like Cordelia and Malachi, or Birdie and John Hay, were on amiable terms already. Others seemed more reserved. Then there was Lily and Pacer. Alex smiled to herself. The young couple stood just outside the gates, staring into each other's eyes, totally oblivious to the confusion around them. Recalling how late it was when Lily had finally returned to the dormitory the night before, Alex was positive the two had made a significant start in getting acquainted.

She turned her attention back to the Kaministiquia, where the brigade of seven canoes, each propelled by short, red paddles wielded skillfully by the voyageurs, was coming into sight. As they neared, Alexandria could hear the men singing.

"Á la claire fontaine . . . Allant m'en promener. . . ."

There was nothing about the appearance of the brigade to indicate to the casual observer the hell it had gone through traversing the hundreds of miles between the Athabasca River, the wildest and loneliest of the Nor'westers' territory, and this tranquil stretch of the Kaministiquia.

The high prows and sterns of the yellow birchbark canoes rode proudly, gaily decorated with freshly painted devices—the rising sun, a rearing grizzly, an Indian peace pipe. The men themselves sat stiffly upright, their straight backs belying the exhaustion of nearly eighty days on the trail, packing heavy bundles of furs over grueling portages or fighting demonic crosswinds on the treacherous open water. In spite of the day's heat, they were dressed in their most flamboyant finery—the traditional blue cloak or *capote*, red woolen caps, and scarlet leggings, with gaudy sashes hanging about their waists. As they drew nearer the waiting crowd, their song grew louder and more boisterous, their white teeth flashing in the sun.

As the first canoes began nosing up to the dock, Dr. McLoughlin moved forward to assist. Shielding her eyes from the glare on the water, Alex shifted her position, standing on tiptoe for a better view. She bumped someone and glanced up to see the young voyageur, Baptiste.

"Good morning, *mademoiselle*. The sighting of a brigade is always a cause for much celebration, no?"

"It would seem so."

One of the lightweight north canoes nudged the dock near them and the man in the prow sprang up, tossing his paddle aside. Casting an arrogant look at the crowded shore, he raised his fist and struck himself on the chest twice, following this gesture with a loud, growling roar and the shout, *"Je suis un homme!* I am a man!" He favored Alex with a wink and a low, sweeping bow. "I have killed more men, loved more women, drunk more whiskey, and risked more danger than any other son-of-a-bitch here!"

Alexandria caught her breath, half expecting the men from the fort to swarm all over the boastful newcomer. Instead, there were a few jovial catcalls and one halfhearted challenge, met with derisive laughter. She glanced over her shoulder and was amazed to find grudging respect for the voyageur clearly evident in the watching eyes. She looked up at Baptiste in question.

He chuckled. "We are used to the men of the north," he explained. "They have the reputation of being the strongest and bravest souls in Canada . . . and we men of Montreal humor them." His dark eyes twinkled as he turned back to the Athabascan.

The voyageur hooked a thumb in the sash he wore and leaned forward, his bold eyes raking Alexandria's figure from head to toe. "Is she your woman, Porkeater?" he asked, using the derogatory nickname given to the Montreal voyageurs by those from the Interior. "I will fight you for her."

He threw one moccasin-clad foot over the gunwale and stepped close to Baptiste. The men were nearly the same height and both had the massive bull necks and powerful upper body of the voyageur, but Baptiste suddenly appeared at a disadvantage. There was something about the other man that made him look dangerously invincible. Alex didn't know if it was his long black hair and sun-reddened skin that gave him such a savage look or merely the menacing way he crouched low in front of Baptiste, as if begging him to fight. She only knew she had to do something to keep the matter from proceeding any further.

"Stop this at once," she demanded. "Leave Baptiste alone."

"Ah, your woman is afraid you cannot best me," the voyageur sneered. "Do you hide behind her skirts?"

Baptiste drew himself up, the affront he suffered visible on his young face. "I do not need a woman to protect me from an Athabascan son-of-a-whore like you."

"Aaugh! You should die for that insult, Pork-eater!"

Instantly, the two men were locked in combat, urged on by the bystanders. The crews from the north canoes stood on the wharf, but not one of them made a move to interfere in the fight. Instead, they alternately cheered or offered advice, hurling epithets at the men from the fort who were backing Baptiste in the fray.

The north man had his hands around Baptiste's throat, his fingers digging deeply into the corded neck. Actually fearing for her friend's life, Alex grew frantic. Without further thought, she flung herself at the Athabascan, clinging to his back, her own arms wrapped around his neck. She kicked her feet, entangling the man's legs in her voluminous skirts. He staggered, losing his grip on Baptiste long enough for the younger man to strike a blow with a hard, swinging fist. The voyageur went down on one knee, nearly toppling over on Alexandria. In the back of her mind, she was aware of Dr. McLoughlin shouting her name, but before she could assure him that she was all right, the voyageur was surging to his feet again and all she could do was hold on. He twisted his massive body, bucking like a wild horse under its first saddle, and, to the amusement of those watching, Alex wrapped her legs around his waist and shouted for Baptiste to have done with him.

Baptiste stood stock-still, humiliated at being saved by a female, and the man from the north country took advantage of the opportunity to send him sprawling to the dock. As the voyageur turned his attention back to Alex, who was now beating him about the head and shoulders, Baptiste clutched him around the knees, causing him to fly forward. Alex let out a frightened squeak as she realized he was careening off the side of the dock and into the river. She immediately released her hold, but it was too late. The icy waters closed over her head as she plunged downward to the river bottom, her skirts opening like a parasol. She used her feet to propel herself upward again, but this time her sodden gown and petticoats swirled around her legs, hampering her ascent. Just when she thought her lungs would burst, her head broke the surface of the river and she saw a dozen concerned faces staring down at her. She managed to blink the moisture from her eyes, treading water as best she could. A few feet away, the man from Athabasca was being pulled from the river by his comrades and Alex couldn't believe it when she saw him and Baptiste exchange handshakes and hearty slaps on the back.

"Alex, are you all right?" Dr. McLoughlin's voice cut through her irate thoughts.

"I'm just fine," she declared through clenched teeth. "Just fine."

The doctor threw back his head and shouted with laughter. "My God, Alex," he gasped, "you are the damndest woman I ever saw!"

Insult or compliment? She hadn't quite made up her mind when two hard hands reached for her, closing around her upper arms and yanking her from the water to stand miserable and dripping before an obviously enraged Rhys Morgan.

"Do you mind telling me what in the holy, blazing hell you thought you were doing?" he ground out, his voice soft but deadly.

"What did it look like?" she snorted, trying to dispel the feeling of being a disobedient child about to be switched by the schoolmaster.

"It looked like you were brawling," he replied quietly.

"I was aiding my friend," she protested. "It was not a brawl."

"Oh? I've seen whorehouse fights that were more respectable."

"What difference does it make, anyhow? Why should you care?" she flared. "I'm nothing to you, after all!" His eyes are the color of a northern lake, she thought, capable of changing from a clear, strong blue to murky gray-green, depending on his mood. And, like the lake, even though the sun might draw forth a pure, warm color, she knew that below the surface, the depths were icy.

"You were the woman to whom I was going to apologize," he stated sarcastically. "I regretted being so harsh with you at Doc's, and I was fool enough to think maybe I should give you a chance to prove you could be a midwife."

"Doctor," she bravely amended, her eyes wide. She took a deep breath. "Do you really mean that?"

"I did. But now I've changed my mind again. Come to my senses is more like it." He grasped her arm and started shoving her ahead of him along the dock. "There is no way I will tolerate a bull-headed, mule-stubborn, hell-raising woman like you in my settlement."

As the amused watchers parted to let him herd her through the gates of the fort, Alex tried to pull away. Rhys's grip merely tightened and his strides lengthened, bouncing her along so quickly her feet barely touched the ground. "Will you listen to me?" she panted breathlessly.

"No, never again. Just forget trying to talk me into anything, woman. This time I mean it — your troublesome little rump will be in the first canoe going back to Montreal and that's my final word!"

Chapter Four

"From now on, you'll stay in your room where you can't cause any more trouble," Rhys announced, as he relentlessly marched Alexandria across the mess hall floor toward the dormitory. His tirade was cut short when they were met at the door by an agitated Gideon Marsh.

"Here she is," he called over his shoulder to someone behind him. "Miss MacKenzie is here now."

"What has happened?" Alex cried, alarmed.

"They hurt Lady Gwendolyn," sobbed Annie, throwing herself at Alex.

"I think they killed her," Tobias stated solemnly.

"Oh, Alex, I'm so sorry about this," Claire said. "I tried to tell Annie there wasn't anything you could do. . . ."

"There is, too!" Annie clutched Alex's wet skirts hysterically. "She's a doctor—she can fix her and make her better!"

"But look at her, Alex." Tobias held out a tangled

mass of cloth and cotton stuffing. "Nobody can fix this."

"Good God, what is it?" asked Rhys, completely baffled by the scene taking place all around him.

Alex glared at him. "Have some discretion, will you?" she hissed. "Anyone can see it's Annie's rag doll . . . or what's left of the poor thing." She patted the little girl's shoulder and raised questioning eyes to Claire.

"We went for a walk with Gideon," the child's mother began. "And—"

"It's all my fault," the carpenter declared. "If I hadn't thought it would be safe to take Claire and the children for a stroll along the river, this never would have happened."

"You couldn't know we would encounter those drunken Indians," Claire assured him. She turned back to Alex. "There were about seven or eight young braves coming down the path and . . . well, Annie and Toby had never seen Indians before and I'm afraid they stared rather rudely. One of the braves took offense and seized Annie's doll."

"They were tossing it back and forth and yelling," Toby said, his hazel eyes wide with remembered fear. "Then one of them tried to grab it away from his friend, and they pulled her head off."

Claire shuddered. "They thought it was a great joke, especially when Annie began screaming and sobbing. They simply proceeded to tear the doll to pieces."

"Damn them," swore Gideon. "I struck two of them before they ran away—I still think I should have gone after them."

Claire laid a hand on his arm. "No, you were very courageous, Gideon, but it wasn't worth your getting injured. Those Indians were so drunk it's impossible to say what might have happened."

"Can you fix my dolly, Alex?" queried Annie anxiously. "She's the only one I have."

"I know, sweetheart," Alex murmured. Heedless of her wet clothing, she sank to her knees to gather the child into her arms. "But I'm not sure what I can do for poor Lady Gwendolyn."

"Will you try?" Fresh tears trembled on the girl's lashes.

"Of course, I'll try, but," Alex turned her gaze to the ruined doll and bit her bottom lip in consternation, "you mustn't get your hopes too high."

"You think she's dead, too, don't you?" whispered Annie, and then broke into a fresh outburst of weeping.

Alex felt rather desperate as she looked at Claire over the child's head. "It isn't that . . . I just think it's going to take her a long, long time to get well again. I'm wondering how you'll manage in the meantime without her." Suddenly her face brightened. "Wait a minute, I have an idea!"

Annie's tears slowed to a stop. She looked up hopefully. "You do?"

"Yes, come along with me. I think I may have something that will make you feel better."

Alex got to her feet and, catching the child's hand in her own, led the way into the bedroom. She studied the trunks lined up against one wall.

"Now, let me see, which one is it? Ah, here we are." She unlatched and opened a brassbound trunk, bending over to rummage through its contents. All that could be seen of her was a shapely rump covered in dripping cotton. "Aha!" When she straightened, she was holding an object wrapped in a shawl.

"What is it?" asked a doubtful Annie.

"Come see," invited Alex, sitting down on the floor and arranging her clammy skirts around her. She began unwrapping the article she held, and the children pressed closer.

"This used to belong to my grandfather," Alex was explaining. "It is very, very old—from China."

She was holding an ornate box of carved ebony; inside, lying on a colorful silk scarf was the ivory figurine of a naked woman, her head resting on a tiny brocaded pillow. The doll had painted black hair, delicately slanted black eyes, and a pink rosebud mouth.

"Oh, she's beautiful," sighed Annie, smoothing the ivory with a daring finger.

"She once belonged to a Chinese lady of high birth," said Alex. "You see, it was quite improper for important ladies to take off their clothing in front of a doctor, so they used these ivory models to demonstrate where they were feeling pain."

"It must be very valuable," spoke up Claire. "Not a child's toy."

"I'm sure Annie will take good care of her."

"You're . . . you're giving her to me?" The little girl darted a quick look at her mother. "Is it all right, Momma?"

"I don't think Alex should—"

"No, really, I want to. If I know Annie has this doll to keep her company, I won't worry so much about how long it takes Lady Gwendolyn to heal."

"Oh, thank you," Annie cried, hugging Alex with fervor. "She's the prettiest doll I've ever seen . . . well, next to Gwendolyn, I mean."

"You'll have to name her, you know." Alex pursed her lips in thought. "Something Chinese, of course."

"But I don't know any Chinese names!"

"You could call her Madame Dragonflower," suggested Alex. "I read that in a book one time."

"Dragonflower is a silly name," groused Tobias.

"No, it's not!" cried Annie, clutching her new toy to her chest "You're just jealous."

Alexandria winked broadly at the boy. "I'll wager it will be Annie who's jealous when she sees what I've got in this trunk for you."

"For me?" Toby came a few steps closer. "What is it?"

Once again, Alex sorted through the trunk's mysterious contents, surfacing with a painted wooden club in her hand. Two bones and a scarlet feather adorned its roughly carved handle. Toby, his face alight with awe, reached for it.

"It's an African medicine club," explained Alex. "My grandfather received it as a gift from an old native chieftain. His people believe the warrior who carries this club will never be defeated in battle."

"Jumpin' catfish!" the boy muttered. "Thanks, Alex. It's the best present I ever had."

From the doorway, Rhys Morgan watched the scene with interest. Doc was right—Alex MacKenzie was the damnedest woman!

She sat on the floor in a soggy dress that must be chilling her to the bone, her damp hair hanging around her shoulders in matted strands. Apparently her own discomfort was unimportant compared to a little girl's hurt—hell, she'd even recognized the boy's guilty envy. Where any other woman would be upset about appearing unattractive, Alexandria seemed completely oblivious to anything but the two children. Not, he found himself thinking, that she needs to worry . . . even a dunking in the river could not destroy her undeniable loveliness. The moisture beaded on her fine skin only enhanced the depths of wide gray eyes, the sheen of her rose-colored mouth.

He wrenched his gaze away from that smiling mouth, but felt no less disturbed when it fell to the bodice of her soaked gown. The thin cotton material clung to her form, leaving no doubt that, slender as she was, she was enticingly curved and rounded in all the necessary places.

Quickly he looked away and unexpectedly met Claire's watchful eyes. She stepped closer, making a remark meant for his ears only. "You see, this is one of the reasons Alex is a fine doctor. She realizes that sometimes more than just the body needs to be healed."

As calm and quiet as the redheaded woman was, Rhys sensed she would be one of Alex's fiercest supporters. But he was already struggling against being too impressed by Alex's handling of Toby and Annie, so he forced himself to shrug, as though he saw scant merit in such an attitude.

"By remaining in those wet clothes, she's inviting a summer chill. Such careless disregard for her own health is disquieting in someone who claims to be a medical expert."

With those sarcastic words, he turned and left the

room.

Stung, Alex watched him go, then surrendered to childish irritation and stuck out her tongue.

Rhys Morgan was nearly halfway across the dining room when he heard the burst of laughter behind him. He stopped short, a curious prickling sensation at the back of his neck telling him more surely than words that he was the object of the mirth. What had the disrespectful little witch said or done this time? For a moment, he was tempted to go back and see, but reason asserted itself and he continued across the room. An amused smile momentarily warred for possession of his features with the scowl he perpetually wore when in Alexandria MacKenzie's presence.

By the time he reached the door, the scowl had triumphed and was firmly back in place.

Hours later, Alexandria sifted through the small pile of twisted fabric and clumps of cotton, trying to sort out arms and legs. But even the challenge of reconstructing Lady Gwendolyn could not divert her mind from the shouts and cheers drifting through the fort. How she longed to be down at the waterfront with everyone else watching the voyageurs race canoes on the river!

Even with the windows up and the door standing open, the room was stifling, and she sighed in self-pity. She was bored. . . .

Seizing a pair of shears and a handful of ecru cloth, she flounced onto the bed. With a sympathetic meow, Nasturtium leaped up beside her, rubbing her head along Alex's knee.

"I know," Alex murmured, "and I appreciate your keeping me company. It's just that I didn't travel thousands of miles to sit in this room like a naughty child. Damn that man!"

Still, she reflected, stroking Nasturtium's head, events had conspired against her, making docile obedience an absolute necessity. She knew as well as she knew her name that she had to take advantage of every remaining opportunity to impress Rhys Morgan with her suitability if she intended to change his stubborn mind.

With resolution, Alexandria picked up the fabric and cut into it, neatly laying the pieces to one side as they fell from beneath the shining blades. As she worked, she hummed a French lullaby her grandmother had taught her long ago. When she laid the shears down, she reached for a needle and thread, taking up the first piece of cloth.

Rhys Morgan stood in the doorway observing the woman sitting on the bed sewing. Now she was neither yesterday's disheveled traveler or this morning's brawling hoyden. She looked placidly domestic, a young wife singing over her mending. Rhys knew the image was probably deceptive, but he enjoyed it anyhow.

Her hair had been dried and wrapped around her head in tidily coiled braids, and she was wearing a plain, cinnamon-colored gown. Several things kept her from appearing in the least matronly, he noticed— the frivolous wisps of red-gold hair that curled about her face, the tatted lace collar of her dress . . . the way she caught her lower lip between straight, white teeth as she concentrated on her stitching.

Alex's first indication that she was being watched

came when Nasturtium sprang to her feet and started hissing, back arched and eyes throwing fire.

"What are you doing?" he asked, choosing to ignore the unfriendly feline.

"Performing surgery on poor Lady Gwendolyn," she replied easily, careful not to show her pique at being relegated to her quarters.

He stepped inside the room. "Somehow you don't seem like the type of woman who . . . well. . . ." Despite his best intentions, he was already headed for her bad side.

"Could sew?" she finished for him. "You shouldn't be surprised—all surgeons learn to be proficient with a needle."

"Oh . . . of course."

"What are you doing here?" she asked. "Instead of being down at the docks enjoying the races."

Something about her tone of voice made it evident that she wished she were seeing the races herself. He felt guilty at knowing he was the reason she was not. At the moment, she looked so harmless he wasn't certain his annoyance with her had been justified.

"I've just come from a meeting in Kenneth Mac-Kenzie's office. As I passed by, I heard you singing and couldn't resist looking in." He glanced about the empty room. "Everyone else down at the docks?"

"Yes." She met his gaze squarely. "They all tried to persuade me to go with them, you know. . . ."

"But you didn't. Why not?"

"I am attempting to show you I do have discipline when necessary."

He grinned. "And I am properly impressed," he admitted. "I appreciate your efforts."

"I suppose I am making better use of my time doing this anyway," she said, stuffing cotton into the doll's leg she had just seamed together. "Poor Lady Gwendolyn needed all new limbs, as you see."

Rhys's eyes wandered over the scattered body parts, coming to rest on the ecru material from which Alex had cut the pieces for them. Suddenly he realized she had sacrificed a very lovely nightgown to repair the doll.

"Why on earth did you destroy a perfectly . . . good nightgown?" he asked, intrigued. He couldn't think of another woman he'd ever known who would have done such a thing.

"The doll was ruined — and this was the only thing I had that seemed the right color for arms and legs." She grinned at him, aware of his disapproval but not understanding it.

He shook his head. It was a damned shame to see something so fragile and feminine hacked to pieces like that. "Surely you could have found a garment less . . . valuable to sacrifice?"

"Don't worry," she said, "I can spare it. I have another one just like it."

He looked up quickly. He suspected the little wretch was laughing at him, at his schoolboy obsession with a piece of frilly nightwear. In a swift change of topic, he said, "I suppose I could escort you to the races. With you on your best behavior, what could possibly happen?"

Alex had just opened her mouth to accept his rather grudging invitation when a movement at the window caught her eyes. Her mouth agape, she watched as ten filthy fingers closed over the sill. The sight was followed by the head and grimy shoulders of the man called Webster who had accosted her at the docks. Her sharply indrawn breath caused Rhys to whirl and look at the intruder, who had thrown one knee up onto the window ledge.

"Oh, Jesus Christ," the man moaned in disbelief as he saw the long-legged backwoodsman start toward him.

"What the hell do you think you are doing, Webster?" Rhys snarled in anger.

"Nuthin'," the man whined. "Nuthin' at all."

"Just passing by, I suppose?"

"Yeah, that's right."

Webster lowered his knee and inched back as Rhys leaned out the window to discover he was standing on a pile of wooden crates.

"Reckon you don't know how those crates happened to be stacked outside this very window. . . ."

"No, reckon not." He squinted at Rhys. "Hey, you ain't thinkin' I did it, are ya?"

"The thought never crossed my mind," Morgan stated. "If it had, I might've had to get riled up, thinking you were trying something foolhardy like bothering the lady again."

"What lady?" Webster gasped, his eyes rolling sideways for a rapid look at Alex.

Rhys leaned farther out the window. "One you'd better forget about if you know what's good for you."

"Anythin' you say . . ." The man pulled back from the threatening nearness of Morgan's chest and shoulders. Suddenly, he lost his balance and, with a hoarse cry, tumbled backward onto the hard ground, cursing as the wooden boxes came down around him. With a short, merciless laugh, Rhys slammed down the window.

He turned to study Alexandria. "I swear, you are the first woman I've ever met who could cause trouble just sitting on a bed sewing."

"Surely you're not going to hold me accountable for that man's actions?"

"You're the one who . . . goaded him. Who else could be at fault? He was merely accepting a challenge he thought you had issued."

"Oh," she fumed, "it is impossible to please you! No matter what I do, it's sure to be wrong, isn't it?"

"Never mind that," he said. "If we're going to see any of the races, we'd better get down to the river."

She looked astonished. "You're still going to allow me out of this room?"

"It would seem the only way to assure that you stay out of difficulty is to keep an eye on you at all times."

Alex gathered Nasturtium into her arms and slid off the bed. "Thank you," she said meekly, hoping he hadn't noticed that the cat hissed and bared her claws at him.

"Don't thank me," he muttered, "just stay right here beside me and don't wander off. And see if you can make that fractious ball of fur behave. I don't trust her any more than I do you."

"Very well," she said, more meekly than before.

By the time everyone sat down to the evening meal that night, Alex was feeling very smug and self-satisfied. The afternoon had gone well. She had remained at Rhys's side, causing not one iota of trouble. No accidents had befallen her or anyone else; she had refrained from involving herself in a single brawl. She was almost positive it was not imagination that made her think Rhys was beginning to feel the tiniest respect for her. Only a few more days of such exemplary behavior and she was sure to win him over. . . .

The scream that tore through the dining hall was high and shrill and rife with terror. Forks stopped in midair, conversation halted abruptly. The scream came again.

"Mmoooommmma!"

Claire jumped to her feet. "Oh, my God, it's Annie!"

Every woman in the hall, as well as most of the men, raced toward the bedroom. Gideon Marsh threw open the door to reveal Annie, her face as white as her nightgown, dancing up and down on one of the beds. Her mouth stretched wide as she let out another shriek.

"Annie, love, what is it?" cried Claire, snatching the child up into her arms.

Annie pointed a finger toward the corner. "Momma, there's a dead man in Alex's trunk!"

All eyes turned toward the open trunk — that is, all but Rhys Morgan's. He stared steadily at Alex.

She flinched beneath his contemplative gaze, realizing he exhibited no doubt whatsoever that she would be perfectly capable of having stowed a dead body among her linens.

"Annie, you must be mistaken," soothed Claire. "Alex wouldn't have a dead man —"

"She does, too! I saw him." The little girl hiccoughed tearfully. "I just wanted to see if there were

70

any clothes for Madame Dragonflower in that big ol' trunk . . . and I saw him!"

Alex's face cleared and she stifled a sudden smile. "I think I can solve the mystery."

As one, the people in the room followed her toward the offending trunk. There, propped in a corner of the chest, on a stack of petticoats, was a pile of human bones, aged to a mellow ivory color. Resting on top was a saucily grinning skull.

"It's my grandfather's skeleton," she explained.

"Your grandfather's?" cried a horrified Cordelia.

"No, I mean it's one he used to have in his office back in Montreal. I brought it along to put in my own office. I'll have to reassemble it, of course."

There was a stunned silence for a few minutes, and then Albert Braunswager made a joke welcoming Grandpa's skeleton to the fort, and everyone laughed in relief. Claire alternately calmed Annie, then scolded her for snooping into someone else's belongings. Doc McLoughlin, grinning from ear to ear, clapped Alex on the shoulder as he passed by on his way back to supper.

"You know, Alex, most women pack dishes or jewelry when they go on a long journey. But not you . . . no, by God, not you!"

She wished she could share the doctor's amusement, but the glowering look on Rhys's face told her that the afternoon's efforts had been wasted. An innocent heap of bones had the man glaring at her as though she were some bloodthirsty female pirate or something.

She tried to tell herself it really didn't matter what he thought of her, but unfortunately it did. . . .

71

For the next few days, Alexandria was kept so busy helping Dr. McLoughlin that she no longer had time to worry about Rhys Morgan's opinion of her. It was as if the arrival of the men from Athabasca had thrown the Rendezvous into full swing, and each day there was a continuous line of patients waiting outside the apothecary.

Alex watched the doctor treat Indians and voyageurs alike for wounds sustained in fist fights or knife fights — he even extracted the occasional musket ball. There was one man who nearly drowned, another who broke his leg falling from the top of the lookout tower. Sadly enough, most of the injuries could be attributed directly to the free-flowing liquor. The overworked physician and his new assistant labored all one night over the victims of a fire that swept through the Indian encampment outside the fort's main gates — a fire that had been caused by a careless brave who overindulged in corn liquor, then passed out too close to his campfire, setting first his clothing and, eventually, the entire area on fire. Besides the man, two women and a child were badly burned. These and similar incidents filled every bed in the outpost's little hospital.

Another establishment that was utilized more during the Rendezvous than the rest of the year was the common jail, a small log building that had once been used as a privy. The stench alone was enough to sober all but the most drunken offenders, and the cries and pleas of those incarcerated for more than a few hours could be heard throughout the fort. It became Alex's duty to administer potions and purges to those arrested for extreme intoxication, because those men too drunk to stand alone were the only inhabitants of Kaministiquia who had no objection to being treated by a female. Alex was always accompanied by Baptiste, and it fell to him to prop up the more senseless patients so that she might pour the medicine down their throats. The ones who managed to remain conscious were so distracted by the sight of the pretty, red-headed lady doctor, they made little trouble—until they tasted the vile brew she was forcing upon them. Even explaining that she was acting under the orders of the fort's proprietor didn't help her cause at that point. The only thing she could do was grasp Baptiste's arm and let him escort her away, head held high as she ignored the shouts and threats of the retching men she left behind. The purges seemed to cure the inebriation faster than merely letting the men sleep off the effects of the liquor, and thus, the enforced stay in the jail was shorter, thereby freeing space for the next offenders. Most of the ones who had received treatment at Alex's hands gave her wide berth when they saw her again, and she was sorely afraid her reputation had suffered greatly.

On the first quiet morning she'd witnessed since coming to help McLoughlin, she was standing at the apothecary window staring out into the fort's main square. She felt more discouraged by her experiences at the fort than anything else, and was beginning to wonder if perhaps Rhys Morgan might be correct. Maybe there wasn't a place for her to practice medicine, even here in the wilderness. Most of the patients that Doc McLoughlin had attended had seemed pleased to have her hold their hands or bathe their brows—few had even objected to her mixing powders or pouring elixirs. But let her reach for a probe or the forceps and they shuddered in terror, begging McLoughlin to do the task himself. He was apologetic, but Alex realized there wasn't much he could do about the situation.

There almost seemed to be too much prejudice and superstition to deal with. An hour ago, when a distraught voyageur from the settlement across the river had come seeking help for his Indian wife who had been in labor a day and a half, Alex was not permitted to even accompany the doctor. When McLoughlin suggested she do so, the voyageur had hastily made the sign of the cross over his chest and backed away, mumbling that he would not allow the white witch inside his cabin, nor would he let his wife suffer from contact with her. Doctor McLoughlin had tried to soften the blow by asking her to keep an eye on his office while he was away, but once they had gone, Alex sank into a chair and, covering her face with her hands, gave vent to her frustration by shedding a few angry tears. How was she to prove her merit if no one would even give her a chance? Was she going to have to struggle against such ignorance no matter where she went?

After a moment she began to recall incidents from the arduous journey out from Montreal. It had not taken her long to gain the trust and respect of the brides headed for Sabaskong Falls. She had treated sunburn and weed itch, head colds and fevers, scrapes and bruises. She had won the confidence of each of them, even the ones who were skeptical at first, like Mellicent and Mrs. Rosswell. By the time their travels were nearly over, she suspected she had even gained the grudging admiration of the reverend himself. More than ever, she knew her future success depended upon her being able to convince the men around her of her capabilities . . . she had proven herself once, she would do it again. Feeling more cheerful, Alex jumped to her feet and began straightening the apothecary. She would be patient and bide her time — surely something would occur to aid and abet her determination to be accepted as a doctor. She swept the floor, then dusted the shelves and their contents, and had just placed a clean sheet on the cot when she heard a shout from outside.

Alex ran to the window, her heartbeat quickening as she saw Baptiste leading a group of men toward the doctor's office. In their midst, three voyageurs were carrying a fourth — a man whose head lolled to one side and whose leg was covered with fresh blood. They were being followed by Waldo Anderson, Malachi Harper, and two Indians.

Alex threw open the door. "What happened?" she queried, stepping aside to make room for the injured man to be transported into the room.

"Jacques got himself wounded in a knife fight, *mademoiselle*," Baptiste explained. "He needs a doctor quickly, so we brought him here."

"But Dr. McLoughlin is away — he was called to the settlement on the other side of the river," Alexandria explained, her eyes already busy with a cursory examination of the unconscious voyageur.

"Then you must take care of him," insisted Baptiste. "He has lost much blood."

Alex nodded briskly. "Put him on the table in the

surgery," she instructed, reaching for the large canvas apron hanging behind the door. "Now, you'll all have to move back and give me some room."

"Rhys!" shouted Malachi Harper, bursting into the storeroom. "Waldo sent me. He says you'd better get on over to the doctor's office."

Rhys looked up from the pelts he was wrapping. "What's wrong?"

"One of the north men got himself slashed in a fight, and they took him over to Doc McLoughlin's . . . only Doc ain't there and that Alexandria woman is working on him."

Rhys tried to hide a smile. "She's wanted a chance to look like a doctor," he said. "Maybe tending a dead-drunk voyageur will give it to her."

"But, Rhys," protested Harper, "you gotta put a stop to it."

"Someone has to patch the man up, Malachi. And if the female makes a mistake and kills him, well, it's what the damned fool gets for drinking and carousing in the middle of the day." He turned back to the pile of furs on the table in front of him.

Malachi shifted feet impatiently. "You don't understand, Rhys—she's got him on that table stark naked!"

"What?" Rhys spun about to fix him with a lethal stare. "Tell me you're joking," he demanded.

"It's no joke. Waldo and me saw her rip off his trousers. Hell, all the men saw it."

"That little idiot," breathed Rhys. "She doesn't have the sense God gave a titmouse."

Furs forgotten, he stalked out of the storeroom,

leaving Harper to catch up with him. When he arrived at the apothecary, he flung open the door and strode inside.

Alexandria looked up long enough to mutter, "Shut the door, please."

Rhys couldn't believe the scene that met his eyes. The room was filled with curious onlookers, amusement showing on most of the faces. Arms folded across his bare chest, the man on the table was, for all intents and purposes, dead to the world. His eyes were closed, and his mouth twisted upward in a blissful smile He was completely naked except for the skunkskin cap Waldo had placed over his exposed genitals.

Alexandria was hovering over him, the silver needle she wielded flashing in the light of the lamp Baptiste was holding for her. Her arm brushed the cap and sent it flying, but when Waldo scrambled to replace it, she said gently, "There's no need for the cap, Waldo—it only gets in my way. Thank you anyway."

Rhys gritted his teeth as he noted the looks that were exchanged around the room. Had she no idea of the gossip this incident was going to spawn? Good God, had she no modesty?

Alexandria worked steadily, as if totally unaware of the voyageur's blatant display of gender. She was stitching together the raw, jagged edges of a wound that started at one hip and curved downward nearly to the knee. Rhys noticed the seam she sewed was every bit as neat as the one she had used on the cloth doll.

When she had finished closing the wound, she sprinkled it with a fine, yellow powder, and then proceeded to wrap the leg in clean gauze bandages. As her hand carelessly brushed the man's most private flesh, Rhy's expression grew even grimmer, and his jaw muscles clenched tightly. He couldn't fail to see the glances the men in the room exchanged, the leers they directed at Alexandria.

She was just swabbing several other nasty looking cuts on the man's body with a pungent lotion when Dr. McLoughlin walked into the room.

"Alexandria?" he said, setting aside the leather case he carried. "What is going on?"

Before she could speak, several of the men began offering explanations.

"You would not believe it, Doc," one of them said. "Jacques and René got rip-roarin' drunk, and then got into a fight about which of them had the biggest. . . ."

"*Oui,* you should have seen them," laughed another. "They stripped off their clothes and commenced to duel with long knives. René would have killed him for sure, but he passed out in the middle of deliverin' the final blow!"

"We put his pants back on before bringing him here," the third voyageur informed McLoughlin. "But the lady, she just tore them off again."

The doctor's eyebrows twitched in amusement as he approached the table, though he kept his voice controlled. "I take it no arteries were severed?"

Alex shook her head. "No, fortunately. He bled profusely for a time, but the deepest part of the wound was in the fatty tissues of the thigh."

McLoughln ran a practiced eye over the man's less serious injuries, then said, "Some of you men put him on the cot, will you? We'll keep him a day or two and make sure he stays off that leg and away from liquor."

"But, Doc," said one of the voyageurs. "Ain't you gonna see that she did it right?"

"No need," replied McLoughlin. "From what I've seen of Miss MacKenzie's abilities in the past few days, I have the fullest confidence she has done everything possible."

Alex's face flushed with pleasure, and Rhys Morgan looked away. He needed no reminder of how beautiful she was—she was the prettiest woman he'd ever seen, even standing there in a bloodstained apron with her hair straggling untidily from its pins. It also disturbed him to see the exchange of warm glances between her and McLoughlin—the two of them were becoming far too friendly to suit him. The best thing that could happen, in his opinion, was for the Rendezvous to end, so that he might put her on a boat departing for civilization. The sooner she was out of his sight, the sooner his life would return to normal.

Rhys stooped and picked up Waldo's skunkskin cap, handing it back to the trapper. "Why don't you men get on back to the cantine now? I'd like a word with Miss MacKenzie . . . in private."

As the grinning men reluctantly filed out the door, heading for the fort's popular Cantine Salope—the Harlot's Tavern, Alex took off the soiled apron and busied herself pouring out water to wash her hands.

Oh, dear, she was thinking, here we go again. What have I done this time?

Chapter Five

"What in the devil did you think you were doing?"
Rhys Morgan towered over her in the stance Alexandria was beginning to recognize as the one he adopted whenever he felt inclined to do battle—hands on hips, one knee slightly bent, shoulders tilted forward.

"What do you mean?" she asked with more courage than she felt.

"You've effectively ruined any chance you might have had to be accepted as a decent woman in this fort. And, even worse, you've made yourself fair game for the men. And not just the bourgeois, but the voyageurs and Indians, as well. How do you intend to keep yourself safe from their advances—or had you even thought of that?"

"Mr. Morgan," Alex said, looking into his shadowed blue eyes and fighting the desire to flinch at the coldness reflected there. "I haven't the faintest notion what you're talking about."

"Alex," interceded McLoughlin, "I think he means—"

"Stay out of this," Rhys nearly shouted. "Good God, man, you're the one who left her in charge. Couldn't you foresee what would happen?"

"Now, look here, Morgan—"

"Excuse me," Alex said calmly, "but exactly what did happen? I saved a man from possibly bleeding to death. I didn't realize that was a crime of some sort."

"Why the hell did you tear his pants off?" Rhys demanded.

"Because I needed to get to the wound as quickly as I could," she answered. "And I didn't have time for niceties."

"Obviously not," he said dryly.

Both were unaware that McLoughlin had turned away to hide the bemused smile that was distorting his mouth.

"Didn't you even consider the consequences?" Rhys continued.

"What? That I might have an unimpeded view of the injury? That I might not be hampered by clothing that would only get in the way and probably spread more filth . . . ?"

"No decent woman risks her reputation by looking at a naked man in public," he stormed.

"The only reputation that concerns me is my reputation as a doctor," she flung back. "And I wasn't *looking at* him!"

"Tell that to the men who were in the room."

"What those men think is of little interest to me—as long as they know I did the best I could to save that voyageur's life."

"You don't care that, in their minds, you're no better than a wanton? A *cantine* whore?"

She gasped angrily, causing McLoughlin to chide, "Now, Rhys, you're going too far."

"Doc, I wish you'd stay out of this. She's got to face the realities of life out here, and the reality is that a woman does not undress a man in full view of an audience — and she doesn't face nudity with a calmness that suggests she sees it every day."

"A woman might not," Alexandria pointed out, "but a *doctor* would. Once I'm accepted as a physician, no one will worry about such trivial matters."

"Trivial?" Rhys sputtered.

"Yes, the matter under discussion was quite trivial." Alex seized her sunbonnet from the peg behind the door. "In fact," she said cheekily, "so trivial I doubt very seriously that the man could have won that contest between himself and the other voyageur."

Before he fully grasped the meaning of her words, she had flung herself out the door, to join Baptiste who was waiting to escort her back to her room. The sound of McLoughlin's delighted laughter followed her all the way across the compound.

"Look at the way that impudent *coquette* is twitching her skirts," muttered Rhys. "Is she trying to catch the attention of every man in the fort?"

"You told me to stay out of it, remember?"

"Is everyone in this place bent on aggravating me?"

"By God, Rhys," chuckled McLoughlin, wiping tears of laughter from his eyes, "this is unbelievable."

"What is?"

"You. Your reaction to that pretty young girl. You know what's wrong with you, don't you?"

"Of course. I've been burdened with responsibilities I don't want. And she's the worst headache of the lot."

"You may choose to believe that, but don't expect me to. Wake up, Rhys, and see your anger for what it really is."

Rhys turned an intense look on the doctor, one black brow rising ominously.

McLoughlin shook his head, still laughing. "You're jealous, man. That's all."

"That's all?" Rhys nearly shouted. "You make a ridiculous statement like that and say '*that's all*?'"

"Calm down. It doesn't obligate you in any way to admit the truth."

"If you seriously think I'm jealous of that flighty little hoyden, you're as wrong as a fellow can be. Why, for all we know, she's one of those . . . unnatural women whose only wish in life is to be a man. Wait long enough and I'll wager you're bound to see her show up in trousers."

McLoughlin's face was red with barely constrained mirth. "Rhys Morgan, for a normally intelligent man, you got mighty stupid in a hurry. If you think about it, you'll figure out there isn't one thing masculine—or unnatural—about Alex MacKenzie."

"Oh, go to hell," Rhys mumbled, stalking out the door.

But, as he made his way back to the storehouse, he knew the doctor was right. And he'd already spent far too much time thinking about that very thing. Since the moment she'd stepped out of the Montreal canoe, Alexandria MacKenzie had been on his mind in one way or another. And from the top of her tousled red-gold hair to the tips of the black boots that peeped so primly from beneath modest skirts, he knew there was nothing masculine about her. She was, in fact, too dangerously, frighteningly female for him or any other six men to handle.

He swore silently. He had to stop letting her dominate his every waking moment, that was all there was to it. He had to become ruthless in exorcising her from his mind. From now on, each time she appeared in his thoughts, he was going to cast her out . . . brutally, if need be. He already had a life of his own, and there was simply no place in it for anyone like Alexandria.

Alex sat on her bed in the dormitory, surrounded by noisy confusion . . . and totally unaware of anything but her own thoughts. How, she wondered, could she have made such a brazen remark to Rhys Morgan? She had spoken the absolute truth when she'd said she hadn't even noticed that the injured man had been naked. She had concentrated solely on the wound and on employing her best knowledge to treat it — and it had angered her unreasonably that Morgan would just naturally assume she'd have stolen covert peeks at the voyageur's masculine attributes. For heaven's sake, if she had been performing surgery on the man's eye, she wouldn't have spared time to admire the fine slant of his nose!

"What's ailin' ye, lassie?" asked Aberdeen, from her position on the floor where she was pinning up the hem in Birdie's wedding gown.

"Oh, nothing." Alexandria casually smoothed Nasturtium's fur and avoided Aberdeen's gaze.

"Nothing, eh? Is that the reason ye keep sighin' and shiftin' about so restlessly?" The Scotswoman slipped another pin into the pale blue satin. "I suspect ye've been talking to Mr. Morgan again."

"Oh, Deenie, why are men so thickheaded?"

"Now I know ye've been speakin' with the man." Aberdeen smiled. "And what has he accused ye of this time?"

"Just because I sewed up a voyageur's leg, Rhys thinks I'm a . . . a wanton, I believe he phrased it."

Claire looked up from her own sewing. "A wanton? Why, how could he think such a thing?"

Aberdeen didn't look nearly so shocked. "Yes, lassie, what would give him an idea like that?"

"How should I know?" Alex responded, lifting her chin defiantly and staring off across the room.

"Lassie," prompted Aberdeen, a knowing glint in her black eyes. "Ye're lookin' a bit too innocent for the likes o' me."

"Oh, all right. I took off the man's pants before I started work on him," said Alex. "And just because he was naked, I've suddenly gotten the reputation of being a loose woman."

She heard several gasps from around the room, and her chin tilted even higher.

"There was nothing else to be done," she explained. "His clothing was in the way—and he really was injured rather seriously."

"And I suppose ye performed this act of medical expediency beneath the eyes of a dozen men?" queried Aberdeen blandly.

"Only seven," Alex corrected. "Until Rhys Morgan arrived on the scene, that is. Lord, was he furious."

"Isn't he always?" laughed Lily.

"Did he shout at you?" asked Judith.

"Doesn't he always?" Alex echoed, then began to smile. "The man is insufferable . . . and why he thinks he needs to be responsible for me is something I don't understand."

"If you don't behave yourself," cautioned Cordelia, "he truly won't allow you to go on to Sabaskong Falls with us."

"The harder I try to be on my best behavior, the worse it gets," complained Alex. "And now I've even started irritating him when I do what I'm supposed to be doing."

"Ooh," squealed Birdie in delight, "it must be thrilling to be able to undress a man . . . and claim it's all in the line of duty."

"Hhmmp," snorted Aberdeen. "Ye'd best get yer mind off such matters and worry about finishing this dress in time for the wedding dance."

"Yes, and then you can undress your own man," spoke up Mellicent. "Big, hulking lump that he is."

"Don't remind me," chortled Birdie. "I'm not sure I can stand to wait!"

"Have you forgotten that you're a lady?" scolded Mellicent.

"Have you forgotten that I'm also a spinster?" retorted Birdie. "And that I've been one for about as long as I intend to?"

"Shameful," muttered Mellicent.

"Honest," corrected Birdie.

"Hush, ye two," said Aberdeen. "Let's have no quarreling. We've got too much to do to waste our time this way."

Alexandria suddenly glanced up to see a determined-looking Lily standing before her. "Alex," she said in a low voice, "there is something important I'd like to speak to you about . . ."

"What is it?"

"Do you remember not long ago when you were gathering those herbs along the trail? And I asked you what they were for?"

"Yes . . ."

"And you recall that you said they were for preventing childbirth?"

Warily, Alex nodded.

"Was that true? I mean, do they work?"

"My grandfather was conducting a study of certain effective plants," replied Alex. "Ones the Indians have used for years. It does appear that there is some merit in their ability to prevent conception."

"Will you let me have some of them?"

"You? But, Lily—"

"You may think it's awful of me, but I don't want babies right away. I grew up in a family with ten children, and I'm simply not anxious to start a family of my own. I'd like for it to be just Pacer and me for a while."

"Have you discussed this with him?"

"Yes, and he feels the same way I do."

Alex lowered her voice even more. "Lily, before . . . when you lived with the man you told me about, what did you do then? Four years is a long time to remain childless."

"Mr. Kerns was sterile, Alex. At least, that's what

he told me—and it seems to have been true. But there's no doubt in my mind that Pacer could father a whole village of children, if he had a mind to." She ended on a nervous giggle, and Alex had to smile with her.

"I find myself in total agreement with you on the matter." She left the bed and went to one of her metal trunks, returning with a small cloth bag which she pressed into Lily's hand. "Here. This is a mixture of three herbs. Put a teaspoonful into a cup of tea every morning, without fail. I hope it works well for you."

"What is that?" asked Birdie, catching sight of the bag.

"None of your concern," snapped Lily. "Alex and I were having a private conversation."

"Oh," said Birdie, beginning to smile. "Were you discussing matters of the flesh?"

"Dear Lord, Birdie!" exclaimed Cordelia. "Is that all you think about?"

"It really is something all of us should think about," Lily said, jumping to her feet. "The lot of you would be smart to talk to Alex the way I did."

Claire hurriedly shooed her children out the door, promising to come get them as soon as the discussion was finished. Tobias and Annie, pleased to be trusted to take care of themselves, skipped off toward the dining hall. "Don't leave the building," Claire called after them before closing the door.

"All right lassie," said Aberdeen, taking a seat on the edge of one of the beds. "What's going on?"

"As Lily said, it's a delicate matter," hedged Alex.

"Since we're all about to become married women . . ." Birdie began.

"Almost all," put in Aberdeen with a grimace.

"You'll change your mind about Waldo the moment you hear the wedding march," prophesied Cordelia.

"Nay. The man is a reprobate . . . and a none too clean one, at that. I'll no' be jumpin' over the broom with him!"

"Now, Aberdeen, you're as anxious to get a man as the rest of us," teased Mellicent.

"Yes, a *man*—and that leaves Waldo Anderson out of the matter. Now, let's quit blatherin' and listen to what Alex has to say."

With all eyes upon her again, Alexandria drew a deep breath. "I don't actually have anything to say. . . ."

"Alex gave me a powder that will prevent having babies," Lily announced loudly. "I think you should all get some for yourselves."

A buzz of voices rose in the room, and Alex tried to calm them. "Ladies, please—this is really between Lily and myself. I can't advocate the use of the preventive for all of you."

"And why not, lass?" spoke up Aberdeen. "Mayhap some of the other women realize that nothing in this world will wear a woman out and make her old before her time the way bearing too many bairns can."

"Yes," said Claire. "Lord knows I love Toby and Annie, but the idea of having more babies right away is an unpleasant one. I want to be sure I'm going to like my new home before I start having Gideon's children."

"But isn't childbirth prevention against the teachings of the church?" inquired Judith doubtfully.

"Think about it logically," Aberdeen said. "With a smaller number of wee ones, a man and his wife can better afford to give them the advantages they deserve. Homes wouldna be so crowded, food so dear. And think what it could mean to a family if the mother was not sickly and worn out from having too many babies."

Alex waited until the next round of comments had faded away before she spoke. "I think it's important that each of you speak to your husbands about this. . . ."

"Why?" snapped Birdie. "It wouldn't be them having the babies!"

"We've given up everything to travel here to the lake country," stated Mellicent. "And we'll be marrying virtual strangers. It's possible that some of us may become unhappy with our circumstances and decide to return to Montreal next spring. Wouldn't it be better if we had only ourselves to think about? With no small children to worry over?"

"Ye have a good point, Mellie," Aberdeen said, nodding sagely. "Going home might be easier if there were no wee bairns who'd be needin' a father."

"Well, I for one intend to make the best of my marriage," spoke up Cordelia. "After all, a bargain is a bargain."

"I hope you are very happy, Cordy," said Birdie fervently. "Nothing would please us more. But . . . just in case, would it be too much to ask you to try to prevent a child—until you know for certain that you and Malachi are properly suited?"

"I don't know," Cordelia said slowly. "Are there ways . . . I mean, how does one go about something like that?"

Again, all eyes turned toward Alex. She cleared her throat, not at all certain she liked the direction the discussion was taking. "My grandfather devoted a great deal of study to the problem of childbirth prevention," she explained. "His own mother died at a very young age, bearing her second child after more than a dozen stillbirths. During his travels, he began noticing that sometimes the most primitive native tribes had better means of curbing conception than supposedly civilized nations, and that they regulated the sizes of their families more judiciously. In attempting to learn why this should be, he came across several highly successful methods of childbirth prevention. All of them involved herbal concoctions, made from formulas which he jotted down in a journal. Over the years, whenever a patient spoke to him of such matters, he encouraged the usage of these herbs . . . with very satisfactory results. But . . ."

"Are these common herbs?" asked Claire, with an interested expression.

"Yes. Fortunately, most of the plants can be found in abundance all over Canada," said Alexandria. "Grandfather had heard rumors that the Chippewa women commonly used one or two of them, and he had intended to do further research when he arrived here."

"How are the herbs prepared?" queried Cordelia.

"The three that I gathered on the way here must be dried and pounded into a powder. One spoonful of the powder in a cup of tea each morning will hopefully prevent conception."

"A cup of tea?" repeated Birdie. "That's all?"

"But it must be taken faithfully," Alex warned.

"Well, I think it's a sound idea," stated Judith. "Even morally speaking, I'm not so sure it isn't better to prevent birth than to bring a child into an uncertain situation."

"Ye may be right about that," agreed Aberdeen. "Were I to be married, I'd try yer herbs, Alex . . . even at my advanced age."

Even Christiana, lying on her bed and looking wan and weak, had to smile.

"Will you give us the powder if we want it?" asked Cordelia.

Alex frowned. "I suppose so, but you must . . ."

Just then a loud knock sounded at the door.

As he'd crossed the dining hall toward the women's dormitory, Rhys Morgan had heard the sound of Alex's voice, and he'd silently acknowledged that she was a natural leader, undeniably looked up to by the others. At times like this, when she was safely within the confines of the dormitory, talking and laughing . . . and not stirring up trouble, he could almost relent and agree to her going to Sabaskong with them. Almost. . . .

Each time he considered it, all the reasons she should not go filtered steadily into his mind—she was too young, too inexperienced, too vulnerable. He sighed. Too pretty, too *unmarried*. God, he couldn't imagine the havoc someone like her could wreak in a small settlement of trappers and backwoodsmen! With no man to protect her, and no sense of decorum herself, she'd fall victim to the first ruthless, unprincipled rogue who came along.

No, he couldn't be responsible for that. He rapped firmly on the bedroom door. He had been put in charge, so this unpleasant duty fell to him. He'd simply do what he had to do and get it over with.

Aberdeen McPhie opened the door and, when she saw Rhys, favored him with a beaming smile. "Ah, 'tis Mr. Morgan. Is there aught we can do for ye?"

"I'd like a word with Miss MacKenzie, if you don't mind."

"Oh, t'won't be me mindin," Aberdeen assured him gaily. "But I'd no' speak for the lass herself."

"Of course I'll talk to Mr. Morgan," Alex affirmed, approaching the doorway. "Is there another problem?"

He shook his head slightly. "Same one, Miss MacKenzie. Unfortunately."

She nodded, warily.

"Uh . . . perhaps we could walk somewhere while we discuss this matter?"

"Certainly." Alex flashed Aberdeen a quick look as she handed Nasturtium over to her. "I won't be long, Deenie."

Once they left the Mess Hall and entered the bustling square, Rhys took her elbow. The warmth of his fingers through the thin cotton sleeve of her gown was disturbing, to say the least, but she did not pull away because she recognized the gesture for what it was, a signal to the men who stopped to watch their progress that she was under Morgan's protection and that he would brook no interference.

"Shall we walk along the river?" he was asking. "It will be quieter there."

"Yes, that would be fine." Alexandria's mind was busy with thoughts of what he wanted to discuss. Perhaps he had reached a decision about hiring her as a doctor. She stole a swift sideways glance, which told her nothing. His eyes were dark and unreadable.

They passed through the main gate, and he steered

her past a throng of half-drunken voyageurs cheering on the bedraggled participants of a fist fight. When Alex's feet slowed to a stop, his grip tightened and he forced her to keep walking.

"Shouldn't we put a stop to that before someone gets hurt?" she protested.

"It's Rendezvous, Alex," he barked. "You can't control everything that goes on."

"But, as a doctor, it's my duty to prevent injury as well as to treat it."

He gave her an exasperated look and muttered, "We've got to talk about this . . . this doctor business."

She followed him more willingly, with only one last doubtful look at the fighters. Time was growing short, and she knew they needed to settle the issue once and for all.

When they reached a quieter section of the riverbank, Rhys released his hold on her arm and allowed her to move at her own pace. She absentmindedly rubbed the spot where his fingers had curled, still feeling his touch.

"I'm sorry if I was too rough," he said.

"Hmm?"

He nodded toward her arm. "Just now. I didn't mean to hurt you."

"Oh! Oh, no, you didn't." Alexandria looked down as if surprised to see her own hand, then dropped it hastily. "What exactly did you wish to say to me?"

A breeze from the wide river whipped her skirts and pulled strands of hair from their anchoring pins. Rhys found himself staring down at her, unable to stop his mind from cataloging every detail of her appearance. She was wearing an old-fashioned gown of plain blue, making him realize that the lightweight Mediterranean fashions so popular in Europe would be totally inappropriate for the climate in Canada. And the last time he had been in Montreal, the ladies had been painted and powdered — but Alexandria MacKenzie obviously didn't employ such artifice. Her skin, pale yet with the faint golden underglow of health, was adorned only by a light sprinkling of freckles across her nose. Her eyes, as gray as a mountain tarn, were fringed by thick, dark lashes whose color reminded him of the young minks who swam and played around the dock back at Sabaskong. And her hair — that glorious mass of shining, shimmering red-gold — it swirled about her head, scorning the modest style she had attempted to force upon it, with all the eager independence of Alex herself.

His eyes fell to her slightly parted lips, thinking how much they reminded him of freshly ripe fruit. Suddenly he became aware that she had spoken and was awaiting his reply.

"I'm sorry . . . what did you say?"

Alex shifted uncomfortably beneath his scrutiny. "I asked what it was you wished to talk to me about. Have I done something despicable again?"

He appreciated her tentative smile a few seconds before making an answer. "No, not this time. Although the fort is still buzzing with the story of you and Jacques."

She shrugged. "I'm certain something else will soon happen to put it out of everyone's minds."

He grimaced. "I do hope you have no plans to be in the middle of *that* incident, as well."

Her squarely stubborn chin rose an inch or two.

"Of course not."

He surprised himself by asking his next question, because it wasn't something he'd even thought about wanting to know. "Why would a woman like you want to be a doctor?"

"I doubt I could ever make you understand." Alex began to walk slowly along the worn path, and he fell into step beside her.

"Give it a try," he commanded softly.

"Well, I suppose it was growing up in my grandparents' house, and seeing Grandfather help so many patients. He was a highly respected physician in Montreal, you know."

"So I understand."

"He cared about what happened to people, and devoted his life to study and research. As I got older, I began to dream about how wonderful it would be to carry on in his footsteps . . . and he encouraged me."

"He had no grandsons?"

"No, but it wouldn't have mattered if he had. Grandfather always declared that gender had nothing to do with one's ability to heal. In fact, as he often pointed out to clients who questioned my presence in his surgery, Aesculapius, the father of medicine, was delivered by a *woman*." She offered him a brief smile. "Female doctors were regarded as extremely competent in Greece, Sumeria, and Egypt, as far back as the periods scientists call the Stone and Bronze Ages. The Chinese and Siamese were allowing women to be surgeons a thousand years before the birth of Christ!"

Her face glowed with earnest conviction, and Rhys had to look away, disciplining his gaze by forcing it to trace the line of trees on the far bank of the Kaministiquia. If he let himself fall victim to her sincerity and beauty, his arguments would amount to less than nothing. He had to be strong, harden his heart against the ease with which she could touch that sensitive spot within him he had thought long since callused over.

"Alexandria," he said slowly, "this is all very interesting, but it has nothing to do with the present situation."

"It has everything to do with it," she insisted. "What I am trying to say is that women have been doctors since the beginning of time. . . ."

"And yet, I don't know of a single one," he pointed out. "If what you say is true, why are there no female doctors today?"

"Because the rise of Christianity brought the downfall of women," she declared. "For some reason, when the church fathers came into power, they decided women's brains were no longer capable of functioning. Suddenly, a female became no more important than . . . than a horse or dog. Less important, in most cases."

"I thought Christianity enlightened the world," he commented.

"Maybe for men," she said. "But for women it meant a period of repression. Our social progress was set back hundreds of years. And it's ridiculous, because women aren't weak . . . and they aren't stupid. Believe me, I debated that point often enough with Reverend Rosswell on the way here from Montreal."

"And did you convince him?"

"Probably not. He's one of those narrow-minded men who think a woman is fit for little besides being a wife and mother—and then, only with strict guidance from her husband."

"While you, on the other hand, promote self-sufficiency for females?"

"Yes, I do! That's exactly what I'm striving for. I'm going to be a doctor my grandfather would have been proud of."

This time it was Rhys who stopped walking. Almost reluctantly, he moved into the path in front of her. "Alex, I actually do hope you can realize your goal someday. But take my word for it, this isn't the time or the place."

"But—"

He dropped both hands onto her shoulders "Wait, let me finish. I've seen too many women leave the cities to try to make a life for themselves out here in the wilderness. In a few years, they're tired and defeated, either running back to the civilization they've known . . . or dying from the need to go back. I didn't particularly want this job, but the men from Sabaskong put me in charge . . . and I just can't allow you to go on with us. I'm sorry."

"But what about the brides?" exclaimed Alex. "I'm better suited for this life than some of them."

"You may be right. But they aren't my concern—you are. They've all got men to be responsible for them, to look after them."

"I don't need anyone to look after me. I'm perfectly capable of that myself. Besides, Aberdeen isn't getting married, and she's planning to travel on to Sabaskong Falls."

"But she isn't going to create the problems you would."

"What sort of problems?"

"You have to stop and think what the appearance of a beautiful, young . . . *unattached* girl would mean in the backwoods. Some of those men haven't been close to a white woman for a decade, especially one like you. With your stubborn disregard for the conventions, your good name wouldn't last a week."

"To Hades with my good name," she stormed. "I don't give a fig for my precious reputation."

He smiled wryly. "I've noticed. However, if you continue to act as thoughtlessly as you did this morning, word of your indiscretions will precede you back to Montreal — and I'm sure you realize what that would mean."

"It doesn't matter. I'm not going back to Montreal."

"Yes you are," he said almost gently. "Alexandria, you have to."

"I won't."

"You have no choice. I'm not going to hire you as Sabaskong's doctor."

The quietness of his tone seemed to convince her, for she tightened her lips over further arguments. She stared up at him, eyes wide and filled with pain. Rhys cursed himself for being foolish enough to touch her — he should have known it would be a mistake. With his hands resting on her shoulders, he could almost feel the misery that surged through her. Her sudden despair was apparent in the way her body slumped, the way she seemed to grow smaller as though shutting herself away from him and the harsh reality he presented.

With a sigh, Rhys dropped his hands. "I'm sorry . . . but this is for the best. Next winter, when you're sitting in front of your fireplace in the city, you'll thank me."

"If I ever think of you again," she muttered, "it will be to revile your name."

"Someone has to protect you from your own rashness."

"But it isn't up to you," Alex cried. "Why couldn't you just have stayed out of this and let me handle my own life?"

She turned and fled down the pathway toward the fort. Unhappy to have shattered her dreams, yet resigned to the fact that he was right, Rhys followed, determined to make sure she got back to the dormitory unharmed. However, Alex did not return to the Mess Hall as he'd expected. Instead, once she got inside the main gate, she headed directly to Dr. McLoughlin's office.

Rhys stalked after her, but just as he stepped up to the front door, he saw Alexandria through the window. She was clearly crying and distraught now, and when she flung herself at McLoughlin, the doctor put his arms around her. Pressing her head to his brawny chest, he patted her back comfortingly.

Rhys's hand fell from the door latch as he turned away. The sight of the doctor listening to Alex's complaints against him made his jaw tighten in anger. Wasn't that just like a woman? To take one man's attempt at reason and twist it, in order to wring sympathy from another? In a way, it only seemed to emphasize the rightness of his decision.

Damn the little fool, he thought. And damn her inborn ability to stir up trouble.

He strode in the direction of the Cantine Salope. He wasn't interested in the boasts of drunken voyageurs or the advances of the giggling Chippewa girls who lingered there, but God knew, he could certainly use a drink!

Chapter Six

Alexandria realized that a tension of sorts was building within Fort Kaministiquia. Perhaps it was simply the fact that Rendezvous was drawing to a close. The agents and partners had nearly finished their business, and the common-men were beginning to sense a need to start on the return journeys to their assorted posts.

Or maybe it was the threat of a summer storm that hung over the fort. Every day the ominous clouds piled high, the air growing hushed and heavy . . . but the storm did not come. Waiting for it, knowing it was inevitable but not knowing when it would happen, seemed to put everyone on edge. The heat became more intense—even the nights were humid and uncomfortable.

Alex wished fervently for the storm to break. Somehow, she had begun to think that, once the weather changed, she would be able to make a decision about what she should do. Surely, if the air were cleared of tension, some sensible solution would occur to her.

She had turned the dilemma over in her mind for hours on end. If she went back to Montreal it would mean defeat for her plan to work as a doctor. And though Rhys Morgan had made it very clear he would not allow her to travel any further with the brides, she could defy his edict that she go back to the city by staying on at Kaministiquia. The thought was a tempting one, and she was beginning to seriously consider it. Perhaps she should speak with Dr. McLoughlin. Surely he could give her some sound advice.

Two hours later, when Alex dashed through the door into the dormitory, Aberdeen was waiting, hands on hips.

"Where have ye been, lass? 'Tis the night of the weddings and ye're going to be late for dinner!"

"No, I won't," Alex promised, flinging aside her sunbonnet and dropping onto her bed to unhook her boots. "Oh, Deenie, you'll never guess—something wonderful has happened."

"And what might that be?"

Alexandria laughed merrily. "Don't look so suspicious. I went to Dr. McLoughlin for advice, and he offered to let me stay on here as his assistant."

"Alex, that is good news," said Claire, turning away from the mirror where she was arranging her hair. "But are you sure it's what you want to do?"

Alex shrugged. "No, of course it isn't what I want to do, but it's the only real choice I have. I am not going back to Montreal."

"I think it is so mean of Rhys Morgan to refuse to hire you just because you're a woman," observed Lily. "Especially after you came all this way."

"What does he expect us to do for a doctor?" queried Judith angrily. "We were told we'd be living in a community with an experienced physician."

"Seems his partner, Scotty McPherson, knows a little about medicine," stated Cordelia. "Morgan says we'll have to make do with him until a replacement for Alex can get here next summer."

"Well I don't like it one bit," groused Birdie. "I was counting on Alex being there to help us. And now, what about the matter of childbirth prevention? How can we ask this Scotty about things like that?"

"I'll be sending the herbal mixtures with Aberdeen," announced Alex, slipping out of her dress. "She'll just have to take my place. And if you are all very careful, perhaps you'll have no need of a midwife or doctor right away."

The sound of low, rumbling thunder could be heard through the open windows.

"Seems as though the storm will finally break," said Aberdeen. " 'Tis a pity it chose the night of the weddings."

Alex chuckled. "Aberdeen, something tells me you and I will be the only ones to notice."

"And don't forget me," spoke up Christiana. "My fiancé isn't here, remember." She turned her head aside and coughed listlessly, causing Alex to frown.

"Christy, hasn't that cough begun to get worse? It has hung on for an interminable amount of time, if I recall."

"It's nothing to worry about," the thin, dark-haired

woman insisted. "Not on an evening when we are all supposed to be happy and excited."

"Nevertheless, I want to prepare some medication before you leave this fort," Alex informed her. "It wouldn't do for you to go out to Sabaskong and get ill."

"Especially since there won't be a doctor there," Mellicent grumbled. She tugged at the bodice of her plain black gown. "Does this low neckline look immodest?" she asked, turning to peer into the full-length mirror the proprietor had loaned them.

"No, you look lovely," chirped Birdie, pinning silk roses into her curled blond hair. "In fact, I think we all look lovely."

"I have to agree," said Alex, pausing in her petticoats to gaze around the room. "This is going to be the most beautiful wedding any of us has ever seen."

The brides were dressed in their best clothing, gowns they had struggled to bring from the city, knowing full well this might be the only occasion for wearing them. There was a variety of lacy shawls and silk flowers, hats and veils, and gloves. Alex was enchanted by the elegance and color the wedding finery had brought to the simple room—she could only imagine the reaction of the men when the ladies appeared in the dining hall.

Reverend Rosswell was going to conduct the weddings after the evening meal, with the ceremonies to be followed by a dance. It was the last night of Rendezvous, and because the festivities would last until dawn, several of the company officers had volunteered their quarters for the night, so that the newly wedded couples might have some privacy. Alexandria thought about coming back to the virtually empty dormitory, and for the first time, she felt a slight pang of envy for the women who would be stealing away with their new husbands. She and the eight brides-to-be had formed a close bond on their journey, but she had only now begun to realize how much she was going to miss them.

"Alex, do you like my dress?" a small voice piped, drawing her away from her gloomy thoughts. Annie stood before her, holding out the skirts of a pink satin dress that exactly matched her mother's.

"Oh my, yes! It looks beautiful on you!" Alex winked at Tobias, who stood nearby looking uncomfortable in a dark suit and ruffled shirt. "But she'd better watch out, hadn't she? Since Aberdeen turned him down, Waldo Anderson is looking for a bride—he might just think Annie is the one for him."

Toby burst out laughing at his sister's outraged expression. "Annie doesn't like the smell of his cap any more than Aberdeen does!"

"Ye're a smart lass, then," stated Aberdeen. "Ye just stay close to me, Annie, and we'll see that Waldo keeps his distance."

"All right, but don't forget that I'm supposed to toss flower petals in front of the brides," said the child.

"Oh, isn't it going to be a wonderful wedding?" sighed Birdie.

"Not if ye're all late," scolded Aberdeen. "Alex, get your dress and let me hook it up for ye."

Alexandria waved her away. "Why don't you all go on to dinner? I can manage without help—besides, I'd like to wash up before I dress. Save me a place, and I'll meet you in the dining hall."

When the others had gone, in a flurry of rustling

106

skirts and nervous laughter, Alex poured water from a china pitcher into a bowl and began a hasty sponge bath. Now that some of the worry over her future was eliminated, she felt almost carefree, ready to enjoy the evening ahead. Staying on at the fort would at least give her the opportunity to continue a practice of sorts and, hopefully, the chance to see some of her friends from time to time.

She slipped her best gown over her head, leaning forward to hook it, then smoothing its wide white satin skirts. The dress was one she had worn to the last Practicing Physician's ball she had attended with her grandfather. On a whim, she had brought it with her to the wilderness, but now that she had a chance to wear it, she wondered if it might not seem a bit daring for the occasion. The neckline scooped low, revealing the upper swells of her bosom, the waist was tight, and the sleeves were short and puffed. Alex studied herself in the mirror, and, thinking of Rhys Morgan's accusation that she cared too little for her own reputation, reached for a shawl. The feather-light scrap of wool, purchased in the fort's mercantile, was the blue and green tartan of the North West Company. Alex decided that it added not only propriety to her attire but festive color, as well.

With a carelessness born of years of practice, she swept her long hair up onto her head, securing it with a handful of pins, and placed delicate gold hoops in her ears.

Before leaving the room, Alex stopped to look out an open window. Black, evil-looking clouds were massing in the west, bubbling up like a foul, witch's concoction about to boil over. Pale streaks of lightning darted from the darkest layer of clouds, flickering and dying in the space of a heartbeat. A slight wind sprang up, creating whirling dust devils along the path to the Council House, where the partners' business had been conducted all week. As it touched Alex's face, she could feel the intermingling of hot and cold air, always the sign of a violent storm.

She felt an odd twinge of excitement. The weather was about to break, the brides were getting married, and her own problems had been temporarily resolved. For the first time in months, since the death of her grandfather, she was truly happy.

Donald MacDonald, a wily old Scot with a wooden leg, was resplendent in the vivid tartan of his clan as he enthusiastically piped the agents, partners, backwoodsmen, and their ladies to dinner.

The dining hall looked festive with the tables draped in white damask, the glassware and china dazzling beneath the glimmer of hundreds of candles. In the center of each table was a vase of scarlet columbine and blue harebells, gathered by the brides for the occasion.

A place had been saved for Alex, between Aberdeen and the fort proprietor, Kenneth MacKenzie, and as she slipped into it, she noticed Rhys Morgan watching her with a grim expression from his own seat just down the way. Instead of his usual buckskins, he was magnificent in evening clothes. He was dressed in black broadcloth, the cutaway coat snug over his wide shoulders, its darkness making him look larger than ever. He wore a snowy linen shirt beneath a jewel green vest, and Alex guessed that, if one were stand-

108

ing face to face with him, his eyes would reflect the deep green color. The thought of the ruggedly masculine woodsman in his fringed buckskins bringing these fashionable, formal clothes with him from a wilderness cabin piqued a curiosity she didn't want to feel.

As the last of the celebrants were seated, MacKenzie stood and lifted his glass of wine, causing a silence to fall over the room.

"I should like to propose a toast," he announced, "to the fur trade and those who labor to sustain it."

"Hear, hear!" came a chorus of voices.

"To the Company," called out one of the clerks, and glasses were raised all around.

"And, in addition," said MacKenzie, "I should like to propose a toast to the men of Sabaskong Falls and their beautiful brides. Here's wishing all of them a wealth of happiness."

"And may God bless their unions and make them fruitful," exclaimed Reverend Rosswell, draining his wineglass.

"Dinna drink to that, lass," whispered Aberdeen. " 'Tis more a curse than a blessing."

As the glasses were being refilled, several young Indian girls entered to start serving the meal. They passed among the tables, bearing trays of meats, bowls of steaming corn or creamed potatoes, and plates of hot bread.

Alex had begun to eat, chattering away to Aberdeen, when she suddenly noticed that Morgan had not taken his eyes off her. Each time she looked up, his gaze shifted and he pretended indifference. And yet, as soon as she turned away, she could feel his eyes return to her. It could only mean that he was, for some reason or another, annoyed with her again, something that was fast becoming habitual with him.

"Oh, fie on the man!" she grumbled half under her breath.

Kenneth MacKenzie chuckled. "And what man would that be, my dear?"

Alex had the grace to blush, but she made an honest reply. "Rhys Morgan," she admitted. "He certainly isn't a very friendly soul, is he?"

"It isn't a requirement that men be friendly out here . . . only that they be strong and dependable. Rhys Morgan has a reputation for being both."

"Who is he, really? I mean, where did he come from?" Alex was surprised by the half-dozen or more questions that so easily came into her mind. Even she had not been completely aware of her interest in the man.

"There are a score of rumors about Rhys," MacKenzie answered. "No one actually knows much more about him than that he came from Montreal. I've heard it said he's a very wealthy man — property in the city, that sort of thing. But I can't tell you why he chooses to bury himself in a little settlement in the woods. Though his men tell me he has spent the last year building a beautiful home. You should hear their stories about the things he had shipped out from Montreal." The proprietor chuckled. "Yes, Morgan is an intriguing man. Who can say what makes him the way he is?"

Alex shook her head. "If those of you who know him can't, then it should come as no surprise to me that I don't understand him." She toyed with a heavy silver fork. "Tell me, what exactly does he do for a living?"

"Good heavens, he's done about everything, so they say. He came out here about ten years ago with some kind of exploratory expedition that opened up new routes across Lake of the Woods for the voyageurs. Later he and a friend became partners in a trading post — and helped build a settlement at Sabaskong Falls. He's been a guide and a mapmaker. Most of the trappers agree that no white man knows Lake of the Woods better than Rhys Morgan — it's a baffling maze of islands, you see, and an easy place to get lost forever."

Just at that point, as Alex was considering several further questions, she saw Morgan look her way again and decided it might be best to hold her tongue. She stirred restlessly, wondering if he could possibly know he was the subject of conversation.

Glad for the distraction, she greeted the serving of cranberry tarts for dessert with a sigh of relief — it wouldn't be much longer before she could make her escape from his unrelenting and apparently disapproving gaze.

After the meal was finished, the tables were cleared and pushed against the walls, emptying the center of the room for the wedding ceremonies that were to take place.

Reverend Rosswell, Bible in hand, stood before a makeshift altar, looking dignified and solemn in a stark black suit. In the far corner of the room, Donald MacDonald took up his station and, having abandoned the bagpipes, now began playing a wedding march on a battered violin. His wooden leg thumped noisily against the floor as he kept time to the music he played.

Standing beside Aberdeen, Alex was suddenly aware of the faint smell of skunk followed by Waldo Anderson's high-pitched voice. "Well, woman, have ya changed yer mind about gittin' married?"

Aberdeen's plain face was transformed by an outraged look. "To ye, ye mean?"

"Yep. Who else'd have ya?"

Alex prudently moved a few steps away, but not so far she couldn't hear her friend's indignant response.

"Are ye gyte? Ye must have the brain of a haggis!"

"It ain't too late to git into this ceremony," Waldo pointed out.

Aberdeen fairly seethed. "Ye'd best get yerself far away from me, man, or I swear, I'll raise a carfuffle the likes o' which ye've never seen."

Waldo glanced at Alex. "Did she turn me down?" he inquired.

Alex nodded, giving him a sympathetic smile. Waldo shrugged, then gave Aberdeen a saucy wink and walked away.

The Scotswoman snorted angrily and muttered under her breath. She didn't grow calm again until the assorted bridegrooms had taken their places in front of the minister. She actually began to smile as Annie, escorted by a very sober-looking Tobias, entered at the back of the room and crossed the floor, strewing bright blue and red blossoms as she walked. The children were followed by the brides, each of whom was claimed by her husband-to-be as she approached Reverend Rosswell. When all the couples had been joined, the children scurried across the room to sit down on a bench with Alex, and the exchanging of the wedding vows began.

Alex studied her six friends and the men they were marrying. Despite a personal aversion to matrimony, she prayed that each of these women had made the right choice, and that their lives would be improved.

Birdie, plump and doll-like in blue satin, stood arm in arm with the massive John Hay, who patted her hand and beamed down at her. Birdie had lived with her querulous, ailing parents in Montreal, taking care of them until they had both eventually succumbed to old age. Alex knew that Birdie's naturally cheerful disposition had sustained her through those long years, and now she hoped the woman would find the contentment she deserved with the blacksmith, who was obviously very taken with her. It seemed evident that Birdie would now be the one being pampered.

Pacer, looking darkly handsome in a new suit of buckskins, was another besotted bridegroom. He gazed at the delicate Lily with fierce possessiveness, and she looked back with an intensity that emphasized the explosive passions that had marked their relationship from the beginning. Lily looked virginal in pale lilac, but she had been forthright about her less-than-sterling past. Having run away from home at fourteen to escape the unwelcome advances of a stepfather, she had been employed as a tavern maid before becoming the mistress of a wealthy man. A man, Alex reflected, whose confessed sterility had protected Lily from bearing children in the four years she had stayed with him. Pacer, on the other hand, was a prime example of virile manhood, and Alex was glad Lily realized the importance of taking the preventative herbs every morning.

Claire, calm and pretty in rose pink, linked her arm with that of Gideon Marsh and looked up into his face with a serene smile. She had confided to Alex the night before that she was well pleased with her husband-to-be and anxious to see her new home at Sabaskong. Gideon had accepted her and the children so readily that she would have gone through the ceremony out of gratitude, but, in addition to that, he had so many admirable qualities that Claire was convinced she had made the best match of all. A young widow, she had grown tired of trying to support herself and her children by working at menial jobs—the trek to the lake country had seemed an opportunity for the kind of life she desired. With the exception of Aberdeen, Alex realized she would miss Claire and her youngsters most of all.

Mellicent was garbed in her best black gown, making a somber and unlikely-looking bride. However, Albert Braunswager didn't seem to notice. Face red and shining, he whispered in her ear from time to time, looking as though he could barely restrain his happy laughter. While Mellicent's face was devoid of all humor at this serious moment, Alex detected an unusual twinkle in her dark eyes and sensed the usually gloomy woman was making a good match. Her first husband had been something of a profligate, assumed dead after he'd disappeared from a local gambling establishment. Alone and in debt, Mellicent had spent the next ten years worrying over his mysterious disappearance. Then she had seen the handbills advertising for brides, and had seized the opportunity to put her old life behind her and embark on an adventurous new one. Not really knowing whether she was a legal wife or a widow, she had chosen to travel to a part of the world where such matters were of little importance.

Alexandria found no fault with Mellicent's reasoning; however, she often wondered what had prompted Judith and Cordelia to make the trip. Judith, a plain, mousy woman inclined to scripture reading, had never seemed bold or brave enough to undertake such adversity, and Cordelia, speaking frequently of the cozy Montreal home where she had a successful business as a seamstress, had given no indication of what had caused her to relinquish that comfortable existence to journey into the wilderness. Still, since both women seemed happy with the men chosen for them, Alexandria assumed the simple need for companionship had probably driven them. She hoped that Hardesty Ames, the quiet, reserved dairy farmer, might prove to be the perfect mate for Judith, and that shy, raw-boned Malachi Harper would continue to look as self-satisfied as he did this moment, standing beside his practical bride.

As soon as the last of the vows had been exchanged, the grooms kissed their new wives amid an outburst of loud good wishes and ribald advice. Then the doors to the hall were thrown open to admit the rest of the fort's inhabitants, along with a select group of Chippewa girls. Outside the barred front gates of the fort, there were other, less civilized parties taking place and, at times, the throbbing of the Indian drums was indistinguishable from the booming thunder of the approaching storm.

The bagpipes droned again, this time joined by a

flute and violin, producing music that was energetic, though somewhat unorthodox. The newly married couples as well as all the Scottish agents took the floor with alacrity when Donald MacDonald announced the playing of the Caledonian Reel, and soon the room was a whirl of colorful skirts among the sober browns, fawns, and blacks of the men's dress suits.

Once the traditional Scottish reels had been dispensed with, the musicians launched into a round of slower tunes to allow the dancers time to catch their breaths. Rhys had been watching from one of the dimmer corners as Alex danced with Dr. McLoughlin. Now he strode forward and, in clipped tones claimed her as a partner. McLoughlin merely nodded amiably and placed Alex's hand on Rhys's broadcloth-covered arm. Seeing the belligerent glint in Rhys's eye, she might have protested had he given her the chance. Instead, he clamped an iron-hard hand at her waist and spun her into the center of the other waltzing pairs.

"Is it true?" he demanded without prologue.

She blinked in surprise. "Is what true?"

"The rumor that's flying all over this fort."

"What, that I treated a naked man? You know it's true."

"No," he growled. "Not that rumor." His jaw tightened even further. "You said there'd be a new one, and by God, you knew what you were talking about."

"I suggest you tell me what you're talking about," she said crisply, suddenly aware of the hot anger that simmered just below his barely controlled surface.

"Is it true McLoughlin has asked you to stay on at Kaministiquia?"

Her chin angled upward, and her eyes met his un-flinchingly. She might have known it would be about that "Yes, it's true."

Morgan swore under his breath, and his hand at her waist grew rigid. "I thought the man had more sense."

"It's obvious he could use assistance," she pointed out.

"During the Rendezvous, maybe. Certainly not the rest of the year. Good God, Alexandria, who knows what his motive might be?"

"You don't trust anyone, do you?"

"Trusting too easily can be dangerous. If you don't curb your inclination to do that very thing, you may find out the hard way that I know what I'm talking about."

"I don't believe you do," she charged. "At least, not when it pertains to me."

"Are you accepting his offer?" he questioned.

"Indeed I am. What choice do I have? And don't tell me to go back to Montreal, because I won't! I want to be a doctor, and if this is the only place I can do that, then so be it. I'm staying."

"You' re a fool, Alex," he bit out. "Why in the hell can't you be like other women?"

He had seen anger flare in her eyes on several occasions, he realized, but this was the first time he had ever seen them go cold and dark with hurt. He was immediately contrite, but before he could frame a redeeming statement, Alex had pulled away and stood glaring at him.

"I'll tell you why," she breathed furiously. "Because I'm not other women—I'm me, Alexandria MacKenzie. I may not want what most females want, but there are things that are important to me . . . things I want to do with my life. Is that so wrong?"

He put out a placating hand, but she struck it away, hardly knowing what she was doing. "I've listened to your sly innuendoes that something must be wrong with me because I don't want to get married and spend the rest of my life cooking and having babies. Well, for your information, Mr. Morgan, it doesn't concern me in the least what you think of me. Nor am I your responsibility in any way. If I choose to stay here or . . . or go to hell, for that matter, there isn't a single thing you can do to stop me."

"Alex . . ."

"Don't touch me," she hissed, backing away. "Just do me the courtesy of staying out of my life!"

Nearly choking on the bitter strength of her anger, Alex turned and, clutching her tartan shawl about her shoulders, marched through the curious crowd and out the front doors. Rhys, hands on hips, silently watched her go. Then, his face dark with fury, he stalked after her.

From their vantage point in one corner, Aberdeen and Dr. McLoughlin turned to each other with beaming smiles.

"Well, it looks as though our little conspiracy may bear fruit, doesna it?" Aberdeen chortled.

"Indeed. Rhys didn't have any problems when he thought Alex was going back to the city. But now that he knows she'll be staying here in my company . . ."

"And that of two dozen other womenless men," put in Aberdeen.

". . . he's in a hell of a quandry."

"Serves him right," observed the Scotswoman.

"Lord, yes. Whatever possessed the man to think he could oppose nine women and get away with it?" He chuckled and shook his head. "Rhys Morgan has a lot to learn about the gentler sex."

The rain was just beginning as Rhys strode out the front door of the Mess Hall. Instead of following the path to his sleeping quarters in the North West House, he veered off, walking along the west side of the hall, which rocked with explosions of noisy laughter and wild music. As he rounded the back corner of the building, the sky was ripped open by a tremendous slashing streak of lightning. Up ahead he caught sight of Alex, her skirts billowing out behind her, but he had only taken a few steps in her direction when the rain suddenly came rushing down in icy torrents.

It was not until he'd found shelter beneath the eaves, his back against the wall, that he realized he was not alone. Standing only three feet away was Alex, her eyes looking enormous in the dim light.

"Does the storm scare you?" he asked brusquely.

"No, of course not. I . . . I find it . . . exhilarating."

Her voice faded, and they studied each other. It was strange they should have come face to face in such an unlikely spot, and the silence between them grew awkward.

"It's late," Alex finally said. "I really think I should go inside now." The clipped tone of her voice told him she was still angry.

As she turned toward the back door to the dormitory, Rhys heard himself say, "Alex . . . wait."

She hesitated.

"Back there at the dance . . . well, I didn't mean to insult you." He ran a hand through his thick hair. "I just couldn't believe you were serious about staying at Fort Kaministiquia."

Her gaze fell to the ground at her feet, as though she were trying to gather her scattered thoughts.

"I certainly don't have much other choice," she reminded him. She shrugged and looked up. "It somehow seems the best thing for me to do."

"But do you actually know what day-to-day life here will entail?"

"I'm sure you will tell me," she replied calmly.

"Yes, I will. Someone needs to . . . you've no idea of the dangers."

"I'm not afraid, Mr. Morgan."

"You don't have the sense to be afraid, Miss Mac-Kenzie. I'm telling you, unless you're a hell of a lot stronger than most women I've met, you'd better find a protector who can keep other men at bay, or you'd better, by God, get your ignorant little ass back to Montreal!"

"Why do you dislike women so?" she asked unexpectedly, her low voice barely audible over the rush of the rain streaming down just two feet from where they stood.

"I don't dislike them, but . . ." He rubbed his jaw thoughtfully, and when he looked up at her again, his expression had grown somewhat milder. "To my way of thinking, there are two kinds of women—and neither of them belongs in the wilderness."

"And, in your opinion, what are the two kinds of women?"

"Weak women . . . and women like you. Women who think they can manage on their own — and eventually discover they need a man, after all." He stared down at her a long moment. "Weak women die in this country, but women like you cause other people to die."

"I don't understand."

"When a man who's lived the last year or so of his life in a place like this finds himself in the company a beautiful woman, he can lose all sense of right and wrong. He'll do any foolhardy thing he has to in order to get her attention. He'll fight his best friend for her, he'll sacrifice his last dollar . . . sometimes even his pride, his honor."

"And do you speak from experience, Mr. Morgan?"

"Look, I'm tired of arguing with you. What I'm saying is, if you insist on pushing your way in where you don't belong, you may not like the consequences. There's not always going to be someone around to rescue you should some drunk want a kiss or some Indian take a fancy to your long red hair. . . ."

"You're only trying to alarm me, and I've already made it perfectly clear that I am not afraid of anything."

At that instant, the night shook with another massive crash of thunder, and blinding lightning forked wickedly across the sky. Alex uttered a shriek and threw herself against his broad chest.

He couldn't prevent the deep laughter from rumbling upward out of his throat. "I thought you weren't afraid."

She wrenched away. "I'm not!

For a long, guarded moment, they looked into each

other's eyes. Then, before he could stop himself, Rhys reached out and, clamping his hands around her upper arms, dragged her against the length of his body. He was immediately overcome with something akin to sweet agony at her touch. His breath grew rapid and harsh as he lowered his head and covered her mouth with his own. She struggled briefly within his hard embrace, then slumped wearily and stopped fighting his fiery kiss. His arms slipped around her, pulling her tightly into the curve of his body, and his mouth roved hungrily over hers.

Alex could feel the low, moaning sound that issued from deep within his chest, and she realized his inner turmoil. She knew he didn't like her, and certainly didn't like admitting any attraction to her, yet it seemed he was unable to regain the control necessary to move away from her. She, too, was stunned by her own reaction to his bold impropriety. She had been kissed by several young men in Montreal, but her feelings had never really been stirred. Now, with the cold rain streaming down all around, she felt such a wave of intense heat wash over her that she almost thought she could go up in flames. This stern, forbidding backwoodsman was awakening some primitive instinct that had been hidden inside her, and the very ease with which he was doing it frightened her more than the raging storm could ever have done.

Torn between the desire to return his kiss and the need to put a safer distance between them, Alex lifted her hands and placed them against his chest. Her mutinous fingers longed to stroke the solid flesh beneath the broadcloth, but she closed her mind to temptation and pressed the heels of her hands into his shirt front, forcing him back slightly.

"I don't think this is a very good idea," she said quietly.

Morgan's chest heaved with the effort of his breathing, and for several seconds a softened expression remained on his face. Then, slowly, it was replaced by his usual cynical one, and he released her. "Of course, you're right. I was only trying to show you the danger of placing yourself in the company of men with . . . with few scruples."

"Yes, I'll keep it in mind," Alex promised solemnly. She took a step backward. "Good night, Mr. Morgan."

He watched her go through the back door of the hall, then turned away, realizing he had made a serious error in judgment. He should never have kissed her—he'd been thinking far too much about Alexandria MacKenzie these past days as it was. No doubt it was for the best that he was leaving in the morning. Something told him that only the broad avenue of rivers and lakes and the still serenity of the forests could push the stubborn redhead from his mind.

Thoroughly disgusted with himself, Rhys walked off toward his quarters, oblivious to the rain that soaked the broad shoulders of his good black suit.

Chapter Seven

Early the next morning, Alexandria, Nasturtium clutched to her breast, stood watching the loading of the canoes bound for Lake of the Woods. She could not help but think how different the departure from Montreal had been in comparison to this one from Fort Kaministiquia. On that long-ago May morning, as the brigade left Lachine, she had experienced a feeling of expectancy, as though she were setting out on the greatest adventure of her life. Even the voyageurs, despite the emotional farewells with their families, had been unable to suppress their excitement.

But now, as she saw her friends preparing to depart the fort and journey deeper into the wilderness, she could only envy them their anticipation. Standing on the wharf in the cold mist of dawn, Alex observed as grim-faced *engagés* efficiently loaded the waiting canoes with the bundles into which supplies had been packed. The reckless joy of the Rendezvous was gone, replaced by reality and the necessity of reaching the outposts before the first snows.

At one end of the dock were piled the trunks and boxes belonging to the new brides. Each husband had been responsible for transporting his wife's possessions to the lakefront, and now the men stood waiting for Rhys Morgan to instruct the loading. The brides themselves were just filing through the gates of the fort, a silent, determined-looking group. Alex felt her throat tighten with tears; she didn't know how she was going to face telling them all goodbye.

The ladies didn't look to left or right—they didn't even acknowledge Alexandria's presence. Instead, they marched straight out onto the dock, past their astonished husbands and into the midst of the luggage. Aberdeen took the lead, settling herself on top of her favorite trunk, and the others followed suit, arranging their full skirts about themselves as they sat down on trunks and boxes. Even Annie and Tobias scrambled up onto their mother's large wardrobe trunk, Annie clutching both Madame Dragonflower and the newly repaired Lady Gwendolyn.

Several of the voyageurs began to mutter, causing Rhys Morgan to look up from the canoe in which he was stashing goods for his Sabaskong trading post. He frowned at the sight that met his eyes, then hauled his rangy frame out of the canoe to approach the women.

"Excuse me, ladies," he said with drawling courtesy, "but you'll have to stand aside now and let the men begin to load this baggage into the canoes."

"We canna do that, Mr. Morgan," announced Aberdeen militantly.

His frown deepened. "And why not, Miss McPhie?"

"Because we've taken a vote, and we have decided that if Alex won't be going to Sabaskong Falls, neither will the rest of us."

Alex's shocked gasp hissed in the still morning air.

"Good Lord!" exclaimed Malachi Harper. "Cordy, are you in agreement with this?"

Cordelia looked a bit sheepish, but when Aberdeen flashed her a dark look, she nodded and replied, "Y-yes, Malachi. I . . . that is, all of us think we need a doctor in our settlement."

"We've been over this a dozen times," Rhys Morgan pointed out with a disgusted sigh. "My partner will be an adequate doctor until we can find a replacement next spring."

"We want Alex, Mr. Morgan," Aberdeen declared. "No other man or woman will do."

"It isn't possible," Rhys said flatly.

"Is that so?" Birdie stepped forward and motioned to her husband. "Then, John Hay, will you carry my trunk back into the fort before you leave?"

The mighty blacksmith looked like a god of thunder as he placed beefy hands on his hips and swung around to glare at Rhys. Seeing the expression on his face, Alex felt the tiniest surge of hope. The man clearly thought little of the idea of leaving his new wife behind; perhaps he would be on her side.

Rhys shrugged. "It's up to you to control your wife, John."

The blacksmith turned back to Birdie, who tilted her head pertly and stated, "No man controls me,

126

Mr. Morgan. I think my husband fully understands the . . . er, advantages of having a wife. But I am staying with Alex, and he is free to remain here with me or go on, whichever he pleases."

John Hay frowned and scratched his head. Albert Braunswager let out a hoop of laughter and clapped the big man on the shoulder. "Married one day and the little woman is already trying to tell you what to do. Lord, man, show her who's boss."

Mellicent snorted indelicately. "As you intend to do, Albert?"

The German trapper looked surprised, then his face grew even redder. "Mellie, my dear, are you saying that you support this . . . this mutiny?"

"Indeed I do."

John Hay allowed himself a broad smile and visibly relaxed. It suddenly began to appear that he was not the only husband with a problem.

Albert sputtered momentarily, but Mellicent calmly stood her ground, apparently without doubt that he would come around to her way of thinking.

"What about . . . ?" Albert leaned closer to her ear. "What about last night?"

Mellicent smiled serenely. "It *was* nice, wasn't it?"

"Damn it, woman, don't defy me in public like this."

"Please understand, Albert, I'm not trying to make you angry. But the truth is, I have known these women longer than I have known you . . . and, well, they're my friends. I intend to back them in this, whether you approve or not."

Braunswager fell silent, stunned to think a mere woman would dare be so calm about disputing her husband's word. Things were not done that way back in the old country. . . .

"Gentlemen," Rhys said in a chilly voice, "I suggest you start loading those canoes. We've wasted enough time."

Hardesty Ames reached for Judith's leather satchel, but her voice rang out sharply. "Leave it! If Alex is forbidden to go, then I am staying here with the others."

"Nonsense," was Hardesty's brief reply.

"You'll think nonsense if you touch that case," she said firmly. "I agree with Mellicent. I owe my first loyalty to my friends—and to my unborn children. I will not reside in a settlement that has no qualified doctor."

"Damn it to hell," raged Waldo Anderson, raking his skunkskin cap off his head and slapping it against one skinny thigh. "Ain't you men got the guts to git these women in line? What are you, a bunch of schoolgirls?"

"Ye stay out of this, ye lang-shankit tattie bogle," snapped Aberdeen. " 'Tis none of yer concern."

" 'Tis, if'n we stand here arguin' til the snow begins to fall."

"We won't be that long," vowed Rhys. "As a matter of fact, this brigade is leaving in twenty minutes. And anyone who cares to see Sabaskong Falls had better be on board."

"Very well, Mr. Morgan," spoke up Cordelia. "Perhaps it might be best if we didn't further encumber your departure. Ladies, shall we return to the fort?"

A chorus of affirmatives rang out over the quiet waters, and the women began the long march along the wharf.

"Wait," cried Malachi Harper. "Cordelia, let's talk about this."

"We've got nothing more to say," Cordelia declared. "If Alexandria stays, so do we."

"Ladies, please don't cause trouble for yourselves." Alex spoke for the first time. "I appreciate what you're trying to do—honestly! But I'm afraid there's simply no use—"

"You're right about that," growled Rhys, angrily tossing a pack into the canoe nearest him.

"But if we give in on something this important," Claire said quietly, "we might as well have sold ourselves as slaves. Don't our opinions matter at all?"

"I think they do," exclaimed Lily, "and I'm staying with Alex."

"You got anything to say about that, Pacer?" queried Albert.

Pacer smiled slowly and dropped an arm about Lily's slim shoulders. "It looks like I'll be wintering at Kaministiquia."

"God almighty, man!" Waldo nearly shouted. "Are you going to let that yeller-haired gal lead you around by yer . . .?"

Pacer's face grew instantly cold and forbidding. "Do not anger me, Waldo," he said with dignity. "I have no wish to carve a turkey as scrawny as you." He fingered the long knife strapped to his side. "But, if necessary, I will."

Lily smiled up at him, and he tucked her close against him. "Thank you," she half-whispered.

"You traveled many months to get to the wilderness," Pacer said simply. "You have married a stran-

129

ger, and are going to an isolated outpost you've never seen. Why should I deny you the one thing you have asked for . . . a doctor?"

"He's right, Rhys," affirmed Gideon Marsh. "It's the least we can do."

"I've been over this too many times already," Rhys said tersely. "I won't go over it again. Miss MacKenzie's last underhanded trick to get her own way isn't going to work."

"My trick?" Alex gasped. "But I knew nothing of this. . . ."

"Don't expect me to believe that," Rhys responded coldly. "This is exactly the kind of trouble you'd make."

"Ye're wrong," interjected Aberdeen. "Alex didn't know a thing about this. We discussed it while she was over at Doc McLoughlin's."

"Don't you think I realize that you'd defend her, no matter what?"

"That isn't the point," said Malachi. "We've got to get underway. What are we going to do?"

"I say let her go," put in Hardesty Ames with a resigned sigh. John Hay nodded in agreement.

"Either she goes or I'm staying here," announced Gideon Marsh. "I've just gained a family. I won't go away and leave them." Claire smiled with gratitude and linked her arm with his.

"Frankly, Rhys, the thought of being with my wife outweighs all the arguments against the lady doctor," admitted Hardesty Ames. "I'll stay with Judith."

Albert heaved a huge, gusty sigh. "I, too, have no wish to leave my wife. Sorry, Rhys, but I have to respect Mellie's feelings on this matter."

Rhys stared at the circle of men in disbelief. Finally, with a disgusted shake of his head, he whirled and started off down the dock.

"Rhys," Gideon said. "Wouldn't it make more sense just to let Alexandria go to Sabaskong Falls?"

Rhys stopped short, and his head snapped up. He studied the pale blue sky for a long, silent moment before slowly turning to face them. "All right, damn it," he ground out. "There's nothing I can do if you're all going to take this stand. But when the trouble starts, just remember that I warned you. And remember, too, that I wash my hands of the whole goddamned situation."

"Rhys . . ." Alex began, but he spun away from her.

"Get the damned canoes loaded and be quick about it," he ordered.

She had no time to worry about his opinion of her—she had to dash back to the sleeping quarters and assist the voyageurs in packing and loading her trunks. Concern over her precious medical books and supplies took precedence over her chagrin at Rhys's hotheaded assumption that she had instigated the scene at the dock.

While her things were being trundled down the hill to the wharf, Alex seized the opportunity to say goodbye to Reverend Rosswell and his wife, and then she sought out Dr. McLoughlin, who walked her back to the river.

"I thought Rhys might come around," McLoughlin was saying, "once he knew you were staying on at the fort."

"Oh, but he didn't come around," Alex informed

him with a wry smile. "In fact, he's livid that the women made such a defiant stand on my behalf. He dislikes being bested."

"He'll get over it in time."

"Perhaps . . . but by then I'll be too old and feeble to care whether I'm a doctor or not." She laughed with sudden exuberance, happy and excited all at once. She felt no triumph over getting her own way, only relief and anticipation that her wilderness adventure had not ended there in the relatively civilized Fort Kaministiquia.

"Just stay out of Rhys's way as much as you can for the next few weeks, and he'll eventually forget his anger," said McLoughlin.

It was then that they saw the canoes had been filled, with each of the brides settled in her husband's craft. The only empty seat left for Alex was in the long canoe with a double-M brand burned into the golden birchbark hull—Rhys Morgan's canoe.

"It's not going to be easy staying out of his way if I have to ride in the same canoe with him," she whispered.

McLoughlin threw back his head and laughed. "God, I wish I were going on this trip with you. It'd be worth a month's pay just to see what Rhys tries next."

Alex stood on tiptoe to place a kiss on the doctor's cheek. "Thank you for everything you've done to help me," she said. "Perhaps I'll see you next year at Rendezvous."

He returned the kiss, patting her shoulder. "I'll look forward to it. Take care, Alex."

Obviously irritated by the delay, Rhys Morgan

moved along the wharf toward them. "Are you ready at last, Miss MacKenzie?"

"Yes, I am."

Footsteps thundered down the wooden planks of the dock, bringing a grinning Baptiste to Alex's side.

"*Mademoiselle,* I could not let you leave Kaministiquia without bidding you farewell."

"No, of course not. Thank you so much for helping me with my belongings." Alex tilted her head and studied the handsome French Canadian who had become a good friend on the trip out from Montreal. "Goodbye, Baptiste. Take good care of yourself on the way home."

"And you take care, also. I will think of you each time I drop a coin into the money box at St. Anne's chapel."

Alexandria smiled, recalling the custom faithfully observed by the voyageurs when leaving the city on a march, as they called their journeys. With a strange mixture of religious fervor and superstition, they stopped at the little church to drop coins into the money box and entreat their patron, St. Anne, for her protection while they were gone.

"Thank you, Baptiste. I wish you were going on to Sabaskong with us."

"As do I, *mademoiselle.*"

Impulsively, the muscular young man threw his arms around Alex and hugged her fiercely, exhibiting more friendly affection than he had previously dared.

"God go with you, Alexandria," he said.

A hand clamped down on her elbow, pulling her from Baptiste's embrace. Rhys muttered tersely, "It's time to go, Alex. Get into the canoe."

"Baptiste, will you assist me?" she asked, not quite trusting Rhys to touch her. In his present mood, he might give in to the temptation to fling her into the icy waters.

Baptiste took the hinged basket she carried, then steadied her as she stepped down into the canoe. Once she had settled herself among the packs, he handed her Nasturtium's basket and, with a final goodbye, stood back to watch the departure.

Rhys, scowling blackly, moved into his position as steersman and, gripping his paddle, set the rhythm that cast the birchbark craft against the swift currents of the river. It was followed by eight other canoes carrying the women, their husbands, and the voyageurs hired to help transport them and their belongings to Lake of the Woods.

As the river caught them, Alex twisted in her seat for one last look at Fort Kaministiquia and found Rhys's stony gaze resting upon her. Even as she opened her mouth to make an apology for her friends' high-handedness, his resentful words reached her.

"You may think you have won the day, Miss MacKenzie, but I hasten to inform you that the battle is far from over. Your scheme to undermine my authority may yet backfire in your face."

"What does that mean?" she asked, all thoughts of humility promptly fleeing her mind.

"I may have been coerced into permitting you to go to Sabaskong, but there is one thing I can do to remedy a few of the immediate problems."

"But I thought you had washed your hands of the matter."

"For the sake of my men, I've changed my mind. As soon as we arrive, I plan to make certain that you are safely married."

Alex fairly sputtered.

"Oh, rest assured," he told her. "I have a decent, honorable man in mind for you."

"I think you are quite insane, Mr. Morgan."

"Not at all. I am only making sure you do not become a disruptive influence in the settlement. My partner, Scotty MacPherson, has long regretted he did not send for a bride. I believe he will be most pleased when I bring him one after all."

"I will not marry your partner or anyone else."

"I will not have an unmarried and highly disobedient woman in my community."

Alex thought the man's set jaw looked as though it had been carved of stone, not realizing her own appeared much the same.

"It's useless to argue with you," she fumed.

"So I've tried to tell you."

"And I've tried to tell you that I do not need your interference in my life. I am quite capable of caring for myself without aid from anyone."

"You're wrong," he stated. "And I intend to prove it long before we reach Rainy River or Lake of the Woods. You obviously think yourself as good as any man . . . well, that's exactly how I am going to treat you on this journey. You won't receive any special concessions from me or anyone else. I plan to push you just as hard as I would a seasoned voyageur . . . and in an hour's time you're going to have to admit you're nowhere near as capable of fending for yourself as you think you are. By the time this trip is

135

done, you'll be damned glad to have someone willing to marry and take care of you."

"Don't wager anything important on it," she said shortly. "I won't let you and your archaic attitudes defeat me."

"We shall see," he promised.

"Yes, we shall," Alex agreed, squaring her shoulders and turning away. She looked straight ahead at the Kaministiquia River unfolding before them, willing herself to remember that each mile brought her closer to Sabaskong and her dream of being a respected doctor.

The journey up the Kaministiquia, which followed an old route used by the early French traders, was beautiful but difficult. The winding river cut between steep, muddy banks covered with dense underbrush and overhanging trees.

The first major portage occurred at midday below a rapids where tea-colored water foamed over the rocks, making it impossible to negotiate with the heavily loaded canoes.

As each canoe approached the bank, the man in the bow, the *avant*, jumped into the water and waded ashore, pulling the craft behind him. Then, after the women had been carried to dry ground, the crew began the process of unloading.

When each canoe was empty, the *avant* and steersman would hoist it, upright, onto their shoulders and start off down the portage trail, while the rest of the men prepared the load for portaging.

Two of the compact, waterproof bundles into which

goods had been packed, were strapped together into a *pacton*, which the voyageurs lifted onto each other's backs. The weight of the *pacton*, about ninety pounds, rested on the carrier's hips, and was held in place by a leather tumpline, or *collier*, fitted around the forehead. As soon as one or two of the *pactons* were secured on a man's back, he lowered his head, leaning into the tumpline, and followed the portage trail with a shuffling step, often whistling or singing.

As Alex busied herself releasing Nasturtium from the basket so that she might run awhile, Rhys stalked by on the trail. He paused just long enough to say, "Hasn't anyone told you this is a mile-and-a-half portage? You'd better start the walk to the other side because we won't wait for you. And if that cat gets lost, it stays lost, because we don't have time to waste looking for it."

"She won't get lost, and no one will have to wait for me."

"This is no damned frolic in the woods," he growled. "It's time you started realizing that."

Alex stood staring after him, fighting back the words she would have liked to throw at his retreating back. He had no right to speak to her in such a way . . . never had she met such an infuriating man! And to think, she had believed him not only handsome but admirable. Lord, now she was consumed by the idea of how easy it would be to hate him! Aware of the sympathetic looks the other women were giving her, she heaved a gusty sigh, called Nasturtium, and tucked the cat under her arm. Then, grasping the empty basket, she started down the trail with determination.

Because the portage was more than a mile long, the voyageurs were moving the cargo by shifts, carrying the first load to a *pose,* a distance of about six hundred feet, where it was deposited while the *engagés* returned to the riverbank for a second load. When all the packs and trunks had reached the first *pose,* they were then removed to a second *pose,* and so on, until the entire load was once again packed into the canoes waiting at the end of the portage.

Dodging the men on the trail, Alex marveled at their strength and speed. No longer dressed in the finery they would have worn upon arrival at Fort Kaministiquia, they now wore only Indian breechclouts, moccasins, and deerskin leggings that reached from the ankle to the knee. Each man also carried a beaded pouch in which he kept the indispensable pipe and tobacco, as well as his firesteel. Long hair swinging, they hied up and down the path, back muscles straining beneath the *pactons,* voices raised in derisive banter or, occasionally, in song.

Alex soon discovered she was dressed far too warmly for the day, which had started out chill and damp, but rapidly progressed to steamy. The heat did nothing to improve her mood. It was becoming increasingly more sullen. Tomorrow, she vowed, she would leave off some of the cumbersome petticoats and change into the lightest dress she could find.

She had assumed there would be a break for the midday meal once the portage was completed, but she discovered her mistake as soon as the last pack was loaded into the canoes. Rhys Morgan, casual in his easy command of the brigade, ordered them to be on their way.

In the other canoes, Alex noticed, the new brides and their husbands were sharing lunches of meat and bread the women had brought from the fort. Her mouth began to water, but she said nothing. Instead, the *avant* spoke up.

"Morgan, should not the lady be given something to eat? She will need to keep up her strength, eh?"

Rhys glanced at Alex, his eyes challenging. "Miss MacKenzie failed to bring a lunch with her, Jean. I expect she did not mean to have a noon meal — after all, she knows voyageurs do not stop to eat." He raised one thick black brow. "You probably didn't want to make an exception of yourself, did you, Miss MacKenzie?"

Wistfully, Alex thought of the breakfast she had only picked at that morning. What she wouldn't give for a slice of warm bread or a juicy ham steak now! "No," she forced herself to say coldly, "of course I wouldn't want that. There will be plenty of time for food when we stop tonight."

Jean looked from one to the other of them, then shrugged. "As you wish, *mademoiselle*. But are you certain you would not like some pemmican to hold you until the evening meal?"

Declining as graciously as possible, Alex swallowed deeply, knowing that, hungry as she was, she would have to be a great deal hungrier in order to accept the offer. Even the tins of dried fish she had brought along for Nasturtium sounded more appetizing! Pemmican was a mixture of buffalo meat pounded with fat and sometimes wild berries, that, when properly stored, was an important staple in the wilderness. It had been her experience that pemmican often contained hair, sand, or sticks, due to the casual conditions surrounding its preparation, and she feared she would relish it only if faced with certain starvation.

By early evening, Alex's back was aching from sitting upright in the canoe for hours on end; her hair had fallen from its combs and pins and was being hopelessly tangled by the river breezes; her skin felt tight and dry, burned by the glow of bright sun on the water. At each bend of the river, she silently prayed that someone would declare it time to make camp for the night.

At last, as a distant roaring became louder and louder, Rhys Morgan, still plying his paddle with energy, slowed his pace to signal to the others, motioning them toward the bank.

"We can make camp here for the night," he shouted. "Kakabeka Falls is directly ahead—that means a long, hard portage. We might as well wait until morning to attempt it."

Again, under Rhys's exacting supervision, the canoes were unloaded, but this time they were pulled onto the bank and turned over to serve as a shelter beneath which the crew would sleep.

Most of the men from Sabaskong were pitching small tents to provide privacy for themselves and their wives, but space was scarce on the narrow shale ledge where camp was being made. A few of them placed their shelters somewhat farther away, but Rhys reminded them it was really not safe to go too deeply into the forest.

The voyageur, Jean, approached Alex, rubbing his chin thoughtfully. "There is no place left to pitch your tent, *mademoiselle*. I will have to put it there on that high bank if you think you can make such a steep climb."

"But I do not have a. . ."

Before Alex could complete her reply, Rhys's gravelly voice cut swiftly into the conversation.

"Why, Jean, I'm sure Miss MacKenzie has no intention of sleeping in a tent—she has claimed not to want preferential treatment. Isn't that right?"

Hands on hips, he turned his inquiring gaze on her, and Alex stiffened in sudden anger.

As a matter of fact, she thought resentfully, I should very much like a tent to myself—*as far away from you as possible.* It would be heavenly to have some privacy so I could take off these dusty, wrinkled clothes and wash from head to toe. I'd like a place to sleep that is out of the wind and away from the dampness of the river. But so help me, I'll die before admitting it!

She forced a brittle smile. "Yes, indeed, Mr. Morgan. You are absolutely right. I have no need to be coddled."

The hell you don't, Rhys chortled to himself. I've never seen such a refined nose so far out of joint!

Alex had to turn away from the humorless grin that lifted his moustache in such an insolent manner. Apparently, he was going to be as insufferable as he could, and she knew she must expect to bear the brunt of his churlish behavior.

The voyageurs soon had a campfire blazing, and while they examined the canoes to make certain none of them was in need of patching, the man designated as cook set about preparing supper.

Alex watched as he swung a large tin kettle filled

141

with water onto the fire. Wondering what supper was going to be, she heard her empty stomach rumble plaintively. She recalled the delicious meals she had shared with the others on the trip from Montreal. Due to their more leisurely pace, the *engagés* had had plenty of time to hunt or fish, so there had always been an abundance of fresh meat, in addition to the food supplies the women had brought with them.

On this night, however, a dearth of preparations on the cook's part indicated that the meal was sure to be something less than elaborate. Alex almost groaned aloud as she saw the man adding several quarts of corn to the boiling water—corn that had been boiled in lye, then washed and dried. Now, dumped into the hot water with a bit of melted fat, it began to split and swell, fluffing up into a thick, white mass. Though she had not eaten it before, Alex knew corn fixed this way was the traditional food of the voyageurs, usually the only meal they were served on the trail.

She wanted to throw a tantrum that none of them would forget, demanding meat and fresh vegetables and decent coffee, but aware that Rhys Morgan was watching, she merely seated herself on a rock and smiled politely as the cook handed her a tin plate with the lyed corn. She glanced about at the other women and saw that most of them were supplementing the meager meal with slices of ham and bread they had packed. But when Aberdeen offered her some of the more appetizing fare, Alex merely shook her head and smiled.

"This will be fine, thank you," she said, pretending not to notice the vaguely surprised look on Rhys's face.

The first bite of corn was bland, almost tasteless, but after Claire passed a small bag of salt to her, Alex found that a pinch of it made the meal at least palatable. And, having gone without food all day, she readily disposed of her supper.

Though somewhat shocked, she did not allow her disapproval to show when one of the voyageurs offered his hat in lieu of a plate; the cook filled the shapeless felt object with the hot corn, and the man, seizing a tin spoon, began eating with vigorous appetite. Another of the voyageurs ladled his dinner into an indentation in a large rock, squatting on his haunches to eat. When two of the others, evidently not owning plates or spoons, simply dipped their fingers into the kettle, Alex displayed no qualms at their lack of manners, though secretly she made a hasty decision against having a second serving.

Darkness was rapidly descending by the time the ladies struggled up the steep bank, seeking a moment's privacy before going to bed. Carrying Nasturtium under one arm, Alex secured a hold on an overhanging tree root and hoisted herself up. Though modesty had prevented the women from simply wandering away from the campfire to relieve themselves, as the men did, they now ventured no further than the shadowed edge of the woods. Alex released the cat and attended to her own needs.

"Rhys Morgan is bein' overharsh, lass," commented Aberdeen before they made the climb back down to the camp. "He shouldna think he can treat ye like a man."

"I won't complain, Deenie," swore Alex. "This is

my opportunity to prove I can take care of myself. If I whine now, I might as well have gone back to Montreal as he wished."

"Aye, it'd be a chance for him to gloat, all right."

"But, Alex, what good will it do for you to become exhausted or ill?" asked Claire. "The man means to drive you to your knees, it seems to me."

"I agree," added Mellicent. "You say the word, my dear, and our husbands will speak to Morgan and put an end to this."

"No, please," said Alex. "Don't say anything just yet. Let me try this my way and see if I can't change Mr. Morgan's mind."

"Might as well try to stop the wind," snorted Lily. "Or make the river flow upstream."

Alex laughed faintly. "You are probably right. Still, I need to prove myself now if I'm ever going to convince him that I can be a reliable doctor."

"But you must promise us that you will ask for help if it becomes necessary," said Birdie. "My John will not let the brute mistreat you."

"Nor will Hardesty," agreed Judith.

"Don't worry about me," admonished Alex. "I'll be fine. You all just hurry on back to your husbands before they come looking for you."

When the others had gone, Alex called to Nasturtium and gathered her up before following. As she scrambled back down the rocky path, she found Rhys waiting for her. His face was nearly hidden in the shadow cast by the broad-brimmed felt hat he wore, and his eyes were darkly unfathomable.

"Here," he said, thrusting a wool blanket at her. "You'll sleep with me tonight."

Alex's mouth dropped open, but before she could give voice to the stunned protest she felt, he had disappeared into the darkness beyond the campfire.

Chapter Eight

Clutching the wool blanket, Alexandria caught up with Rhys.

"Would you mind repeating what you just said?"

Rhys stopped in midstride, turning to give her a cold look. "I said that you had better sleep with me tonight."

In her arms, Nasturtium stiffened and growled. "I cannot believe you would make such a ludicrous suggestion," Alex stated. The cat hissed angrily and Alex set her on the ground.

"I'm only thinking of your well-being."

"And my good reputation, no doubt."

"No doubt."

"Oh, I see," Alex suddenly exclaimed. "This is merely part of your scheme to punish me."

"Punish? Hardly that." He shifted his stance as the gray tiger-striped cat sniffed the fringes of his knee-high moccasins. "I'm only complying with your wish to be treated as an equal."

"Surely such sleeping arrangements could have nothing to do with equality."

"Let me simplify this for you," he said slowly. "There are a limited number of overturned canoes where the engagés will sleep—in pairs. It's safer that way. Now. You can have your choice of sharing a sleeping space with me . . . or with any member of the crew you choose. I can promise you I have nothing more than sleeping on my mind, though I find myself unable to state with authority that the rest of the men feel the same way."

Alex tossed her head impatiently. "Oh, very well, Mr. Morgan, have your little jest."

She tucked the blanket beneath her arm and started toward the line of canoes on the rocky shore.

"One more thing," Rhys said shortly.

She whirled about to pierce him with a sharp glare.

"What now?"

He pointed at the cat. "Take Ol' Nasty with you."

Alex's glare grew even more fierce. "Her name is Nasturtium," she murmured frostily, scooping up the animal. Ignoring the feline's testy hiss at the sight of Rhys, Alex raised her head and walked away with dignity.

"Good night, Miss MacKenzie," Rhys Morgan uttered. Then, in a soft half-tone, "Good night, Nasty."

The prow of Rhys's canoe rested on a large rock, and Alex had to drop onto her knees to crawl under it. She rolled up in the blanket, wincing as her hips and shoulders made contact with the unyielding rock beneath. She could not help but recall the soft beds of fragrant pine boughs upon which she and the other women had slept on the earlier journey. Every night after supper, Aberdeen had teased her about the voyageurs vying for the privilege of constructing Mademoiselle Alex's bed. As the men had tried to out-do each other, her beds had gotten progressively larger and softer.

She allowed herself a small sigh of self-pity, which was immediately interrupted by a yawn. She cushioned her head on one arm and closed her eyes. Nasturtium snuggled against her back, purring noisily — a comforting sound in the darkness. The only other sound was the faint snore of the nearby voyageurs, the roar of the waterfall, and the monotonous lapping of waves on the rocky ledges.

Not much later, her purr ending in a grumpy hiss, Nasturtium leaped across Alex's body to crouch in affront, back arched and green eyes sparking fire. The canoe tipped sharply to one side and Alex heard a heartfelt curse. There was a muffled rustling of cloth, the canoe settled back into place, and then her back was jostled by what felt suspiciously like another human body.

"Who are you?" she gasped, knowing the answer before she asked. She turned clumsily, entangled in her petticoats and the blanket, and her hands struck a solid object. To her horror, she realized she was positioned against a wide, masculine chest.

"Cold?" Rhys Morgan's sardonic query was edged with laughter.

"You!" she choked out, pushing away from him.

"So you weren't joking, after all?"

"Did you think I was?"

"I had hoped . . . what are you doing?"

"Trying to get settled for the night."

"Why must you settle here?" she snapped, keeping her voice low.

"It's my canoe."

"Yes, but . . ."

Alex thought she detected a small chuckle, and her anger burned. "Are you laughing at me?"

"God forbid. Now go to sleep."

"How can I . . . with you bothering me?"

"I'm not bothering you."

"Oh, yes, you are."

He heaved a weary sigh. "Look, Miss MacKenzie, I thought you didn't want any favors on this trip, yet now it seems you expect me to bother you. Well, I'm sorry to disappoint you, but I'm simply too tired. Maybe another time?"

With that, he eased away from her, pulling his own blanket around his shoulders and shutting his eyes.

"Oh! You wretched backwoods boor!" In those first few moments of embarrassed ire, Alex seriously entertained the thought of kicking him, but gradually, the childish urge was mastered.

His next words were muffled by the blanket. "If you must know, I overheard a couple of the men making a little wager about your . . . friendliness. I thought it might be a good idea to stay close enough to you to ward them off, but I can leave . . . if you insist."

"No," she said slowly. "But I don't want you to

149

touch me."

He made no answer, leaving her with the feeling of dissatisfaction an unfinished argument can bring. Tossing the blanket aside, she rolled away from him.

"Where do you think you're going?" Rhys's voice was softly menacing.

"I'm going to sleep out here."

"Don't cause me any more trouble, Alexandria. Just stay put and go to sleep."

"It's not my purpose to cause you trouble," she replied, grasping the edge of the canoe in an attempt to move from beneath it. "But I believe I will be more comfortable in the open."

A brawny arm clamped about her waist, and she felt herself being yanked backward.

"Let me go," she commanded in a wrathful whisper. "I asked you not to touch me."

He half-rose over her, his hard hands pressing her shoulders flat against the granite rock. "I'm tired, and I don't have the patience to put up with you. Now, either you lie still and go to sleep or, I swear, I'll lie on top of you to keep you here!"

"My God, you wouldn't dare!"

Even in the dark, she saw the challenging smile that curved his mouth upward.

"Wouldn't I?" He flung one long leg over her hips, but before either of them could make another move, the air within the confines of the overturned canoe was suddenly so charged with tension that they simply froze. Alex found her breathing almost hurtfully restricted, but knew it was not from his weight upon her. The press of his body was intimate, even through the clothing she wore, and a flood of wholly new emotion swept over her.

There was nothing new about the emotion racing through Rhys's mind and body, but never before had he been forced to deny those feelings. Struggling to control his urge to consign propriety to hell, he closed his eyes and came closer to praying than he ever had in his life.

It wasn't until Alex found herself free from his intense gaze that she could speak again. Shakily, she murmured, "I . . . I won't leave, if you'll please get off me."

Rhys rolled away to lie on his back, one arm across his face. Without opening his eyes, he said, "It's just that you'll be safer here, Alex."

"Yes, all right."

Neither of them spoke again, and after a time, she implemented a little more decorum by withdrawing further from his disturbing presence. She slid to the edge of the shielding canoe, letting her gaze drift across the star-sprinkled night sky, and fell asleep in the middle of a wealth of confused thoughts.

One drop of rain, and then another, struck Alex on the forehead, causing her eyes to fly open in alarm. In the hours she had slept, the sky had been transformed into plain black velvet, and now there wasn't a star to be seen. Somewhere on the high bank behind them, trees were moaning in the rising wind, and she could hear the sizzle of raindrops as they began to fall into the campfire.

Chilled by the damp wind, Alex moved back beneath the shelter of the canoe. To her surprise, Nasturtium was curled up asleep on Rhys's chest, and he, completely unaware of the animal's trespass, was sleeping soundly, one arm flung above his head. Even as she sidled closer, Alex could feel the comforting warmth of his body. She was intrigued, for, never having shared a bed in her life, she'd had no way of knowing the heat and comfort another human body could give.

Rhys stirred in his sleep and turned his face so it rested on her unbound hair.

"Alex," he mumbled drowsily, lost in a dream.

The cold rain, now falling steadily, drummed on the canoe and dripped in rivulets from its edges. Alex lay quietly and tried to believe it was the noise of the storm that prevented her from falling asleep again.

"Lève! Lève, nos gens!"

The strident call rang through the camp just before daybreak, causing Alex to wake with a start and sit up, striking her head on the bottom of the canoe. Rubbing her forehead, she recalled where she was and darted a quick look at the blanket beside her, filled with relief to find Morgan gone.

"Lève!"

She peered out from beneath the canoe and found that it was Rhys himself rousing the others. When he saw her, he smirked complacently, as if pleased by her early morning grumpiness. She knew immediately he had not thrown off the surly mood of yesterday. Resolutely, she tossed the soggy blanket aside and stiffly crawled forth into the chill of dawn.

The voyageurs' breakfast was a dismal event, she soon discovered, for the cook had prepared extra rations the night before and now the lyed corn was served cold. Her stomach rebelled as she saw the voyageurs attack the gelid mass on their plates, and she felt no remorse at turning down her own share. She only regretted that, in order to save time, the campfire had not been rebuilt, so there was no hot tea or coffee to sustain her.

She was pleased to notice, however, the men from Sabaskong had built a small fire for their wives, who were busily brewing up their morning cups of tea. When Birdie cheerfully offered her a cup of plain tea, Alex was tempted to accept . . . until she became aware of Rhys's glance in her direction.

"No, thank you, Birdie," she said through gritted teeth. "I'm so anxious to see the waterfall, I think I'll go on ahead while the rest of you have breakfast."

At the far end of the rock ledge on which they had camped was the beginning of the rough track that skirted the waterfall. Alex wrapped a shawl about her shoulders, put Nasturtium into the hinged basket, and started down the portage trail.

Kakabeka Falls was magnificent, its ferocious beauty almost frightening. The river hurled itself over jagged rocks, the dark waters crashing and foaming nearly one hundred and thirty feet below. Ghostly mists rose up from the churning boil to float in ethereal splendor.

Called the Mountain Portage, this was perhaps the most difficult between Fort Kaministiquia and

Lake of the Woods. Only the spectacular view made it bearable at all, Alex decided, as she strove to reach the top of the escarpment.

Despite the steepness of the trail, the heavily laden voyageurs soon began to pass her, and determined they would not have to wait on her, she quickened her pace.

The loose shale underfoot was treacherous. More than once, she lost her footing and stumbled. The first time she fell, she skidded on her knees, scraping them painfully. But, thankful no one had witnessed her indignity, Alex rose and trudged on. However, the mud left by last night's rain and the clutter of slippery shale combined to create her downfall. Though she felt herself starting to slide, there was nothing she could do to prevent it, burdened as she was by the unwieldy basket. It seemed her feet were suddenly higher than her head. Arms flailing, she gave a low cry of alarm and landed on her back in the wet grass and weeds growing along the trail. Feeling as if the air had been knocked from her body, she wanted to give in to the urge to simply lie there.

Unfortunately, a deep masculine laugh rang out, causing her head to snap up. Rhys Morgan, a *pacton* strapped on his back, was regarding her, hands on hips and devilish delight in his eyes.

"Having a rest already, Miss MacKenzie?" he inquired, raising one hand to tip his hat back on his forehead. "But, really, I shouldn't have to tell a doctor it is unwise to lounge about in poison ivy."

"Poison ivy!" Alex cried, springing quickly to her feet. He was right—she was standing in a thick growth of the noxious, three-leafed plant. "Oh, no!"

Chagrined, she momentarily hid her face in her hands, and when she looked up at him again, muddy prints of each palm remained on her cheeks. As a wide grin spread across his face, she bit back a curt remark, seized the basket, whirled, and tramped away. His mocking laughter mercilessly followed her all the way down the winding trail.

Again, there was no stop for a midday meal, and Alex stubbornly refused the food the brides offered her, even though the sight of them munching crusty bread and cold meat as they made their way along the portage path caused her mouth to water. She vowed that as long as Rhys didn't give in to a need for food, neither would she, though by late afternoon she was wondering how much longer she could go on. Although thirsty and weak from hunger, her most serious problem was the torturous itching that had begun when the day grew hot and humid. Small red blisters appeared on the backs of her hands and behind her knees, and it seemed the skin on her entire body crawled and twitched.

A deep and abiding anger at Rhys Morgan added to her discomfort. That disturbing sentiment had reached a dangerous point at the last portage where, seeing one of the voyageurs preparing to lift her from the canoe and carry her ashore, Rhys had suggested she be allowed to wade like the men.

"You may not realize it," he'd said, transfixing the astonished *engagé* with a harsh glare, "but Miss MacKenzie doesn't require such attention. She is hoping to prove herself as hardy as any man here."

Clearly at a loss, the voyageur turned his inquiring gaze on Alex, leaving her no choice but to politely decline his offer of help and splash angrily to shore unaided. On the bank, she watched Pacer wade through knee-deep water with a smiling Lily in his arms. He whispered something in his wife's ear and gave her a quick, hard kiss before releasing her on the granite rocks and turning back to the canoe. When an obviously bemused Lily asked after Alex's well-being, it was all she could do to keep from snapping at the girl. After all, none of this was Lily's fault, Alex reminded herself as she set off through the woods. As to whose fault it was . . . well, a firm image of Rhys Morgan remained fixed in her mind.

Alex's misery was soon compounded by boots that sloshed water with each step and rapidly wore blisters on her heels. Not long afterward, she limped into a dark swarm of mosquitoes, and though they did not appear to bother the voyageur's naked flesh, they attacked her even through her clothing. She draped her black woolen shawl over her head, but found it inadequate protection at best.

Thinking she had surely reached the limit of her endurance, she considered it nothing less than a miracle when she arrived at the end of the portage trail. She released Nasturtium and sank down onto a small boulder to rest while she watched the tireless voyageurs reload the canoes.

Her eyes closed briefly . . . until she heard Morgan's snide comment as he passed by. "Don't get too comfortable — we're about to push off and we won't wait while you have a nap."

"Nor would I expect you to," she replied coolly.

She got to her feet, flinging the shawl over her head again, and reached for the hinged basket.

Nasturtium! she thought with alarm. She's in the woods. . . .

Alex glanced behind her, relieved to see they were still securing the cargo in some of the canoes. Quickly, she dashed into the trees, softly entreating, "Here, Nasturtium! Kitty, kitty, kitty!"

The woods were quiet except for the subdued trills of a few birds. Alex walked farther into its dim coolness, calling again, "Kitty . . . here, Nasturtium."

Where is that cat? she worried silently, eyes searching through the shadows. Why doesn't she come when I call? What could have happened to her?

A tight knot of apprehension formed in her stomach. Morgan had already warned her he would not wait for anything, and he'd certainly told her that if her cat got lost, it could stay lost.

Her voice sounded strained and anxious as she shouted again and again, wandering ever deeper into the forest.

A slight, rustling noise caught her attention and she stopped short. It came from the underbrush off to her right. With a weak cry of joy, she dropped to her knees, peering under the straggling clumps of buckbrush. Seeing a huddle of light-colored fur, she reached out a hand, then recoiled in fright as a terror-stricken rabbit bolted, frantic in its haste.

Alex's throat ached with fear. "Oh, Nasturtium," she moaned beneath her breath, "where are you? I can't leave you here. . . ."

The thought of what it would be like to be left alone there in the darkly forbidding woods made her heart sink like a stone.

Damn that arrogant, coldhearted Rhys Morgan! she raged silently, tears springing to her eyes. How could he be so mean? So unfeeling?

The dampness of the muddy ground began seeping through her skirts, so she got to her feet but stood motionless, shoulders slumped in utter dejection.

"Alexandria?" Morgan's deep voice sounded close behind her and, startled, she turned on him.

"I don't give a damn if you leave me here," she cried furiously. "I won't abandon my pet!"

"But—"

"You're a monster," she ranted, "hateful and uncaring—you're a brute!"

Once she had released herself from the usual civilized restraints, she could not seem to stop the flow of wrath. "I know you don't care that I'm tired and hungry! Or that I itch all over and have horrible blisters on my feet! Or that swarms of mosquitoes have nearly devoured me alive! All you care about is making this trip in the shortest time possible. Well, I'll tell you something, I'm tired of your bullying! And I think I'd rather be left here than forced to go on with you!"

Just as suddenly as it began, her spate of irate words was over.

Rhys Morgan studied the small woman standing before him as if he'd never really seen her before. She was certainly mad—mad as hell. And though she was a strange sight to behold, something told him he had better not display one sign of humor at the situation.

She was glaring at him, arms akimbo and legs spraddled, the light of battle in her eyes. Her bronze hair straggled down around a face smeared with mud and tears; her neck and hands were clearly marked with a reddening rash; her dress was streaked with filth, the hem torn and ragged, the useless shawl askew around her now-squared shoulders.

Rhys swallowed deeply, conflicting emotions sweeping through him.

I've put her through hell, he thought, just trying to show the impudent little baggage she doesn't belong out here.

But now he wasn't certain he'd proven his point at all. Until this moment, whenever he'd harassed or rebuked her Alex had only stiffened her back, thrust out her chin, and persevered. Rhys took another long look at her and realized a grudging admiration. She wasn't as weak as he'd expected her to be.

He took a step toward her. "Is this what you were searching for?"

Alex caught her breath in amazement. Her fury had kept her from noticing Nasturtium, nestled in the crook of Rhys's arm. Her gray eyes flew to his as she hesitantly reached out to accept the animal.

"When I saw the empty basket by the trail, I figured what must have happened," Rhys explained. "I found her chasing a ground squirrel through a hollow log."

"Thank you," Alex said, sounding meek after her tirade.

Rhys stared at her face, permitting himself a moment of pleasure. Even through the grime of mud and tears, she was beautiful. But the sudden recollection of his plan to marry her to his partner came into his mind and his pleasant mood vanished.

"We'd better go," he said shortly.

With a return of spirit, Alex said, "Yes, I know I kept you waiting and I'm prepared to apologize."

"Be glad we didn't leave you."

"I am, especially after you said. . . ."

"I know what I said." He shifted impatiently. "And if this happens again, you can believe I will enforce it."

"I'll remember that."

"We'll make camp within the hour," he said abruptly, "and then you can rest and have a hot meal. The men were going to catch some fish while they waited for us. We'd better treat those blisters on your feet and put some salve on that poison ivy." His hand moved to her shoulder to remove the shawl "As for mosquitoes," he said with an unexpected grin, "wearing this thing won't help. Dark colors only attract mosquitoes."

The smile had a most unsettling effect on her, so she ignored it, stepping around him to follow the path back to the river.

Aberdeen and Cordelia met them at the edge of the forest. "Is everything all right?" Aberdeen asked.

Alex took only a few seconds to reassure her, and then they got underway once again.

Rhys Morgan was as good as his word. Before

another hour had passed, camp was made on a sandy crescent of beach which cut into the thickly overgrown riverbank. The canoes were unloaded with alacrity while the cook prepared the evening meal. As the kettle of water heated for the lyed corn, he spooned fat into a shallow iron skillet and began frying the pike the men had caught. So appetizing was the aroma that everyone gathered around the fire, plates in hand, long before supper had finished cooking.

Perched on a rock, Alex ate every bite of the large serving the cook handed her, and thought it the most delicious meal she'd ever eaten. Even Nasturtium displayed approval of the tidbits of crispy fish the diners shared with her, by rolling onto her back in the cool sand and stretching her hind legs out in sensuous abandon, the pads of her feet looking startling pink in the growing darkness.

Alex sipped a tin mug of tea sweetened with maple sugar, and let herself be lulled by the gentle slapping of waves upon the beach, the low murmur of voices as the men and their wives sat around the fire talking. When she could no longer see the line of trees on the opposite shore because of the oncoming night, she rose and, calling softly to the cat, slipped out of the circle of light cast by the campfire. As she passed the brides' tents, she heard Aberdeen call her name.

"What is it, Deenie?" she asked, stifling a huge yawn. Then she heard a faint strangling cough from inside the nearest shelter.

"It's Christiana," the Scotswoman said. "She's been coughing since early morning."

"No doubt from the dampness of the waterfall," Alex said, forgetting her own tiredness. She lifted the canvas flap at the front of the tent and went inside. The two pallets where Christiana and Aberdeen were to sleep took up all the floor space; Christiana was huddled on one, wrapped in a blanket and looking pale and miserable.

"How do you feel?" Alex asked, laying her hand against her friend's heated forehead. "Any pain?"

"Only a tightness . . . here," Christiana replied, tapping her chest. "And something of a headache."

"I expect the headache's from hunger and exhaustion. It's the cough I'm worried about." Alex sat back on her heels. "This has bothered you off and on since we left the city, hasn't it?"

Christiana nodded, looking faintly guilty. "I've tried not to . . . not to act sick, but lately I've felt worse. I don't know why that should be."

"You're not getting proper rest, for one thing. And, for another, mornings and evenings are getting damper and cooler. Perhaps that has had some effect on you." Alex shook her head. "The main thing is, we've got to get you to Sabaskong without letting you succumb to this illness. It will be difficult treating it on the trail, but I'm afraid we have no choice."

Alex left the tent and began giving brisk orders. She sent Aberdeen for food and tea, insisting that Christiana eat something whether she wanted it or not. While one of the men built a fire outside the tent, Alex rummaged through one of her trunks until she found the items she sought. Herbs were scattered into a pot of boiling water, with a blanket

162

draped from the door of the tent to a makeshift frame which stood over the small fire. Alex was hopeful that enough of the aromatic vapors would steal inside to ease the congestion Christiana was suffering. She placed a poultice on the woman's chest, then firmly commanded her to take two spoonsful of thick, syrupy medicine that would, she promised, help the cough. Alex did not leave the tent until her patient had fallen into a deep sleep.

"I'm worried about her," she confessed to Aberdeen. "Really worried. I only hope we can get her to Lake of the Woods before she starts getting too much worse."

"Ye think she'll get worse, then?"

Alex nodded. "I'm afraid so." She heaved a weary sigh, and Aberdeen patted her shoulder.

"Ye'd best get some sleep yerself, lass. The last two days have no' been easy for ye." Aberdeen smiled suddenly. "Though I understand the dour Mr. Morgan has relented somewhat and allowed the men to pitch a tent for ye. 'Tis said he had a proper dressin' down from a certain fire-haired she-cat. . . ."

Alexandria grinned impishly. "Is that what they're saying?"

"Aye, lassie. There was many a chuckle over it at the campfire tonight. Now, get ye off to yer bed."

A short distance away, on another, narrower stretch of sand enclosed by sheltering bushes and stunted willows, was the evidence of Rhys's apparent contrition. A small tent stood bathed in the welcome blaze of a campfire.

How wonderful even a few hours of privacy will

163

be, she thought gratefully. Just to be all alone. . . .

With a quick glance behind her, Alex pulled off her boots and began loosening her gown, dropping it onto the beach.

Tentatively, she eased her tired, blistered feet into the cold water and sighed with delight. The short, choppy waves soothed and refreshed, though each time she moved and they splashed higher on her bare legs, she drew a sharp breath. Soon the inflamed and stinging flesh on her face, arms and shoulders, began to crave the chill touch of the river and, without further consideration, she untied her petticoats and stepped out of them, hurling them onto the sand behind her.

Then, dressed only in a chemise and pantalettes, she plunged forward into deeper water before her courage could desert her. Shock sent her mind reeling as the iciness closed around her, but along with the shock came almost instant relief from the itching she had endured all afternoon. She dipped her head back, letting her long hair fan out behind her. She wished she had brought a piece of soap with which to wash it, but at least she could rinse out the dust. She ducked beneath the surface, grateful for the numbing effect of the water on the multitude of mosquito bites she had suffered. Though she had never had an opportunity to learn to swim, she was not afraid of the river—not as long as her feet could touch the clean sand and rock bottom. Feeling liberated from the restricting clothing and emboldened by her buoyancy, she let her body float, laughing softly at her own clumsiness.

As she played, she caught sight of Nasturtium's

shadowy form lying on a flat rock at the water's edge. Knowing the animal's complete disdain for water, she could well imagine her feline curiosity.

"Alexandria, for God's sake! What do you think you are doing?"

The irate voice boomed out, frightening both Alex and the cat. Nasturtium gave a discordant yowl and fled into the underbrush, while Alex bounced upright in the water, flinging back her wet hair, which slapped against her bare shoulders.

She could see a man standing on the shore, and even though darkness obscured his face, she knew it was Rhys Morgan by his aggressive stance.

"I said," he repeated with exaggerated calm, "what the hell do you think you are doing?"

Alex felt childishly defensive once again. "I was merely trying to ease the sting of poison ivy and mosquito bites," she answered. "I thought the cool water might help . . . and it did. Tremendously."

"Well, I suppose I must bow to your medical logic. Drowning would be a most effective means of ridding oneself of an unwanted itch."

"Drowning?" she murmured faintly.

"Yes, something that happens to people foolish enough to go into the water alone. In a strange river. At night."

Each phrase sounded more damning than the last, and Alex felt completely chastised.

"I didn't realize I was being careless," she admitted. "All I could think about was how hot and dirty I'd been all day, and how good the water would feel against my skin."

"I guess no real damage was done," he conceded.

"But you'd better get out now."

"Yes, I will."

Rhys stood patiently for a moment. "Well . . . ?" he finally said.

"I'll get out when you leave."

"No, come out now. I want to make sure you do as you say you will."

"Oh, all right. But turn your back."

Surprisingly, he obliged without argument. "And next time you get a half-witted idea like this . . ." His words trailed away as he glanced back over his shoulder, then turned to stare.

Aware that she was dressed in only the barest of clothing, and those items were nearly transparent with wetness, Alex crossed her arms over her chest and hurried past him to seize the profusion of petticoats lying on the beach. Using them to shield herself from his intense look, she glared back, waiting for him to finish his reprimand.

"You were saying . . . ?" she prompted.

"Hmmm? Oh, yes! I was saying that next time you should tell someone of your intentions."

"Very well."

"I came to bring this and make certain you were going to treat those blisters." He held up her black leather medical bag. "No sense in taking a chance on blood poisoning, as I expect you know."

"Yes, of course." Alex, still clutching the petticoats with one hand, held out the other for the bag.

"Do you have something for the poison ivy?"

"Yes."

"Good." Then, instead of bidding her good night and going as she'd expected him to, Rhys said, somewhat gruffly, "Sit down on that rock by the fire, and I'll have a look at those blisters."

Giving her no chance to protest, he knelt and waited until she had seated herself. She could not control a start of alarm as she felt his warm fingers close around her ankle, lifting her foot so he might survey the blisters worn by her boots. More conscious than ever of her state of undress, she compressed her lips and stared into the darkness over his left shoulder.

"Where's the medicine? In the satchel?"

At her nod, he dug through the bag's contents until he found the appropriate tin and a roll of soft gauze bandaging.

"I can manage this," she said.

"It'll be easier for me to do it. Now sit still."

He braced her bare foot against his thigh while he pried the lid from the tin, releasing the pungent odor of the salve. He leaned forward and the large muscles of his upper leg shifted and rolled beneath Alex's foot, causing all thought of anything else to flee her mind. Before Rhys, she had never touched a man so intimately—this was nothing like the impersonal contact she had with a patient. His thigh seemed as hard and solid as the granite rock underlying Canada's thin soil. Bemused by the thought, she cautiously wriggled her toes, feeling the immediate response of the sinew she rubbed against.

Slightly aghast at her own daring, she raised her eyes and saw him watching her.

At first, Rhys had been amused, and surprised that she could dissemble so well. She had reacted to him with the curiosity of an inexperienced virgin, and yet he himself had seen her laboring over the naked voyageur not more than a week ago. He tried to believe that her playful naiveté was distasteful, but the truth was, as he applied the salve to her injuries and began wrapping her ankle and heel in strips of gauze, he was becoming all too cognizant of the seemingly innocent rub of her foot against his thigh. As false as he thought her action to be, it nevertheless sparked an answering curiosity in him.

Her legs, naked from the knees down, looked slender and well-shaped in the dim light of a new moon. As he slid his hand upward, taking her bare calf in his hand, she stirred restlessly—almost, but not quite, resisting his touch. Her skin was soft and smooth, still cool from the water, and very pliant beneath his fingers.

With an effort, he wrenched his mind away from such reflections and finished the bandaging.

"There. Now, where's the lotion for that rash?" he asked brusquely.

"In that bottle . . . but I can do it myself."

Still on his knees, he uncorked the bottle and handed it to her. She merely looked back at him with a blank expression on her face.

"Well, go ahead and start applying it."

Because she did not want to drop the shielding petticoats, Alex stalled for time. "I suspect you think I've been a terrible nuisance," she said.

"Yes, but it's what I expected." For some reason, it irritated him that she didn't seem particularly contrite, even under the current circumstances, and he allowed his impatience to show. He all but snatched the bottle away from her, saying, "I don't know why you don't get on with this so you can go to bed. Turn around and hold your hair out of the way, and I'll spread this on your neck and shoulders."

"But I can—"

"Don't argue, Alex."

With a sigh, she swiveled about on the rock, pulling her wet hair forward, wringing it dry, and leaving it hanging in a damp twist.

Behind her, Rhys began stroking the lotion along her shoulders and upward onto her neck, and she stiffened. But slowly, she relaxed beneath his ministrations, her shoulders slumping forward, her face turned away.

Looking at the curve of her averted cheek, Rhys thought, for the hundredth time, that she was beautiful. Beautiful in an elemental way that shook him completely, causing his hand to slow and stop. Her skin was still beaded with drops of moisture, her thick lashes tangled with wetness. In that light, her eyes were lustrous, mysteriously almond-shaped, and exotic; her high cheekbones thrown into relief by the pale moon.

Leaning closer, Rhys determined what he already knew, that her beauty did not end with her facial features. In an unguarded moment, her grip on the discarded petticoats had loosened, and now the size and shape of her breasts, loosely constrained in the soaking wet chemise, were revealed. Rhys felt himself tense and tighten in response to the sight of their shadowy loveliness, and he silently cursed. How had he come to such a state? He was nearly panting with lust at the merest glimpse of a female body, and that body belonged to a woman who, for all intents and purposes, was the embodiment of all he despised and distrusted in women.

"Lord help me," he muttered under his breath.

Alex turned to look at him, her lips softly parted, her eyes wide with question. "What did you say?" she inquired.

It took every bit of strength Rhys could summon at that moment to pull his gaze away from her mouth. He thought it most tempting, and wondered if the innocent invitation it offered was only his imagination. The calm and practical Miss Alexandria MacKenzie sat among the moonbeams looking very much like a royal princess holding court. He pondered what her reaction would be if he should suddenly yank her up into his arms, kissing her until her breath came fast and ragged. Would it affect her as little as that first kiss had seemed to do? Or had she grown to dislike him enough to struggle angrily? Or would her lips open beneath his in passionate reply?

My God, he thought wryly, she'd probably dislocate my arms, then scream the needles off the pine trees!

Abruptly, he thrust the bottle at her. "I'm sure you can finish this," he said, his voice harsh. He rose and started to stalk away, then, pricked by some devil even he did not understand, he spun back to face her. "Look, Alex, my partner is an honorable man . . . somehow I can't think that, as your future husband, he would approve of your behavior tonight."

Shock equivalent to that caused by the icy water washed over her, and she gasped in outraged surprise. "I don't know what you're talking about."

"An engaged woman does not entertain men in such a state of undress."

"I never asked you to come here," she cried, but he had turned and was striding away into the dark, and she found herself addressing his retreating back.

Nearly strangling with wrath, she buried her flaming face in the drift of petticoats on her lap. How could he pretend such concern one minute, then accuse her of the basest immorality in the next?

Had she ever detested anyone as much as she did Rhys Morgan?

Chapter Nine

Despite her new privacy and the exhausting experiences of the day, Alex did not sleep well that night. Over and over, she heard Rhys's insulting accusations and, because she knew how unfounded they were, her temper fairly simmered.

The following morning, she dressed and, folding her tent into a neat pack, joined the men for breakfast. On that day, the meal was hot, and even though she appreciated the fact, she did not reveal her pleasure by so much as a word or glance in Morgan's direction. She knew it was silly to sulk about his treatment of her, so she vowed not to fall into another such situation. From that point forward, she fully intended to keep her distance, ignoring him whenever possible.

Likewise, she was determined not to cause further delays as they continued the journey. Over the next several days, she dressed less warmly, protected her skin with a brimmed hat borrowed from one of the voyageurs, and kept the medicinal salve close at hand. On the portages, she was more careful, avoiding mudholes and poison ivy with a vengeance. Even Annie and Tobias hung back, daunted by her stubbornness as she tramped alongside the men, teeth gritted in resolution, shoulders squared.

The Great Dog was one of the worst portages between Athabasca and Montreal, for the two-mile trail rose nearly five hundred feet at its highest point. Densely wooded, the path was eerily dark in some places, with muddy ruts underfoot and fallen logs that tripped up even the most experienced men. It was with heartfelt relief that Alex finally arrived at the pebbly beach of Dog Lake, which marked the end of the portage.

Dog Lake was the first expanse of open water they had encountered since the beginning of the march. She thought it a welcome change to sit comfortably in the canoe as it skimmed lightly along the west edge of the lake, with no rapids or falls for a distance of twelve miles. Even after they reached the shallow, reed-choked mouth of the Dog River, there were no major obstructions for twice that distance. The river wandered aimlessly for miles before straightening and widening into a long, narrow lake, with thick cedar forests crowding both shores. At one point, as the canoes made their silent passage, they came upon a cow moose feeding along the marshy banks. She raised her enormous head and stared at them, then resumed her meal, moving awkwardly through the water lilies.

As time passed, Alex knew the constraint between herself and Rhys must be obvious to the others, for she had noticed several of the brides observing the two of them with speculative gazes. As for Rhys, he seemed intent on ignoring her just as studiously as she ignored him.

To Alex's surprise, their arrival at Height of Land Lake was marked by a ceremony. It was at this spot that the rivers no longer flowed to the south, into Lake Superior and the St. Lawrence River system, but northward into Hudson Bay. From this point on, all travel would be downhill, with no more arduous struggle against the prevailing current. And, the smiling voyageurs informed the women, to mark the passage over the divide, any tenderfoot traveling into the northern wilderness for the first time must be initiated.

Alex, chosen to go first, considered putting a stop to such frivolity until she saw Morgan watching her. Certain that he expected her to balk, she calmly inquired about the details of the initiation and submitted graciously.

She knelt on a wide, flat rock, head bowed, while one of the voyageurs dipped a cedar bough into the north-flowing stream, then splashed her with it. She gasped under the onslaught of cold water, and the men who were gathered around, laughed heartily. Tossing Rhys Morgan a challenging look, two of the *engagés* broke out a keg of rum and declared travel over for the day. Morgan, leaning casually against a tree, his arms crossed over his chest, watched through narrowed eyes, but made no objection.

Tin cups of rum were passed, and when one of them was handed to Alex, she good-naturedly took a small sip. The fiery liquid seared her throat and brought tears to her eyes, but even though she was fighting for breath, she managed a feeble smile, causing the men to cheer. Darting a quick look at Rhys, she saw amusement on his tanned face, and, irritated, she deliberately raised the cup and took another swallow. When someone passed a cup to Rhys, he inclined his dark head in her direction and lifted the mug in a silent, sardonic toast.

After the brides had been officially welcomed to the north country, the men began steadily emptying the keg. By evening, they had grown more and more boisterous. When they tired of swimming and wrestling, they found a sandy place to play a daring game that involved tossing hunting knives at each other's moccasined feet. Looking on from the sidelines, Alex was amazed that no one was hurt; even copious amounts of rum and the duskiness of approaching night did not seem to lessen their skill.

Alex herself had taken all afternoon to drink the one cup of rum presented to her, but even though she had sipped it slowly, she could feel its effect in the lassitude that possessed her. She had stayed with the voyageurs, even when the other women had set up a camp some distance away and were spending the unexpected leisure time in washing out clothing or cooking food for the days ahead. She enjoyed the antics of the crew, and wished she felt free to join in their silly games. She decided she must be a little drunk, the thought mildly scandalizing her.

Suddenly, an *engagé* named Louis called a halt to the merriment by announcing, "But we have forgotten something — the *mademoiselle* has not yet taken the oath!"

The knife-throwing was forgotten as the men circled around Alex.

"What oath?" she asked cautiously, looking from one drunken face to another.

"You must promise to uphold the laws of the wilderness," one of Morgan's men explained.

"And you must vow never to steal from a voyageur," cried another.

"But, most important of all, you have to swear you will never kiss a voyageur's wife if she is unwilling!" A shout of laughter greeted this remark, and even Alex had to smile.

"That should be simple enough," she said.

"Ah, but wait one moment," put in Louis. "Considering that Miss MacKenzie is a female, should we not reverse the oath? Should not she have to swear she will never kiss a voyageur who is unwilling?"

The men called out cheerful assent, and one of them stepped forward. "And I, for one, am most willing!"

With unexpected swiftness, he threw his arms about Alex, drawing her into a rough embrace to place a smacking kiss on each of her rose-tinged cheeks. Before she could struggle free, he whirled her into the waiting arms of the next man, who also announced his willingness and kissed her soundly.

Seeing that the men intended only chaste kisses, Alex forgot her alarm and laughed with them, growing dizzy from the speed with which she was passed from man to man. And then, before she realized it, she was held fast within Louis's grip and his grinning face was lowering to hers. Something in his expression warned her that his kiss was not meant in fun, and just as his mouth brushed hers, she turned her head, causing his lips to fall on her cheek.

Louis gave a growl of anger, and his fingers tightened on her arm. "So! *Mademoiselle* chooses to tease?" He gave her a shake. "I do not like to play such games. Shall I show you what happens to women who tease . . . ?"

Rhys Morgan's rough voice cut the threat short. "Don't be selfish, man. You've kissed her — now pass her on."

"And if I don't?"

"I will kill you." Rhys raised a hand, and the wide blade of knife gleamed wickedly in the last rays of the sunset.

Louis's hand fell to the hilt of his own knife, opening and closing with nervous indecision.

Seeing the glitter of drunken hatred in the man's eyes, Alex's heart sank. What in God's name was she doing in the middle of nowhere, surrounded by a handful of inebriated men who might, at any moment, try to kill each other for the flimsiest of reasons?

"Either unsheathe that knife or pass me the woman," Rhys said coldly, taking a step toward them.

Something about his stance told Alex that even he was not entirely sober, and her fear took on new intensity. Despite everything, she had come to think of him as her protector, as a buffer between herself and danger. Now, if he chose to abandon civility, what could she do? For the first time, she began to understand something of her own vulnerability.

Her anxiety increased as Louis and Morgan glared fiercely at each other. Then, suddenly, Louis shoved her toward Rhys. "Take her, Morgan . . . after all, this is a celebration and not the time to have such differences, eh?"

"You're right." Rhys took Alex's arm and said, "Come along while I put up your tent." He glanced back at the watching men. "Someone sober up the cook and tell him to fix supper."

Alex allowed him to pull her along behind him until they were separated from the others by a stand of pines. When he stopped, she slipped out of his grasp and, kneeling, began to unroll the canvas tent. It, and the small carpetbag in which she had packed her essentials, had been dumped into the scanty grass at the edge of a flat granite shelf. Nearby, perched atop a roll of bedding, was Nasturtium, eyeing them owlishly.

As soon as the tent was freed from its cords, Rhys erected it with swift, practiced motions, and Alex, thanking him politely, turned away to spread the blankets for her bed. Instead of leaving as she had expected, Rhys stood and watched her, making her feel awkward and self-conscious, certain that he was amused by her ineptness.

Far from amused, Rhys was feeling the combined effects of the rum and days of enforced closeness to the most exasperatingly attractive woman he had ever met. Each morning as they left camp and continued on, gliding from one lake to another, he would renew his intention of concentrating only on the task at hand. And then, as he gazed straight ahead, sighting the best route for the brigade to follow, her clear-cut profile constantly interfered with his line of vision. How many times had his *avant* had to warn him of shallows or rocks or the rotten, floating logs the voyageurs called deadheads? And how many times on the portage trail had he found himself purposely walking behind Alexandria, completely entranced by the inviting sway of her hips beneath the thin cotton gowns she wore? He was thoroughly disgusted with himself, but seemingly unable to get his growing lust under control. Sometimes, when he made himself stop to think that he might be putting all of them into danger by his blind fascination with the woman, he would remind himself that she was promised to his partner and best friend—that he himself intended to see that particular marriage take place as soon as possible. And then he would be filled with an unreasoning jealousy toward Scotty, the gut-twisting intensity of which puzzled him, because his friend hadn't even met Alexandria and had no idea she was to become his wife. Rhys despised being so weak and emotional. His feelings confused and irritated him, and drove him to disprove them once and for all.

Alex straightened, then turned slowly to face him. Her gray eyes seemed to snap, but her voice showed no sign of temper.

"I suppose you are waiting for my apology . . . and an admission of weakness. Well, I won't disappoint you. Thank you for getting me out of that situation with Louis. I imagine it could have become rather ugly, since he had been drinking."

Ignoring her words, Rhys raised a hand to lightly caress her neck, capturing her chin and jaw with a broad palm and lean fingers. Startled, she tried to move away, but he placed his other hand on her back, at waist level, drawing her firmly up against him.

"What are you doing?" she muttered, struggling. "Release me at once!"

"Not on your life."

"I've offered an apology. . . ."

"An apology is not what I want," he said.

"Then what?"

"You kissed every man in the brigade. Surely you don't expect me to give up my turn?" The hand along her jaw tightened, and he pressed his thumb beneath her chin to lift her face to his.

"But I . . ." Her words faded as she tensed, anticipating the touch of his lips on hers. Instead, his mouth gently grazed first one cheek, then the other. His moustache swept softly over her skin, causing a delicate shudder to skim down her spine. He smelled of rum and cedar and fresh sunshine. . . .

Alex looked into his eyes and saw that they were

a deep, shaded green—as dark as a night forest, and just as frighteningly mysterious. Stunned by the sudden, bone-melting sensation washing over her, she shut her eyes and drew a deep, shaky breath. In the next instant, his mouth closed over hers and her mind went spiraling away into senselessness.

No, not senselessness exactly, she thought wildly, for her senses were almost agonizingly acute. She was aware of the soothing warmth of his lips, of their yielding firmness beneath the slight harshness of the moustache. She could hear the faint groan that came from deep within his throat, could feel the easy strength in the splayed hand at her back. The feel and taste and scent of him was overwhelmingly masculine . . . and like nothing she had ever experienced before. She sagged weakly in his embrace, suddenly finding no resistance to his kiss, no will to fend him off.

After a timeless moment, Rhys raised his head. "Welcome to the North Country," he said, with a crooked grin. "God, I must be drunk—I know better than to start something like this."

"Then don't do it," she whispered, but only half-heartedly, for his lips were playing over hers again. They rubbed lightly, teasingly, until she stood on tiptoe and pressed her own mouth to his, her fingers tangling in the fringe of the buckskin shirt he wore. Both his arms went around her as the kiss deepened, dragging her close against the entire length of his muscular frame.

His tongue caressed the tiny cleft in her upper lip, and she was filled with an unexpected bloom of passion that threatened to engulf her with its heat, leaving her powerless to stop his sensual invasion. She parted her lips tentatively, and felt an answering shock surge through the body of the man holding her. It was both thrilling and terrifying to know she could affect him in the same way he was affecting her.

Alex moved closer to him, enjoying the feel of his lean legs bracketing her own, intrigued by the hard thrust of his hips against hers. Her hands slipped upward to his shoulders, bringing her breasts into intimate contact with the breadth of his chest. Rhys's hands began an almost feverish exploration of her back, sliding down to her waist, then lower, cupping her against him in a way that sent piercing stabs of pleasure through her body. Alex was caught up in a dark undertow of desire that pulled at her, holding her prisoner while the wild tides of reason washed over her and ebbed away.

Eyes closed, she felt Rhys's shoulder dip, and then he was lifting her into his arms. He didn't remove his mouth from hers as he began to walk. Alex neither knew nor cared where he was taking her, and it was not until he knelt and she recognized the scratchy wool of blankets beneath her palms and smelled sun-bleached canvas that she realized he had entered the tent.

She opened her eyes to see his shadowy figure looming over her. Instead of fear or outrage, or any number of other emotions she might have expected, she was relieved. This thing had been between them long enough — since the first moment they had spoken on the dock, she reckoned—and it was time to resolve it. Alex was not the kind of woman to shy away from new experiences, and this was no exception. Her only rational thought was surprise at the sense of delight she felt that it would be Rhys Morgan who initially acquainted her with the joys of lovemaking. That it would be joyous, she had no doubt. It was her opinion that passion was one of the advantages of being human, she was only amazed that it did not seem to require a partner whom one loved. She had always assumed that when she did actually give up her innocence, it would be with a man she truly cared for. Surely it wasn't possible to *love* someone you very nearly detested?

No, it couldn't be. Alex prided herself on her honesty, and now she had to face the fact that apparently she was one of those unusual women who could separate love and lust. She moved one hand to cover Rhys's where it rested on her waist. Touching the sinewy fingers, sliding her own upward to his hair-hazed wrist, then along the rigidly muscled forearm, she realized that he was no doubt attractive to her because he was such a splendid specimen of manhood—sternly handsome, tough, strong, and exciting in some disturbing, primitive way. Her reaction to him was purely physical, prompted most likely by her having arrived at the advanced age of twenty-four with only limited personal knowledge of the act of love. Perhaps love was for the young only, and when a spinster reached a certain age or hormonal condition, she was capable of dispensing with the need for declarations of affection. Alex wasn't certain, but her breathing quickened with the determination to find out. . . .

Rhys shuddered under her questing hand, and flung himself down beside her. One leg crept across her hips, just as it had that night beneath the overturned canoe, but this time neither of them withdrew from the pleasure that resulted from his action. Alex nestled more deeply into the blankets, sighed, and lifted her arms to enfold his shoulders and draw him closer to her. Once again they shared a long and searching kiss, one that ignited fires that leaped and burned within Rhys's dark eyes, to meet an answering flame within hers.

"Alex . ." He whispered her name in a ragged voice, and the very sound of it sent ripples of desire skimming through her.

"Hmmm?" she murmured softly.

"You are so beautiful—and you feel so damned good to me. . . ."

She could tell that he still resented being drawn to her, and she briefly wondered how they were going to feel once they had made love. Would it intensify their animosity toward each other . . . or soften it? At this rate, their relationship was never going to stagnate, that seemed certain. An amused smile sprang to her lips at the thought, then died immediately as she felt his fingers on the buttons down the front of her gown.

Rhys sensed her sudden tension and soothed her with sweet, nipping kisses along the side of her neck. Once she had relaxed beneath the tender onslaught, his hand returned to the buttons, which he undid slowly, one by one. The whiteness of her chemise glowed in the dark, and her skin was only a few shades darker. He slipped his hand inside the fabric of her dress and cupped her shoulder, finding that it fit perfectly into his palm. Then, with a deliberate lack of haste, he allowed his hand to stroke downward, slipping over the smooth contour of her breast to her ribs, and then back upward. He cradled the breast gently, almost reverently, awed by the full, velvety softness of it . . . fascinated by the hard, pebbly texture of the nipple that blossomed beneath the small, circular movements of his thumb. Alex twisted at his touch, but moved into his caress rather than away from it. The increased jerkiness of her breathing indicated her enjoyment of the sensations he knew he must be stirring within her. The same blinding need for fulfillment was building inside him, and he knew he was nearing a point of no return. He felt an almost frantic urge to accelerate the lovemaking, to push both of them beyond the ability to think. He needed to hurl himself over the brink of reason and sanity into the mindless sphere of pure animal gratification. He wanted this woman, wanted to experience the shattering release he knew she could give him—he didn't want to think of anything else.

Alex lay still, loving the feel of his callused thumb bringing her such agonizing delight. Then without warning, his hard, dry hand was replaced with the sweet, hot moistness of his mouth, and she could gladly have swooned at the piercing thrill that shot through her, galvanizing every nerve ending in her body.

"Oh, God, Rhys," she moaned, her fingers tightening almost painfully in his hair. "What are you doing to me?"

The gently wrenching pull of his mouth ended in a soft kiss, and then he moved away, leaving her to shiver as the cool evening air struck damp, bared flesh.

He couldn't help it—her response had been so spontaneous, so . . . so stunned, almost as if she had never held a man to her breast before. It was unnerving for her to act like an innocent virgin, sparking some protective instinct inside him. Why couldn't she just be honest and accept her own need for a purely erotic encounter? Why did women have to create such a major issue of something as simple as making love?

"Damn," muttered Rhys and rolled away from her.

"What's wrong?" she whispered, sounding stricken.

He couldn't answer, simply because his throat was suddenly choked with self-loathing and disgust. Her innocence or lack of it wasn't what had stopped him, and he knew it.

Damn it, the woman was going to marry Scotty! He sat up and swept a trembling hand through his hair. His best friend, for God's sake! The man he loved and trusted above all others—a man who was closer to him than a brother could have been.

"What in the hell am I doing?" he raged viciously.

"Rhys . . . ?"

"What were we thinking of, to let something like

186

this happen?" he groaned, still fighting hard to loosen the grip of passion.

"We weren't thinking . . . we only wanted each other."

Her blunt way of putting the matter in perspective only irritated him further. "Well, I'm thinking now," he growled. "For both of us, if need be. We aren't doing this to Scotty."

"Scotty?" Her tone was as incredulous as if she had never heard the man's name before. "Your partner?"

"The man you're going to marry," he amended. "My best friend."

"Oh . . . that's it," she murmured, a smile lurking behind her words. "You're having an attack of guilty conscience."

"As you should be," he said shortly.

"Would it make any difference if I told you that I have no intention of marrying your partner? That I never did?"

His hands curled into fists where they rested on his thighs. Hell, he might have known.

"It was a part of our bargain. The only reason I allowed you to make this trip to Lake of the Woods."

"It may have been a part of your bargain," she pointed out, "but I certainly never agreed to it. And as for you letting me make this journey, I beg to differ. Have you forgotten so quickly how the ladies convinced you?"

"You're marrying Scotty and that's final." He surged forward and out of the tent.

Alex got to her knees and stuck her head

187

through the canvas flap. "I won't!"

She could see that he had stopped, turning back to look at her, but she couldn't make out his expression in the darkness. "Alex . . . oh, hell!" He came a few steps closer. "Look, I'll take the blame for what just happened between us. I lost sight of . . . well, that doesn't matter now. The important thing is, I came to my senses in time to stop what could have been a disastrous mistake. From now on, it'll be up to both of us to see that nothing like this happens again."

"However, whether it does or does not has nothing to do with your friend. I'm not marrying anyone, Rhys, and I mean that."

"Can't you get it through your thick head that as long as you are an unattached female, men are going to be . . . that there's always going to be someone bent on having his way with you?" He heaved an aggrieved sigh.

"Can't you get it through your thick head that that isn't necessarily something to run from?" she dared to tease. "Perhaps I knew exactly what I was doing. . . ."

"And now you sound like a well-experienced waterfront jade," he exclaimed. "Lord, who knows how promiscuous you actually were back in Montreal? Maybe I'm doing Scotty a disservice to bring him such a bride."

"You're doing yourself a disservice if you persist in believing you can coerce me to do anything," she returned, suddenly angry. "And the amorous encounters in my past are none of your business."

His whole body twitched wrathfully. "Jesus, that's

exactly the sort of thing I meant when I opposed a single woman making this trip. It's insane."

"I'm beginning to think you may be insane," she accused.

"And I'm beginning to think you may be right. But let me hasten to assure you that I was in my right mind until the moment you stepped out of that canoe and professed to be, by all the great, flaming fires of hell, a *doctor!*" He ended his tirade with a short, explosive profanity that Alex had seldom heard in her somewhat sheltered life. She sat back on her heels and felt her eyes grow wide with amused surprise. The man was thoroughly irate, if his language was any indication.

"I am a doctor, you know," seemed to be all she could think of to say in reply.

"Yes, I know," he stormed. "And you're also a troublesome, temperamental female with a devious mind and a stubborn streak as wide as the Kaministiquia."

"If you find me so loathsome," she said with dignity, "why don't you simply leave me alone?"

"That's the first sensible idea you've had yet. I'll be only too happy to comply."

"Good."

"I'll deliver you to Scotty, then leave you alone for the rest your life."

"Fine. Maybe your partner is a man who will listen to reason. He probably won't want to marry me any more than I want to marry him."

"We'll let him decide, shall we?"

"Fine. Good."

They glared at each other through the nearly impenetrable darkness. Finally, with an impatient shrug of his shoulders, Rhys said, "It's getting late . . . I'd better go check on the cook."

Alex declined comment, and after an awkward silence, he turned on his heel and stomped away. She sank back onto the blankets, letting the gloom of the tent's interior settle around her. Realizing that the front of her dress was gaping open, she began buttoning it, reluctantly recalling the earlier interlude with Rhys.

His rejection of her stung, she admitted to herself. She had been uncaringly lost in the heat of the moment, how unflattering that *he* had been able to keep his head. How frustrating, as well. She had been a woman on the brink of discovery; now she felt like a chastened little girl.

Times without number, Alex had read the clinical details of the male-female relationship. In the course of her studies, she had encountered all the textbook explanations, thinking it sounded rather dull and uninspiring. Now, at an age when she thought there could be no more to know about human sexuality, she had begun to find that the reality far surpassed the written word. No schoolbook could have prepared her for the heady actuality of passion, for the way her blood had sung in her veins, for the way her heart had jolted in her chest. No mere medical prose could have fully expressed the thrill of being crushed to a hard male body, or the miraculous sense of compassionate power that came to a woman when she finally recognized the hold she had over a man becoming lost to desire.

Alex's hand faltered, forgot the undone buttons, and moved to her mouth. She traced her faintly swollen lips with a light touch of her fingers, and dreamed of Rhys Morgan's ardent kiss.

"Damn him," she whispered softly. It was difficult to be a free-thinking woman when the man she chose happened to be a hidebound throwback to the Dark Ages!

With a regretful sigh, Alex lay back on her makeshift bed and drew the blanket up around her shoulders.

She didn't go to supper that night.

Chapter Ten

The brigade bound for Sabaskong Falls left the brown-colored lakes of the south behind and began traversing the clear, green waters of the north. The late-summer days dwindled swiftly as they made their way down long corridors of pine, beneath daunting rock bluffs and over wild, foaming rapids, all the while striving to maintain the North West Company's standard of forty paddle strokes a minute.

Though he seldom spoke to Alexandria, Rhys was always near, and she sensed that his attitude was one of coldly silent protectiveness. She assumed he had decided she was indeed a loose woman, one he had better keep a close eye on until she could be safely delivered to Scotty MacPherson. Each time she talked with any of the voyageurs, she could detect his watchful gaze upon her. She supposed that now he had managed to escape her wiles, he intended to safeguard what was left of her virtue until matrimony transformed her into a staid matron. The absurdity of that notion set her mouth to twitching merrily.

Until coming to the wilderness, Alex had lived a curiously sheltered life that had allowed for no exposure to the depth of feeling that could exist between a man and woman. She had been very young when her parents died, and by the time she was old enough to even think of such things, her grandmother was already afflicted with poor health. Though her grandparents were obviously devoted to each other, there was no passion between them. Thus, Alex had to form her own opinions, and since most of these were inspired by the romantic novels she read, she developed the idea that love, based on mutual respect and affection, was essential for the existence of passion, and that, naturally, existed only within the confines of marriage. However, her recent experiences with Rhys Morgan had since caused her to discard that theory completely, leaving her in need of new definitions.

She had not been prepared for the sensations his kiss had aroused within her. A little shocked at first, she had quickly found intense pleasure in the feel of his mouth against hers, the brush of his hands over her body. She wasn't surprised to find passion in her character so much as she was surprised that it could exist without any serious commitment. Childishly, she had assumed it took a wedding and all the trappings to nurture certain feelings in a woman—how many times had she mourned the fact that, by denouncing marriage and family, she had also given up all rights to love and desire? It was a wonderfully satisfying thing to have learned those emotions might not be beyond her reach after all. She had no plans to love Rhys Morgan, and heaven only knew, marriage to him wasn't even the remotest possibility, but it would be a lie to say she did not desire him. She watched him covertly, wondering if and when the flames would be reignited, and though the idea was alarming, it was also strangely appealing.

Rhys, on the other hand, thought he was treating Alex with a deference that was meant to demonstrate his regret over the incident in the tent. He purposely tried to remain aloof, but as they pressed farther into the interior, her genuine pleasure in everything they saw gradually won him over, loosening his tongue in spite of his intentions. He found himself pointing out Indian paintings high on the rocks or the deer watching from the forest's edge. His eyes, dark, unreadable, and no easier to discipline than his mouth, could not seem to stay away from her.

Rhys constantly cursed himself for his recklessness. Why had he ever gotten close enough to touch her? Lord, he knew how hot her temper could be, he should have suspected the presence of other fires as well. Now, having had a brief taste of her warmth, he found his mind filled with her. At least a hundred times a day, he reminded himself that she was too disruptive an influence not to be married to someone strong enough to control her. That someone had to be Scotty, since Rhys himself had long ago sworn never to make the mistake of taking a wife. That he had even considered such a thing for the briefest split-second since meeting Alex sent him into a fury of self-disgust. He began to feel a need to get home, to put Alex into Scotty's hands and get on with his own life . . . at a safe distance from her.

The brigade crossed big, windswept Lac des Mille Lacs, Windigoostigwan Lake, French and Pickerel Lakes. They passed sandy beaches, stands of white pine and cedar, marshy swamps guarded by blue heron, and huge granite boulders. At Lac La Croix, the Kaministiquia route joined the more southerly one used by the American traders. It was a beautiful lake filled with densely wooded islands, and that night they camped within sight of the mai, or lobstick. This was a tall spruce tree, trimmed of all its branches but those close to the top. One of the most famous landmarks in the Northwest, it marked the place where the road from Fort Kaministiquia branched off from the "new road."

After that, they moved through a succession of lakes — Loon Lake, Lake Vermilion, Sand Point Lake — until they reached Namakan Lake, a large body of water swept by such vicious headwinds they were forced to make a degrade. They went out of their way in search of a protected shore along which they crept, hoping the wind would blow itself out. When it did not, they had no choice but to halt their journey in midafternoon and make camp.

That night a nearly full moon rose over the lake,

shedding its red-gold light lavishly over the roughened waters. Alex sat on a boulder near the beach, Nasturtium asleep on her lap. There was a new chill in the nights now, and she pulled her shawl closer about her shoulders.

"Pretty moon." Rhys's quiet words came from some point behind her, and she realized she had been waiting, as if somehow she had known he would seek her out.

"Yes . . . I hadn't even noticed," she said, surprised that she had not.

"Something bothering you?" he asked. He moved forward, into her line of vision, but stood with his back to her, head raised as he gazed at the hazy red moon high in the night sky.

Alex smoothed Nasturtium's thick fur absent-mindedly. "It's Christiana. Her cough seems worse this past week."

"The medicine isn't helping?"

"Not much—probably just enough to keep her going."

"We'll reach Rainy Lake tomorrow," he stated. "That's where our brigade heads north. It won't be much longer after that."

"If we can only get her to the Falls, perhaps she can start to rest and get better." Alex shook her head. "I'm becoming more worried every day."

"What do you think is wrong with her?"

"I have a feeling Christy has suffered from a weakness of the lungs since she was a child. But if that's the case, I can't imagine why she ever left Montreal. She surely knew the journey would tax her strength."

"Her reason for coming must have been greater than her fears for her health," Rhys reasoned.

"Perhaps." Alex rose and draped Nasturtium over her shoulder. "But if we don't arrive at Sabaskong soon, her life could be endangered."

"We'll get her there," he said quietly, and Alex believed him. As much as she denied needing anyone, she knew she was becoming more and more dependent upon him, for some reason, trusting him to ease the way for all of them. It cost her dearly to admit such a thing even to herself, and she made a silent promise to do better at being self-sufficient. It had never been her plan to come to the wilderness and become any man's responsibility.

Alex's serious, contemplative face and the quiet beauty of the night surrounding them began to make inroads on Rhys's concentration. Unwilling to trust himself in what suddenly seemed an intimate setting, he attempted to lighten the moment.

"Ol' Nasty makes a pretty decent-looking fur piece. If you don't watch out, some unscrupulous trapper or another will be after her hide."

Alex looked horrified. "Oh, my God!" she cried. "Do you mean that?"

He put out a placating hand, which somehow ended up on her shoulder, next to Nasturtium's whiskery face.

"Alex, I was only joking," he said. "I'm sorry. I never thought you'd believe me."

"But I did." She swallowed deeply, her eyes looking huge. "I couldn't bear it if something happened to Nasturtium—she's such a sweet, loving animal."

Against his better judgment, Rhys laughed. "Sweet? Ol' Nasty?"

The cat in question stirred, opened its eyes, and saw Rhys's hand lying within reach. With no compunction whatsoever, the feline growled warningly, then lashed out with a wicked claw.

"Ouch!" Rhys yelped, pulling back his hand. "That damned cat clawed me!" He studied the thin red line that snaked across his knuckles.

"You startled her," Alex protested, soothing Nasturtium. "Besides, it's only a scratch."

"Men have bled to death from less serious wounds," he said sarcastically.

Alex's snort of derision was her only reply.

"Hell, I should have left that miserable flea bait in the woods," Rhys declared.

"Yes, and me with her," commented Alex. "You might as well say it as think it."

"Maybe you're right about that."

Alex drew herself up to her full height, tossing her hair angrily. "I refuse to stand here and debate this subject with you, Mr. Morgan. Good night."

He watched her go, absurdly disappointed that the peaceful mood of the night had been destroyed. Blast that cat, anyway! It had been as meek as a lamb the day he'd rescued it from the forest, leading him to assume its unreasonable dislike of him had been overcome. Now it was evident that the animal was just as fractious, just as testy and illogical as its mistress.

He shrugged. Once and for all, he'd learned his lesson. He would avoid them like the plague, and, please God, they would soon be at the Falls and he would no longer have to deal with either of them!

The next day Rhys Morgan led his brigade of canoes down a crooked passageway and past the mist-shrouded Kettle Falls into Lac la Pluie — Rainy Lake. As far as the eye could see, there was only open water, somber blue-gray and challenging in its immensity. It was nearly forty miles from one end to the other, and with that expanse of water, the safest route was along the northerly shore, as far from the effect of the prevailing wind as possible. Again, by the middle of the afternoon, the gale made travel too dangerous, so an early camp was made.

The brides were greatly cheered by the announcement that it would be only a few more days until they reached their new homes at Sabaskong Falls, and they decided to fix a special supper in celebration. Cordelia, taking charge, sent Alex, Aberdeen, and Lily in search of blueberries for dessert. They had wandered through a small stand of spruce trees, emerging onto a long, narrow spit of land that jutted out into a sheltered bay.

Just as Alex caught sight of two canoes pulled up onto the rocks, Aberdeen said, "Ach, it looks as if we've wandered into someone's camp."

"Ladies?" The mellow French-Canadian voice came from behind them, and the three women whirled about in unison, startled. At the sight of the man facing them, Alex's mouth went dry and Lily's short shrill scream rang in her ears. Even Aberdeen failed to control an involuntary gasp.

The man's face held their horrified attention. At one time he would have been extremely handsome—olive-skinned and dark-eyed, with a thin black moustache outlining a sensual mouth. Now a deep and puckered scar, dull mulberry in color, slashed through the right side of his forehead, through that eyelid and down his cheek, running into the hairline just below his ear. The skin of his forehead and eyelid bunched, drooping over the eye, which was almost totally obscured. Even so, in the bright light of afternoon, Alex could discern a telltale shine behind the overhanging skin and knew he was not, as she would have expected, blind in that eye.

Ashamed of her stunned hesitation, Alex made herself step forward to explain their presence in the strange man's camp. "How do you do? I'm Alexandria MacKenzie and these are two of my traveling companions. We were looking for blueberries when we stumbled into your ca—"

"Yer sudden appearance startled us," Aberdeen said bluntly.

"Ah, poor ladies," he said with a beaming smile that did not lessen the frightening impact of his ruined face. "You cannot have expected to meet up with such an ugly man!"

He did not flinch beneath their scrutiny, as if he had long since come to terms with his unsightliness and was willing to give others the same opportunity.

Alex thought he was much too tall to be a voyageur, and though his body was thin and lanky, there was a look of wiry strength about it. He was dressed in greasy buckskins, sweat-stained and snagged; a bear claw necklace hung about his throat, and on his feet were Indian moccasins. Hanging from a beaded belt slung low around his hips was a curved hunting knife, the bone handle worn smooth from years of use. Even standing as he was now, the fingers of his left hand rested caressingly on the ivory-colored hilt. He wore a discolored, flat-brimmed hat adorned with an ostrich feather, the symbol of a wilderness guide, over oily black hair that fell to his shoulders. In one ear was an earring fashioned of a large gold hoop, from which dangled several short strings of beads.

Alex cleared her throat nervously. Her companions remained mute and staring, so she felt it was up to her to make polite conversation. She was frantically casting about in her mind for a topic when, with relief, she heard a familiar shout.

Pacer, an evil-looking hunting knife clutched in one hand, burst into the campsite. He was followed closely by Waldo and Rhys, armed in a similar fashion. The men stopped short, for, although the stranger looked sinister enough, he was clearly engaged in nothing more threatening than talk. Nevertheless, Pacer crossed immediately to Lily's side.

"Are you all right?" he asked gravely. "I heard you scream."

Lily uttered a faint laugh. "We stumbled into this man's camp by accident. He . . . he startled us."

Pacer's dark gaze took stock of the scarred man, who, with a friendly smile, stepped forward and extended a hand.

"Allow me to introduce myself, if you will. My name is Bacconne—Robber Bacconne."

"And where do you hail from, Bacconne?" Rhys spoke for the first time.

"Fort Lac la Pluie," came the easy reply. "My men and I are doing a little fishing."

One black brow arched upward, but Rhys didn't question the information. Instead, he asked, "Where are the others?"

"As I said, fishing. Just along that point there."

"I see 'em," confirmed Waldo. "There's three more."

"That's right," agreed Bacconne. "I assume your party is camped somewhere close by?"

"Around the bend," said Pacer. "Why?"

Bacconne smiled at the young man's frankly suspicious tone. "I thought perhaps we might share some of our fish with you for your evening meal."

"Reckon that wouldn't hurt none," Waldo commented, glancing at the others to gauge their reaction. "Some fresh-caught fish might taste real fine to the ladies."

"You're welcome to join us for supper," Rhys said, though the invitation was offered somewhat grudgingly. "You'll find our camp on the other side of that stand of trees."

As the six of them walked back toward camp, Alex caught snatches of a whispered exchange between Rhys and Pacer. It was obvious the two did not trust Bacconne and were planning to keep him under close observation.

Alex shared their distrust of the woodsman. There was something sly about him, something un-

202

nerving in the way he quietly watched. She imagined that she could feel his intense gaze burning into her back all the way across the clearing, and it took every bit of her self-control not to turn and look.

Darkness had fallen before the men appeared. Bacconne was accompanied by three scurvy-looking trappers whose buckskins were filthy and strong smelling, and whose long black hair hung in greasy hanks about their thin, watchful faces. Bacconne did all the talking, making every effort to be amenable, while the others fell upon their food with all the restraint of starving animals.

And with about as many table manners, Alex thought, as she saw one of them sucking the meat from the long, curved backbone of a walleyed pike. She noticed that while the horrified brides stared at the ravenous men in disgust, Bacconne's furtive gaze moved over each of the women in turn, as though storing away information for later use. The thought was chilling, especially when she felt his black eyes taking her own measure. She wanted to run from his scrutiny, to hide in the darkness where she would feel safe from his rapacious intent. Instead, she raised her chin defiantly and stared straight back at him, refusing to be cowed. Her stomach lurched fearfully as he lowered the lid of his undamaged eye in a bold wink. His teeth gleamed in the firelight, and Alex fancifully imagined him to be the embodiment of the world's worst evil.

She assumed that Rhys Morgan felt very much the same, for he volunteered no information to the man and deftly changed the subject each time Bacconne inquired about their destination. As the evening wore on, the husbands moved closer to their wives, most wrapping protective arms around their shoulders; even Aberdeen made no protest when Waldo Anderson settled his bony frame not more than three feet from her. There was a general feeling of relief when the strangers finally rose and departed for the night, but for the first time since leaving Fort Kaministiquia, Rhys Morgan appointed sentries to keep watch over the sleeping camp.

Alex's uneasiness over their undesirable neighbors gave way to worry about Christiana when she woke in the early morning hours to hear painful coughing. She found the pale, brown-haired woman huddled in her blankets, shivering miserably from the chill that seemed to have wrapped her in its icy grip.

Between harsh, gasping breaths, Christiana admitted to feeling much worse, and as Alex labored over her, she fought back fear. They were so close to Sabaskong now, what if they couldn't get her there in time?

Taut nerves made her want to snap at the woman, to demand why she had so endangered her life by leaving the city behind, but reason told her it was not the time for such a discussion. Rhys was surely right in thinking Christiana's motives had been strong ones, and, Alex reminded herself, a physician's duty was not to pry but to heal. She sighed deeply, wondering how possible that was going to be in this case. She had seen many cases of chronic bronchial congestion, and normally the prognosis wasn't good.

"Alex," Christiana whispered, "why am I getting so much worse? I've been taking the medicine you gave me. . . ."

"I know. I expect your condition is being aggravated by anxiety over finally meeting the man you're going to marry."

With a low, keening moan, Christiana turned her head away, but not before Alex caught the gleam of tears on her thin cheeks.

"Christy, what's wrong?" she softly demanded.

"Alex, I'm so afraid. How can I marry a man I've never seen?"

Alex sat back on her heels. "You can't mean to say that you've never given this any thought!"

Christiana looked more miserable than ever. "You wouldn't understand, Alex. You're too strong and . . . and too brave to ever be like me."

"You can't help being ill," Alex said.

"No, I don't mean that. I mean I'm a coward . . . and a weakling. I needed someone to take care of me . . . and a husband seemed the best choice. But now I'm frightened. What if I've made a terrible mistake?"

"You haven't. Look how well things have turned out for the other brides."

"But they're all healthy and well. Maybe Joseph Patterson won't want me. I'm not like you, Alex. I can't manage on my own."

"You've got to stop fretting over this. There's no

sense in getting so upset before you even get to the Falls and meet Joseph. You're only making yourself feel worse."

"I've tried not to worry . . . I just can't help it. I don't know what I will do without a husband to take care of me."

"I'll help you," Alex promised. "Now take another spoonful of this syrup and go back to sleep. I'll stay with you."

The tall pines were black silhouettes against the dawn sky before Christiana fell into an uneasy sleep. Alex sat beside her, smoothing the hair from her fevered forehead and murmuring words of comfort and encouragement.

What is wrong, she wondered, with a world where women must be so dependent upon the whims of men? She thanked God that she was strong and capable, and had no need to run crying to a man for help. She shivered in the cool morning air. Life was wonderful, but sometimes it was difficult to accept its inequalities.

On the following day, the brigade left Rainy Lake behind and, traveling through a series of smaller lakes, headed north toward Sabaskong Falls. There was no further sign of Bacconne and his companions, though Alex couldn't help but notice the men's discreet watchfulness after leaving camp. She even found herself looking over her shoulder, half expecting the horribly scarred Bacconne to suddenly appear. She couldn't believe he would not come back—like a bad dream.

The warm, sunny days of summer slipped away as they completed the last segment of the journey. Imperceptibly, the woods that edged the lakes and streams through which they traveled began to turn beige and gold, with brilliant flashes of pure, deep crimson that sometimes delighted the eye. There was a new crispness to the air, a sharp edge that hinted at stormy gales to come, and all in the party sensed that the forest and its inhabitants were preparing for the onslaught of winter.

The shorter the distance to Sabaskong, the harder the men pushed. They had grown anxious to settle their wives in their homes before the autumn rains began, and there was hunting and harvesting to be done before they were ready to face the long, cold season ahead. The trip from Fort Kaministiquia had been relatively leisurely, despite Rhys Morgan's constant demand for haste, but now an almost fevered urgency seemed to propel them headlong toward their destination. After what seemed months of endless travel, the women were growing weary indeed by the time the canoes glided rapidly across the smooth surface of Kakabikit-chiwan Lake to the wide expanse of falls that meant they had arrived at Sabaskong Bay.

When the canoes were beached for one last portage, Alex leaped ashore, eyes sparkling with excitement. There below them was the settlement where they would be living. Knowing she wouldn't be heard over the roar of the waterfall, she merely grasped Aberdeen's shoulder and pointed out the trading post, then the broad arm of the bay that eventually led to the more open waters of Lake of the Woods.

Sabaskong Falls, she thought with eagerness. Home!

A sudden, light rain started falling as the unloading began. Alexandria followed Rhys Morgan as he carefully trod the slippery path that skirted the waterfall, a blanket-wrapped Christiana in his arms. "Halloo!" he shouted, throwing back his head. "Is anybody home in this Godforsaken place?"

Almost immediately a face appeared at one of the narrow windows of a good-sized log building identified by the weathered sign over its front steps: Falls Trading Post, A. MacPherson and R. Morgan, Proprietors.

" 'Tis about time ye decided to come back, ye heathen rogue!" The man striding toward them had a shock of bright auburn hair; that and the brogue with which he spoke proclaimed him as the Scotsman, Andrew MacPherson—the man Rhys called Scotty. "Lord, what have we here?" he asked, blue eyes clouding with concern as he noticed Christiana's pale, strained face. She tried to speak, but her words were cut short by yet another bout of harsh coughing.

"Please, can we take her inside?" asked Alex. "Somewhere she can lie down and rest?"

Scotty nodded briskly. "To be sure. Right this way."

He led them through the main room of the trading post, past a curtained door and into his living quarters. "Put her in the bedroom, Rhys, while I bring in some wood to get a fire going. The poor lass looks chilled to the bone."

Alex set aside Nasturtium's basket and the case she carried and pulled back the bedcovers. Rhys placed Christiana among the pillows, where she huddled miserably.

"If you'll leave us a moment," Alex said, "I'll get her into a nightgown."

"I'll see to the unloading," Rhys replied, giving the woman on the bed one last, worried look. "Shall I send Aberdeen in to help you?"

"Yes, thank you. I'd appreciate that."

Thirty minutes later, an exhausted Christiana had taken a cup of tea and her medicine, and had fallen into a peaceful sleep for the first time in a week. A fire hissed and sang on the hearth, while a kettle of steaming water projected the pungent smell of herbs throughout the cabin.

Alex and Aberdeen left the bedroom just as Rhys Morgan came in from outdoors, raindrops spangling his black hair. Scotty stepped toward his friend, seizing his hand and giving him a hearty slap on the back. "I was beginning to wonder if ye were ever coming home, man."

Rhys grinned. "You didn't think I'd leave a scoundrel like you in charge for too long, did you?"

The affection between the two men was obvious, and Alex was intrigued. Here was a new and unexpected side to the complicated backwoodsman. He had not seemed the type to need friendships, yet he appeared genuinely glad, even relieved, to see his partner. She recalled that this was the man Rhys expected her to marry, and decided his relief was simply because he thought the Scotsman was going to take her off his hands at last. Her chin rose abruptly at the thought.

Rhys caught her movement and smiled grimly, as though he knew exactly what she was thinking. "Scotty," he said, "let me introduce the ladies. This is Alexandria MacKenzie. . . ."

"How do ye do?" Scotty inquired, bowing over her hand in a courtly manner. " 'Tis a pleasure to meet such a beauty. And a Scottish one, at that, if I'm not mistaken."

"I was born in Montreal, but my family came from Scotland."

"Well, ye certainly have the look—hair as red as a Highland autumn and eyes like a rain-drenched loch. Ach, ye make me homesick, lassie."

Rhys snorted. "Lord, Scotty, it's not like you to spout sentimental drivel. I think you've been alone in the wilderness too long."

"I think his words were very poetic . . . and charming," Alex stated diplomatically.

Just then the lid of the hinged basket raised slightly to reveal a sleepy-eyed Nasturtium.

"Ach, would ye look at the wee beastie!" cried Scotty, stooping to fondle Nasturtium's head. "We MacPhersons are inordinately fond of cats. There's one on our clan crest, ye know."

"How appropriate," drawled Rhys with a knowing look at Alex.

She suspected he had suddenly remembered his vow to see her wed to the Scotsman, and decided to move the conversation in other, safer directions "This is my friend, Aberdeen McPhie. Now she truly is from—"

"The Old Country," Scotty finished for her. He and Aberdeen were silent for a long moment, as though taking stock of each other. "Aberdeen, eh? Is that where ye came from?" he asked.

"Aye. I was born there, and my father was a romantic fool." Aberdeen's dark eyes gleamed with humor. "I've always been thankful I wasna born down the road at Blackdog."

Scotty's laugh rang out. "Well, I'm a Grampian man myself, so I understand your father's sentimentality. Welcome to Sabaskong Falls, ladies. I've been anxious to meet the brides."

"Oh, we're not brides," Alex quickly informed him, ignoring a sardonic glance from Rhys.

"The truth is," Aberdeen interjected, "I was to be a bride . . . until I met that peelie-wally puddock named Waldo Anderson!"

Scotty chuckled again. "I must say, I've never thought of Waldo looking like a sick frog before."

Aberdeen sniffed. "The man has a face like a chanty."

Alex clapped a hand over her up-curved mouth and turned away. She came face to face with Rhys, who had stepped close behind her.

"What the hell is a chanty?" he asked, one black eyebrow quirking upward.

"A chamberpot," she murmured, walking the short distance to the fireplace and stretching her hands to its warmth.

"So," Aberdeen continued, "since Alexandria will be busy being a doctor, I've decided to become her housekeeper instead of jumping over the broom."

"A doctor?" exclaimed Scotty. "A fair lass like Al-

211

exandria is a doctor?"

"Yes, despite what some people might think." Alex said the words innocently enough, resisting the urge to look straight at Rhys.

"Well, ye seem to be doing everything ye can for the poor woman in the other room. Tell me, what do ye think she ails from?"

"I believe she has a chronic lung congestion— what we call asthma. It has been aggravated by lack of rest, and by the damp, chilly weather, I suppose."

"Aye, I've seen cases like that," Scotty replied. "I've a tad bit of medical knowledge myself, though I must admit, I'm merely an amateur, pressed into service when there was no one more proficient around."

"Rhys told us you were skilled," Alex murmured. "In fact, I had a somewhat difficult time convincing him I should be allowed to come with the brides. He seemed to think you were as qualified as anyone need be."

Scotty turned a questioning look on Rhys, who shifted his stance impatiently. "Look," he said in a graveled tone, "I can explain all that to Scotty later. Right now we need to get people settled."

"Yes, ye're right, man. Why don't you show the ladies their cabin? I'll keep a watch over Christiana."

"Poor thing," Aberdeen said, "she needs a husband at her side. I only wonder when she will be well enough to wed."

"She's not married yet?" Scotty inquired, an odd expression on his face. "Is she the one promised to

Joe Patterson, then?"

Rhys nodded. "She is."

"Well, there's a bit of a problem on that score . . ."

Rhys looked grim. "All right, Scotty, what has happened?"

"Ye knew that Joe was . . ." Scotty cast a swift glance at the women, then went on speaking. "Ye knew he was living with one of Chief Talking Elk's daughters?"

Rhys nodded again, his expression becoming a scowl.

"It seems the girl . . . er, she discovered she was to . . . to have a wee bairn, so Talking Elk demanded Joe take her as a wife."

"Damn," Rhys muttered. "What was Joe thinking of?"

"I think he always was taken with the girl anyway," admitted Scotty. "I don't believe he was too upset over the matter."

"Yes, but he was contracted to marry a woman from Montreal. How in the hell could he justify his actions?"

Scotty's mouth formed a wry grin. "Let's just say that Talking Elk and his sons can be a persuasive lot."

"That's fine for Joe," raged Rhys "but what in the world are we going to tell that poor woman in there? She came hundreds of miles to marry a man who couldn't be bothered to honor the agreement he'd made with her."

"Perhaps you could marry her yourself," Alex suggested. "Wouldn't that be a wonderful solution

213

to Christiana's problems?"

"But not to my own," he snapped. "No, we'll have to find some alternative."

Alex smiled demurely. "Surely we can think of something. I'll be glad to ponder the matter."

"I'm certain of it," he mumbled.

"Right now, however, would you mind showing us our cabin? I'd love to see where we'll be spending the winter."

Picking up Nasturtium's basket, Alex started for the door, leaving Rhys and Aberdeen to follow.

Pausing at the curtained entrance, Rhys stared after her, then heaved an affronted sigh.

"Let me take care of the ladies, Scotty, and I'll be back. There are several matters we need to discuss."

"Miss Alexandria MacKenzie among them?" the Scotsman asked, with a grin.

"Yes . . . as usual."

Chapter Eleven

Alex pulled the hood of the cloak she wore up over her hair and followed Rhys through the rain. She caught glimpses of log cabins here and there among the trees as they hurried past, and Birdie waved gaily from the front door of the one nearest the doctor's cabin.

Her new home was situated in a grove of pine trees, with a pocket-sized stretch of grass that met the flat, granite rocks along the lake. Somewhat isolated from the others, Alex's cabin consisted of two main rooms, with an office and a three-bed hospital at the back. The rear entrance boasted a freshly painted sign that identified the doctor's office; the front door, which faced the bay, had a tiny porch and a long window with a flower box.

As they went into the house, Alex trailed her hand along the edge of the flower box and gave

Aberdeen a beatific smile. Inside, in the main room, the voyageurs had neatly stacked her trunks in one corner, and someone had built a fire in the stone fireplace. Besides the window by the door, there were two others—a small one that faced back toward the trading post, and a large square one that looked out over the water. Alex stepped up to it, spreading her fingers over the cold glass.

"Glass windows," she said in awe. "I didn't expect that. . ."

"We had the glass brought down from Montreal," Rhys explained. "Several of the cabins in the area boast real windows."

"It must have been dear, paying for it to be brought all that way," Aberdeen commented. "Aye, dear indeed."

Rhys only smiled and leaned against the door frame to watch the women explore their new living quarters. Aberdeen went immediately to the cupboard where the dishes and cooking utensils were stored, while Alex looked about the room, approval shining in her eyes, and then disappeared through the doorway into the bedroom. Rhys followed.

"We'll bring in another bed," he said. "We didn't expect two of you to be living here."

"That sounds fine," she murmured, setting Nasturtium's basket on the bed. As soon as the cat was released, it leaped onto the pine dresser and stood on its hind feet to look at itself in the oval mirror hanging on the wall. When she saw Rhys's reflection behind her, the animal hissed.

"Hush, Nasturtium," Alex scolded, puzzled as always by the usually docile feline's distrust of the

216

man. She reached up to pull the damp hood from her hair. "Now I'd like to see my office," she said, crossing the room.

Instead of moving aside as she had expected, Rhys stood his ground, and she had to sidle past him to get through the doorway. For a split second, their eyes met and held, and she realized that, in some situations, she barely trusted the man herself. Or, she wondered, hurrying down the short hall that led to the office, was it herself she didn't trust?

"Oh, this is wonderful!" she cried, stepping into the square, tidy room where she would do her work. There was a desk and chair near the window, a small cot along one wall, and rows and rows of shelves, just waiting for the addition of her belongings. The hospital itself was furnished with three beds and a large wooden chest for medicines and supplies.

Alex circled the room, even opening the door to admire the sign with an attitude bordering on reverence. When she shut it, she was careful to keep her back to him as she said, "This is a beautiful cabin . . . please tell me whom I must thank."

"All the men worked on it," Rhys told her. "It meant a great deal to them to have found a doctor willing to live here."

Alex lowered her head, seemingly to study the hands she had clasped in front of her. Thinking it odd she would not look at him, Rhys murmured, "Alex? Is something wrong?"

"No, not at all. . . ."

He crossed the room swiftly and, putting a hand

on her shoulder, turned her to face him. Something tensed painfully within him at the sight of a huge teardrop that clung to her thick lashes a long instant before spilling over to trickle slowly down her cheek.

"Why are you crying?" he asked softly, tracing the teardrop's path with his thumb. When he reached the curve of her jaw, he did not remove his hand, but rested it there, gently forcing her to look up at him.

She smiled tremulously. "I'm not, really."

"Oh? That certainly looked like a tear."

"It's only that I'm so very pleased," she half-whispered. "This is a beautiful cabin . . . and my very first home."

"What about your grandfather's house in Montreal?"

Her gray eyes looked dark in the gloominess of the room. "I loved it there," she replied. "I was happy, of course. But it was my grandparents' house, not mine. This is the first time I have ever had a place that was mine alone." She lowered her lashes, embarrassed. "I even brought flower seeds with me—and next spring when I plant them in the window box, it's going to symbolize my putting down roots at last." She raised her eyes to his again. "Do you think that is . . . silly?"

His lips tightened as he experienced a barrage of emotions, but he shook his head. "No, it's not silly. What kind of seeds?"

"Heart's ease," she answered. "And that's what this place is going to bring me."

"Alex . . ." His hand moved slightly, as though

he would like to caress her face. "I only hope you are right."

She smiled again. "I am."

It seemed that a lengthy silence grew between them, although they were both aware of several sounds—Aberdeen moving about in the other room, the ticking of the clock standing in the corner, their own suddenly labored breathing.

Rhys moved his hand, letting it drop to her shoulder, then slide easily down her arm. She shuddered as his strong fingers closed about her wrist, filling her entire body with warmth. He tugged her closer to him and, his eyes dark with intent, lowered his head.

"Lass? Where are ye?" called Aberdeen.

Regret knifed through Alex as she managed a reply. "I'm in here, Deenie. What is it you need?"

"I want ye to tell me which trunks ye want in yer office."

"All right. . . ."

She thought Rhys would release her wrist, but instead his hand engulfed hers and he lifted it to his lips, turning it so his mouth brushed her palm. She felt his heated breath against her skin, then the soft scrape of his moustache . . . and then the heart-stopping press of his firm lips. Her response was immediate and powerful—the strength went out of her legs and surged into some secret part of her that only this man had ever reached.

He freed her hand as they heard Aberdeen's approaching footsteps. "I'll go now and leave you to your unpacking," he said.

Alex watched as he ducked through the doorway

and disappeared into the slow, silent drizzle. Never had she felt less interest in her bottles and pills.

There was to be a wedding in Sabaskong Falls, but it was not the ceremony everyone had expected. The morning following the brigade's arrival, Joseph Patterson had brought his new wife to the trading post, seeking an opportunity to explain and apologize to Christiana.

Standing quietly at her patient's side, Alex noticed several things. Joe Patterson seemed a decent young man, and his Indian bride was obviously smitten by him. Alex knew of the white trappers' habit of taking *country wives*, as the Indian women were called, and she also knew it was unusual for such a couple to legally wed, no matter how many children their union produced. Therefore, even if he had been prodded somewhat by a concerned father, Joe's willingness to do the right thing was admirable. Most importantly, she noticed that Christiana did not seem at all upset by the latest turn of events. She clung to Scotty's hand as though she had known him a lifetime, and trustingly deferred to anything he suggested.

When the Pattersons had gone, Christiana obediently took her medicine and returned to bed for a nap. Her coughing had abated somewhat, and her color was much better. As she fell asleep, Alex sat by her side, listening to the conversation Scotty was having with Rhys Morgan in the next room.

"Scotty you've lost your mind."

"Because I want to marry the girl?"

"Because you don't need a sickly wife."

"That's not the point, Rhys. Christy needs a strong husband—she needs me."

"Christy?" Alex could almost see Rhys's black eyebrows shooting skyward. "Are you so familiar with her then?"

"I feel I have known her forever," the Scotsman replied. "We sat up talking most of the night . . . Rhys, ye don't know what her life has been like." His voice receded, then grew louder, telling Alex that he was pacing back and forth. "When she was a child, her father would beat her whenever she grew ill. He was ashamed if she had a coughing spell before company. God, can ye imagine what that must have been like for a bairn? Trying to breathe without coughing, and all the while the anxiety making it worse."

"And you feel you should make that up to her?"

"Someone should. And I think I can. Aye, I'd like to give it a try."

"But why?"

"I like the girl. I like the looks of her . . . and I like the way her mind works."

"But she's nearly an invalid," Rhys protested. "You need a healthy wife—someone like Alex."

"As you know, we've already discussed my marrying the lass. Alex is too strong and too independent for the likes o' me. Now she's a fine woman, and a beauty, there's no doubt about that. But the fact is, Christiana needs me . . . and Alex doesn't."

"What if Christiana dies?" Rhys had lowered his tone, but his voice reached Alex's ears nonetheless.

"If that's what the Almighty decrees there's

naught I can do about it except make what remains of her life as happy and comfortable as possible."

"Damn it, Scotty, I never knew you to be so mule-headed."

"Ye'd best get used to it, my friend." Scotty's words had the sound of finality. "Christy will be staying here with me, and we'll be married the next time the preacher passes through Sabaskong Falls."

"What about Alex?"

"What about me?" Alex left the bedroom doorway to stand directly in front of the man.

Rhys ruffled his hair with an agitated hand. "What am I to do with you if Scotty marries someone else?"

"You've delivered me safely to the Falls, so your obligation to me has ended. Besides, you know I never intended to marry Scotty. Please, just let me make my own decisions from now on."

"You only made this trip because I allowed it," he reminded her. "And the stipulation was that you marry."

"I never agreed to that, and anyway, how can I marry if there are no available men?"

"There's you, Rhys," observed Scotty. "If ye think the lass is going to create problems by being unwed, perhaps you'd better marry her yerself."

"Stay the hell out of this, will you?" Rhys shouted. At the sound of Alex's muffled laughter, he turned on her. "I'll find you a husband yet, don't think I won't. You're a spoiled, stubborn, disagreeable female . . . but somewhere in this camp there is someone desperate enough to marry you. And I won't rest until I find him!"

Alex's laughter died. "Desperate enough?" she echoed in disbelief. "How can you insinuate such a thing?"

But her question came too late — he was already gone.

It was midafternoon before Alex finished straightening the shelves of her apothecary. She had just removed her apron, washed her hands, and tidied her hair when she heard a knock at the door. She was surprised to see Waldo Anderson standing there, twisting his skunkskin cap in his gnarled hands.

"I'm sorry, Waldo," she said, "Aberdeen isn't here. She's over at Mellicent's helping her unpack."

"It ain't Aberdeen I came to see," Waldo said. "Although I think the woman has finally started to take a likin' to me. Why jist yesterday, when I was helpin' her unload them trunks, she called me a sweetie wife. Whatd'ya think of that?"

Alex didn't have the heart to tell him that the term was a Scots phrase meaning an effeminate, gossipy old man, so she merely smiled and said, "How nice, Waldo. I'm glad the two of you are getting along better."

"Well, that's sorta what I'm here about . . . I jist wanted ya to know I didn't mean nuthin' personal when I refused ya. It was because of Aberdeen, ya see."

"Wh-what do you mean, Waldo?" Alex stepped

223

back and opened the door wider. "I think you'd better come in."

Waldo glanced around the small room nervously, then dropped onto the high-backed bench near the fireplace. "I hope ya understand why I turned ya down, Alex. As I said, it ain't nuthin' personal—yer a fine, good-lookin' girl and all. But I jist got my heart set on Aberdeen."

"What exactly do you mean when you say . . . you turned me down?" Alex's mouth felt suddenly dry.

"Why, when Rhys came askin' me to marry ya," the white-haired trapper said.

"Rhys?" Alex took a deep, steadying breath. "Let me get this straight—Rhys asked you to marry me?"

Waldo nodded, pink scalp gleaming through his wispy hair. "Yup. He said you was needin' a husband right bad, and would I do the honors. Well now, it ain't every day an old geezer like me gets a chance at a gal like you, but, Alex, I swear I'm plumb taken with that Scottish bag of bones. I'm real sorry, but I had say no."

Alex tried valiantly to disregard the violent temper boiling up within her. She smiled faintly, patting Waldo's scrawny shoulder. "I understand, Waldo. Truly, I do. And if there is anything I can do to further your cause with Deenie, please let me know."

"No hard feelin's then?"

"No hard feelings," she assured him. "At least not toward you."

The trapper was clearly relieved. "I sure hoped

ya wouldn't take it too hard. That's why I figgered I'd better come talk to you like a man . . . I wouldn't want ya to hear this from someone else."

"I appreciate your consideration, Waldo. I just wish everyone was as thoughtful."

"Well, reckon I'll wander on over to Mellicent's and see what Aberdeen's doing."

"That's a splendid idea, and thank you so much for . . . for breaking the news to me in this way."

"It was the least I could do. 'Bye now, Alex."

She did not slam the door, nor did she throw any of the numerous items she could so easily have gotten her hands on. Instead, burning with a white-hot anger, Alex scribbled a note to tell Aberdeen where she had gone, then grabbed a shawl and went out the door. This time she did slam it, but the satisfaction she felt at the gesture was fleeting. She struck off down the path that edged the forest, leading away from the Falls. She had been told that Rhys Morgan's cabin was at the end of the trail and at that moment, there was nothing she wanted more than to have a few words with the man.

The path wound through the pines, sometimes rising high above the shoreline, twisting between boulders of smooth rock, and sometimes dropping low onto the floor of the forest, where the carpet of fallen pine needles muffled her footsteps. By the time she had covered half the distance to Rhys's cabin, her wrath had calmed enough for her to pause occasionally and enjoy the beautiful views that opened up each time the trail made a turn that brought it out of the sheltering woods.

Scotty had told her that Sabaskong—the Indian name for "water with many bays"—stretched for nearly two hundred miles before reaching the central part of Lake of the Woods. Those miles were filled with thousands of pine-crowned islands, making the long span of water a treacherous maze. Now, in the September sunshine, the lake looked like blue satin, scattered with an infinite number brilliant diamonds. Alex was fascinated, for only that morning it had been somber and mist shrouded, an almost forbidding sight. It was quite evident that the lake took its mood from that of the unsettled autumn weather.

The low, eerie cry of a loon drifted over the stillness of the late afternoon, startling Alex and reminding her of her mission. When she thought of Rhys Morgan so arrogantly trying to arrange another marriage for her—and with Waldo Anderson, at that!—she grew livid again, and set off striding purposefully down the trail.

A few minutes later, she rounded a bend and saw the first canoe. Dull red in color, it looked familiar—and, suddenly, she knew where she had seen it. Though the craft was too far out in the water for her to recognize the faces of the two men in it, she knew it belonged to Robber Bacconne or his companions. Hoping they had not seen her, she began to walk faster, glad when the trail snaked back into the woods.

At the next curve of the pathway, she sighted the second canoe . . . and knew immediately the men in it had sighted her. It headed with unerring speed straight for the shore. Alex walked faster, longing to break into a run, but unwilling to show her fear. She heard the men yelling back and forth to each other, and then the first canoe altered its course and started toward her.

"Mademoiselle," called the man she now distinguished as Bacconne. "What are you doing in the woods alone? Are you lost?"

"No," she shouted. "I'm not lost, and I'm not alone. Someone's waiting for me. . . ."

Alex walked as fast as she could, spurred on by the prickling at the back of her neck and the clammy perspiration on her palms.

For quite some time the canoes followed her, never getting too far ahead, never falling behind. At first, Alex ignored the lewd remarks the men made, simply putting her chin in the air and walking faster. But eventually the words Bacconne spoke began to sink into her consciousness, and she experienced the beginning of terror.

"We followed your brigade from Rainy Lake, *mademoiselle,*" he called out "We wanted to see the place where so many lovely women were going to live. We have been watching for any sign of you . . . or the pretty little golden-haired Lily." He laughed cheerfully. "It is fortunate for us that you chose to leave the settlement alone, eh? But, perhaps, not so fortunate for you. . . ."

Alex was all but running, eyes straight ahead, straining for any sign of Rhys's cabin. How much further could it be? Was Bacconne only playing a cruel prank on her, or did he, indeed, intend to harm her?

"Mademoiselle," he taunted, "you seem to be fright-

ened of me. Why is that? I have done nothing to make you fear me, have I?"

The sound of the other men's laughter chilled her through and through. How was she going to get away from them? If she screamed, would there be anyone to hear?

"Oh, Rhys," she murmured breathlessly, "where are you?"

"I grow tired of waiting for your reply, *Mademoiselle*," Bacconne called out.

Alex's head jerked up as she realized he sounded much closer. The canoe was skimming past her, just beyond the small rounded stones at the edge of the water. From that distance, she could see his ruined face clearly, and the expression on it turned her blood to ice.

"Why don't you stop trying to run away from me?" he asked, his mouth curving in amusement. "I could be very nice to you . . . if only you would be a little more accommodating. What do you say, Mademoiselle Alex? Ah, I see you are surprised that I remembered your name. Rest assured, little one, I remember many things about you . . ."

"Why don't you leave me alone?" she cried.

"Oh, no, *mademoiselle*, that would never do. One as beautiful as you should not be alone. I cannot understand what is wrong with the men of Sabaskong. I would not treat you in such a way."

After a muttered exchange with his companion, Bacconne suddenly plied the wooden paddle he held, swinging the nose of the canoe toward the sandy beach. As he leaped over the gunwale and began splashing to shore, Alex gathered her skirts in her hands and started running. She was already nearly winded from her frantic walk. Now her breath seared her throat with every step she took, and she could hear her own moans of fright.

Bacconne's cruel hands grasped her from behind, clamping onto her waist and swinging her around to face him. She fell to her knees and heard the laughter of the other men, watching from the canoes.

Alex surged to her feet and with every ounce of strength she could summon, swung her right arm, landing a blow on his temple. Amazingly, Bacconne laughed, increasing her fear.

"I think you are going to be a challenge, *mademoiselle*. And Bacconne, he likes a challenge!"

He grabbed her forearm, jerking her toward him in one vicious movement. The fingers of his other hand closed over her chin and jaw, forcing her face up to his. Alex struggled, aware of how perilously weak she was against the man. Her breath was coming in furious, sobbing pants.

"Let me go," she hissed.

Bacconne pulled her against his chest so tightly she could feel the bear-claw necklace he wore digging into her flesh. He rested his chin on the curve of her shoulder, and when he spoke again, his breath was hot along the side of her neck.

"Do not fight me until you have heard the proposition I offer, eh?"

When she did not answer, he shook her viciously until she nodded her head.

"Out here," he continued, "no woman can survive without a man—and I've decided to become your

man, Mademoiselle Alex. You should be grateful
to me. . . ."

"No!"

"I am a strong man, one who can teach you
many ways to pass the long, cold winters of the
North." He put his other hand up to caress her
throat, then slid it downward, moving it slowly
over her breasts.

"Stop it," she ground out through clenched teeth.
"I'll scream for help. Surely your men will not sit
by and let you abuse me!"

He chuckled, the sound low and evil. "My men
have been given orders not to interfere. They will
do nothing."

"I demand that you let me go . . . ."

"Ah, but you are no longer in a position to
make demands, my dear." His mouth touched the
side of her neck, moving greedily over her skin.

Alex felt nausea rising from the pit of her stomach, and she groaned in desperate anguish, twisting
within his hold.

"Don't touch me," she choked out. "I can't bear
it!"

Bacconne grew very still. "You think that because I am ugly, I cannot be a good lover?" His
words were quiet, edged with ice. "That because I
am no longer handsome, you can treat me as less
than a man?"

He gave her a violent shove, tumbling her backward onto the ground. "I will show you there is
more to me than a ruined face!"

With a swift, savage movement, he tore away the
buckskin shirt he wore, displaying a smooth, heav-

ily muscled chest. Tapping it with a fist, he said, "A jealous husband may have spoiled my face, but my body is unmarred. It is still perfect. Mother of Christ, look at me, woman!"

Alex deliberately turned her face away, but in the next instant, he fell to one knee beside her and, burying his fingers in her hair, dragged her face upward. Tears began to trickle from the corners of her eyes, and with a surprisingly gentle touch, Bacconne used the thumb of his free hand to wipe them away.

"Do not turn away again, Mademoiselle Alex." His words were a soft warning as he released her and stood up. His hands fell to the waist of his buckskin pants. "I am a man in every way, and I will give you much pleasure."

Knowing she must fight him, Alex gathered the tattered remains of her courage about her. In a sudden motion, she scrambled to her feet and, giving him a hard push, fled down the shadowed trail. Bacconne cursed and came after her, his fingers catching the sleeve of her gown, ripping it loose. She wrenched away, but he seized her about the waist and flung her to the ground, going down onto his knees, straddling her body.

Bacconne laughed triumphantly as she writhed beneath him, a strange excitement lighting his undamaged eye. Dimly, she was aware of the cheers of the men in the canoes. Alex's curled fingers reached out, clawing at his face but, as she raked the unprotected flesh, he cursed and rocked backward on his heels, delivering a brutal blow to her jaw with the back of his hand.

Stunned, Alex fell back and lay still. She did not even move when he gripped the front of her dress and tore it open to the waist. She was so tired of struggling. . . .

Suddenly, she felt his slobbering mouth moving over her bared skin, and the urge to fight him came back with startling force. Her hands flew upward to fasten in his greasy hair and pull with as much strength as she could manage. She heard his grunt of pain, and dreaded the blow that would follow. Instead, his hands closed around her throat, and he was lifting her face to his.

When his mouth clamped over hers, she nearly gagged. His breath was sour as his ravaging tongue invaded the recesses of her mouth, a horrifying display of his masterful strength.

Alex's hold on his hair tightened, and as his head moved backward to ease the pain, she turned her face and screamed. Even as she did so, she knew the effort was useless.

Bacconne reached upward, catching her wrists in a crushing hold, pulling her numb fingers from his hair to twist her hands behind her. As her back arched, his leering gaze fell on her naked breasts and, with a pleased chuckle, he bent his head to hers.

"No," she panted, still struggling. "No! Rhys, help me . . . Rhys!"

Rhys Morgan had spent the last hour cursing himself for a fool. What had possessed him lately, robbing him of his usual good sense? There was no reason in hell he should feel so responsible for that stubborn, red-headed woman, but Lord help him, he did. Even as he thought it, he knew responsibility really had nothing at all to do with it. What he felt for her transcended duty.

Unable to rid himself of the guilt he'd felt after offering her to Waldo, Rhys had gone to the doctor's cabin to apologize and explain that it had all been in jest. When Aberdeen told him Alex had left the settlement to go to his cabin, he was filled with a peculiar disquiet. Some inner alarm warned him to go after her, to find her quickly.

He had almost covered the distance to his cabin when Alex's scream echoed through the trees. Her second scream, the agonized crying of his name, hit him like a fist in the stomach. Despite his shortened breath, he began running, and when he came upon Bacconne bending over her, his mind filled with the red haze of fury.

"God damn you to hell, Bacconne!" he yelled, pulling the scarred man to his feet and smashing a deadly fist into his shocked face. The Frenchman cried out as he reeled backward, stumbling. Before he could regain his balance, Rhys struck him again, and the crack of knuckles against bone sounded loud in the still afternoon. Like a beast gone wild, Rhys systematically pummeled Bacconne, dealing him punishing blows that left him bruised and bleeding, begging for mercy. Rhys felt an ironic laugh crowd into his throat. Mercy—something Bacconne had been prepared to deny Alex.

"You cowardly son-of-a-bitch," he snarled, seizing

the man and dragging him toward the water. "If you ever lay a hand on this woman again, your life won't be worth living, I promise. You'll beg me to kill you and put you out of your misery." He gave Bacconne a shove that sent him sprawling into the lake. "You men can save him or let him drown, whichever you please. But, I'm warning you, you're not welcome here. Take Bacconne and get as far from here as you can before the snows come, or I will personally hunt you down, one by one."

The men made no move toward Rhys, and it was only after he'd turned away that they put forth the effort to pull Bacconne from the water.

"Alex," Rhys murmured, kneeling. "Are you all right? Did he hurt you?"

She shook her head. "No . . . I'm fine." Then, shuddering, she whispered, "He was going to—"

"Shh, I know. Don't think about it anymore. Let's just get out of here."

Rising, he lifted her into his arms and cradled her close against his chest. Without another glance at Bacconne, Rhys began striding along the darkening path.

"Where are we going?" Alex asked.

"I'm taking you to my cabin—it's close by."

"I can walk," she protested faintly.

"Alex, just this once, don't be stubborn." He rested his chin against her tangled hair. "Be quiet and let me take care of you."

She didn't speak, merely turning her face toward his shoulder, the fingers of one hand twining in the row of fringe across his chest.

Behind them, a bloodied Bacconne watched from

the security of his canoe, and there was no mistak-
ing the malice that glittered dangerously in his
eyes.

Chapter Twelve

Rhys's cabin stood on a point of land surrounded by water on two sides. The yard was filled with the long shadows of pines and the silvery music of wind in the quaking aspens. A high, sheltering bluff rose behind it, so that the forest seemed to hover above, protectively.

Rhys felt a sense of relief when he carried Alex through the front door, into the welcoming haven. Slowly, he lowered her to her feet, but stood supporting her until she moved away to kneel in front of the fireplace.

"I feel so cold," she murmured, lifting her hands to the hint of warmth the dying embers afforded.

Rhys could tell she was shivering, but whether from cold or shock, he didn't know. In either case, he deemed it imperative they have a fire, and after draping a blanket about her shoulders, he hurriedly went about rebuilding one. As he worked, he wondered what effect Bacconne's attack might have on Alex. Grimly, he reflected that he should have killed the man while he had the chance.

Alex stayed on the hearth rug beside him, seemingly unaware that her hand rested on his leather-clad foot. Her need for reassurance easily reached the tenderness he ordinarily tried to keep hidden, especially from her, and he felt himself responding to her rare defenselessness.

As soon as he had a small, cheerful blaze going, he sat back and took stock of Alex's condition. She was huddled within the blanket, shivering slightly. Rhys's eyes were anxious as they rested on her face.

"Would you like something hot to drink?" he asked. "Are you still cold?"

"I'm all right." Her huge gray eyes met his with candor. "I don't know where you came from, Rhys, or how you found me, but I thank God you were there. I never saw anything more beautiful than the sight of you running down that trail." She laughed shakily, drawing a deep breath. "And you needn't hesitate to point out that you warned me about just such dangers as . . . as Bacconne."

He managed a casual shrug. "No one knew the man was anywhere within a hundred miles. You couldn't have guessed he would appear so suddenly."

"Still, I should have listened to you."

"I'm getting worried," he gently teased. "It's not like you to be so contrite. Can this be the same little hellcat I met at Fort Kaministiquia?"

Unexpected tears sprang into her eyes and ran unchecked down her face.

"I don't know. I almost feel as if Bacconne turned me into some sort of stranger . . . even to myself." She looked up at him. "He meant to r-ravish me, didn't he?"

"Alex . . ."

"H-he touched me, and I feel so—"

"Hush, now," he scolded as calmly as he could. "He won't touch you again, I promise."

Alex choked back the sobs that threatened, uttering a small laugh. "I always seem to be crying these days—and I hate crying!" She returned to a study of his face, her eyes solemn and tear-drowned. "It seems strange that, when you kissed me, I liked it . . . but with Bacconne, it was horrible!"

She shuddered and laid a hand on Rhys's sleeve. "Please . . . would you do something for me? Will you kiss me again . . . now? I want to forget how awful it felt when he—"

Rhys seemed to sense her anxieties and, without hesitation, leaned forward to cup her wet face in his hands. His lips were warming and smooth as he moved them softly over hers, rubbing tenderly, erasing the horror of Bacconne's degrading touch. Fresh tears trickled past the corners of her mouth, and he kissed them away, bringing his salty lips back to hers in a healing, cleansing kiss. Alex moaned faintly, and her mouth trembled beneath his. A jumble of emotions—pity, relief, passion, and others less easily identified—raged through him, and his arms went about her, tightening protectively.

A small warning voice at the back of his mind entreated him to remember his oath not to become too involved with this woman, but for once he refused to listen. She was no longer promised to his best friend—and she herself had turned to him for comfort. He found he could not deny her that.

Alex raised her chin, leaning slightly forward to press

238

her lips to his again, and he breathed in the enticing fragrance of her hair and skin. In that unguarded moment, he admitted to himself that she was, to him, the most desirable woman on earth and that he wanted her with an almost frightening intensity. Never before had he felt so at the mercy of any female; never had he dreamed he would have so little pride in the matter.

When Alex lifted her arms to encircle his neck, the blanket dropped away from her shoulders, and the sight of her torn gown and the bruises on her neck renewed his frustrated wrath.

"God, Alex," he muttered, against her hair, "I wish I had killed Bacconne."

"Destroy my memory of him — that's all I ask."

"Tell me how to do that," he whispered, turning his head to kiss her temple.

"I think perhaps you should make love to me," she murmured, thick lashes shielding her suddenly shy eyes. "If . . . if you want to, I mean."

"Alex, you're upset . . . you don't understand what you are saying."

"Yes, I do." She pulled away from him, no longer making an effort to conceal the generous glimpse of bosom revealed by the tattered fabric of her dress. "You yourself have cautioned me that . . . that unscrupulous men will constantly try to . . ." She swallowed deeply, striving for some semblance of composure. "I realize now that I might not always be able to avoid them. Had you not arrived when you did, Bacconne would surely have used me cruelly — and then, no doubt, have given me to his men."

Rhys ground out a curse, the hands he rested on her back clenching into fists. "Damn the man."

Alex's smile was poignant. "Rhys, what if he had succeeded? What if he had been the first . . . ? I couldn't have stood that." She softly kissed the corner of his mouth. "That is why I want you to make love to me. Please."

"Alex, I . . . This isn't a good idea."

She looked stricken. "You don't want to?"

"God, yes, I want to, but it isn't right."

His expression suddenly altered as the import of her words struck him. "What do you mean, the first?"

"I've never been with a man before," she said, alarmed by the fierce look that sprang into his eyes—eyes that were gray-green at the moment, with a hint of flame behind them.

"But I thought . . . well, you being a doctor and all . . ." he stammered.

"I tried to tell you that even though I know certain medical facts, I'm not worldly or experienced—nor am I a woman of easy virtue. And, while I may have seen naked bodies in the course of my work, I have never gazed upon one in an intimate situation."

"You're a virgin?"

"Why is it so hard for you to believe that?" she asked.

"I don't know . . . because you're so damned beautiful, I suppose. Because you know so much, and have done so much. I didn't see any way you could still be an innocent."

"Perhaps you were prejudiced against me because I'm a female who has dared to seek a place in what is considered a man's profession," she suggested. "Many people feel that innocence goes hand in hand with ignorance, therefore, with my physician's training, I must be immoral."

He smiled crookedly. "I suppose I felt the same way—oh, not that you were immoral, but that you . . . well, you simply knew too much not to have learned part of it somewhere besides a book."

"Trust me when I tell you there is a great deal about . . . certain matters that I do not know."

His mind was instantly intrigued by the thought.

"Rhys?"

"Hmm?"

"I truly want to learn about those things from you. . . ."

Rhys felt a jolt of pure, unadulterated passion pierce through him. The guilelessness of her eyes in combination with the boldness of her words excited him unbearably, making rational thought suddenly beyond the sphere of possibility.

"Alexandria," he murmured, pulling her to her knees and rising up to meet her. His hands flattened against her back, then slid lower to grasp her hips, fitting her closely to his body. His mouth, now bereft of sensible words, had no choice but to seek hers in a deep, probing kiss.

Alex did not pull away. Instead, she pressed herself into the hard curve of his body, letting his strength and warmth melt away the last chilling memories of Bacconne's unwanted touch. She tried to tell herself that she would gladly have accepted comfort from any decent man at that moment, but her heart was far too stubborn to believe such a ridiculous notion. It might be permissible for another to dry her tears or pat her back in sympathy, but comfort of this sort she wanted only from Rhys Morgan. It was a relief to have finally reached this moment with him.

She loved the feel of his taut thighs against her softer ones, the granite hardness of his hips. She reveled in the commanding clasp of his hands on her body, thrilled to the sweet crush of his lips on hers, the teasing thrust of his kiss. She gloried in the low, uncontrolled moan that rose from Rhys's throat, sensing he was as lost in the moment as she.

His hands moved to her waist, and then he was standing up, scooping her into his arms. The blanket fell unheeded to the hearth rug.

As Rhys strode from the room, Alex had only a glimpse of the luxuriousness that was unusual for a wilderness home. He crossed the planked floor, taking her into a bedroom washed with flickering gold from a fireplace that opened into both rooms. He placed her on the wide brass bed, and Alex sank deeply into the feather mattress. She lifted her arms in invitation.

Rhys stretched out on the bed with her, his big frame partially covering her slender one, his hands gripping her shoulders. He took her mouth in a fevered kiss, and Alex felt herself open to him like the late daisies in the woods opened to the autumn sun. It seemed he was drawing forth a response from her very soul.

She experienced dizzying thrills of pleasure as his heated mouth left hers, and moved downward to the ravaged bodice of her gown. He kissed her breasts through the torn fabric, then released her shoulders to let his hands unbutton and gently push aside the gown and chemise. His face was still and intent, his breath harsh in the silence of the room. His tanned hands trembled faintly as they shaped themselves to the sides of her breasts, whose smooth fullness looked pale by contrast. His first unencumbered look at her nakedness

242

shook him powerfully, filling him with a confusing mixture of awe and carnality. Reverently, his thumbs stroked the small, upthrust nipples.

"These remind me of the wild raspberries in the forest," he murmured, lowering his head. "I wonder if they taste as sweet. . . ."

Alexandria's body arched in sheer, exalted delight at the fierce, piercing thrill that streaked through her chest . . . and downward. So easily could he plumb the unexplored depths of her hidden other self. So very easily.

"Mmm," he whispered, "sweeter."

She raised a hand to caress his tumbled black hair, and he turned his head to kiss her palm, then trailed moist kisses along the sensitive skin of her inner arm. He gently tortured her with swift, grazing nips of his teeth before satisfying the longing building within each of them by crushing his mouth to hers again. Rhys's loss of restraint was evident in the way he kissed her, his lips parted, his tongue teasing, tasting, then withdrawing . . . only to return with renewed fervor. Alex twisted beneath him, struggling to get as close as she could to his unfamiliar and fascinating maleness. Rhys's answering moan was so pain-filled that she thought she must have hurt him.

"God, Alex." He wrenched his mouth from hers, dragging in deep breaths. His eyes were black with desire, his mouth softened from its usual grim lines. "I can't—I can't do this."

An agony of frustration welled up inside Alex. "But I want you to. . . ." She placed a pleading hand upon his chest, and where her fingers touched bare flesh beneath the loose buckskin lacings, they were nearly burned. She lowered her head to his shoulder, fighting the despair that his withdrawal brought. "Please!" She turned her head slightly, letting her mouth graze the smooth, bronzed skin of his neck. She touched him lightly with her tongue, pleased by the hot, salty taste of him, and felt his heart jerk under her hand. Abruptly, he flung himself away from her.

The thought that Rhys might not want her was as frightening as Bacconne's fearsome advances had been earlier, and Alex doubted she could survive his rejection now.

"What is it?" she asked, in a low, uncertain voice. "What have I done?"

Sitting on the edge of the bed, he buried his face in his hands. "It's not you, Alex . . . it's me. I've got to get myself under control."

Puzzled, Alex sat up and, slipping her arms around his broad shoulders, leaned against his back. The pliant buckskin felt very much as she imagined his bare flesh would feel. "Why?" she queried softly.

He drew a deep breath, dropping his head to stare at the floor. "If I tried to make love to you while I'm in such a state, I'm afraid I'd hurt you. I can't seem to hold back."

"There's no need to hold back," she assured him. "I don't want you to."

"Alex, listen to me. You need a man who can proceed slowly and carefully, not some clumsy fool who can't keep a sane thought in his head."

Rhys was entirely sincere, but even as he spoke, the image of another man bending over Alexandria in passion caught him by the throat. He twisted about, and, seizing her by the waist, pulled her onto his lap. "Damn my eyes," he swore violently, "I don't want anyone else

244

making love to you. God help me, I want to be the one."
He rested his face against her hair, forcing himself to
gentle the hold he had on her. "But what if I hurt you?"

"You won't. I'm not so very fragile, you know."

He thought she *looked* fragile lying there within his
arms. Her skin was translucent ivory, fine and delicate,
and she seemed so small and vulnerable. But he
couldn't resist the sweet softness of her mouth, and
when the kiss had ended, neither could he resist the
insistent heat that rose within him again.

"Help me go slowly," he entreated, getting to his feet.
He allowed her body to rub easily down his until her
feet reached the carpeted floor. "Help me keep my
senses about me."

Alex raised her eyes to his and said frankly, "How can
I, when all I want is for you to help me lose mine?"

She bent to remove her boots and stockings, then
unfastened the waistband of her dress and let it drop.
She smiled gently. "I think it would be all right for us to
lose our senses together."

She untied the ribbon that released her petticoats.
Stepping out of them, she reached for his hands, placing them on the ragged edge of her chemise, her only
remaining garment. His eyes were as black as obsidian
in the darkened room, and they never left hers as he
deliberately tightened his fingers on the chemise and
slowly ripped it in half, tossing the remnants aside.
They both caught their breath — she in an effort not to
cringe before his burning look, he in an effort to still the
desirous flames that consumed him as he gazed upon
her unshielded beauty.

"Alex," he whispered, his voice more graveled than
usual. "You are the most perfect woman I have ever

seen. . . ."

His avid scrutiny filled her with a sudden disquiet, and all her boldness stole away. Looking much calmer than she felt, Alex reached past him to turn back the bedcovers and slip hastily beneath them. She had suddenly become a miserable coward again, hiding behind a flannel sheet and wool blanket. Why had he said that? Why had he made her start speculating about the number of women he had seen and loved in the past? She certainly hadn't needed the worry of whether or not she could measure up to those mysterious females . . . whether any one of them had meant anything special to Rhys.

Without speaking again, he pulled his fringed shirt over his head, then rested one foot on the side of the bed to unlace the knee-high moccasins he wore. It seemed only seconds before both had been dispensed with, and his hands fell to the front lacing of the buckskin trousers.

Alex could no longer watch as his splendid nudity was revealed in such a tantalizing manner. New fears were gripping her, and regret roiled in her stomach. The man himself was more beautiful than any human she'd ever seen—how could she have been so foolish as to think herself a match for him? He was bound to think her too thin, too inadequate, too spinsterish!

She felt the mattress give beneath his weight, and panic spurred her into action. She rolled away from him, planning on slipping out the opposite side of the bed. Instead, his ironlike arms went about her waist, hauling her back against him. She could feel heated skin, the coarseness of body hair and the terrifying strength of his arousal against her bare buttocks. She wriggled wildly, her fingers clutching at his.

"Stop it, Alex," he said, close to her ear. "What's wrong with you?"

"I . . . I've changed my mind," she panted.

His groan was filled with real anguish. "Damn it, woman, I wanted you to help me go slowly — not stop me completely!" He swallowed so deeply that she could hear it. "Don't do this, Alex. You can't. I can't just call a halt to this — not now!"

His lips nuzzled the back of her neck and she stiffened. His kiss was as persuasive as ever, she found. His need for her was obvious, and it was her fault. Alex lectured herself silently, even as she turned in his arms. No mature woman would lead a man on so and then abruptly change her mind. She had instigated this moment, she knew, and she accepted the fact that now she must be willing to go through with it.

"I'm sorry. I . . . I lost my nerve, I guess."

"Are you all right?"

She nodded.

"You're certain?"

She placed a palm along the side of his face and lifted her mouth to his. "Yes," she told him, her lips brushing his lightly. "I'm through being a frightened child."

Rhys deepened the kiss, pulling her body into alignment with his. As his mouth whispered over hers, straying to her temples, to her ears and the tender spot below her finely carved jaw, one hand roved in like fashion, stroking her breasts, tracing the line of her hips . . . moving to the smoothness of her thighs. When he touched her intimately, she stiffened within his embrace, then settled deeper into it, with a pleased sigh.

"That feels so . . . oh, Rhys . . . so wonderful!"

247

Her fevered cries of delight fueled the fire burning inside him, and yet, he kept a tight rein, cautioning himself to move slowly, to bring her steadily and without haste to the edge of fulfillment. His own pleasure was not even a consideration, so it came as an unexpected surprise to find that her enraptured response only heightened his own.

He regretted this was not the first time for him . . . and yet, in a sense, it was. It was the first time he had ever loved unselfishly, had ever given of himself without the slightest need to receive anything in return. Alexandria's happiness was all that mattered. Her bliss was his — it would be enough for the two of them.

And yet, encouraged by each enthralled gasp or sigh from Alex, happiness seemed to be pushing up from someplace deep inside him . . . to unfurl and grow, bursting into blossoms of purest joy that vined slowly throughout his body. As incredible as it was, he knew the self-proclaimed spinster, as untutored in the ways of love as she might be, was teaching him things he hadn't realized he didn't know.

"Rhys," her voice rasped into his ear, "I'm not . . . at all certain how . . . oh! How this works, but I . . . I don't think I can go on . . . much longer. Oh, Rhys!"

Her head lolled back on the pillow, her hair a riotous mass of bright curls. The angles of her face were taut with the tension she felt, and her eyes revealed her deep pleasure before being masked by thick lashes. Her lips were softly parted, freely offered for his kiss.

Rhys raised his body to cover hers, tilting her hips with gentle, guiding hands. He paused, striving to accustom himself to the feel of her, then carefully eased his way, unaware of the endearments he was murmuring.

Her body's resistance was merely token, for Alexandria welcomed his loving intrusion.

"Am I hurting you?" he whispered, his nerves ragged from the excitement that gnawed at him. "Should I stop?"

"No," she cried, aghast at the suggestion. "Besides . . . it only hurts a little. Oh, Rhys, don't stop now."

Her fingers clutched at his shoulders, her nails scoring the skin in her frantic need. She writhed against him, arching up to meet him. Her cry of pain was short and sharp, and Rhys took it into his mouth, soothing her with his kiss.

After a moment, the pain had faded, and when he began to move, tentatively at first, she moved with him. Instinctively, she met every thrust, and with each astonished, yet ecstatic, response from the dark-haired man above her, she grew bolder. With the boldness came an overpowering sense that something wonderful was about to occur, and Alex quickly became incapable of controlling her own reactions. Taken captive by an overwhelming frenzy, she moved with even more abandon, and soon Rhys could no longer sustain his caution. He was lost in desire such as he had never known, spiraling toward a release that was as vital to him as his next breath.

"God, Alex . . . I'm sorry," he muttered. "I can't . . . seem to . . . wait . . ."

His words trailed upward into a harsh cry as he felt himself caught up in a storm of passion. His last rational thought was that Alex was right there with him, clinging to him as they were whirled away into that sunless, moonless, timeless place where there is nothing but a great, pulsating surge of breath-taking pleasure, followed by soul-shattering contentment.

Several minutes passed before Alex stirred and opened her eyes. Rhys was gazing at her, looking exhausted by the strength of the emotions they had just shared.

"Do you feel all right?" he asked.

Her gray eyes glowed. "I feel wonderful."

He pulled the sheet up to cover her shoulders, and dropped a soft kiss on her smiling mouth.

"Go to sleep, sweetheart," he murmured.

Sweetheart? she thought drowsily. For once he didn't say I was mule-headed or stubborn. He didn't even call me a troublemaker . . . just sweetheart.

She snuggled deeper into his arms, and slept.

When Alex awakened, several hours later, she was alone. But the lighted lantern on the dresser and the plaid wool shirt thrown across the foot of the bed were evidence of Rhys's proximity. She had just slipped out of bed and into the shirt when he stepped to the bedroom doorway. Alex's hands faltered on the buttons, and her face grew warm with sudden embarrassment. She was glad the room was so shadowy.

"Did you rest well?" he asked.

"Y-yes. What time is it?"

"Half-past eight. . . ."

"Oh, my heavens, Aberdeen must be worried sick about me!"

"No, it's all right. I've sent her a message saying that you are safe, and will be staying the night here."

"You told Aberdeen I was spending the night . . . with you?"

"Now, don't start throwing things until I explain," he said with a chuckle.

He took a few steps into the room, and Alex found herself backing away. Her buttocks struck the edge of the mattress and she sat down abruptly.

"I employ a married couple—Pierre and Jacquetta," he was saying. "They live in a small cabin not far from here. Pierre helps me with the livestock and planting, and Jacquetta does the cooking and cleaning. I sent Pierre into Sabaskong to tell Aberdeen what had happened between you and Bacconne, and to let her know you would be staying here with me. Don't look so mutinous, Alex. He also mentioned that I have two bedrooms, and that Jacquetta will serve as a chaperon. You may wish to tell her the truth later, but that will be your decision."

"Well, I suppose you did the best thing. And if there is any kind of medical emergency, at least they will know how to find me."

"Right. For the time being, however, why don't you have a hot bath? Afterward, we'll have the supper Jacquetta has fixed." He indicated the metal bathtub placed in front of the fire. "Shall I fill that for you now?"

"That would be wonderful." She was suddenly very aware that, despite the large size of the shirt she had on, there was a considerable length of naked leg showing. "Uh, where are my clothes? I'll need something to wear."

"I'm afraid you'll have to make do with what you've got on, until Jacquetta gets your dress repaired. You'll be warm enough by the fire."

Being warm had not been Alex's first concern, but she merely nodded and said nothing. Rhys looked as though he would like to say something more, but he, too, seemed to feel the constraint between them. He eventually left the room, returning with pails of steaming water, and then disappeared completely while Alex had her bath.

She soaked in the tub until the water began to cool, then hastily dried herself and again donned the black and white plaid shirt. Jacquetta had sent a brush and comb for her hair, and she was sitting in front of the fire using them when Rhys came to tell her supper was ready.

A small drop leaf table, set for two, had been placed on the hearth rug in the living room. Rhys held one of the chairs for Alex, and when she had seated herself, he handed her a blanket to cover her bare legs. Unable to meet his amused eye, she took it and murmured her thanks as she unfolded the blanket and draped it over her lap.

Alex was somewhat dismayed that Pierre and his wife were not joining them for the meal. Although it would have been uncomfortable meeting them under such circumstances, she was not altogether certain that wouldn't have been preferable to being alone with Rhys. Just the recollection of her impassioned response to him made her breath grow shallow and her cheeks burn. Why hadn't she thought past the first moment of desire? Why hadn't she realized her relationship with Rhys wouldn't end when they left his bed? That they would continue to see each other in any number of situations, and that she would have to learn to accept his newly altered opinion of her.

"Alex?"

She gripped the edge of the table and forced herself to look up at him. Instead of the knowing, or even contemptuous, look she expected, Rhys was gazing at her, his eyes warm and faintly puzzled.

"Is something wrong?" he asked. "You've barely looked at me."

Alex shook her head. "No, everything's fine."

There was a short pause, and then Rhys spoke, his voice a shade too hearty. "Hand me your plate, and I'll give you some of Jacquetta's stew. It's the best in Upper Canada, I guarantee."

Though they ate in silence, Alex found her spirits rising as she finished the delicious meal. With her usual honesty, she reflected that none of this was Rhys's fault — she had been the one to disregard the danger of wandering off alone. She had been the one in need of rescue, and then in need of comfort. Just because Rhys had so adequately supplied both did not mean that he could be blamed for anything. It would be best for all concerned, she decided, if they could go on as though nothing out of the ordinary had happened. And it was up to her to restore a normal atmosphere between them.

"You have a beautiful home," she said, finally seizing upon a safely neutral topic. "I wasn't prepared for so much luxury here in the wilderness." She waved a hand at the room's elegant furniture, which included an upholstered sofa and chairs, a Welsh cupboard filled with china, and glass-fronted bookshelves.

"When I made the decision to live here instead of Montreal, I wanted as much civilization around me as possible."

"You've made a very comfortable home. Tell me, did you grow up in the city? Is that how you came to be so well educated?"

"My parents were from Montreal, but I was born north of here — up on the Red River." He hesitated, then added, "We went back to the city when I was twelve."

"And you attended university there?"

He nodded, toying with the wineglass at his plate. "My mother had taught me before that."

Alex sighed, recognizing that the conversation was stilted, but knowing it was better than letting their minds drift back to the afternoon's happenings.

"Why did your family leave the wilderness?"

"My father and I left the wilderness," he said softly. "That's all the family there was by then."

"What do you mean?"

When he looked up, his eyes had become such a cold blue they resembled a winter lake. Alex shivered involuntarily, and he came instantly to her side.

"I'm sorry," he muttered. "My . . . reaction to your question has nothing to do with you. Thinking about those early days always affects me this way."

"But why? What happened to you then?"

He remained kneeling beside her chair, taking one of her hands into his. His thumb rubbed the back of it absently, and she knew he didn't realize he was hurting her. His thoughts had turned inward, his eyes reflecting some long-endured pain.

"Maybe if I tell you this, it will help you understand my objection to your coming to Sabaskong with us. Maybe you'll see why I feel the way I do about women living in the wilderness."

"I'd like to hear it," she said quietly.

He nodded, but it was a long moment before he began the explanation. "My mother was the finest lady I've ever known — soft and gentle, quiet spoken. She was from one of the oldest families in Montreal and had been raised in affluence. When she met my father, he was different from any man she knew—she was fascinated by his ruggedness, by the sense of adventure that dominated him. They had only been married a short time when he became a Wintering Partner in the North West Company. She made no objection when they were sent to an outpost on the Red River, because she had been trained to believe it was a wife's duty to follow her husband."

"But she was unhappy in the wilderness?" Alex prompted.

"Unhappy?" he growled. "It killed her." His grip on her hand didn't lessen. "All the while I was growing up, I was aware of how much she had come to hate the place where we lived—the loneliness, the harsh winters, the primitive cabin. The only time I ever saw her truly happy was when my sister was born. She'd given up hope of more children, and then, suddenly, there was a little girl for her to love. She was a different woman . . . until Jenny died of smallpox. I think I knew she had given up then, just by the look in her eyes."

"Oh, Rhys, how sad. . . ."

"It was more than sad. Up until that time, she had never said a word about going back to the city. But after my sister's death, it was all she talked about. Do you have any idea what it's like for a ten-year-old boy to lie awake at night, listening to his mother sobbing and pleading with her husband to take her home? I felt so guilty, because I loved the forest—and yet, I grew to hate my father because he denied her the one thing she ever asked of him. He'd always promise they'd go back someday, just as soon as he made a little more money

. . . one more season, he'd say. One more shipment of prime furs.

"She killed herself when I was eleven," he said bleakly. "Simply walked into the river, and let the current take her away."

"Rhys, I'm so sorry." Alex caressed the dark head bowed before her. She was filled with compassion for the man she had once thought so stern and strong. For the first time, she saw beyond the carefully constructed facade, to the hurt, frightened child who was still such a part of the grown man.

"We buried her there," he went on, "beside Jenny. In the place she hated so much. Within the year, my father decided to go back to Montreal and took me with him. During the course of conducting his business, he met a wealthy young widow and married her—and built a house in the city because she didn't want to live in the wilderness.

"I couldn't forgive him for that. I finished my education because I knew it had been important to my mother, but as soon as I could, I left Montreal and came here to Lake of the Woods. I never saw him again, but I didn't forget the way he had treated my mother."

"That explains so much," she said. "So much about your attitude toward women. Dr. McLouglin told me you had a cynical view of marriage, but he didn't explain why."

"I haven't told anyone else that story, except Scotty. But every time I see some bright-eyed backwoods bride, I think of my mother."

"You know, there are undoubtedly women better suited to life in the wilderness than she was. Most of the brides haven't had her sheltered upbringing— most of them are strong because they've had to be. You mustn't think all women who come here will end up sick and unhappy like her."

He suddenly seemed to realize he was holding her hand too tightly, for he loosened his grip and gently rubbed her fingers. "Since meeting you, Alex, most of my ideas have changed—of necessity. And now, for the first time in years, I've begun to think things could be different for me, if only I'd be brave enough to take that chance."

When he raised his face to look at her, she couldn't deny an unexpected urge to lean forward and kiss his mouth. His hands crept to her shoulders, pulling her toward him.

"You don't know how beautiful you look sitting there." He kissed her softly. "Come back to bed and let me love you again."

"But, Rhys . . ."

He nuzzled his face against her neck. "Alex, I need you."

She smiled to herself. That admission was probably the closest he would ever come to telling her he no longer considered her weak and helpless.

Earlier, he had warmed and comforted her . . . now it was her turn. She accepted the responsibility with gladness.

"Yes, whatever you want," she murmured, allowing him to lead her back to the rumpled security of the feather bed.

Chapter Thirteen

Streamers of mist floated eerily over the lake, as the haunting cry of a loon pierced the predawn stillness.

Standing by the open window, Rhys breathed in the fresh, damp air and recognized the underlying tang of autumn. These last warm days of the year ordinarily filled him with a nostalgic regret, a reluctance to see winter force itself upon the land. This morning, however, he could summon no such dread. His bemused mind was, instead, busy with images of long, cozy evenings before the fire, just himself and Alexandria, sharing a companionship he had never known.

He pulled the window shut and latched it, turning back to look at Alex as she lay sleeping, her fiery hair spread across the pillow. Never had he allowed himself to envision her in his home, his bed. But now that it had happened, he realized it seemed right and natural.

He eased his naked body back into bed beside Alex, grateful for her warmth. She stirred in her sleep, and he gathered her into his arms. Her head came to rest upon his shoulder, and one hand curled against his chest. Rhys breathed in the fragrance of her red-gold tresses with the same appreciation he had just shown the pine-scented morning air.

He wanted to resent her, and might have done so under other circumstances. But their night together had come about so unexpectedly, and for such compelling reasons, that he couldn't actually blame her. Bacconne's attack had distressed her, and she was in need of comfort, leaving him at a loss as to what else he could do but hold her and offer solace. He had not intended to discover he cared for her; that was the worst part. He didn't want to love any woman or be responsible for her happiness. He had vowed a long time ago he would never take a wife, and now, suddenly, for all intents and purposes, he was as good as married.

He studied Alex's face, relaxed in sleep, and felt tenderness well within him. She would probably be just as shocked by their situation as he. She had proclaimed her desire to be a doctor many times—never had she admitted any inclination to be a wife . . . or, Lord forbid, a mother. His arm tightened about her. After last night, she, too, would have to face reality.

He considered what marriage to Alex would mean, and smiled sleepily. Life would never be dull, he'd wager. He supposed he could become accustomed to having such a lively wife underfoot all the time—he couldn't deny wilderness living was sometimes a solitary and lonely existence. And then his smile slowly faded. What if Alex became ill? Or frightened of the rigors she was bound to face? What would he do if she grew bored with the tediousness, the isolation?

He rested his cheek against her hair. He'd just have to deal with those possibilities if and when they occurred. Right this moment, fate had intervened in his life and he was left with very few choices. He had to do the right thing—and that was to marry Alexandria.

The morning sun was burning away the mist that drifted across the small bay in front of Rhys's cabin by the time Alex awakened. She yawned and stretched languorously, surprised to find herself alone. Filling a washbasin from the steaming kettle that hung on the hearth hook, she hurriedly washed, then dressed in the neatly repaired clothing she found draped over the bed posts.

Alex quickly made up the bed, her thoughts a confused tangle of elation and dread. Her relationship with Rhys Morgan had changed drastically, and now she was uncertain as to what to expect.

When she walked into the kitchen, she was relieved to find it empty, although she knew she would have to encounter Rhys sometime. Or, more to the point, she admitted, face what was between herself and him. In the intimate darkness of the night, they had proceeded far beyond the initial constraint of a man and woman who have surrendered to sudden, gripping passion. They were now at an emotional crossroad, a place where they must stop and get their bearings anew.

She glanced through the window and saw a short, plump woman and an even plumper man turning two milk cows out of a log barn to the grassy lawn behind the cabin. As she watched, Rhys walked into the clearing, his face lighted by a broad smile as he said something to the couple. The three of them laughed heartily, and Alex was stricken by how young and happy Rhys looked. He had never appeared so carefree.

A feeling of warmth crept through her as she allowed herself to wonder just how responsible the night they had spent together was for the contentment that seemed evident in every line of his body.

Quickly, Alex turned away from the window and let her gaze wander over the room before her. A fresh, yeasty aroma emanated from a loaf of bread left in the warming oven set into the stones of the fireplace, making her realize how hungry she was. Besides the bread, Rhys had left butter and jam on the scrubbed pine table, as well as a tin of tea. Grateful for his thoughtfulness, she cut a slice from the loaf and buttered it, carrying it to the fireplace with her as she went to get the teakettle. She had just taken a bite when the door to the cabin opened and Rhys came into the room. He caught sight of her and stopped, then slowly closed the door and crossed the floor to stand in front of her.

"Good morning," he said softly, his eyes a dark green. "Did you sleep well?"

Alex wanted to flinch beneath the unwavering intensity of his gaze, but she forced herself to return it as calmly as she could.

"Yes, I did, thank you. And, thank you for the breakfast. This bread and butter is delicious."

A wicked glint came into his eyes. "Mmm, it looks delicious . . ."

Before she could anticipate his action, he stepped close to her, one hand cupping the back of her head, the other sliding around her waist. His mouth touched hers, his slightly open, his tongue gently lapping at the melted butter along her upper lip. Alex experienced the familiar weakening sensation to which she seemed prone each time the man touched her. It came as something of a surprise—she had thought the passion between them well sated. But her reaction to his audacious kiss told her the fires had only been banked, waiting for an opportunity to flame up again.

"Rhys," she protested lightly, turning her face so that his heated lips trailed across her cheek. "We shouldn't . . ."

She wanted nothing more than to kiss him back she suddenly realized, but her momentary caution had broken the spell. Rhys moved away, though his eyes were still twinkling. "I couldn't let you meet Pierre and Jacquetta with butter smeared on your mouth, could I?"

"No, of course not," she replied, her own face stretching into a smile. "Now, if I am suitably presentable, perhaps you could make the introductions, and then I really should start back to the Falls."

"Yes," he agreed, with a more serious tone.

"There is a great deal to be accomplished today. Pour your tea while I get Pierre and his wife."

Alex declined the use of one of Rhys's horses, preferring to walk. She was not surprised when he declared his intention of walking with her. Undoubtedly, he wanted to make certain Bacconne and his men were no longer lurking in the vicinity, and she welcomed his company. It was not until they were nearly halfway back to the settlement that she had the first hint something was amiss.

"Do you think my cabin is too isolated?" Rhys asked, unexpectedly.

"Why . . . no, I suppose not." She glanced sideways at him. "You wanted it set apart from the others, didn't you?"

"It suited me. But what about you? Do you think it's too lonely a spot?"

"I don't know. I hadn't thought about it, actually." Alex's skirt swished against the browning fern fronds that bordered the worn path. "Why do you ask?"

"I know that it isn't going to be easy for you at first, Alex. Getting used to being away from the others I mean. And I understand how you feel about doctoring . . ."

Alex stopped in midstep, her eyes widening in alarm. "I think you had better explain to me what it is you're talking about," she said quietly. "Why would I be away from the others? And why are you asking all these questions about your cabin?"

Rhys faced her, hands dropping to his hips as he

noticed the stubborn set of her jaw. "I won't give up my home, Alex," he warned. "I've only just finished building it."

"Rhys," she said, striving for patience, "what on earth are you trying to say?"

"When we marry, I want to live in my cabin . . ."

"When we . . . what?" Alex's voice echoed sharply against the wall of trees.

"I realize that it isn't what you might have chosen," he began.

"Excuse me," Alex interrupted. "Did you say marry?"

He shifted his feet. "Yes, of course. What did you think we were talking about?"

"I didn't know. I'm still not sure I do . . ."

He grasped her shoulders firmly. "Hadn't you realized we'd have to live one place or the other when we're married?"

"No . . . and I can't figure out where you got the idea we were going to get married!"

"Surely after last night . . .?"

Alex felt her face grow hot, her temper keeping pace. "Oh, of course," she muttered. "Now I see. You feel you have to redeem my reputation once again, don't you?"

"It isn't only a matter of your reputation. Good God, Alex, you're a doctor. You should know the risk we took better than anyone else."

"Let's just consider the risk mine, shall we?" Her voice had grown frosty. "And you can forget this nonsense about making an honest woman of me. I don't intend to hold you to some outdated code of

264

chivalry."

"We are not discussing chivalry," he growled. "We are speaking about reality—a discussion I thought might take place in an atmosphere of calmness and serenity. I should have known you wouldn't allow that."

"I'm not trying to be obstinate, Rhys. I am only attempting to reassure you that you need feel no obligation toward me."

"Well, I do—whether you want me to or not. What kind of man do you think I am?"

"One who has declared his contempt for matrimony at every opportunity. No, I would never force you to marry me . . ."

"You're not forcing me, damn it."

"I will not permit circumstances to force you, either." She shrugged away from his restraining hands and continued along the trail. He stared after her for a few seconds and then, with a sigh of frustration, started after her.

"Alex, listen to me. I have given this serious thought. I don't mind marrying you—I want to!"

"I'll not have a husband who was prompted by guilt," she said shortly. "In fact, I have no need of a husband at all."

"What about last night?"

"What about it?"

"Oh, come now, Alex. Surely you don't expect me to believe you aren't somewhat worried about the possible outcome?"

"I only expect you to believe that I fail to see it as a reason for so severely altering our lives."

"Altering our lives? How can you be so goddamned unfeeling about this?" As they came into the Sabaskong Falls settlement, heads turned and Rhys realized he was shouting. In a quieter voice he added, "I thought you had changed, Alex — grown up a little."

At the porch of the doctor's cabin, Alex turned to face him. "Have you ever noticed that you only think I'm immature when I don't agree with you?"

"That's not true," he fumed. "Besides, I'm thinking of your welfare . . ."

Alex yanked open the door. "I'm not marrying you."

"What if there's a baby?" he asked.

"I —"

"Good morning, Alexandria." Aberdeen stood on the threshold, her face grim. " 'Tis past time you were home . . . obviously."

Like a guilty child, Alex darted a quick look at Rhys. He looked properly daunted by the sight of the sternly disapproving Scotswoman.

"Thank you for your . . . services, Mr. Morgan," Aberdeen said coldly. "It would seem you have gone above and beyond what the situation warranted."

He nodded curtly. "Alex and I have some things to discuss . . ."

"No doubt." Aberdeen's usual smile was well hidden. "But now isna the time to do it. The girl looks fair worn out."

"Aberdeen," Alex hissed in embarrassment.

"Then I'll come back later," Rhys insisted, "after she has rested."

"There's no need," said Alex. "Your idea of a discussion is you giving orders and me obeying them. I'm not interested."

"Suit yourself."

Aberdeen stood aside to allow Alex to enter the cabin. "Now, if that's settled there's a nice hot cup of tea waiting for you, lassie. *Herbal* tea."

Alex blushed deeply, but obediently headed for the kitchen.

"Coming to Sabaskong Falls was the wisest decision I ever made," declared Cordelia, pausing to thread the needle she held. "And Malachi Harper is a wonderful husband, even if he is a bit careless with his clothing." She smiled indulgently as she held up a shirt with ragged cuffs and collar.

"My Hardesty, on the other hand," spoke up Judith, "rarely needs his clothes mended. It's my cooking he favors. I'll bet I've made him a dozen pies since we've been here."

Birdie, perched on a wooden bench by the fire, smiled sweetly. "It isn't cooking or sewing that John Hay has grown fond of. I'll swan, if there were enough hours in the day, he'd—"

"Spare us the details," snapped Mellicent, setting a tray of china cups on the table. "Now, who would like a nice, hot cup of tea?"

The brides had gathered at Mellicent's cabin to chat and catch up on the latest gossip as they did their mending. Though the largest cabin in the settlement, it was still crowded, the chairs and benches lining the wall to make room for everyone.

As Mellicent distributed cups of tea, Claire

267

stepped to the door to call her children. Tobias and Annie, playing in the nearby aspen grove, came running at the offer of maple-sugar cookies and glasses of fresh milk from the Ames's dairy.

"Looks like the bairns have settled in well," commented Aberdeen.

"Yes," replied Claire. "And they've even made a few friends—the children of some of the trappers and their Indian wives." She accepted a cup of tea from Mellicent. "We really should organize some kind of school for them, I expect."

"I might try my hand at teaching them." Cordelia smoothed back a stray lock of hair. "I used to be a schoolteacher once . . . a long time ago."

"If you do start a school," Lily said in a quiet voice, "would it be all right if I came and learned to read? It's something I've always wanted to do."

"Then, by all means, you'd be welcome to come," Cordelia assured her.

Christiana coughed lightly. "Perhaps I could help out—on the days I feel up to it.

"Ye know that handsome Scotsman of yers wouldna like that notion," chided Aberdeen. "I'm surprised he let ye out of his sight long enough to come to Melly's this afternoon."

Christiana's laugh was faintly embarrassed. "I'm sure Scotty wouldn't mind. I'm feeling so much better these days." The remark was met with a round of teasing laughter, and Christiana's cheeks grew pink as she bowed her head over the mending in her lap.

Alexandria stood by a window, staring out into the sunny afternoon. The idle chatter flowed around her, but she might as well have been deaf for all she heard. She was watching the group of men who were helping Gideon Marsh build another room onto the cabin he now shared with Claire and her children. Or, rather, she admitted with self-disgust, she was watching one of those men — Rhys Morgan.

He had stripped off his shirt and tossed it aside, and the sight of his bared chest and long, lean legs encased in clinging buckskin and knee-high moccasins was having a disturbing effect on Alex. She had not seen or talked to Rhys since the morning following their night together, and she wasn't prepared for the feelings this unexpected glimpse of him generated.

Rhys was notching a log, and as he raised the axe and swung it downward, the muscles in his arms and shoulders stood out in bold relief, polished by a sheen of perspiration despite the coolness of the day. Alex's undisciplined eyes touched the dark mat of hair that covered his chest and crept enticingly lower, along the spareness of his ribs and belly. When he turned, presenting her with a view of his naked back, her hands curled slightly, remembering the smooth warmth of that flesh. With a strangled sigh, she dropped the curtain and moved away from the window.

"What's ailin' ye, child?" asked Aberdeen, a worried frown on her plain face.

"Nothing," Alex lied. She glanced around the room to find most of the other women watching her. "I . . . I was just thinking . . ." She drew a deeper breath and continued the improvisation,

". . . that what we need in this settlement is a . . . a community building. Someplace we can meet to talk or work where we wouldn't be as crowded as . . . as minnows in a pool."

"Why, Alex," exclaimed Claire, "that's a wonderful idea. If we had such a building, we could use it for a school, also."

"And a church," chimed in Judith.

Alex suddenly found herself quite taken with the suggestion that had surfaced so unconsciously. "Perhaps the men could start work on it as soon as they finish Gideon and Claire's cabin."

"And they could put it on that point of land near the trading post," said Cordelia. "It seems to be community property, and there would be a fine view of the bay."

"I think we should approach our husbands with the idea tonight," spoke up Christiana. "I'm certain Scotty, for one, will think it a marvelous plan."

"Aye, tisn't fair that any community event must take place in the trading post simply because it's the biggest building in town," agreed Aberdeen.

"Oh, it isn't that," Christiana murmured, blushing a second time. "It's just that . . . well, the next time a preacher comes through, it would be nice to be married in a real church."

Alex sneaked another quick look out the window, and felt her heart leap nervously as she saw Rhys again. A new project was exactly what she needed to take her mind off that irritating man, and this was something she could justifiably immerse herself in.

"Then that settles it," she said briskly. Reaching

270

for a cup of tea, she raised it high. "Ladies, shall we drink to the new Sabaskong Falls community center?"

The men had only been at work a few minutes the next morning before Albert Braunswager broached the subject of the new building.

"Melly tells me the women have thought up some wild scheme about a community center." His jolly laugh boomed out. "I told her we'd done fine without one this long . . ."

"I tried to tell Cordelia the same thing," said Malachi, shaking his head. "The woman has a temper, let me tell you."

John Hay grinned, then nodded his head. The gesture spoke most eloquently of the response he'd gotten from his own wife.

"Of course," commented Joseph Patterson, "we all know whose idea it was in the first place."

Rhys suddenly found all eyes on him. "What?" He lowered his axe. "Don't look at me — I haven't heard a word about any of this."

"Odd. Since the person behind it is your little red-headed doctor." Malachi's amused gaze swept the circle of men. "Isn't that so, boys?"

"Now wait a damned minute," Rhys ground out. "I don't know anything about a community building. And as for Alexandria MacKenzie, the last thing she is, is *my* little red-haired doctor. *Or my anything else!*"

Waldo chuckled and aimed a stream of tobacco juice at a nearby tree. "No need to get all riled up,

Rhys. No matter whose idea it was in the first place, I reckon these fellers put a stop to it."

"Danged right we did," declared Albert. "Can you imagine, with all we have to do before winter sets in, those females thinking we'd have time to cater to their whims?"

Gideon Marsh spoke for the first time. "It isn't a bad notion, really. If only we hadn't started this addition to my cabin—"

"It was necessary under the circumstances," said Hardesty Ames.

"And them women will have to learn we can't drop everything just to please them," offered Waldo.

Pacer and Scotty exchanged amused looks. "You know," Pacer drawled, "if some of you would ever try pleasing your women, you might find out it has its advantages."

"Naw," argued Waldo, lifting his cap to scratch his head. "Keep 'em in their place, is what I say. Keep 'em in their place."

Rhys took up his axe again. "There's work to be done. Let's get back to it."

"So they've refused our idea," Alex commented a few days later, looking around at the disappointed faces before her. "Well, we aren't going to let this be the end of the matter."

"We aren't?" queried Birdie doubtfully.

"We can't. Don't you see, they're using this issue to demonstrate their authority. They can't deny the need for such a building, so they tell us how busy they are, how much there is to get done before the snow falls."

"There is a great deal to do," said Mellicent reasonably.

"And I agree that some of it should receive immediate attention," Alex affirmed. "The rest of the harvest must be attended to, and the barns readied for the livestock. And Gideon's cabin has to be finished. But after that, there isn't anything more pressing than church or school—or a place where the entire settlement can gather for meetings or festivities. It's important that we insist on a measure of civilization for the Falls."

"Alex is right," Claire added. "If we stand firm on this, it will set the pattern for the future. If we're going to live here and be happy, we'll have to demand at least a few amenities."

"But what can we do?" asked Judith. "The men are adamant about this."

"Let's see how adamant they are if we refuse to cook or clean anymore," suggested Mellicent. "A week of no meals and dirty clothes ought to change their minds."

"I'm not sure that's the best way . . ." Alex began, but her words were lost in the general shout of approval.

"Aye," cried Aberdeen, rubbing her thin hands in glee. "If it's a war they're wantin', 'tis a war we'll give them!"

"Rhys! Wait up!"

Rhys had just started down the path toward his cabin when he heard his name called. He turned to see Hardesty Ames hurrying toward him. The tall, rawboned farmer looked agitated.

"Something wrong, Hardesty?"

"There sure as Hades is, but I didn't want to say anything about it in front of the others. Not yet, anyway."

"Look, if it's about this community center—"

"It's not," Hardesty assured him. "I wish that was the worst thing she had done."

"She?" Rhys heaved a weary sigh and let his gaze follow the lazy flight of an eagle, high over the treetops. "Why do I get the distinct feeling you mean Alex?"

"Because she's a troublemaker, Rhys, and whenever there's trouble, it's just natural to assume she's caused it."

"What has she done now?"

"Well . . . it's a little hard to . . . well, to talk about."

"Hardesty, for God's sake! I'm tired and I need to get home to do chores. If you have a complaint to make, get on with it."

Hardesty Ames's face flamed a dangerous red. "I don't think Alexandria MacKenzie has any right to intrude into what goes on between Judith and me . . . in the privacy of our bed."

"What?" Rhys's eyebrows shot upward in surprise. "What the hell has Alex got to do with that?"

"It seems our Miss MacKenzie is opposed to women bearing children. She has given all the brides some sort of herbal mixture that will prevent them from having babies."

274

"You're demented," muttered Rhys, but without much conviction.

"Ask Judith. She admitted it to me when I questioned her about starting our family. Says Alex thinks it would be best for the women to make sure they want to stay with us before they begin having babies. Have you ever heard of anything more preposterous?"

Rhys nearly choked. *All* the brides? Are you sure?"

"I am. Rhys, we can't have this kind of interference from Alex, even if she does claim to be a doctor. A thing like that should be decided by a man and his wife."

"I agree. But just what is it you expect me to do?"

"Talk to her. Make her take back all her potions and herbs. Judith has hidden hers and refuses to hand them over to me. And she was such a meek, God-fearing woman before that . . . that trouble-maker got her clutches into her."

"I can't promise to do much good," Rhys said, "but I'll try. Just as soon as I figure out some way to . . . to approach the subject."

He stood and watched Hardesty return to Sabaskong. So, he thought, that's why she wasn't worried about our night together.

Apparently, Alex had stumbled upon some kind of relatively effective childbirth prevention, and that must account for her lack of worry and fear. And for her confidence in scorning his offer of marriage.

She looks so sweet and old-fashioned, Rhys silently admitted, but in reality, she's got an unholy knack for being far too progressive.

"Just wait until I get another word with you, Alexandria," he swore, stalking off down the crooked trail toward home. He knew he needed time to ponder the situation and devise the best means of dealing with her, but he hadn't yet realized he was more than a little pleased by the challenge.

The last thing Rhys expected was a knock at the door of his cabin on a cold, wet night.

He flung the door wide, knowing it would take something important to bring anyone out into the soaking autumn rain.

"Albert, Malachi . . . Hardesty."

The three men crowded past him, followed by John Hay and Waldo Anderson. Taking off their wet oilskins, they faced Rhys with grim determination.

"We've reached the end of our patience," said Albert, his customary joviality nowhere to be seen. "If you don't step in and put a stop to this nonsense, we'll be forced to take drastic measures, I'm warning you."

"What now?" Rhys rubbed his forehead tiredly. He'd had two sick horses to care for and hadn't been to the settlement in three days. He'd known better than to hope things might have been calm in his absence.

"Do you know what she has our wives up to now?" asked Malachi, moving to the fireplace to warm his backside.

Rhys shook his head. There was no need to ask who *she* was.

"Them durn fool women ain't cooked a lick all week," spoke up Waldo. "And they ain't washin' no clothes or doin' no mendin'."

John Hay, his smile slightly less bright than usual, stepped closer and pointed out the foodstains on his wool shirt. Then he displayed the tattered knee of his trousers and made a disgusted face.

"It's their way of getting revenge," explained Albert.

"Revenge for what?" queried a confused Rhys.

"For us refusing to build their community building," replied Malachi. "That female doctor advised them to bring us around by not doing their housewifely duties. And then, when several days of eating our own cooking and wearing dirty clothing didn't work, the termagant hatched a new plan . . ."

Waldo chuckled merrily. "Damn, but it was a sight, Rhys! Now, you know I don't cotton to women getting all uppity, but I never seen anythin' like it."

"This morning, your Miss MacKenzie led a work party of women," said Malachi. "They announced that if we were too disinterested to build their meeting hall, why, they'd simply build it themselves."

"They came with axes and saws and hammers . . .," said Albert. John Hay nodded vigorously.

"And what did this work party accomplish?" asked Rhys, fighting a sudden urge to laugh. He could just see Alex, a militant look on her face, wielding an axe with a handle half as long as she was tall.

"They measured off the dimensions for the darned building," snorted Malachi. "And scalped the ground in preparation for the flooring. And to-morrow—"

"They're going to start marking the trees to cut for logs," finished Albert. "Even in the rain. I tell you, Rhys, this has gone far enough."

"Why not let them see how much hard work is involved?" Rhys asked calmly.

"Because one or more of them is bound to get hurt," Albert pointed out. "They're our wives, damn it . . ."

"Then why don't you control them?"

"Maybe we could, if something is done with that MacKenzie hoyden," said Hardesty. "She's a disruptive influence, misleading our womenfolk with drivel about their rights—and about that other matter . . ."

"Oh, hell, Rhys," chortled Waldo, "that's a good one, too. Wait'll you hear."

"I've already heard," Rhys commented dryly. "Gentlemen, just what is it you want me to do?"

"Take her in hand," answered Albert. "Lay down the law to her and make her behave."

"Tell her to quit meddling where she doesn't be-long," added Malachi. "Since she doesn't have a husband, it's up to you to handle her."

"Why me?"

"You're in charge here—our leader, so to speak. It's your duty, man." Albert's beefy face was seri-ous. "It's up to you to get this mess straightened out."

"Oh, all right," Rhys conceded. "I think we'd better call a town meeting for tomorrow night. Inform the others, will you, and make sure every man in the community shows up."

Rhys lay awake late into the night, hearing the drip of rain along the eaves. Inevitably, his thoughts were on Alexandria. But he wasn't thinking of her misguided campaign for childbirth prevention or even her daring scheme for obtaining a community center. He was thinking, instead, of that other night when she had lain in his arms, so sweetly compliant and loving.

Damn, what he wouldn't give to have her there again . . .

Chapter Fourteen

At the trading post the next night, Rhys faced a group of disgruntled men and nearly laughed despite himself, thinking how Alexandria had single-handedly stirred up a hornet's nest of admirable proportions. The laugh died abruptly when the doors opened and in came every woman in the settlement, led by none other than the flame-haired lady doctor.

"What's the meaning of this?" exclaimed Albert Braunswager, jumping to his feet to glare at his wife.

"This is a town meeting, is it not?" inquired Mellicent.

"Y-yes . . ."

"Surely it cannot have escaped your notice that we women are citizens of the community, too, and, as such, are entitled to be present at all public meetings."

"I never heard o' such a thing," grumbled Waldo

Anderson.

"Well, ye have now," snapped Aberdeen, pointedly taking a seat on one of the benches. Most of the other ladies followed suit, settling themselves with an air of having come to stay.

"Alexandria, are you responsible for this?"

Rhys knew his question was rhetorical. Just the way the woman seated herself, carefully spreading her rain-spotted skirts and demurely folding her hands on her lap, seemed to demonstrate her smugness. It was obvious that, once again, she thought she had scored a major victory in this everlasting battle of wills.

Well, thought Rhys stubbornly, the ladies can sit in on our meeting, but, by God, that doesn't mean they'll get the chance to talk!

"Now then, let's get this underway," he shouted, and the room gradually quieted. "I understand some of you men have complaints to voice."

"You're darned right we do," said Malachi Harper, getting to his feet and turning to address those gathered. "I say we put a stop to this community building nonsense before it gets completely out of hand."

"It is not nonsense," objected Cordelia.

"Here now," remonstrated Rhys. "Malachi has the floor—let's give him the chance to speak his mind."

"Very well," the woman conceded, but the look she threw her husband was so filled with malice that the man coughed twice, loosening his collar, and sank back into his seat.

"Uh . . . that's all," he muttered. "I just thought

281

we should . . . discuss the matter."

"What in thunderation do we need a new community hall for?" asked Albert Braunswager. "There's plenty of room here at Scotty's."

"Don't be such a dunderhead, Albert," scolded his wife, Mellicent. "This is no longer a settlement of men. There are women and children here now, and the needs of the community will naturally change. We need a school and a place to hold church. And Alexandria has suggested we ladies form a cultural club for the enjoyment of literature and music. Who has a home big enough to accommodate us?"

"I feel certain Scotty would permit you to meet in the trading post," Rhys replied.

"Don't you think that would tend to disrupt his business?" Mellicent inquired sweetly. "Besides, we are already planning to raise funds to buy an organ. Where would we put that? Among the dry goods? Or between the pickle barrels?"

There was a smattering of laughter, mostly feminine in nature, and Rhys gritted his teeth, trying to remain patient.

"And what about the library we intend to start?" queried Lily. "We need a permanent place to store the books we get."

"Books?" squeaked Waldo. "What in th' hell do we need books for?"

"Because we hope to bring a wee bit of culture to this part the wilderness," spoke up Aberdeen. "Even an uneducated gowk like yerself might find it enjoyable to read a good book on a cold winter evening."

"In a buffalo's hump," Waldo snorted.

"Yeah. He'd have to learn how to read first," commented Joe Patterson, slapping the older man on the shoulder.

"And here's another thought on the subject," Claire said, rising to her feet. "If we did have such a building. . . ."

As she talked, Rhys found his attention straying to Alex. She sat quietly, letting the arguments ebb and flow around her. It was evident to him that she had instilled such incentive in these women, she herself did not need to speak. She set the other ladies in motion, like toy tops, then sat back and waited to watch the results.

But, he thought, just what benefits does she hope to gain? She doesn't seem the sort to simply make trouble for trouble's sake, yet she has no husband or children. As a doctor, she can't always expect to have time for music and books.

Could it be that she was just thinking of the good of the community? Was she worried that the others might find life there too dull or lacking? Instead of trying to cause trouble for the men of Sabaskong, was she actually trying to aid them in keeping their wives contented? Rhys rubbed his chin thoughtfully. There was something to the theory, one way or another. If the end result of Alex's domestic revolt was the betterment of the Falls, maybe it hadn't been so ill conceived after all. And if it served to keep the other women happy, might it not work the same way for Alex? He let his eyes roam over her trim figure clad in blue wool, admiring her serene loveliness. Considering her reputation as a hell-raising crusader, she looked perfectly harmless.

Even as he had the thought, other, less innocent pictures of Alex slipped into his mind, and he knew she could never be considered harmless—at least, not by him. He knew all too well the harm she could do, had already done. Such a short time ago, his only concern had been how to get her away from the fort and back to Montreal. Now, strangely enough, he was occupied with schemes to make her stay. What had happened to him, and how had it happened so quickly?

"I'd like to say something," he heard himself announcing. The natural authority in his voice silenced the others immediately, and all eyes rested upon him. "This community hall—I don't think it's such a bad idea. The ladies are right. We do need a regular meeting place, one big enough to hold all of us comfortably. And it's a poor town that can't provide a school for its children and a church for its citizens."

A few male mouths dropped open in surprise, but unperturbed, Rhys continued. "If those of us who are interested start to work on the building as soon as we're through with Gideon's cabin, we can have the exterior done before snowfall. As long as we have the fireplace working, we can finish the inside even after the weather turns bad."

"A good idea," agreed Pacer. "I will be glad to assist."

"Count me in, too," spoke up Scotty, laying an

arm along Christiana's shoulders. "I think the ladies have a most commendable idea."

"Listen to you, you bunch o' lily-livered babies." Waldo clapped his skunkskin cap on his head. "If you give in to them women every whipstitch, they'll run you around like trained pups! You ain't gonna see me bendin' like a willow in the wind."

With that, he stalked out of the trading post. For a few moments, several of the other men looked as if they would like to follow, but when they did not, a hum of voices started, and in a short while the evening had been altered into a purely social event.

Later, as she was saying her goodbyes, Alex found herself face to face with Rhys. He leaned against the doorpost and studied her, his eyes as dark as the night beyond.

"I . . . I'd like to thank you for supporting our cause," she said softly. "I was surprised that you did."

He grinned. "Frankly, so was I. But your arguments made sense, once I'd thought about it."

"Well, I'm truly grateful for whatever made you change your mind."

She slipped past him, aware that his nearness was having its usual effect on her silly heart.

"Alex?"

She paused, but didn't turn around. She heard his footsteps as he crossed the front porch of the trading post and came to stand close behind her.

"Yes?"

"Would you like me to walk you to your cabin?"

"Oh, no, that isn't necessary. It's only a short distance."

She left so hurriedly that it almost seemed she was running away, and Rhys realized he was disappointed that she had refused his company. His earlier anger had faded, leaving him with only unanswered questions and a growing desire to know more about the seemingly indomitable Alexandria.

"Something on yer mind, Mr. Morgan?"

Rhys turned to face the unsmiling Aberdeen McPhie. "Nothing more than the usual," he calmly replied.

"Alexandria?"

He nodded. "I don't understand her, Aberdeen."

"And just what is it about the lass ye don't understand?"

"Well, for one thing, how can she have garnered such a reputation as a hell-raiser when she's always so prim and proper?"

"I'd no' say Alex is prim," Aberdeen said with tightened lips, "but then, neither would I say she's a hell-raiser. Where did you get that idea?"

"From the men."

"Pshaw. What would they know?"

"They seemed to know that Alex was behind the movement for a new community building."

"She suggested it, aye." Aberdeen eyed him shrewdly. "But 'tis my opinion she only did so because she was tryin' to put other, less pleasurable thoughts from her mind."

"Meaning what?"

286

"Oh, nothing in particular."

"I see."

"Besides, ye canna deny the idea was a good one."

"But her means of getting that across were somewhat unscrupulous," Rhys pointed out.

Aberdeen raised a questioning eyebrow. "What means were those?"

"Talking the women into refusing to cook or do laundry. She shouldn't have interfered in such matters."

Aberdeen's sharp laugh rang out. "If ye think Alexandria was behind those shenanigans, ye're mistaken. 'Twas Mellicent's idea . . . and my own."

"What?"

"I'm tellin' ye the truth. Alex had nothing to do with that."

"But she did lead the women out to work on the building themselves, did she not?"

"Of course. She's no' a meek lamb, ye know."

"I know." Rhys couldn't control a brief grin, thinking just how very far from meek Alex really was. Then his smile faltered and died. "What about the herbal medicines she's giving the women to . . . uh, to discourage . . . ?"

"Bairns?"

"Yes."

"What about it?"

"How did she determine that such a thing was her business? Wasn't she taking on more than her rightful share of responsibility?"

"A doctor must meet the needs of her patients,

Mr. Morgan. When the brides went to Alex and asked for help, would ye have had her refuse them?"

"Wait a minute. They went to her?"

Aberdeen inclined her head. "Indeed they did. Did ye think the lass had forced the medicine upon them?"

Rhys swallowed deeply. That was exactly what he had thought . . . what he'd been led to believe.

"Aberdeen, are you telling me that Alex has never deliberately stirred up trouble among the women?"

"It purely riles me that ye should think so," the Scotswoman snapped. "Alexandria is trying her best to prove herself to the likes o' ye. She doesn't have time to do half the things ye seem to be accusing her of."

"I think I've been misled about her," he said slowly. "Maybe I should make an effort to get to know her better."

"Oh, I think ye know her verra well, as it is."

Rhys's gaze was steady. "It's not my intention to hurt her, Aberdeen. It never has been."

"Good. Then I suggest ye make haste with yer plan. What time shall I tell her to expect ye tomorrow?"

"Tomorrow?"

"Might as well get started with it. I think the two of ye need to go off somewhere alone." She shook a severe finger in his face. "And talk. There's a great deal about the lass ye dinna know."

"Very well. Tell her I'll come by in the early

288

afternoon to take her for a canoe ride. But don't be surprised if she refuses to go."

"Oh, she'll go, all right. Leave that to me."

Alex leaned back against the cushions in the prow of the canoe and watched the man before her. Rhys held a paddle, which he moved through the water with long, rhythmic strokes, propelling the craft swiftly along, past pine-topped islands. Occasionally, Alex had seen trappers' cabins nearly hidden among the trees, and once they had encountered a small group of Indians who raised their hands in silent greeting as their canoes sped past.

"Before the wild rice was all harvested, we'd have seen dozens of Chippewa families out among the islands," Rhys told her. "Most of them are moving to their winter campgrounds by this time."

Alex knew that winter could not be far away now, for there was an edging of ice along the lakeshore every morning, and several times during the day she heard the plaintive cries of the last, straggling flocks of geese as they migrated southward. Even the lake itself was changing. Gone was the wild, rough-and-tumble water of late summer. In its place was the smooth glassy mirror of dark, autumn water that reflected back all the colorful glory of the dying year.

"What are you thinking about?" Rhys asked suddenly, startling her out of her dreamy reverie.

"That it is beautiful here. And that I am grateful

to have had the chance to come and see all this." She swept her hand in an arc that included the still water, the jagged treeline and the robin's-egg blue sky overhead.

"And when the landscape is a monotonous stretch of white?" he asked quietly. "When you can't determine where the snow-covered ground ends and the winter white sky begins?"

"Winter in Montreal is not exactly mild," she reminded him. "I assure you, I know what to expect."

"I wonder."

"Rhys, what is there about me that makes you think I can't survive here? Do I seem that weak?"

Weak? It had been a long time since he had thought of her as weak.

"No, of course not. I'm only afraid you don't really know what life in such an isolated spot entails."

"I've got friends here . . . and duties. It doesn't seem isolated to me."

Rhys fell silent then, guiding the canoe into more open water. Alex turned her head to look into the distance, enchanted by the bluish haze of far-off islands and sky. A pair of gulls wheeled past the prow of the birchbark canoe, chattering noisily. She sighed in contentment and nestled deeper into the cushions behind her.

Presently, Rhys spoke again. "It's rare to see this stretch of water so calm. Usually it's boiling like a cauldron." He delayed paddling long enough to point out an island laying ahead. "That's Wolf Island—we'll go ashore there for a while before starting back to the Falls."

The island he indicated was good sized, with flat granite rocks along the northern edge. Just off the tip of it was a small cluster of rocks, with one spindly pine tree standing like a sentinel upon it.

With practiced skill, Rhys nosed the canoe into shore, beaching it on a narrow crescent of sand. From that angle, Alex could see that the center of the island was thickly wooded.

Rhys jumped ashore and held out a hand to assist her. She was glad he did, for she moved awkwardly in the heavy woolen greatcoat he had brought her to wear. He had warned her not to be fooled by the sunshine, for it would be cold out on the water. Rhys himself was wearing a jacket of buckskin, with some sort of fur lining. It was fringed and decorated with beads and quills, adding an exotic, almost savage distinction to his rugged appearance. Alex found him compellingly attractive, though she had chided herself silently since they'd left the settlement.

She almost flinched when Rhys's warm hand engulfed her own. She hadn't realized her fingers were tingling with cold.

"Didn't you bring any gloves?" he asked, reaching for her other hand and chafing both of them between his larger ones.

"Yes, they're in my pocket. I . . . hadn't realized my hands had gotten so chilled."

She stared up at him, aware of little else but the intent look his eyes. Somewhere in the distance,

291

the shrill cries of the gulls sounded again.

"Alex," he murmured hoarsely, tightening his hold on her hands, drawing her imperceptibly closer. "Alex, I . . ."

She raised her face, feeling suddenly breathless. She detested hypocrisy too much to try to tell herself she had not missed his kisses. From the moment she had stepped into Rhys's canoe, she had known they would come to this, and now her lips parted softly in anticipation.

Rhys looked down at her, feeling a jumble of emotions crowding his chest "God, I . . ." Suddenly he dropped her hands and stepped away. "I didn't bring you here for this," he said severely. "Better put on your gloves."

He moved back toward the canoe, leaving Alex staring at him in confusion. With conscious thought, she reached into her pocket for the gloves and began drawing them on over her stiff fingers.

Rhys seized a blanket and the cushions from the canoe and, stalking up the grassy knoll toward the front side of the island, tossed them down. "Look, Alex," he said, running a hand through his dark hair, "I asked you to come with me today because I wanted to talk to you. I didn't mean for . . . well, for anything else to happen. I hope you believe that."

"Yes, I do. Of course." Slowly, she approached him. "What was it you wanted to talk about?"

"I thought Aberdeen might have told you."

"No, she only insisted I hear you out."

He grinned wryly. "She's not one to make these

things easier, I suppose. Probably thinks I deserve to simmer in my own broth for while."

Alex's answering smile was tentative. "Just what is it you're trying to say?"

"Aberdeen set me straight on a number of things I've been blaming you for. Apparently, you are much more innocent than I wanted to believe."

"What things?"

"The domestic difficulties of the men at the Falls, for one. I thought it had been your suggestion that the women forgo cooking and laundering. I was told you were behind that entire insurrection."

"Perhaps some of the men believed that because it was more palatable than believing their own wives might be involved," she suggested softly.

"Possibly. But then the matter of the herbs, the childbirth prevention . . ."

"Oh. You know about that, too?"

He nodded, then smiled. "But Aberdeen tells me it was never your idea. That the others came to you first. Is that how it happened, Alex?"

Her chin rose sharply, but she kept her voice calm. "I'm not certain why I must defend myself to you."

He sighed heavily. "You're right. There's no need."

"Thank you."

"But, Alex, I just wanted to say that . . . well, I'm sorry I thought the worst. And my men thought the worst. I'll make sure they know the truth."

"Don't say anything that will cause more trouble

between them and their wives," she entreated. "The past week has already strained relations enough."

"I agree, and I promise to be tactful."

Alexandria let her eyes travel slowly along the misted horizon, sensing something of the vastness of the lake that lay beyond. Its very immensity made her feel small, insignificant. Involuntarly, she shivered.

"You're cold, Alex. Why didn't you say so?" Rhys bent and grasped the blanket and cushions again. "Here, let's move back into the shelter of the trees. We'll be out of the wind there."

Skirting the edges of the pine grove that covered the island was a tangled thicket of smaller trees. Ducking his head, Rhys pressed into them, finding a clear space where he spread the blanket.

Following him, Alex cried out in delight. "Oh, look," she exclaimed. "How beautiful!"

The winter-bare saplings were choked by trailing vines laden with bright orange pods. Some of the pods had burst open to reveal the red-orange berries beneath. The unexpected color glowed warmly against the dull gray wood.

"What are these called?" Alex was standing on tiptoe, dragging a branch down for closer inspection. "Can I take some back with me?"

Wasn't it just like a woman to be so thrilled over something as ordinary as wild berries? Rhys shook his head slightly, unable to prevent a tolerant smile. "That's what we call bittersweet," he told her. "Not the herb, just a wild vine. And, yes, you can take all you want. However, I don't know what it's good for."

"Why, it's pretty," she said. "Isn't that enough?"

"I . . . well, I never thought of it that way. But, yes, I suppose that's enough."

The branch Alex had been holding slipped out of her grasp and snapped back into place with enough force to shower her with a fall of dried pods. She cast a pleading look at Rhys.

"Would you mind breaking off that branch for me? I'm not quite tall enough."

He stepped close to her and reached up a hand, but the movement was arrested by the sight of her standing so near, her hair spangled with spiky orange pods.

"Did you know those pods look like little stars in your hair?" he asked, his voice sounding harsh and dry.

"No. . . ."

His hand fell to her hair, gently freeing one of the bittersweet pods from the shining strands that held it. He displayed it on his open palm.

"You're right, Rhys, they do look like stars."

Delighted, Alex took it, then smiled up at him. Her eyes were caught and held by the burning brilliance of his. This time the depth of feeling between them was so great, she knew he wouldn't move away.

She could feel the iron grip of his hands on her shoulders even through the thickness of the coat she wore. He dragged her against him without ceremony and began kissing her—her ears, her cheeks, her eyes—and finally, just as she thought she would go mad with impatience, her mouth. His heated breath mingled with her own as his lips mastered hers, demanding and insistently rough in the beginning.

"My God, I've been starved for this," he rasped. "For you."

His hands moved downward to splay themselves across her back, holding her to him. Alex's own arms slipped inside his coat, to embrace the wonderful heat of his body.

Gradually the kiss became more gentle, more coaxing, and altogether more devastating in its effect. Alex melted against him, lost to everything but the tumult of feelings raging within her. Time and place no longer had any meaning for her—her need for Rhys was suddenly all that mattered.

As they sank slowly onto the blanket, Rhys's ragged voice reached her ears. "Lord, we can't do this—it's too cold. Alex, we've got to stop. . . ."

All the while, his hands were slipping beneath her coat, stroking her shoulders, sliding the heavy wool garment backward, out of the way. Freed from the cumbersome coat, Alex's arms encircled his neck, drawing him closer as she returned his feverish kisses.

"No, don't stop," she whispered, aware that her words were responsible for the shocked tremor that ran through his body. "I don't feel the cold at all. . . ."

And it was true. His mouth and hands were arousing the most wonderful warmth within her, dispelling the chill of the October day. Each place he touched her seemed to glow with a slowly spreading fire.

Rhys shrugged off his own coat, tossing it aside. As he leaned over her again, Alex searched for the lacing at the front of his shirt, opening it to her caressing fingers. As her fingertips grazed the bronzed skin of his neck, she could feel the heavy thud of his heart and knew it was keeping time with her own.

Rhys unbuttoned her dress with eager haste, letting the warm weight of his hand rest against her breast a moment. "I'd like to feel you naked against me," he moaned, his lips brushing along her collarbone, "but it's too cold. God, what are we thinking of?"

Alex stroked his thick, soft hair. "Giving each other pleasure?" she whispered, almost shyly. "Or, perhaps, doing the only thing we seem to be able to do without arguing."

She felt his chest rumble with laughter, and the intimacy of the moment filled her with happiness. Why couldn't it always be like this between them? When her heart and mind were filled with the wonderful sensations caused by his bold touch, there was no room for doubt or anger.

Rhys clasped her tighter, letting his mouth glide slowly down the gentle swell of her bosom to the place where his hand lay. Curling his fingers to cup the side of her breast, he nuzzled his face against her, letting his lips capture and sweetly torture the tightly gathered nipple. Alex released a gasping sigh and wriggled beneath him, as though trying to align her body more closely with his.

"Rhys," she murmured. "Oh, Rhys . . ."

He raised his head to look at her, and the cool air stung her moist skin. She was glad when he returned his incredible warmth to her bared flesh, this time lavishing attention on the other breast. His brazen fingers slipped to her waist, squeezing, tucking her more tightly beneath him before wandering on, downward to the hem of her gown. In a haze of enervating passion, she felt his heated touch on the calf of her leg, soothing, petting, stroking upward along her thigh to her hip. He gripped her body, pulling her into the hard junction of his own legs, letting her realize the strength of his desire. Then he loosened the ribbon at the waistband of her pantalettes and his hand insinuated itself beneath the thin material. Shaken by his emboldened explorations, Alex cried out and, wrapping her arms about his neck, buried her face against his throat.

He even smelled warm, of sunshine and smoky autumn air. He seemed the embodiment of a pagan sun deity, sharing his glorious heat and fire, and Alex was hopelessly drawn to him. She basked in the radiance emanating from him; she burned with a slow, soft, simmering warmth.

Eager for him to come to her, Alex lifted her hips to ease the removal of her undergarment. To Rhys, that simple gesture revealed the depth of her arousal, and he was instantly inflamed. Uttering her name in a tense whisper, he lifted her skirts and petticoats, pushing them aside. Shielding her from the slight, lake-born breeze, he fumbled with his own clothing and then swiftly moved over her.

Alex cried out in pleasure, and Rhys, framing her face with his hands, kissed her deeply, his lips enticing, wooing. Alex's mouth opened in response, returning the kiss and further igniting him. With a low, gratified moan, he began to move, keeping himself under a rigid control that cost him dearly. Sweat beaded on his forehead, his features grew tense.

Looking up into his face, Alex saw that his eyes had darkened to the clear, deep green of the water found just offshore of the pine-studded islands. Though shadowed, there were fires burning within like refracted sunlight, striking straight to the depths. Behind him was the unclouded blue of the sky, and overhead, the bittersweet, a myriad of bright orange sunbursts.

Alex's softly parted lips and glowing eyes, as well as her somber contemplation of his face, stirred Rhys, stoking the fires of his passion ever higher. He felt his control slipping away, felt himself being gripped by an unbearably sweet frenzy. His movements became rapid, thrusting . . . and Alex gladly surrendered herself to the sensual chaos he was generating. Wildly, they clung together, as they reached a sudden, shattering release. Their faint, joyful cries lingered on the crisp air, echoing their pleasure.

As they lay locked together, Rhys shifted to one side, holding her against him. One hand slid beneath the tangled mass of her hair to curve about her neck and draw her face up to his. Tenderly, his mouth covered hers, softly yet insistently. Alex sensed that he was attempting to convey something for which he had no words. She leaned into the kiss, still thrilled by their intimate contact, still reeling from the force of their spent passions. Some elusive emotion lingered within her, as well, and though the feeling was overwhelming, it was too nebulous to analyze, too fleeting to express aloud. Rhys's thumb stroked and caressed her cheek, and he buried his face in the fiery softness of her hair.

"I could stay here with you forever," he murmured.

Forever? It seemed a rash overstatement and yet, straining her imagination to peer ahead down the long corridor of time that was her life, Alex could not envision ever wanting or needing anything more from a man than what she had shared with Rhys today. Laughter, companionship, splendid passion—what more could there be? *Love,* a tiny voice in her mind offered hesitantly. *What about love?*

What about it? she thought impatiently. In the life I have chosen there is no room for love. I'm dedicated to science—it would be impossible to find time to love a man . . . be a wife and mother.

Despite the notion, she raised her face in invitation and Rhys began kissing her again. An errant wind shook the branches above, showering them with a storm of orange stars.

Alex swallowed deeply and closed her eyes. Bittersweet . . . how apt a symbol for the tangle of emotions she now felt. While it had been undeni-

300

ably sweet being swept away by the powerful persuasion of Rhys's lovemaking, it was bitter to realize that their future must be confined to brief, stolen moments like this. As long as she remained true to the course upon which she had set her life, her feeling for Rhys Morgan could go no farther.

With a sigh, Alex brushed the bittersweet pods from his hair, closing her mind to any more unhappy thoughts.

Chapter Fifteen

The trip to Wolf Island marked a change in the relationship between Rhys and Alexandria. For the first time they had spent time together simply for the enjoyment of each other's company. Rhys's need to talk to her had been an excuse, and neither of them bothered to deny it.

For the remainder of their afternoon on the island, Rhys had not mentioned marriage or indeed anything concerning the future, nor had she. But in the two days since then, he had appeared at her door each evening, as though they were any ordinary courting couple, and she worried that her silence might have caused him to think they had some sort of understanding. Still, during the course of the evenings — on one they had visited Scotty and Christiana at the trading post, on the other they had strolled along the falls — she could find no way to broach the subject. Rather than ruin their new association with an argument, she had kept quiet.

Alex was presently standing in her office, gazing at a vase filled with the gnarled branches of bittersweet she had brought home, when a sudden commotion at the front of the house caught her attention. Thinking it might be Rhys, she smoothed her hair and hurried toward the source of the noise. Disappointment swept through her when she saw that it was Waldo Anderson at the front door. It took her an instant to realize he was being blasted by Aberdeen's wrath.

"What's going on here?" Alex cried.

The Scotswoman drew herself up to her full height. "This . . . this puir excuse for a man had the nerve to . . . to . . ."

"Waldo, what did you do to Aberdeen?" Alex demanded angrily. She hadn't yet forgotten the old trapper's part in the conspiracy against her.

"I didn't do nuthin'." Waldo twisted his skunkskin cap in his freckled hands. "I just come around like any gentleman caller."

"Gentleman?" shrieked Aberdeen, advancing on the man, who rapidly backed away, across the small porch. "Ye dare to call yourself a gentleman? Ye must have the brain of a foust neep if ye think there is a female alive who would welcome ye."

Alex followed Aberdeen out onto the porch, feeling somewhat ashamed of her friend's ungraciousness.

"What is a fawst neep?" Waldo asked her, ignoring the enraged Aberdeen.

"A . . . well, it's a moldy turnip," Alex faltered. "But, Waldo, I'm certain Deenie didn't mean to insult your intelli—"

"I did, too," the other woman stated firmly. "The man has no intelligence. Else he would never have

303

graced our home with his coo breath and his breeks that are so filthy they could stand alone."

Waldo cocked a bushy white eyebrow at Alex.

"Coo?"

"Cow," she interpreted for him.

"Breeks?"

"Trousers."

"She thinks I smell like a cow?"

"Ye smell like that black and white cat ye wear on yer haid!"

Nasturtium, who had been stretched along the porch railing, sleepily observing the altercation, now leaped down and stalked away, her tail stiff with indignation.

Albert Braunswager and Malachi Harper, who were approaching the doctor's cabin, laughed uproariously at the sight of the scrawny trapper suffering the sharp side of a woman's tongue.

"What seems to be the trouble, Waldo?" jeered Albert. "The little lady not in the mood for courting?"

Aberdeen turned on them with a scowl. " 'Tis none of yer business, to be sure."

"Ain't it a hell of a note," Waldo complained loudly, "when a man comes to give an old maid one last chance to git married, and she throws 'im out of her house?"

Aberdeen's outraged gasp echoed through the yard, and Alex quickly seized the woman's arm.

"Now, Deenie, don't forget you're a lady," she admonished. "You've hurt Waldo's feelings and made him angry."

"And now I'll make him blind and lame," Aberdeen screeched furiously. "Let go of me!"

"Now, Miss McPhie," soothed Malachi, a twinkle in his eye. "What fault could you possibly find with a fellow like Waldo? Why, he's a fine man."

"He's a great, scurvy gowk," retorted Aberdeen, tearing her arm from Alex's grip. "I'd no' look at the likes o' him until he'd had a proper bath — and combed the beasties from his hair. And burned every last bit of that evil-smellin' tobacco he chews."

"Well, if that's all it takes, Malachi and I can remedy that," stated Albert. "We'll see to it that he has a good bath. Right, Malachi?"

The other man grinned. "I reckon it's our civic duty, seein' as how we want Waldo to have the same chance at married happiness we have."

"Now what do you boys have in mind?" growled Waldo, backing down the low porch steps. "I ain't gonna have to hurt ya, am I?"

"You can try, old man," sneered Albert, making a grab for one of Waldo's arms. "Get him, Harper!"

Waldo gave Aberdeen a last, reproachful look. "Yer a mean one, Aberdeen McPhie — as mean as a bee-stung rattlesnake!" Then, with a shrill cry of alarm, he began running through the trees with Albert close on his heels. Malachi paused long enough to say, "By the way, Miss MacKenzie, Cordelia sent me over to tell you she wants to come by in the morning so you can treat her for the earache she's been having."

"Tell her that will be fine. I'll be expecting her."

As Malachi joined the pursuit, Waldo circled a boulder and came racing back through the yard, emitting a stream of vigorous curses.

Aberdeen chuckled uncertainly, and Alex gave her

a severe frown. "Shame on you," she scolded. "What if they hurt Waldo?"

"What the hell's going on?" Rhys rounded the corner of the cabin, stopping to stare after the three men.

"They're going to give Waldo a bath," Aberdeen said, a satisfied smile dancing about the corners of her straight mouth.

"Can you stop them?" asked Alex.

Rhys grinned. "What for? You can't deny the old coot needs a bath in the worst way."

"Not in the lake," she protested. "It's too cold."

"They won't hurt him, Alex. They may even be doing him a favor."

"A favor? How can you—?"

"Alex," he softly interrupted, "I didn't come here to discuss Waldo with you. Get your coat, I want to show you something."

"I'll fetch it," Aberdeen offered, disappearing into the cabin.

"Are you certain we shouldn't do something to put a stop to this?" Alex gestured toward the lakeshore where the two men were attempting to push a struggling Waldo into the water.

"They're not exactly overpowering him," Rhys pointed out dryly. "Stop worrying. He'll be all right."

When Aberdeen returned with the heavy woolen coat, Rhys held it while Alex slipped it on. Then, grasping the lapels, he pulled the collar up to frame her face. "It'll be dark before I bring her back, Aberdeen, but I promise to take good care of her."

"Where are we going?"

"You'll see. Come on. . . ." He took her hand,

curling his larger one around it. As they started down the path that skirted the settlement and eventually led to Rhys's cabin, they could hear Waldo's infuriated threats above the sounds of splashing water.

"Here we are," Rhys said, bending to speak directly into her ear. They had arrived at the banks of a small, circular lagoon that Alex recognized as being near his cabin. She glanced about before turning back to him, but when she opened her mouth in question, Rhys put a finger lightly across her lips. "Shhh . . . over there."

He nodded toward the far shore and in a few seconds, Alex caught sight of a small, dark head moving through the water.

"What . . . ?" she whispered.

"Beaver," he mouthed. "Look."

The animal, its pelt sleek and shining with wetness, pulled itself out of the water, awkwardly dragging its body onto the grassy shore where it began feeding on a small birch sapling growing nearby. It was round and plump, looking so much like a rotund little man that Alex had to stifle a giggle. Even the muffled laugh was enough to alert the beaver, who grew very still, looking toward them, his whiskery face soberly intent. Alex hardly dared breathe until, satisfied that there was no immediate danger, the beaver returned to his evening meal.

A few minutes later, he was joined by two more beavers, smaller in size but just as sleek and whiskery.

"The female is his mate," Rhys murmured. "The

other is one of their offspring—a yearling, I'd say."

"They only have one baby?" Alex whispered.

Rhys smiled, dropping into a kneeling position in the tall grass. "There are probably several young ones in the lodge." He nodded toward a rounded structure of logs and mud that hugged the opposite shoreline. "Maybe a couple more yearlings and some of last spring's kits."

Growing interested, Alex settled herself beside Rhys, tucking her coat and skirts about her legs for warmth. The sun had just slipped behind the spiked stand of trees on the west side of the lake, and the air was becoming increasingly chilly.

"Does the family always stay together?" she asked, looking up at him.

"Until the youngsters are fully grown, and go off to build lodges of their own . . . usually in the same body of water."

"Have you ever seen the inside of a beaver house?"

"Once or twice," he replied. "I've dived down a time or two to explore. The space inside is dry and well vented— very snug when a foot of ice covers the lake."

"Did you . . . did you ever trap beavers?"

"When I was a boy I hired on to help an old trapper." He shrugged, looking somewhat sheepish. "I lasted about two days. Just didn't have the stomach for it, I guess."

Alex was stunned to hear such an offhand confession from a man she had believed incapable of admitting any weakness. She studied his face as if searching for some proof this was the Rhys Morgan she thought she knew.

308

Half under his breath, Rhys groaned. "Don't look at me like that, Alex. Please."

"I didn't mean to stare," she replied. "It's just that I thought everyone in the wilderness made his living from exploiting the beavers."

"Not everyone—and certainly not me. Having seen too much of senselessly cruel slaughter, I think it's a ridiculous and shameful state of affairs that thousands of beavers must be killed every year so that British *gentlemen* can have fashionable hats to wear." He tapped her chin lightly with his forefinger. "You're looking at me that way again."

"I-I don't mean to." She smiled faintly, teasingly. "But I'm so astonished to learn that you have a heart."

"Oh, I have a heart all right. Here, feel." He took one of her hands and placed it inside his jacket, against his chest. "And the way you are smiling at me is surely making it beat faster than is healthy."

Rhys's free arm slipped around her waist, lifting her closer to him, settling her against his side. Slowly, deliberately, his mouth lowered to hers, its heat almost a shock in the cool air. Against the palm of her hand, his heart thudded alarmingly, and she began rubbing her fingers soothingly over the flannel material of his shirt. Within her chest, she could feel her own heart responding in a similar fashion, frantically pumping liquid heat to every portion of her body.

His lips moved over hers with searing thoroughness, leaving her breathless and longing for so much more. He had taught her body lessons it was loath to forget. . . .

309

"Stay with me tonight, Alex." His husky whisper effectively scattered her thoughts. "Come to my cabin — Pierre can take a message to Aberdeen."

She rested her face against his neck for a few seconds before looking up to meet his eyes. "Rhys, I can't . . . I'm sorry."

"Did the old spinster lecture you?" he queried, so fiercely that Alex had to chuckle.

"No, it isn't Aberdeen. I have a patient coming for treatment in the morning. I need to be there."

Rhys seemed to do battle with himself for a long moment, and when he spoke again, his tone was resigned. "I understand."

"Perhaps next time?" she suggested in a small voice.

He smiled broadly. "Then there will be a next time?"

She nodded. "I promise."

At that instant there was a slight splashing sound from across the lagoon, and several more dark heads appeared in the water. "Oh, look," Alex cried in a low voice. "There are the younger ones." Four more beavers, smaller and even more roly-poly, began clambering up onto the slippery bank. In only moments, the silence was filled with noisy chewing sounds as the beaver family continued eating.

Rhys studied her rapt expression as she watched the scene before them. Until now, he'd only seen that look in a woman's eyes when she had been paid an outrageous compliment or given an expensive gift. It seemed each time he was with Alex, he discovered another way in which she destroyed his previous conception of women.

Presently he touched her arm to draw her attention. "We'd better go back now. It's almost dark."

"Can't we stay a while longer?" Alex pleaded. "I love watching them."

"We'll come back tomorrow, if you like."

"The beavers will be here again?"

"They'll come out to feed every evening until winter sets in."

With one last look at the animals, Alex allowed him to pull her to her feet. With an arm about her shoulders, he guided her through the trees to the well-worn trail.

"Thank you for taking me to see the beavers," she said. "I'm so glad you thought of it."

"So am I. I sometimes forget that things I take for granted might be new and interesting to someone from the city."

As they approached Alex's cabin, they saw a silent figure standing near the porch, gazing upward.

"Aberdeen?" queried Alex. "What are you doing out here?"

"Looking at the Merry Dancers," came the woman's reply. She pointed toward the night sky. "That's the Scottish name for the Northern Lights."

Overhead, through the lacy tops of the pine trees, they could see the shimmer of pale green that swirled across the firmament. As they watched, bands of the luminous color shifted and swayed, like curtains blown by the wind.

"How lovely!" Alex breathed in wonder, reaching for Rhys's hand without thought.

Surprised, he smiled down at her. "Surely you've seen the aurora borealis in Montreal?"

"Well, yes, but never so brightly. Nor so . . . close. It's truly beautiful."

Aberdeen started toward the cabin. "I'll just leave ye to watch. . . ."

"Deenie, is something wrong?"

"Nay." The woman paused, then turned back to Alexandria with a heavy sigh. "Och, 'tis that nuisance of a man, Waldo Anderson. Ye should have seen him when Albert and Malachi were finished. He was standin' in the lake wearin' only his drawers—and mad as an old wet hen." A small, rather forlorn laugh escaped her. "I shouldna have suggested such a thing."

"But you never suggested those two get involved in the matter," Alex protested. "You can't blame yourself for their actions."

"Still and all," muttered Aberdeen, "I feel a wee bit sorry for the old coot."

"He'll recover," Rhys assured her. "He's lived through worse things than a bath. And God only knows, he was well past needing a dip in the lake. But you'd better watch out, Aberdeen, because he may take to courting you in earnest now."

"Do ye think so?" she asked, cocking her head to one side in contemplation of such a thing. "Well, it certainly won't do him any good. No good at all." She crossed the wooden porch and opened the door to the cabin. "Good night, ye two."

"Good night, Deenie."

When she had gone, Rhys stepped up behind Alex, pulling her back to lean against him, his arms wrapped about her waist. "She didn't sound all that distressed at the possibility of Waldo coming around again, did she?"

312

Alex snuggled her shoulders into the breadth of his chest. "Not really. You don't think . . . ?

He grazed her neck with soft kisses. "Who knows? Anything can happen out here in the wilderness."

She turned in his arms, her eyes serious. "That's true. Look at us. Not more than a month ago we could hardly speak a decent word to each other, and now, well, now we're . . ."

"What, Alex?" he murmured. "Just what are we now?"

Unable to answer his question, Alex stood on tiptoe and drew his face down to hers, silencing him with a long, deep kiss that completely stole his attention from nature's elaborate display above—and from further questions about what they were beginning to mean to each other.

Alex hurried along the path toward Rhys's cabin, her face wreathed in smiles. She could hardly wait to tell him about the latest event in Sabaskong Falls. Waldo Anderson had come to supper—at Aberdeen's invitation!

The man had appeared at the door just as Alex was leaving, and she was grateful that he had. Otherwise, she might never have believed Aberdeen's account. Waldo was, for the first time since they had met him, spanking clean, from his pink scalp to the newly trimmed fingernails on his gnarled hands. He no longer smelled of skunk, possibly because he had discarded the fur cap and was now carrying one of felt, but more likely because he was wearing a slightly wrinkled suit that smelled of camphor. Incongruously, he was still wearing battered moccasins on his feet.

When he saw Alex stealing a glance at them, he grew defensive. "I cain't help it—them damned boots hurt my feet." He looked up to see Aberdeen standing directly behind Alex and his face reddened. "Er, excuse me, Miss McPhie. I meant to say that my boots are too discomfortable to wear."

Alex stepped aside to let her friend handle the situation, but she couldn't bring herself to leave just yet.

"Here," Waldo said, thrusting a small wooden box at Aberdeen. "I brung you a present."

Obviously, Albert and Malachi had done more than initiate Waldo to bathing. Aberdeen smiled graciously, even after opening the box and perusing its contents.

"My, how lovely," she said in a perfectly normal voice. "Look, Alex, Mr. Anderson has brought me some pemmican."

Her snapping black eyes dared Alex to make one untoward statement. Managing to quell the laugh that bubbled inside her, Alex merely said, "Wasn't that nice of Waldo! I've heard pemmican is quite tasty."

"Well, lass, I'll be delighted to share with you." Aberdeen's smile was only a little grim as she invited Waldo inside the cabin. Alex chose that moment to snatch up her coat and slip out the door.

"I'm going down to the lagoon to watch the beavers," she said, lowering her voice to add, "Don't worry if I don't come home tonight, Deenie."

"Hmm?" The Scotswoman was clearly preoccupied with thoughts of her gentleman caller. As she closed the door, Alex heard her say, "Won't you sit down, Mr. Anderson? Why, yes . . . I suppose I could call you Waldo."

Alex could hardly believe she had escaped so easily. For the past two nights, Rhys had pressed her to stay with him, but to her chagrin, she hadn't been able to summon the bravery needed to tell Aberdeen she wouldn't be home.

Bless Waldo for his timely arrival, she thought. Now at least Deenie can't say I didn't warn her about my plans.

As she reached a point in the trail where there was a clear view of the lake, she recognized the spot where Bacconne had accosted her. How long ago that day seemed now. So many good things had happened to her since then that she seldom thought of the evil French Canadian, and she certainly harbored no fear of him. She had been up and down this path many times, and not once had she been frightened.

Her life, she reflected, had indeed improved since coming to the Falls. Her dream of working as a doctor was taking form at last. The women and children of the settlement had provided her with a slow but steady supply of ailments to treat, and just that very afternoon, she had seen her first male patient. One of the trappers who lived in the forest near Sabaskong had slashed his leg with an axe while chopping wood, and his partner had brought him to Alex. Of course, while she had worked to staunch the flow of blood, the other man had gone for Scotty, just as a precaution. As she cleaned and stitched the wound under Scotty's somewhat embarrassed observation, Alex had refused to permit herself any feeling of resentment. After all, the trappers had come to her first, and she realized that this was the only way she could prove herself once and for all. Apparently satisfied with the treatment she had given his injured friend, the second man had asked her advice about a troublesome bunion before they'd made their departure.

Scotty had assured her that her reputation as a physician had received a genuine boost, and that it might not take as long as she feared to overcome the remaining prejudices the local men had about a lady doctor.

"And I never fail to put in a good word for you myself," he'd said. "Not after all ye've done for Christy."

Alex had to admit that the sickly woman had made wonderful improvement lately, but she wasn't certain it was due so much to the herbs, rest, and rich diet she had prescribed as to the tender, loving care Scotty himself had lavished on her. But, whatever the cause, it was heartening to see Christiana growing stronger and happier every day.

With an inward smile, Alex considered her own state of happiness. How much of it did she also owe to a man? And not just to any man, but to Rhys Morgan, whom she had once thought an irritating, ill-mannered oaf. Finding herself more than a little anxious to see him, she began walking faster. The prospect of an entire night with Rhys made her feel light enough to float—right through the feathery pines to the glowing pastel sky beyond.

Rhys met her on the path a dozen yards later, clasping her in his arms to give her a warm kiss of welcome before even speaking a word.

"Alex," he said, finally lifting his head, "can you go on to the lagoon and wait for me there? Pierre needs help with the milking. I won't be long, I promise."

"That's fine," she said, "but please hurry—I have so many interesting things to tell you."

He kissed her again. "I'll be there as soon as I can."

Alex made her way through the sparse woods to the edge of the lagoon, whose waters were bathed in gold from the last, long rays of the setting sun. She seated herself on a small boulder hidden by the shadows and began the vigil that was quickly becoming a nightly ritual.

She didn't have to wait long before the beaver family made its appearance, one by one. They were so earnestly industrious, their mannerisms so charming, that they had endeared themselves to her. They acted exactly like a human family, the father protective, the mother scolding when her kits misbehaved. Alex and Rhys had shared much laughter over their antics.

For all his grace in the water, the male beaver was clumsy moving about on land. Alex watched as he took his time selecting just the right sapling to gnaw, waddling slowly away from the lake's edge. Following not far behind was his mate, and two of the young ones, frolicking about with total disregard for their mother's reprimands. They clambered up onto the bank hissing at each other in mock menace, and the female tried to soothe them with a rhythmic sound that was something between a sigh and a murmur. Alex had heard the strangely comforting noise every evening, thinking it quite beautiful as it drifted softly on the quiet air.

A slight movement from the rapidly darkening lake caught her eye, and Alex turned, half-expecting to glimpse a moose or some other elusive woodland animal. Instead, she saw a canoe moving over the still water, drifting into the lagoon with silent, ominous purpose. Positioned in the prow of the birchbark craft was the immobile figure of a young Indian man dressed only in a leather breechclout. In his hands he held a bow, fitted with an arrow and drawn back tautly. An extra arrow was clamped between his strong, white teeth in readiness for a second shot. Behind him, kneeling on the bottom of the canoe to paddle, was another brave. As he dipped the oar into the water, it made no more noise than a feather falling onto the surface.

Alex's mouth went dry with fear. Suddenly she knew—they were hunting the beavers! Knowing when the animals would come out to feed, they had set their canoe adrift, silently guiding it into the lagoon, downwind of the unsuspecting animals. Before any sort of alarm could be given, the hunter could shoot and kill the two adults, leaving the rest to flee in panic. The destruction of the family and the possible danger to the kits left on their own would never occur to such men. They would be well pleased to acquire two prime pelts, as well as meat for their cooking pots.

Alex wished for Rhys, all the while realizing that if anyone was going to save the beavers, it would have to be her. Certain there was a wilderness protocol she would be breaking, she nevertheless sprang to her feet and began yelling.

318

"Stop!" she shouted. "Don't you dare kill those beavers!"

Everything seemed to happen at once. The male beaver wasted no time diving back into the lagoon, issuing a strident warning by slapping the water with his broad, flat tail. Shrilly chattering, the female shepherded the young ones to safety, and, in an instant, every dark head had disappeared beneath the surface.

The hunter grunted out several harsh words, and the paddler stroked furiously, nosing the canoe toward the bank where Alexandria stood, holding her ground for lack of any better idea of what to do. The nearly naked man leaped ashore, flinging his bow and arrow angrily into the canoe behind him.

He approached Alex, still grumbling Indian words that had no meaning for her other than their obviously threatening tone. Finding it difficult not to break and run, Alex stayed still, glaring unflinchingly at the man. The moment he paused for breath, she added her voice to the argument.

"I couldn't very well just stand by and let you murder those innocent animals, could I? They . . . they're like friends to me — something you probably could never understand."

His reply was somewhat less vehement, and Alex knew he didn't speak any English at all. Somehow, that made her braver.

"Don't you have better things to do than skulk about half-dressed, preying on helpless creatures?" Forgetting her fright, she shook an indignant finger in his astonished face. "You should be ashamed of yourself!"

Unbelievably, the smallest flicker of a smile came and went from his lips. He turned to the other brave, motioning for him to come closer as another series of short, harsh words rumbled forth.

The huntsman looked back at Alex, his black eyes frankly appraising. He reached for a strand of her hair, but Alex slapped his hand.

"Don't touch me," she warned, backing away.

"Alex!" Rhys burst through the trees, stopping short as he saw the unexpected tableau. "Jesus Christ, what have you done now?"

Alex and the Indian both began talking at once.

"They were going to kill the beavers," she explained, stung that Rhys would immediately surmise she had been the one at fault. "I couldn't just let them do it, could I?"

"Oh, hell, no," he replied, sounding weary. "You couldn't have managed anything that simple."

The brave repeated his query, and, impatiently, Rhys answered in the same language.

"You think I should have let them do it?" Alex nearly shrieked. "My God, how could you?"

"Alex, this is the chief's son. When he is still-hunting beavers, it isn't up to you or me to interfere."

"And why not? You said yourself you wouldn't kill one. Why then would you allow him to?"

"This is a different situation."

"How?"

"At least the Indians use the meat for food."

"Oh, so that makes it acceptable?"

The brave, who had been watching their argument with a stoic amusement, now clamped a hand on Alex's shoulder and asked Rhys several short, terse questions. While Rhys paused to answer them, she shrugged away from the Indian's touch, making him laugh.

"What is he saying?" Alex asked. "What are you telling him?"

"He wants to know who you are," Rhys said. "Whether or not you have a husband."

"Why should he want to know that?"

"Probably so that he'll know whether or not anyone will try avenge your death when he drowns you in the lagoon."

Alex paled. "I hope you are making a jest, Rhys Morgan. Am I in danger?"

Rhys shifted his weight to the other foot, hands dropping to his hips in the old attitude of disgust that she hadn't seen in so long. "Hell, yes. What do you think? Hunting is a serious business to these men, and they don't take kindly to a . . . a squaw sticking her nose in where it doesn't belong."

The two Indians seemed to recognize the word *squaw,* for it elicited low-pitched laughter and raised eyebrows. Seeing their reaction, Alex fell silent and permitted Rhys to reason with them as best he could in the awkward language. After what seemed an interminable length of time, they finally seemed to reach some sort of agreement. The chief's son stepped close to Alex, holding his hands up to her hair as though warming them at a fire. He said a few words to Rhys, then nodded at Alex.

"He says to tell Woman-with-Hair-of-Flame farewell," Rhys said reluctantly. "And, if the Grandfathers are willing, the two of you will meet again."

Alex gritted her teeth. "Tell him it will have to be

321

over my cold, dead body."

Rhys said something to the man, but Alex doubted if he had repeated her words as the Indian nearly smiled again. With a dignified nod of his head, he marched back to his canoe, followed by the other man. When they had gone, as silently as they came, Rhys turned an angry gaze on Alex.

"Someday, woman, you are going to get yourself into trouble and I'm not going to be around to get you out."

"Oh, so you think you came to my rescue once again, eh?"

"It would appear so."

"For your information, those men didn't scare me at all. I was in the process of speaking my mind when you came on the scene. Don't flatter yourself by thinking I needed you."

"It isn't safe to let you go out alone, Alexandria. You don't seem to realize that some silly incident like this could stir up more Indian trouble than we've seen around here in years."

"Oh, pshaw!" She started stalking away, sensing they were teetering on the brink of a monumental argument.

"Oh, pshaw?" he repeated, following her. "Is that your mature opinion on the matter?" He seized her arm and pulled her around to face him.

"We both know how little you value my opinion," she countered. "So just take your hands off me and let me go home."

"All right, I will." He released her arm abruptly. "But don't come running to me for help if the chief or his son demand some kind of retribution."

"Don't worry, I won't. In fact, from now on, I'll do my best never to come to you for anything."

As she hastened through the trees toward the path leading back to the Falls, Alex heard his last, shouted words.

"This isn't the end of the matter, Alexandria. You offended those men, and they're going to demand repayment. Mark my words!"

Too hurt and angry to be frightened by his warning, she merely pulled her coat more tightly about her and ran through the darkening autumn night toward home.

Alex heard from the Indians sooner than she expected, but their method of communication was nothing like what she had anticipated. The next evening, as she returned to her cabin from a visit to Annie and Tobias, who were sick with the croup, she found three spotted ponies tied to her front porch railing. All of them wore braided leather bridles, with the same decoration of beads and eagle feathers the chief's son had worn in his black hair.

Alex couldn't prevent a pleased smile. Instead of being angry with her, the huntsmen had sent a peace offering. She allowed herself a full minute to enjoy thoughts of the look on Rhys's face when he learned they had apologized.

Of course, she couldn't keep such a valuable gift. Horses were far too rare here in the wilderness. But she could feed and water them tonight, then figure out how to go about returning them in the morning.

Still smiling, she led the placid animals toward

John Hay's barn next door. Perhaps this would finally prove to Rhys Morgan that she was perfectly capable of taking care of herself—and without any help from him.

Chapter Sixteen

The following morning, as John Hay helped Alex lead the three ponies from his barn, Rhys came storming into view. Alex turned to face him with a determinedly bright smile.

"Rhys! You're just the person I needed to talk to . . ."

"When did these horses arrive?" he asked brusquely, not bothering with a polite greeting.

Alex flashed John Hay a startled look, and he smiled encouragingly.

"Last night," she replied. "Why?"

"Last night?" he echoed, obviously displeased.

"Yes. I found them tied to my porch railing. It would seem those Indians weren't as angry as you thought."

"No, they weren't angry at all," Rhys agreed. "In fact, it seems I've made one more colossal miscalculation about your ability to charm the male of the species."

Alex couldn't prevent a smile. "I'll have to return the horses, of course. That's what I wanted to talk to you about."

"Don't you think it's a little late to return them?"

"I couldn't very well have taken them back last night," she pointed out.

"No, but you could have left them tied outside. You could have refrained from feeding them."

"I wouldn't neglect an animal that way."

"You should have." He jerked his head toward the lake, and both Alex and John Hay looked in that direction.

Leaning against a pine tree near the dock was an Indian. He was so perfectly immobile that he might have been carved of wood.

"Isn't he the one who was with the chief's son at the lagoon?" Alex asked, startled.

"Yes." Rhys fixed her with a piercing gaze. "He's here as an emissary for Killing Sky, the chief's son."

"Oh?" Alex's tone was suddenly uncertain. She had the feeling there was something she didn't understand. "What do you mean?"

"Alex, what the hell did you think finding those horses tied to your porch meant?"

"That the men were ashamed of trying to kill the beavers, that they were offering some sort of . . . apology."

Rhys practically snorted. "Apology? Good God, Alex, you're unbelievable."

Her chin came up, thrusting her straight nose into the air. Hastily, John Hay took a step backward. He had been married long enough to recognize that particular gesture.

"Suppose you explain why it is you think I am so unbelievable," Alex suggested in an even voice.

"For one thing, Indians don't ordinarily apologize for doing something that is second nature to them. Those men were hunting, and they saw nothing wrong with it."

"Then what do the horses mean?"

"The fact that they were left on your doorstep means Killing Sky was making an offer for your hand. . . ."

Alex gasped. "What?"

"And the fact that you took them in and fed them means you accepted."

"No! No, there's a mistake." Alex whirled, her skirts flaring out around her. "Excuse me, there has been a mistake," she said, bearing down on the watching Indian. He straightened, looking from her to Rhys, who followed.

"He can't speak English," Rhys reminded her.

"Then you tell him there's a misunderstanding," she demanded fiercely. "Tell him I didn't know what the horses meant. Tell him I won't marry his . . . his friend."

Rhys crossed his arms over his chest. "Wait a minute, my dear Miss MacKenzie. I seem to recall that you recently vowed never to come to me for help again."

"You think this is amusing, don't you?" she cried.

Rhys's smile died. "No, actually I don't. This is the biggest mess you've landed in yet. I'll be interested in seeing how you extricate yourself without causing a major incident."

"Why should it cause any sort of incident? I'm not accepting the man's gift."

"That's the point. By caring for the ponies last night, you did accept it—now you're rejecting it. That will be a matter of shame to Sky. Besides, I don't think you understand just how much trouble he went to in getting those animals here. His father's band has moved in from the islands to their winter camp on the mainland . . . but the easiest way to get there is still by water. Can you imagine the difficulty in transporting three lively horses on a log raft?"

Alex glared at him for a few moments, at a loss as to how to respond. Finally, with a resigned sigh, she motioned for John Hay to lead the horses to the dock. The raft Rhys spoke of was tied to one of the pilings, and Alex pointed to it as, with an earnest expression, she faced the Indian.

"Is that how you brought the horses here?" she asked, carefully enunciating each word. The young brave stared at her, apparently without a hint of what she was asking.

"You will have to take them back," Alex said, her voice growing a bit louder. "I cannot marry your— Killing Sky."

He must have recognized his friend's Anglicized name, for the Indian looked at Rhys and muttered a few words.

"Did he understand me?" Alex asked.

Rhys shrugged. "This is your problem, Alex. I won't interfere."

"You are the most damnable man I know," she

328

ground out.

"Then we make a fine pair," Rhys returned, "because you are the most damnable woman I know."

John Hay grinned broadly.

"Stay out of this," Rhys warned, and Hay's smile grew even wider.

"If you refuse to be gentleman enough to help me," Alex said, "the only thing I can do is go with this brave when he returns the horses. Perhaps there is someone in the tribe who will understand me."

"The only way you will go anywhere with him is if you incapacitate me first."

"A tempting offer," Alex murmured. She stepped close to the Indian and laid a hand on his forearm. He tensed, but did not move away.

Leaning close to look into his face, Alex spoke slowly and clearly. "I want to go to your camp with you. I must explain that a mistake has been made. We'll take the horses back . . ." She pantomimed leading the horses onto the raft and pointing out across the water, in the general direction she believed the winter camp to be. "I-go-with-you."

Rhys's hands clamped around her shoulders, and he easily set her aside. Before she could round on him in anger, Rhys began addressing the brave in his own language, and Alex fell silent.

The conversation continued for four or five minutes, then came to an abrupt halt when the Indian reached for the bridle on the first horse. One by one, he led the large creatures onto the raft, and Rhys helped him secure them. Then he turned back to Alex.

"I'll have to go on the raft with him—the horses are too much for one man to handle."

"Then how did he get them here in the first place?"

"Two other men were with him on the raft, and a third followed in a canoe. They expected you to keep the horses, so the others returned to camp last night."

"But how will you get back here?"

"You're going to follow us in a canoe."

"I don't know anything about paddling a canoe," she protested.

"Well, you'll never learn any younger."

"John, will you go with me?" Alex asked, turning toward the big blacksmith.

The man warded her off with both hands, a horrified expression on his face.

"Going voluntarily into an Indian camp is something John Hay will never do," Rhys informed her. "Have you forgotten he was once tortured?"

"Oh, John, I'm so sorry," Alex exclaimed. "No, of course you wouldn't want to go."

"Maybe you could ask another of the men from the settlement," Rhys grudgingly suggested.

"No, I'll just have to do it," she said with sudden conviction. "I seem to have brought this on myself, so I might as well get it settled without involving anyone else."

"You're certain?"

"I am," Alex affirmed.

"Whatever you say, then."

"But you'll be there, won't you?"

"As your translator," Rhys answered. "You'll have

to come up with your own reasons for rejecting Killing Sky — something that will allow him to save face. If you simply march in there and inform him you aren't the least interested in marrying him, we may both end up as food for the gulls. Think about that as you're paddling your canoe."

He exchanged a few more words with the waiting brave, then took Alex's arm. "Come on, we've got to get some supplies and warm clothes. This may take more than a couple of hours."

"Rhys . . . ?"

He paused. "What?"

"Thank you for helping me — again."

He nodded. "But remember, once we get the ponies out to the islands, I'm simply an interpreter. And you, sweetheart, are on your own."

Throughout the long journey from Montreal and even during the more strenuous one from Fort Kaministiquia, Alex realized she hadn't fully appreciated the canoemen. They were so skilled at their job that they made it look easy, but Alex knew she would never again take them for granted. Not now that she had spent a long morning paddling her way across the bay, and through a maze of islands. Her back and shoulders were stiff and aching, her joints burning with pain. She had long since shed her heavy coat and opened the throat of her woolen gown; still perspiration beaded her forehead.

She had learned the essentials of canoeing the hard way — by trial and error. As Rhys and the Indian poled the heavily laden raft through the shallower water, then oared it through deeper passages, she had managed to follow closely enough to keep them in sight at all times. Her canoe wandered crazily at first, with her paddling furiously to right its wayward patterns. Finally, as she tired, she slowed her pace and tried to conserve some energy—she had no idea how far they had to go—and simply concentrated on keeping the raft in sight.

Most of the islands looked so much alike that Alex began to understand how easy it would be to get hopelessly lost. At that point she started seeking out landmarks to remember, in the event she did find herself separated from the others. She listed these landmarks softly:

"Dead pine with eagle's nest, trapper's shack, rock shaped like a buffalo . . ."

Not only did she commit them to memory, but by doing so, she also took her mind off the task at hand, and when she relaxed, the paddling became easier.

Fortunately, they reached their destination at about the same time Alexandria decided she could not go on. When she saw the raft being guided into a small natural harbor and the ponies being untied and taken ashore, she summoned the last of her pride, and, happily, it was sufficient to enable her to beach the canoe and step out. She hid her blistered hands behind her back and conjured up an insouciant smile, all too aware of her strained arm muscles and shaking legs. How nice it would have been at that moment to lean on Rhys, meekly putting herself into his protective care. Straightening her shoulders, she stepped past him and started along the narrow path that led to the winter camp.

When the various members of the Chippewa band noticed their arrival, they gathered about, curious and friendly. As the ponies were walked into the village, there was a surprised murmur, then one or two derisive laughs. Alex swallowed deeply. Perhaps she hadn't really comprehended the interpretation that would be put upon her returning Killing Sky's gift. How could she avoid humiliating the man in front of his people?

"Morgan?" The name was spoken in strongly accented tones by a man who stepped from one of the dome-shaped birchbark wigwams. He was elderly, and as plump and wrinkled as a prune. Wearing buckskins and wrapped in a blanket, he raised one hand in greeting, his inquisitive gaze drifting immediately to Alex.

"Alex, this is Chief Talking Elk," Rhys said. She nodded and smiled, and solemnly the chief returned her greeting. He then addressed several remarks to Rhys, who answered somewhat warily. When the old man turned away to speak to the brave who had accompanied them, Alex whispered, "What was he saying?"

"He's not pleased that you have chosen to bring back his son's gift. He's sending for Killing Sky now."

Alex grew frantic, discarding one excuse after another. Somehow, she didn't think these Indians would understand a woman's desire to be independent and live alone. As a chief's son, Killing Sky probably had expected her to be flattered, grateful to accept his offer of matrimony. Good Lord, what was she going to do?

The time for a decision was rapidly at hand, for Killing Sky seemed to materialize out of nowhere, looking tall and menacing. And not at all happy to see the three spotted ponies. His face was reproachful as he turned to Alex and muttered a stream of words that were totally unintelligible to her.

"He wants to know if his ponies were too inferior to please you," Rhys interpreted.

"Oh, no . . . they're beautiful," she cried. Then realizing the man couldn't understand her, she urged Rhys to relay the message. "Tell him the horses are beautiful, but that I cannot accept them."

Killing Sky's answer was short and harsh, and she knew he was asking why. She drew a deep breath and plunged into what her grandfather had always insisted was the best policy — the truth.

"Tell him that I am not interested in being married — not to him, or to anyone else." At Rhys's sardonic look, she hurried on. "Explain that I am a doctor, and as such, I really cannot have a personal life. Tell him I am flattered by his offer, but that I must regretfully decline." She cast another glance at Killing Sky's glowering face and added, "Emphasize the regretful part, Rhys."

The Indians who had gathered around hung on every word as Rhys spoke to Killing Sky. Smiling faces sobered, then brightened again, leaving Alex in an agony of curiosity. The Indian asked another question, and Rhys replied, his gravelly voice sounding almost hoarse as he uttered the strange Chippewa dialect.

Killing Sky studied Alex for a long moment, then shook his head and clearly issued an ultimatum. Rhys heaved an exasperated sigh, running a hand through his hair in an agitated manner.

Alex felt a chill creeping up her spine. Something had gone wrong. The two men had lost their polite air, and now a certain antagonism was evident.

"What is it?" she asked anxiously, tugging at Rhys's sleeve. "What is he saying?"

Ignoring her, Rhys posed another question, and the Indian's answer was swift.

"Oh, hell." Rhys started unlacing his shirt. "Go wait over there with those women, Alex. Hopefully, this won't take long."

"What is going on?" she cried. "I demand to know."

"I'm going to wrestle the damned fool for you." Rhys pulled his shirt off over his head. "Killing Sky never was one to listen to reason."

"You're going to do what?"

Rhys took her arm and led her toward a knot of giggling women. "We're going to have a wrestling match."

"But why? Was he angry about what I said?"

"For God's sake, Alex, you don't think I could really have used that lame excuse of yours, do you? I had to give him a reason he would understand."

"And just exactly what was that reason?" she inquired, her dry tone indicating that she didn't believe his method had been any more satisfactory than hers.

"You may not like to hear this, but I told Sky you couldn't marry him because you were already my woman. I—"

"You told him what?"

"Well, I expected it to work a little better than it did. But it seems he is so enchanted by your red hair, he doesn't mind the fact that you're soiled goods."

"Soiled goods?" she repeated, a storm building in her gray eyes. "That is about the most insulting thing you've said to me yet."

"Look, Alex, he's waiting. Now, either stay here and pray like hell I beat the man, or reconcile yourself to being his squaw. Which will it be?"

She raised huge eyes to his. "What do you mean . . . pray you can beat him?"

"Exactly that. When two Chippewa braves desire the same woman, they hold a wrestling match and the woman goes to the winner."

"No matter what?" she whispered.

"No matter what."

Alex groaned. "I'm praying," she said.

Killing Sky had stripped down to his breechclout and now, poised and ready for the match to begin, looked tough and dangerous. Alex, refusing to believe she could soon belong to a stranger, fastened her attention on Rhys.

Bare-chested, his lean hips encased in clinging buckskin, he was a splendid physical specimen, she had to admit . . . but could he best the bulkier man? He stood half a head taller than his opponent, but Killing Sky easily outweighed him by thirty pounds.

Though Alex's mouth was dry with fear, she refused to let herself even consider the possibility that Rhys would lose the match. Naturally, if he was victorious, he would be more arrogant and self-satisfied than usual, but dealing with that situation would be the lesser of two evils.

The match began suddenly, with no prelude. Killing Sky made a lunge for Rhys, and they grappled wildly for a few moments, occasionally falling to their knees but staggering upward again like two woodland stags locked in mortal combat. The other Indians were delighted at the unexpected entertainment, and they cheered and called out advice.

Alex gasped as Rhys went sprawling, but before Killing Sky could fling himself upon him, Rhys was up, charging like a crazed bull. Head lowered, he crashed into the shorter man's belly, knocking him backward onto the thin, sandy soil. Killing Sky grunted in pain as his hip struck a rock half-buried in the ground. Rhys halted his attack while his adversary got to his feet, and Alex silently cursed his ridiculous code of ethics. But then, she reminded herself, it wasn't his future at stake. She felt a pang of remorse as her conscience scolded her—Rhys hadn't needed to get involved in this at all, and she'd better damned well be thankful he had!

Killing Sky surged to his feet, but as he came up, he hooked an arm beneath Rhys's knee and jerked. Off balance, Rhys landed on his back, with the Indian suddenly straddling his chest.

Alex loudly protested the brave's lack of scruples, and the onlookers nearest her smiled and nodded, pleased by her interest in the outcome of the struggle.

Rhys paused long enough to cast her a reproving look and, in the split second that Killing Sky also glanced her way, twisted to one side, spilling the brave onto the ground. For a moment, as they scrabbled about in the sand, he had the upper hand, but then Killing Sky seemed to gather himself, and he began muttering a slow, monotonous chant.

Rhys knew the chant was a ploy Indians sometimes used to unnerve an opponent, and for an instant, he feared it would work. As muscle strained against muscle, it had become apparent that neither man was superior to the other in physical strength; therefore, the end of the match might be influenced by mental stamina. Rather than let himself be bested by Killing Sky's wiliness, Rhys forced his own mind to conjure up images that would inspire him to greater energy.

The first of these was a picture of Alex being led away to Killing Sky's lodge. This was rapidly followed by a kaleidoscope of scenes too painful to contemplate: the man's burnished hand upon her paler flesh, his face bending to hers . . . her gown lying crumpled and discarded next to Killing Sky's sleeping mat.

Rage burned through Rhys's veins, spreading into his brain with deadly efficiency. An outraged cry burst from his lips as he lifted the Indian bodily and flung him aside. Then, moving with the

338

speed and accuracy of a cougar, he pounced upon the astonished brave and in a matter of seconds, tossed him facedown in the sand, one brawny arm twisted cruelly behind his back.

Though disappointment showed briefly on his features, Talking Elk signaled the end of the wrestling match, reluctantly recognizing Rhys as the victor. The old chief beckoned to Alex and, when she approached, placed her hand on Rhys's arm and muttered an invocation that was obviously meant to bind the two of them together.

"What did he say?" she whispered, but Rhys ignored her, putting out a hand to help the defeated foe to his feet. Killing Sky took Rhys's hand willingly enough, and as the two faced each other, they grasped forearms in a gesture of goodwill. The Indian, his ruddy skin gleaming with sweat, managed a smile for Alex.

When he spoke, Rhys calmly translated his words. "He says he is very regretful to have lost you to me, and that, if the day should ever come when you . . . tire of my attentions, he would be grateful if you seek him out."

"Thank you," Alex said, speaking directly to the brave.

Rhys repeated Killing Sky's reply with less enthusiasm. "He wants you to know that he considers your hair more beautiful than even the most fiery sunset."

Alex smiled gently. Savage or not, the man was a graceful loser. "There is something I would like to know about him," she told Rhys, her cheeks tinged with faint color. "Ask him how he came to have such an unusual name."

"There was a tornadic storm the night he was born," Rhys said shortly. "It tore hell out of the surrounding forest, but didn't touch the camp. The elders considered it an omen."

"Why didn't you let him answer my question?" she asked, surprised at his brusque tone.

Rhys glared at her, his chest still heaving from the exertion of battle. "Look, Alex, are you sorry I won?"

"Lord, no!"

"Then why are we standing here chitchatting with the man, for God's sake?"

"I—I don't know. I assumed it was protocol or something."

"The only protocol you need be concerned with now is obeying me. These Indians will expect to see you jump when I say 'jump,' so just be sure you do it."

Alex's eyes grew wide with disbelief, then clouded with anger.

"Why are you treating me this way?"

Talking Elk addressed Rhys, then turned aside to add a comment to his son, who laughed in agreement.

Alex raised a finely arched eyebrow, but before she could ask, Rhys offered a translation. "First, the chief invited me to sit by the fire and smoke the pipe of peace with him. And then he told his son that perhaps it was the Grandfathers' intervention that caused him to lose the match. The red-headed woman, so he says, is too vocal and too disobedient to make a good wife."

"I'd like to give him a piece of my mind," she snapped.

"Fortunately, that won't be necessary." Rhys's smile was wry. "Now, you are to wait with Sky's mother and grandmother while I sit with the men. Try to behave yourself, won't you?"

Without another word, Rhys joined the chief and his son as they strode toward the central wigwam. A Chippewa woman touched Alex's shoulder timidly, then inclined her head to indicate she should follow her to another, smaller dwelling.

The inside of the wigwam was warmed by a central fire, which was surrounded by woven mats. The woman and her mother took their places only after Alex had seated herself on one of the mats. They resumed their task of stitching fur-lined moccasins, conversing in quiet murmurs interspersed with occasional soft laughter.

Presently, unable to talk with the women and having no work to occupy her hands, Alex grew drowsy. She stretched out on the mat and, turning her face away from the others, drifted into a deep sleep.

A tentative touch on her hair and soft, scolding words woke her an hour later. Startled, she sat up and gazed about. There, beside her on the mat, sat a small girl whose round brown eyes held a mischievous glint as she listened to reprimands from her elders. The resemblance was so marked that Alex realized the child must be Killing Sky's youngest sister. The women murmured and shrugged apologetically.

"Please don't worry," Alex said, even though she

could only hope her tone of voice would convey the meaning of her statement. "She didn't disturb me at all."

The little girl smiled broadly and stroked a none-too-clean hand along the sleeve of Alex's gown, as though fascinated by the soft wool. She uttered a few words, and Alex nodded and smiled.

"Yes, it's pretty, isn't it? But look at you—you're very pretty, also."

And, indeed, she was beautiful. Huge eyes dominated an oval face the color of maple sugar, and a charming smile revealed rows of small, very white teeth. Gleaming black hair had been braided into two long, thin plaits that framed her face and hung to her waist. Dressed in a fringed doeskin dress with matching moccasins, she was a miniature copy of her mother and grandmother. The only flaw in her appearance was an angry-looking boil on one cheek. Alex frowned and leaned closer to inspect it.

"I'll wager this hurts you a great deal doesn't it?"

The little girl stiffened, expecting pain, but Alex patted her shoulder reassuringly. "I won't hurt you, honey. I only wish I had brought my medical bag. I could have lanced that and put some salve on it."

The child bent her head to reveal a second boil at the nape of her neck, just into the hairline, and then pointed out another on her upper arm, hidden by the fringe of her dress. Alex cried out in frustration.

"I know I could help you if only I had that blasted satchel. I usually take it wherever I go. Why did Rhys have to be in such a hurry this morning?"

At the thought of Rhys, she wondered where he was and what he was doing. She got to her feet and walked to the door of the wigwam, but the Indian women shook their heads, plainly telling her she was not to leave their company.

The little girl, sensing her distress, began rummaging in one corner of the lodge, through a tidy stack of cooking utensils and supplies. From a basket she took a doll, made of leather and dressed in buckskin, and proudly showed it to Alex. Joining the child on the mat once more, Alex allowed herself to be entertained. She watched as the doll was undressed, her clothes changed and her hair braided. Thinking of Annie and her dolls, Lady Gwendolyn and Madame Dragonflower, Alex wished Claire's daughter could be there to play with the Indian child. Even though they couldn't communicate with words, she suspected there was a special language through which children made themselves understood with no difficulty.

Before much longer, the two women laid aside their handiwork and began preparing the evening meal. Tamping down a growing anger at Rhys for abandoning her, Alex observed their quiet, efficient movements, soon finding herself becoming more and more interested in their strange, nomadic way of life. When the chief, his son, and Rhys appeared for the meal, she was calm enough to avoid a scene, merely meeting Rhys's questioning eyes and glancing away, as if completely indifferent.

The food was odd but tasty, and Alex found she was nearly famished. She ate corn cakes and fish stew, declining some of the more mysterious dishes.

When the men had eaten their fill, the chief spoke to Rhys, indicating Alex with a brief nod of his head. All eyes were suddenly upon her as Rhys translated his words.

"We'll spend the night, Alex, and go back to the Falls in the morning."

"But—"

"Come with me now. A special place has been prepared for us to sleep."

"You're mistaken if you think I intend to sleep with you tonight," she said, smiling falsely as she tried to disguise the waspishness of her statement.

"Do try to be obedient, Alex," he said wearily. "They expect it of you."

"Expect it?"

"You are my woman, remember. My property. You will do as I say."

Seeing the militant set of her chin, he merely reached out and grasped her arm, pulling her along with him as he followed the chief out of the wigwam. Moments later, they paused at another such birchbark structure and Rhys thrust her inside.

"This is where you will sleep," he said firmly.

"I'm tired of being told what to do," she replied tartly.

"Well, you'd better put up with it a while longer," he informed her. "I could still change my mind and relinquish you to Killing Sky, you know."

"Morgan?" The old chief's heavily accented voice broke into their argument. The guttural-sounding sentences he uttered next caused Rhys to smile, then shake his head in denial. Out of the corner of his mouth, he said, "Talking Elk thinks you are sorely in need of discipline, Alex. He can't believe I would relish sleeping in your lodge."

"And just what does he suggest you do?"

"He's offered me the company of his eldest daughter." Rhys turned to study her reaction. "It's a Chippewa custom of hospitality."

Alex seethed. "Hospitality? It's barbarian! Of course, I don't suppose you would think so. Are you going to take him up on his offer?"

"That depends on you." His face was grim, his eyes intent.

"Why should it depend on me? It's a matter of small concern to me."

"Do you mean that?"

Her gray eyes flashed. "I do."

Turning his back to her, Rhys spoke to the chief, who began to beam. He clapped his hands in delight, shouting for his daughter. When she appeared, her face shyly downcast, Alex felt her heart stumble. The girl was strikingly lovely, slender and delicate, with a curtain of black hair that reached to her waist. She raised adoring ebony eyes to caress Rhys's face, and Alex knew this was not the first time the two had met. Jealousy raged through her, making her tremble with the urge to fling herself into Rhys's arms and make her apologies for being such a shrew. He had brought her here to extricate her from a touchy situation, and she had done nothing but complain. Shame finally loosened her tongue, but just as she was about to ask for a second chance, Rhys slipped an arm about the Indian maiden's shoulders and, with a few words to

345

her father, led her away. Stunned, Alex stared as they disappeared into a wigwam only a few yards distant. Talking Elk met her incredulous expression with a triumphant smile, shaking a finger at her in gleeful reproach as if reminding her that this was all her fault. No doubt he thought she had learned a well-deserved lesson.

Eyes filling with tears of misery, Alex stepped inside the birchbark hut and covered the doorway with a blanket of skins. She felt so alone, with no one to comfort her—not Nasturtium, not Aberdeen—no one! Not one soul knew or cared how she felt at this moment, and it surely must be one of the worst moments of her life.

She seized a folded blanket and dropped onto a sleeping mat. What made the whole thing nearly intolerable was that she had brought it on herself. She had goaded Rhys, thrown his chivalrous gesture right back into his face.

Alex could not have guessed the pain she would feel at the thought of Rhys Morgan in the other woman's arms, sharing her sleeping mat. Jealousy tore at her, filling her mind with unbearable images. Why had she thought he cared for her? Why had she not realized how much she cared for him?

When Rhys flung open the door of the wigwam the next morning, he was stricken with remorse. Alex, startled from sleep by his abrupt appearance, sat up and gazed at him like a frightened doe. He knew she must have spent a restless night. Her russet hair swirled about her shoulders, snarled as if she had tossed and turned, and her wide eyes were heavily shadowed.

Her vulnerable state caused him to speak more gently than he had intended. "The women have breakfast for you, Alex . . . and then it's time to go."

She nodded. "I'll only be a moment." Obedience came more easily to her after the long, lonely night she had just spent.

"Alex, about last night . . . ."

"Wait, Rhys. You don't owe me any explanations. I . . . I understand."

Did she? he wondered. He reconsidered the wisdom of telling her the truth, and found he was hesitant to destroy her present acquiescent mood. He made a hasty decision to wait, at least until they were gone from the Indian village.

Thirty minutes later, they walked through the cluster of wigwams, saying goodbye to Talking Elk and his band. Alex, still numbed by Rhys's easy unfaithfulness, was glad when Killing Sky's youngest sister ran up to her, taking her hand and providing a much-needed distraction. Several other children followed, obviously in awe of the little girl's intimate acquaintance with the stranger. Alex couldn't help but notice that most of them had one or more boils on elbows, knees or faces. She busied her mind trying to determine what dietary deficiency might have caused such an outbreak of the painful affliction. Perhaps in her medical books back home . . .

"Give me your hand, Alex." Rhys's deep voice sounded close in her ear as he attempted to assist her into the canoe for the return to Sabaskong Falls. "What's this?"

Feeling an unaccustomed roughness on her palm, he turned her hand over and saw the blisters she had earned the day before.

"Why didn't you tell me you were hurt?" he asked softly.

"It was nothing," she replied, very aware of the warmth of his fingers as they cradled her hand. "I'll treat them when we get home."

For once, he didn't dispute her use of the word home. It seemed natural to hear her speak of the Falls that way. As he shoved the canoe out into the water and leaped into it, Rhys pondered the oddities of fate that now made him accept the fact that Alex had come to the wilderness to stay. As he took up the paddle, he experienced a curious light-heartedness.

"You know, Alexandria MacKenzie," he said, his eyes a brilliant forest green, "now that you are officially my woman, I think we are going to have to discuss some drastic changes in our association."

Chapter Seventeen

Alexandria wielded a cloth listlessly, dusting the items on the bookshelves without really seeing them. In the two weeks since she and Rhys had returned from the Indian camp, it seemed she had done little else but clean her office and reorganize her medical equipment and supplies. Somehow, her dream of being a practicing physician was not materializing in exactly the way she had planned.

With the exception of a splinter she had removed from Gideon Marsh's hand and the elixir she had prescribed for Birdie's dyspepsia, Alex had done almost no doctoring. It would appear that no one really needed her.

The Falls women had no time for complaints about their health. They were too busy storing potatoes and other vegetables in their dug-out cellars in preparation for the onset of winter, or curing and salting down the fish and game brought in by the hunters. The men who were not helping with the hunt had set about putting up the exterior of the new community building, and were working long hours each day the weather permitted. Everyone had a job to do and was determined to get it done before the heavy snows drove them indoors. Even the children were kept occupied, helping their mothers in the mornings and attending school in the afternoons. Until the new building was completed, they had to crowd into Cordelia's cabin for their lessons.

One of the major changes taking place concerned Aberdeen. She was spending more and more time with Waldo, inviting him to supper nearly every evening, and sometimes going out for walks with him. Surprisingly, the trapper had diligently kept up his newly acquired cleanliness, and Alex hadn't seen him within ten yards of a plug of tobacco since Aberdeen had issued her ultimatum against it. Although she was amazed at the direction the relationship between the crusty Scotswoman and Waldo Anderson had taken, Alex could only wish them the best. After all, Aberdeen had left Montreal with the idea of finding a decent man to marry, so Alex had to hope the current situation led to something permanent. For herself, she tried to subdue the occasional pangs of envy she experienced, regretting that things had not worked out half so well with her and Rhys.

She could never deny the hurt she had suffered when Rhys spent the night with the daughter of the old Indian chief, but she had not considered it the end of whatever feelings they shared. She had lectured herself sternly, prepared to forgive him, knowing she really had no choice. This was the wilderness, and certain arrangements surely existed between the Indian women and the men who lived here. Logic told her that Rhys must have been with the native women from time to time, as would any man of normal appetites. For all she knew, he may even have had an Indian wife in the past. It was not her place to offer a judgment on the morality of the situation, for it was born of the unique way of life in Upper Canada.

And, of course, there was the matter of the cursed male vanity. She realized that her rebellious attitude toward Rhys was as demeaning as her rejection of Killing Sky's marriage proposal. Damn her hotheaded independence! She had really left him no choice but to turn away from her to save face. Had she only swallowed a bit of pride, he would have been with her that night and there wouldn't be this coldness between them now.

For a few moments, as they were leaving the Chippewa village, she had thought Rhys meant to make his apologies, to right the wrong he had committed—and, possibly, bring up the advantages of marriage to him. But then a sudden, dismal rain had sprung up, and all their energies had been devoted to getting back to Sabaskong Falls as rapidly as they could. They'd been greeted at the dock by those curious enough to brave the weather, and as soon as Rhys had recounted the tale of his struggle with Killing Sky, Aberdeen had hurried Alex away to change clothes and eat a hot meal. In the days since, she had seen Rhys several times, but never alone. If he came to visit in the evening, Waldo and Aberdeen were there. If she happened by the building site, at least half a dozen men would stop work, lean on their axe handles, and watch with open interest. Rhys's eyes followed her, but their message was so enigmatic she couldn't interpret it. That he came by her cabin from time to time made her think he was not yet thoroughly disgusted with her, but the fact that he made no effort to get her alone, or into his bed, confused and worried her. With a heavy heart, she sensed the trip to the winter camp had proven to Rhys once and for all that she wasn't worth his trouble.

Alex sighed as she gazed at the bare spot on the top of her walnut desk. Ordinarily, when she was in her office, Nasturtium was curled up there asleep. But lately even the cat had deserted her. As soon as she'd had her morning bowl of milk, Nasturtium had gone to the front door, meowing plaintively until Alex had finally let her out. Her good humor evidenced by the cocky tilt of her striped tail, Nasturtium had headed straight for Joe Patterson's cabin, and a short while later, Alex had seen her pet in the company of the Pattersons' yellow tom, happily scavenging through the woodpile for mice.

A knock sounded at the door of her office, and Alex, pleased by the diversion from self-pity, called out, "Come in."

Scotty MacPherson ducked through the door, a worried look on his face. "Am I disturbing you, Alex? I've a need to speak to ye. . . ."

"Of course you're not a disturbance. I was only dusting." Alex tossed the cloth aside and smiled. "Here, pull up a chair. What can I do for you?"

"It's Christiana," he said, a frown marring his forehead.

"Is she coughing again? I thought she was so much better. . . ."

"It isn't the cough, Alex. Nay, 'tis something else entirely this time."

"Scotty, tell me what's wrong."

The man studied the freckled hands lying on his knees for a long moment before raising troubled eyes to Alex's. "I think Christy is . . . with child. I'm almost certain there is to be a bairn."

Alex felt the blood drain from her face as she sank into the other chair. "My God," she whispered. "A baby? Oh Lord, Scotty . . . what was I thinking of?"

"You?" he said with a bitter laugh. "I canna blame this on ye. I'm afraid the fault can only lie with me, fool that I am."

"No, don't you see? All the other women in this settlement are taking precautions to prevent childbirth. But I overlooked Christy because she was so ill. Scotty, I should have realized . . . I should have spoken to her."

"It's not your fault, Alex. We could have come to ye for advice. It's just that . . . well, things happened very quickly. Christiana was so sick at first, and then, when she got better, and we knew we wanted to be married, we didn't see any need in waiting. The preacher won't make an appearance until next spring most likely, and we simply couldn't deny our need to be together." He buried his face in his hands. "Damn me for a fool! I'm no simpleton—I knew what could happen."

Alex patted his shoulder sympathetically. "Perhaps you're mistaken, Scotty. It's possible, you know."

"I wish it were, but Christy has been sick every morning for the past two weeks. She can't eat a bite until afternoon, and then she feels fine."

"I see." Alex's hand dropped to her lap. "In that case, there doesn't seem to be much doubt, does there?"

Scotty shook his head. "What are we going to do? She can't survive having a baby. Her health is too delicate, Alex. The saints help me, I should be horsewhipped for allowing such a thing to happen. Of all God's creatures, man is surely the most un-thinking!"

"You mustn't be so harsh with yourself, Scotty. I know Christiana doesn't feel that way."

"No, she's delirious with happiness—that's why I came to see you alone."

"We can't make any decisions without consulting Christy," Alex pointed out.

"There's no decision to be made, really. We can't undo what's already been done. There'll be a baby whether we want it or not."

"Now, you know you'd welcome a child, Scotty."

"Under ordinary circumstances, of course I

would. But not at the risk of Christy's life. Alex, I can't bear the thought of her being in danger. If she comes to harm because of me—"

"I know it's risky, but maybe Christy can come through this without too much difficulty. With our help, of course. We'll have to watch over her every moment, make certain she gets her rest and follows a proper diet. Look at the way she has improved just since arriving at the Falls."

"Yes, I canna deny that. But a baby. . . ."

"We'll have to start thinking in a positive fashion. Right away, Scotty. First, I'd like to examine Christy. Even though it's too soon to know for sure about the baby, at least I can rule out a few other possibilities and can check on her general state of health."

"I'll go get her now," he said eagerly. At the door he paused. "Promise that you'll help me watch over her, Alex."

Alex swallowed around the lump in her throat. "I promise, Scotty. Between us, we're going to take very good care of Christiana."

Forty-five minutes later, that determined confidence was wavering badly. Alex had examined Christy, finding that every sign seemed to confirm her worst suspicion. Cheerfully, she had outlined a regime of light exercise and plenty of sleep, cautioning Christy about the need to eat healthfully. But the moment she had seen the relieved couple to the door, she had sat down at her desk and laid her head on her arms.

Dear Lord, how could she have failed so miserably in her capacity as a doctor? Why hadn't she been perceptive enough to foresee the likelihood of such a thing happening? Of all the brides in the settlement, Christiana was the least able to withstand the rigors of childbirth, and her welfare should have been foremost in Alex's mind. The obvious truth of the matter was, by the time they had gotten to Lake of the Woods, Alex had been too concerned with the details of her own life to spare much thought for anyone else. She'd been so caught up in proving she could be a doctor that somehow she had lost sight of the one precept every good physician lived by: the patient's welfare was the most important thing.

Alex raised her head and glanced about at the neatly appointed office. Was she here under false pretenses? Did she actually have the proficiency to practice medicine? Lately, she had not been of much use to anyone.

Her gaze dropped to the leather-bound medical book she had been dusting earlier. A memory of the hours she had spent poring over such books with her grandfather sprang into her mind, and she wondered what he would say if he were with her. Without doubt, he'd be displeased by her carelessness, but it was his way to temper criticism with praise. Something told her that he'd urge her to admit her error, do what she could to correct it, then move on to the next project and make sure she did a better job on it.

A smile trembled on her lips as she idly turned pages of the book. Just the thought of her grandfather bolstered her spirits and gave her the determination to renew her efforts to be the kind of doctor he was.

Carbuncle . . . the word nearly jumped off the page at her. Instantly, she remembered Killing Sky's little sister and the painful boils that plagued her. Of course, the Indian children! By doing something to treat the outbreak of boils in the winter camp, she could rebuild her faith in herself and, more importantly, do something to assist someone who truly needed her help.

Knowing that it would not be much longer before the lake froze over, Alex began making plans to leave for Talking Elk's village the following morning. With any luck at all, she could go there, treat the children, and be back at Sabaskong Falls before anyone even knew she was gone.

Her mood greatly improved, she stood and reached for her grandfather's black satchel. To do something useful would help her forget the feeling she had shirked her duty as far as Christiana was concerned. And it would strengthen her resolve never to let such a thing happen again.

Her plan had worked so well that Alex felt ashamed. She hadn't actually lied to John and Birdie Hay when she'd told them she needed to borrow a canoe to take medicine around the point—she just hadn't clarified how far around the point. John, ever helpful, had made it clear he would accompany her, but she had assured him she could manage on her own. It made her feel guilty to see their trust in her as they stood at their dock to see her off. She felt equally guilty at remembering how she had waited until Aberdeen stepped out of the cabin to go to the trading post before scribbling a short note and slipping out the back way. Caution had prompted Alex to write her true destination in the note, in the event she suffered some misfortune and it became necessary for someone to come after her.

The possibility of that occurring had seemed remote until she found herself out of sight of the Falls, entering a succession of identical islands. Strangely, the pines appeared taller, towering menacingly over her small craft, and the water seemed darker, deeper, more turgid and threatening. But when Alex caught sight of a landmark she remembered from her first trip to the Indian village, she breathed easier, laughing at her fears. She knew where she was now, and taking relief to the children of the tribe would make all the stealth and deceit worthwhile.

Rhys looked up from the doorsill he was planing and saw Aberdeen walking past, going toward the trading post. He was startled when she glanced his way, a coy expression settling unexpectedly over her usually somber features. She raised one hand and wriggled her fingers at him. Stunned, Rhys waved back.

"You ain't thinkin' of tryin' to steal my woman, are ya?" growled a voice behind him.

Turning, Rhys found Waldo Anderson glaring at him. "Oh, hell, Waldo, I thought she was waving at me."

"Well," the trapper commented, a twinkle appearing in his blue eyes, "I guess I'll let you off this time. Jist don't make a habit of it."

Rhys laughed shortly. "I've got enough trouble with one woman, Waldo. Why on earth would I want another one?"

"Since you mention it, I don't reckon you would." Waldo's gaze followed Aberdeen's straight figure as she sailed down the path. "Believe I'll jist go along with that little female. She's sure to need some help with her purchases at the post. This here community building can wait a whit."

Rhys watched the man go after Aberdeen and felt the sting of envy. His thoughts, as usual, swung to Alexandria, and squinting against the bright autumn sunshine, he stared toward the doctor's cabin and wondered what she was doing at that moment.

He had a sudden urge to stop work and go find her. He'd been biding his time ever since their return from the Indian camp, hoping she would come to him and demand some explanation of what had happened there. At first he'd been anxious to clear the air, but then, as time elapsed and Alex showed no sign of jealousy or even concern over his having spent the night with another woman, he'd grimly decided to wait her out and see how long it would take for her to broach the subject. As each day passed, he grew more stubborn. Surely she cared!

But what if she didn't? The ominous thought occurred to him for the thousandth time. He'd been tortured by that possibility, more than he cared to admit. Maybe she really did regard him as a protector and nothing more. To her, he might only be someone to rescue her from trouble when the need arose, but not anyone she could make a permanent part of her life.

Rhys stood up, handing the wood plane to Malachi Harper. Why should he wait any longer? It was time to find out once and for all just how Alex felt about him. And it was time for him to reveal his own feelings toward her. They were both acting like children, and he was tired of it.

"I'll be back later," he said to no one in particular and stalked away.

A sharp wind had sprung up, stinging Alex's face as she labored at paddling the canoe. Her shoulders ached beneath the heavy coat, and yet the day had grown too cold for her to take it off.

She had passed the last landmark some time ago and the islands all looked frighteningly alike. If she didn't find the camp soon, she was going to have to assume she was lost. Uneasily, her eyes scanned the forest that rimmed the lake to her right. It looked like the arm of the mainland where the Indians had camped, but how could she be sure?

Was this going to be another misadventure, she wondered. If so, it was definitely of a more serious nature than most of her others. Losing her way on the huge lake at this time of year could quite easily prove fatal. She'd known that when she'd left the Falls, but her enthusiasm and self-confidence had been so great she had never really considered that anything would go wrong. With a sigh of self-disgust, she realized she was still as naive as ever.

And then, suddenly, she caught sight of three or four thin plumes of smoke rising above the trees and knew she had stumbled upon the village after all. Holding back the cry of relief that crowded into her throat, she centered all her concentration on getting across the last stretch of water.

Alex's arrival at the log dock was greeted by surprised shouts of welcome, and soon nearly everyone in the camp had swarmed down to the lakeshore. The cluster of people parted to let Talking Elk and his son through. The men greeted her in their grunted Chippewa dialect, their faces friendly but puzzled. Alex hoped that Killing Sky would not think she had changed her mind about his offer of marriage, and for the first time, she foresaw the difficulty in making her purpose understood.

Reaching into the canoe, she held her black bag high, then lowered her other hand to indicate a child's height. Seeing a small boy peeping out from behind his mother's skirt, she pointed at him and beckoned him forward. His mother clutched the child, a look of fright on her face, but Alex smilingly shook her head, trying to convey her good intentions. She could see a series of infected boils on the boy's elbow, so she touched her own arm in that location, then opened her satchel to display her medicines. She pantomimed rubbing salve on her elbow, holding out the tin and nodding encouragingly to the boy.

"This will help you feel better," she said, frustrated by the apparent lack of understanding. "I'm a doctor. I want to make you well."

Killing Sky and his father held a brief conference, then the younger man said something to Alex and started off down the path to the camp. Assuming she was to follow, Alex closed her bag and hurried after him.

To her relief, Killing Sky summoned his young sister from one of the birchbark wigwams, and bringing her to stand in front of Alex, he pointed out the boil on the child's round cheek and raised his eyebrows in question.

"Yes," Alex cried in excitement. "Exactly! I can treat those awful sores so they will go away."

The man inclined his head, as though granting her permission. With a suppressed sigh, Alex sat down on the ground and reopened her satchel. "Now, before I can put medicine and a bandage on those boils," she said in what she hoped was a reassuring tone, "I will have to lance the boil and let the infection out. This won't hurt. . . ."

As she drew a scalpel from the bag, the little girl's smile of welcome faded abruptly, and the air was pierced by her shrill scream. She jerked her arm from her brother's grip and fled like a terrified fawn. Several other children who had been watching disappeared into the forest behind her. An angry buzzing erupted from a group of onlookers, and Killing Sky growled out a short, harsh question.

Alex felt like crying. Had she come all this way only to be thwarted at every turn?

"Damn the woman!" Rhys shouted, raking a hand through his hair. "What in the world was she thinking of?"

"She was thinking of those bairns," Aberdeen said softly, crumpling the note Alex had left. "That's all she could talk about when you first came back from the Indian camp. She wanted to help them."

"But she's putting her own life at risk by doing so. It's too damned late in the year to be out on the lake." Rhys shifted his stance. "There's been a skim of ice across the bay every morning this week. Maybe tomorrow it won't break up in the wind and waves. Maybe she'll be caught out there somewhere."

Aberdeen cast a wary glance at Waldo, who nodded sagely. "It's happened to men with more experience than that gal has," he confirmed. "What are ya gonna do, Rhys?"

"The only thing I can do—go after her. And when I catch up with her, I'm going to give her the hiding she has deserved since she arrived here."

"We'll go with you," Aberdeen hastily interjected.

"No, there's no sense in risking the lives of two more people. But I'd appreciate it if you could help me round up some supplies. I'd better be prepared for the worst."

And so had Alexandria, Aberdeen thought with a grimace.

Even expecting the worst couldn't keep Rhys from plunging into the direst of moods once he got out onto the lake. The water in the bay had been almost syrupy, which came as no surprise. What did upset and worry him was that even the water farther out had changed, indicating the onset of the freeze-up. If he couldn't find Alexandria and get her safely back to the Falls, they could get caught in the ice and die.

The entire northern half of the sky was a sullen metallic gray color, with layers of snow clouds building. Curse Alex! She had used the poorest judgment imaginable. If the weather turned nasty too fast, they might be forced to spend a good deal of time at the Indian camp. Although returning to Sabaskong Falls overland was possible, it would be a lengthy and hazardous journey at best, and he wasn't convinced she would be hardy enough to withstand it.

Why couldn't she have come to him with this scheme? Somehow he'd have made her understand it was simply too late to start out across the lake. He'd have promised to take her in the spring, as soon as the ice went off. Nobody died from boils.

The children would have survived the winter, as they had always done.

After an hour of furious paddling, Rhys's anger calmed enough for a deadly fear to enter his mind. He had rehearsed his tirade over and over again, relieving his emotions by practicing the burning words he would say once he'd found her at the camp. But what if she never made it to the village?

He realized how fatally easy it would be for her to lose her way. She had only traversed the route one time. No greenhorn would be able to follow it again without help, and certainly not a woman. Hell, she could barely paddle the goddamned canoe. . . .

He felt as if a cold fist were curling in his chest, squeezing his heart slowly and painfully. He would not let himself think that he might not see Alex again, that she could die and her body never be recovered. It had happened before, to men who should have known better. What chance did a foolish, fragile woman like Alex have against such deadly danger? Once the ice actually started forming on the lake, it solidified with alarming swiftness, but until it had hardened completely, usually in a matter of two or three days, it wasn't firm enough to walk on. Alex's canoe would become icebound, and she could die from exposure to the elements while sitting within sight of land. Even if she had the forethought to take an axe with her, to chop her way through the ice-crusted water, as the ice thickened, the shards would rip her canoe to pieces, leaving her at the mercy of the lake. If she went into the water, chances were the shock would kill her immediately. If not, she couldn't survive more than a moment or two. He closed his mind to the horrible image of Alex's body being dragged below the surface of Lake of the Woods by a heavy coat and sodden woolen skirts. He began paddling so furiously that his shoulders ached, and his heart kept beating at the same rapid, terrified pace within his heaving chest.

I'll find her, he silently promised himself. And when I do, I'll give her a tongue lashing that will blister her reckless hide. For once, the imperious Miss MacKenzie is going to hear me out, whether she likes what I have to say or not.

His mouth tightened as he surveyed the overcast day. The temperature was falling now, and the cold wind had accelerated, bringing with it the scent of snow.

As his canoe labored onward, Rhys's eyes scanned the lake ahead, hoping for a glimpse of another boat, of Alex's bright hair. He saw nothing more than endless water, endless islands, and endless gray sky.

Alex wished she had thought to bring along some kind of trinkets with which to bribe the children. As it was, nothing would induce them to come near her. She had made an impassioned appeal to Killing Sky, but after seeing the scalpel, he, too, seemed distrustful.

366

There was nothing she could do but return to the Falls, admit her failure and face up to the inevitable condemnation. Aberdeen would lecture her, and Rhys. . . Lord, she didn't dare think of what Rhys would say or do! He'd be absolutely incensed, ready to commit mayhem. This latest scheme of hers was turning out to be the worst of all.

She hadn't expected to fail in this mission, it simply hadn't occurred to her that anything would hamper her good deed. At this point, even she had to admit her greatest downfall was that she didn't think things through thoroughly enough before acting. She should have asked for help, she knew that now. Once again, the independence of which she was so proud had gotten her into serious trouble. Well, she'd tried and that was all she could do. It was time to consider her own well-being and start for home before the weather got any worse.

She knelt by her satchel to return the medicine and bandages, then closed it with a discouraged snap. Beside her, Killing Sky uttered a few words, but when she glanced up, he was looking beyond her. Still on her knees, Alex turned to follow his gaze.

Looming up against the pewter sky was Rhys, his face carved into a fierce scowl. He strode directly to her, his eyes burning into hers, and instinctively Alex shrank backward. She didn't want to cower in fear, but she had never seen him look so threatening.

"Alex . . ." He grasped her upper arms and

pulled her to her feet. For one long, tense moment his gaze devoured her and then, unexpectedly, he wrapped both arms around her and drew her against him in a bone-crushing hug. "Thank God, you're safe," he muttered. "I didn't know if I would find you or not."

Before Alex could offer any response, his mouth closed over hers in a searing kiss that expressed the maelstrom of emotions he was feeling—worry, relief, anger, and heartfelt caring. His kiss made it evident that he truly had doubted finding her, and Alex, fully aware of what he must have gone through, answered it with all the pent-up emotion she herself was experiencing. They clung to each other, striving for control. At last, Rhys drew back to look into her face.

"Don't ever do this to me again, Alex," he pleaded, his voice low and gravelly. "Promise me."

"I promise," she whispered.

She recalled the times when she had thought Rhys's eyes resembled a northern lake, changing colors in the way a lake reflects back the hue of trees or sky. Back then she had believed that, also like a wilderness lake, there were icy depths beneath the surface. But now, looking into those same eyes, she couldn't imagine why she had ever thought Rhys cold. His gaze was a pure, smoldering blue—like sapphires bathed in flames. Despite the cold wind swirling around them, his look warmed and comforted her.

"I'm not interested in an idle promise," he warned, giving her a small shake. "I'm serious about this."

"So am I. I've gone off on my own for the last time, Rhys. From now on, whenever I get an idea, I'll come to you first. You can trust that I've finally learned my lesson."

"I hope so," he said, a slight smile tugging at the corners of his mouth, "because sometime today I discovered that I can't live without you."

"You did?" she murmured, her eyes widening in surprise. At her skeptical look, Rhys had to laugh.

"Alex, I love you," he said. "And I can't think why I haven't told you before. You don't know how scared I was that something had happened to you . . . and that you would never know how I feel."

"Rhys, I . . . you . . ."

"You're stuttering, sweetheart," he teased, lowering his mouth to brush it gently across hers.

"I expected anything but this," Alex said gravely. "I thought you would be furious with me."

"I am—but only because I love you so damned much." He kissed her again. "Unfortunately, we don't have time to discuss the matter now. The way that sky looks, we'd better start back to the Falls."

"But, Rhys, I haven't treated the children yet. They're afraid of me. Do you think you could help convince them that I won't hurt them?"

"I'll try, but we've got to make it fast. The way the temperature is falling, the lake is bound to freeze up tonight sometime."

Rhys turned to Killing Sky, who had been watching the scene with interest, and explained Alex's objective.

"The boils will be much more painful if left to rupture on their own," Alex added. "Tell him that the one on his little sister's face could leave an ugly scar."

Rhys related her warnings, and with a decisive nod, Killing Sky began issuing orders for the children to be rounded up and brought to Alex.

"I've got something that might help," Rhys said. "I'll be right back."

When he returned from his canoe, Alex had reopened her bag and was assembling the necessary items.

"While I was getting some supplies ready, Scotty fixed this up for the children." Rhys held out a leather sack filled with sticks of hard candy. "Guess he figured you might have need of it."

"Bless him," Alex breathed. "That just might win them over."

But even though they eyed the candy hungrily, the children still hung back, reluctant to come too close. Finally, after Rhys had carefully explained the procedure and promised the candy as a reward, a young girl of about sixteen came forward. She had two large boils on her neck, obviously irritated by the chafing of her buckskin dress. With a courageous smile, she sat down beside Alex and indicated that she was ready to undergo the needed treatment.

"Thank you for being so brave," Alex said, giving the girl an encouraging pat on the shoulder. Working as swiftly as possible, she lanced the boils, ignoring the gasps of the onlookers, and used gauze pads to press out the infection. Then she smeared the boils with a thick salve and bandaged them.

When Rhys handed the girl a stick of the candy, she murmured her thanks, then turned to a small boy standing nearby and offered it to him. The child hesitated only a moment before taking the candy and dropping down beside Alex.

"He's her brother," Rhys said. "She has challenged him to be as brave as she was."

"Give her another piece of candy for herself," Alex suggested. "She may have provided the start we need."

When the other children saw the boy sitting quietly, stoically eating his candy while Alex lanced and bandaged the boils on his knees, they began to crowd closer, and before long, were arguing over who would be next. Even Killing Sky's little sister clamored to be included.

When she noticed that, Alex raised her head to smile triumphantly at Rhys and was stunned to find him standing a short distance away, talking quietly to the beautiful woman with whom he had spent the night during their recent stay with the Indians. As she watched, the woman said something and laughed, and laughing in reply, Rhys shook his head.

Was she offering herself to him again? And was he forced to decline only because he had to escort the reckless lady doctor back across the lake? Alex's jaw clenched, and her mouth tightened in jealous anger as she returned her attention to the waiting child.

371

By the time she had finished, Rhys was standing by her side again. Without meeting his eyes, she said, "Would you please ask Killing Sky if these boils occur in the summer, or only after the return to the winter camp?"

Rhys repeated her question, then said, "Only in the winter camp."

"Then tell him that I suspect the water here is contaminated, and they should look for a cleaner source. For some reason, this sort of thing seems to mainly affect the young. Of course, the boils could be caused by something the children are eating that the adults are not. They should make an attempt to discover whether or not that is the case."

While Rhys translated her words, Alex took bundles of gauze and tins of salve from her case and handed them to Killing Sky's mother.

"Tell her that the bandages should be changed every day and new medicine applied until the boils have healed. And inform the children that when we come back in the spring to check on them, we will bring more candy."

Rhys's eyes lingered on her as he echoed her words, his smile warmly approving. "Did I ever tell you that you're an unbelievable woman?" he asked, wrapping an arm around her waist to pull her close to his side.

Frowning, she glanced up at him. "Yes, more than once."

Though he was amused by her irritation with him, there was no time to deal with it then. Both of them recognized the very real danger they would

372

face on the trip home. Keeping a cautious eye on the darkening November sky, they rapidly prepared for the journey back to Sabaskong Falls.

Chapter Eighteen

In the first hour after their departure from the Indian village, Rhys and Alex made good time. Having left John Hay's canoe at the camp until spring, they set out in Rhys's more heavily loaded one. With both of them paddling, it skimmed along at a fairly rapid pace. However, as the afternoon turned colder, so did the waters of the lake, making passage more and more difficult. Moving among the islands, Rhys began noticing ice crusting upon the rocks and his mouth thinned into a grim line.

Alex was tired, but she forced herself to match the pace Rhys had set. She knew that haste was the most important thing—the only weapon they had against the freeze-up. She determinedly kept her thoughts away from her aching arms and concentrated instead on Rhys's arrival at the winter camp. Never had she been so surprised in her life. She had expected anger and accusations; nothing had prepared her for his tenderness, his relief at finding her safe. Remembering how he had told her he loved her, she felt warm despite the creeping chill that surrounded them. Strangely enough, Rhys had asked her for nothing. His affirmation of love had been freely given, not contingent upon her feelings for him. She tightened her grip on the wooden paddle and smiled to herself. As soon as circumstances allowed, she needed to make those feelings known. It didn't seem fair for her to harbor the secret of her love for him when he had bared his heart and mind so readily. Instinctively she knew it was not something that had come easily for him, nor was it something he had done many times in his life.

The sudden sting of sleet against her face wrenched Alex's thoughts away from pleasantries and back to the danger at hand. She met Rhys's eyes and saw worry reflected in them.

"Damn, I hadn't counted on a storm," he said. "Why the hell couldn't it have held off until we'd made it back?"

"But we're not that far from the Falls, are we?"

"Only an hour or two. It's just that I'm not sure how much longer we can go on," he said tersely. "The temperature's dropping by the minute now."

"What else can we do?"

"Find shelter on one of the islands. We can't take a chance on getting caught out in the canoe."

Alex swallowed deeply. "Do you mean that . . . that we aren't going to make it back?"

"Not tonight, at any rate." He surveyed the rapidly darkening sky. "We'll push on for another thirty minutes, maybe an hour. But after that, it won't be safe. We'll have to stop and make camp."

"Oh, my God . . ."

"It won't be so bad," he assured her. "I brought plenty of supplies. We'll only have to stay there until the ice hardens enough for us to walk on to the Falls — two or three days, most likely."

"If you knew this might happen, why did you come after me?" she asked, shaking her head. "Why didn't you let me stay with the Indians?"

His teeth gleamed whitely in the gathering dusk. "Because I know you well enough to realize you wouldn't stay put there. As headstrong as you are, you'd never have given up trying to get back to Sabaskong. I just wanted to make sure you did."

"But I didn't mean to put you in danger, too."

"I know, and you haven't. With any luck at all . . ."

Their luck held for the next hour, then ran out with an abruptness that nearly caught them unaware.

As the temperature of the water fell, it became more thick and syrupy, hindering the movement of the wooden paddles. When the ice began hardening, it was necessary to break the top crust with the paddle, moving the canoe forward before the ice could re-form. Rhys had kept them close to the long chain of islands through which they were passing, but now they were entering a small area of open water with the next island nearly a quarter of a mile away.

Testing the slushy water with the oar, he shouted over the howl of the wind. "When we make it to those islands ahead, we'd better take shelter. It won't be safe to go on any longer."

Alexandria merely nodded, looking in apprehension at the projections of granite rock just barely visible through the driving sleet. It seemed an impossible distance away to her, but she knew that every foot they covered shortened the distance they would eventually have to walk.

As the canoe lurched forward, a maniacal wind caught them, rocking the craft dangerously. Rhys leaned into the gale, his face set and stern, his eyes squinted against the sleet and snow that lashed at him. Beneath the heavy coat he wore, his shoulders flexed and strained.

"Hell," he muttered, "this wind is working against us. The ice is closing up too fast."

Alex felt chilled despite the perspiration trickling down her back beneath her own coat. The ice was thickening with enough speed to keep the canoe from responding to their efforts. Now when she lifted the paddle from the water, it was encased in an ever-thicker coating of ice; on each downward stroke, she had to use the sharp edge of the paddle to break the crust before she could slip the oar beneath the surface. Behind them, the water in the canoe's wake was freezing over as soon as the birchbark boat cleared it. With a sudden, wrenching motion, the canoe settled into the ice and refused to move. They were bogged down.

Rhys snatched up one of the canvas-wrapped bundles laying on the bottom of the canoe. "Alex," he commanded, "you'll have to paddle. I'll try to keep the ice chopped away."

He leaned over the prow, using a sharp axe to break up the ice. In a matter of moments, the crust had hardened to a thickness of half an inch in places. As Rhys strained to clear a path, Alex used her waning strength to propel the canoe forward. Slowly, inch by inch, they proceeded.

The only sounds to be heard beneath the keening moan of the wind were Rhys's laborious grunts and the scrabbling of his booted feet as they sought a firmer purchase on the ribbed floor of the canoe. Alex filled her mind with silent prayers, refusing to believe they might not make it to shelter.

"We're almost there," Rhys shouted. "Can you keep going just a little longer?"

Alex didn't think she could, but she wouldn't admit that to him. Not when it was her fault they were in such a predicament in the first place. "Yes, I can," she called back, unaware that tears of fright and exertion were freezing on her cheeks.

Even when the rocky shoreline of the island was only thirty feet away, they had to keep struggling. The water was too dangerously frigid to risk. Now, as Rhys swung the axe with desperation, the ice broke away in chunks and slivers. Fragile by comparison, the hull of the canoe was pierced again and again by the jagged ice, and slushy water began to ooze into the craft. Alex cast a frantic look over her shoulder, but seeing how close they had come to the island renewed her energies and she paddled with all the vigor she could muster.

"That's good, Alex," Rhys encouraged. "We're going to make it!"

Close as they got, however, he was forced to leap

from the canoe and plod the last ten feet, crashing through the ice and slipping on the round rocks on the lake bottom as he forced the craft from the grasp of the freeze. With his last remaining strength, Rhys secured the canoe between two boulders at the edge of the lake, then collapsed onto the frozen sand.

"Rhys." Alex breathed out his name, scrambling out of the canoe and kneeling beside him. "Are you all right?"

"My hands and feet," he moaned, shivering uncontrollably. "Can you help me get these wet boots off?"

Alex tugged the water-soaked leather gloves off his hands, and began pulling off his boots. She was thankful he had not been wearing the usual moccasins, for they would have provided little protection. She stripped away soggy woolen socks and began gently warming and massaging his feet with her own gloved hands. Where the leather boots had not shielded his calves, blood welled from a dozen cuts made by the sharp edges of the ice.

"Rhys, you've got to get your feet warm. Did you bring other boots?"

"My moccasins and some socks are in one of the packs."

"I'll get them."

Ignoring his protests, Alex climbed back into the canoe and handed out a musket and the bundles of supplies Rhys had brought with him. As soon as he located the clothing, he put on dry socks and the knee-high moccasins.

"The next thing we have to do is find some shelter," he said, glancing about them. "And get a fire going."

The island was small, with a sparse covering of trees along the south edge. Dragging the packs with them, they made their way to the opposite side of it, heads bowed against the force of the snow-filled wind. That end of the island was a sandy bluff that bordered the water.

"This is our best bet," Rhys said, tossing the packs he carried to the bottom of the bluff. "The hill behind us will cut off the wind."

With Rhys's help, Alex half slid down the embankment. There was a ledge of rock between the wall of sand and the lake, and because it was sheltered from the sleet, it was relatively dry.

"This will be a good place to start a fire," Rhys stated, leaning the musket against a small boulder and opening one of the packs to search for the firesteel. "Do you think you can find some kindling?"

Alex unshouldered the pack she had carried and looked about. Trees towered above them, so the ledge was covered with small pine cones and dead branches that had blown down during the autumn. She made a pile of the cones, then began breaking up dry sticks to add to it.

"See where that pine has fallen?" she asked Rhys. "Its roots have left a big hole—almost like a cave. Think we could make a shelter in there?"

Rhys looked up from his task and grinned. "You just may make a wilderness woman, after all."

Alex crept beneath the overhanging limbs and found a hollowed spot some four feet deep. By using her hands to dig, she knocked away enough sand and soil to widen the shelter a little more, and to cover the rock floor with a thin layer of dirt.

"We need some pine boughs to make it warmer," she announced, emerging from beneath the roots.

A thin column of smoke curled upward from the pile of kindling, and Rhys carefully laid a few bigger pieces of wood on the fire. "Let me get this to blazing, and then I'll cut some branches for you. We're going to need a good supply of firewood first."

Alex busied herself picking up the larger pieces of driftwood along the shoreline, while Rhys took the axe and climbed back up the steep bank. She could hear him crashing through the underbrush, and after a while, there was the ring of a blade on wood. Shouting a warning, he rolled the larger logs over the side of the embankment; then an armload of brush and smaller branches followed. Alex hovered near the blaze for a moment or two, warming her cold face and hands before turning away to stack the wood Rhys had tossed down. He was halfway up the bank again when she heard his shout.

"Alex! Look out — your skirt!"

The smell of burning fabric filled her nostrils at the same time she realized something was hampering her efforts to rise from a crouching position.

Rhys dropped the axe and hurled himself down the embankment. Just as he reached Alex, her skirts burst into flame and she uttered a short, terrified scream. Seizing the burning log with his bare hands, Rhys threw it aside, then shoved Alex to the ground and flung his body over hers. Clasping his arms around her, he rolled from side to side, smothering the flames. Alex clung to him, sickened by the smoke and the odor of scorching wool.

"Are you hurt?" Rhys gasped, releasing her and surveying the ruined gown.

"N-no, I don't think so. What happened?"

"You knelt too close to the fire and a small log shifted, then rolled onto your skirt. Thank God I could get to you in time."

Alex looked at her dress with wide, disbelieving eyes. The blackened material continued to smolder.

"You'd better take it off," Rhys said. "I've got extra clothes in the packs. You'll just have to put on a pair of men's pants."

Alex was so shaken she had no desire to argue. On wobbly legs, she went inside the shelter and unfastened her gown while Rhys found her a pair of pants and a woolen shirt. The air was icy against her bare skin, allowing her little time for modesty. She scrambled into the clothing he handed her, grateful for its heavy warmth. Rhys cut a length of rope for a makeshift belt, then knelt to roll up her pantlegs.

Alex moaned in horror. "Rhys, your hands!"

Surprised, he turned them over and studied them. Streaked with soot, his palms and fingers looked as if they had been charred, and they were already blistering from contact with the burning log.

"Oh, my God," she cried, "the pain."

"I can't feel a thing," he replied in wonder.

Alex knew it was a state that wouldn't continue, but she didn't want to tell him so. Instead, she began scraping up a handful of the snow that filled the crevices of the rock on which they stood. "This will help," she said, gently smoothing the snow over his damaged hands. "My grandfather never believed in treating burns with warm water, as so many physicians do. He thought it made the pain more intense." She broke off, biting her lip. She was positive Rhys did not yet realize the seriousness of his injuries.

"I'll have to clean and bandage them," she went on softly. "The skin is broken in several places." She held her breath as she again examined his hands. It was difficult to hold back the self-blame she felt, but she knew there was still too much to accomplish before she could allow herself time to think about it.

Working as quickly and gently as she could, she cleaned Rhys's burns and coated them with salve. Because she had left all her gauze with the Indians, she had to tear her petticoats into strips to use as bandaging. Throughout the process, Rhys sat quietly, but the strained lines of his face told her that he was already feeling the onset of pain.

"Now, you stay here by the fire," she said briskly, dropping the tin of salve back into the leather bag, "and I'll cut some pine boughs to make our beds."

"No, I'll do it," he protested, getting to his feet. "The axe might slip and—"

"Rhys, your hands are going to be too tender for you to do anything," she stated firmly. "I know it won't be easy for you, but you're going to have to sit back and tell me what to do—and how to do it."

"I can't do that."

"I'm sorry, but you have no choice." She laid a hand on his arm. "Please, don't argue with me. There are things that must be done before dark."

"Surely there's something I can do. I hate like hell being helpless."

"Just get in out of the wind and rest. I'll be back as soon as I can."

Without waiting for his answer, Alex struggled up the embankment, stopping to pick up the axe Rhys had dropped. She knew chopping the lower branches of pine was going to be easier than cutting wood for the fire, but she pushed the thought aside. She'd worry about that when the time came.

When she returned to the fire, Rhys was sitting with his back against the hill, his face drawn and pale. Forcing a cheerful smile, Alex spread most of the fragrant boughs on the floor of the shelter, then draped the rest across the roots overhead, creating enough of a roof to keep out the worst of the weather. The sleet had turned to snow, and the flakes were growing larger.

There were four woolen blankets in the packs, and Alex used them to complete the beds. As soon as she had finished, Rhys crawled into the makeshift shelter and lay down. She rolled two empty canvas packs together to make a pillow, then covered him with two of the blankets. With his bandaged hands lying awkwardly across his chest, Rhys closed his eyes. There was a small amount of laudanum in her case, but Alex feared he would need

384

it more later.

She spent a few moments going through the additional packs, finding a tin pail, cooking and eating utensils, and a bundle of food, as well as the inevitable pemmican. That she put carefully aside, aware that it could possibly save their lives if their stay on the island lasted more than a day or two. Taking the axe and the pail, she walked to the water's edge. Already the ice was over an inch thick. She chopped through the top crust and drew a pail of water. Once it warmed somewhat, it could be used for drinking, and the ever-present danger of fire made it imperative to keep water handy.

The fire, close enough to the mouth of the shelter to provide a certain amount of heat, yet not so close as to set the tree roots or pine boughs aflame, needed tending. Alex determined that the supply of wood Rhys had already cut would be enough to last the night, but in the morning, cutting more would have to be her first duty. She piled additional logs on the fire, then positioned a kettle of water on two stones at the edge of the flames. There was tea in the food pack, as well as a loaf of bread, slices of venison, and a few potatoes. No doubt those things had been Aberdeen's contribution to the supplies.

Hunkered by the fire, Alex thought of the people back at the Falls and wondered if they were concerned because she and Rhys had not returned. For all she knew, emergencies of this kind were commonplace, alarming no one. But, with Rhys sleeping so soundly inside the shelter, and the frigid winter night closing down around her, Alex felt very frightened and alone. The sound of the wind was enough to freeze one's blood. . . .

As soon as the tea was made, Alex crept inside the shelter and found Rhys awake. When he saw her, he struggled into a sitting position.

"Can you manage this mug of tea?" Alex asked.

Rhys reached for the steaming mug and held it close to his face to breathe in the steamy fragrance. "This seems like a miracle right now," he said. "I'm starving."

He took a sip of the hot liquid. "What kind of tea is this? It tastes . . . odd."

Alex hastily took a drink from her cup, and her look of alarm changed to one of amusement. "I believe Aberdeen sent us herbal tea."

"Herbal? You mean the kind the women . . . ?"

She nodded, grinning mischievously.

Rhys grinned back. "Well, at least it's hot. I suppose Aberdeen didn't want to risk . . . uh, anything."

Alex studiously ignored him as she set out the bundle of food and used his hunting knife to slice the bread. Wrapping a piece of bread around some of the meat, she held it for Rhys to eat, knowing he would be virtually helpless with the bulky bandages on his hands. It was obvious his injuries were becoming more painful when he had to set the mug of tea aside once the warmth of the cup penetrated the layers of cotton fabric.

"I'm worse than a baby," he fretted. "How are we going to get along when you even have to feed me?"

"Everything will be fine. Don't worry." Alex flashed him a reassuring smile. "This will be a chance for me to show you that I'm not a helpless female."

"I'm afraid you don't understand what we're facing."

"Rhys," she said sternly, "stop looking for trouble. I'll do what needs to be done, and that's that. Now, would you like more to eat?"

"No, I've had enough. You'd better have your own meal."

Alex took a slice of bread and some meat, then rewrapped the remainder and put it aside. "If we're conservative with this, it will last another day or two, I think."

"And then?"

"If we're still stranded here, I'll think of something," she assured him.

"Can you shoot the musket?"

"N-no."

He sighed. "It's just as well. It doesn't look like there's much game on this island anyway."

She smothered a wide yawn, prompting him to continue. "You're worn out, Alex. Why don't you come to bed? It'll be warmer if we share the same one."

"I agree. Just let me see to the fire."

After throwing more wood onto the blaze, Alex crawled back into the shelter, burrowing down into the bed of pine boughs beside Rhys. They lay on one blanket and covered themselves with the other three, sharing the canvas pillow. They were silent for a time, watching the clotted snowflakes that fell outside their den, silhouetted against the orange firelight.

"Do you think the people back at the Falls are worried about us?" Alex finally asked, voicing the fear that had nagged at her for hours. "They won't come looking for us, will they?"

"No, they understand the situation. It's an unwritten rule of the wilderness that no one risks his life needlessly. And that's what anyone would be doing by setting out before the freeze-up is complete. They're trusting us to take care of ourselves."

"At least it's a relief not to have to worry about anyone but us," Alex murmured, yawning again and snuggling deeper into the bedding.

They were quiet then, drifting quickly into exhausted sleep. Beyond their shelter, the fire hissed and crackled bravely as the cutting north wind swept across the lake country, driving the icy snow before it.

Rhys's long, low moan of pain woke Alex sometime in the depths of the night. Raising herself on one elbow, she gazed down at him. There was enough light from the fire to show that his face was etched with anguish, his forehead bathed in sweat. His head thrashed from side to side on the pillow, and he muttered, "Alex . . ."

"Yes, Rhys, I'm here," she softly assured him.

His eyes slowly opened and focused on her face. "My hands hurt like hell," he half whispered, a note of surprise in his voice.

Alex felt overwhelming compassion for him. He was a strong, self-reliant man suddenly finding himself in pain and at someone else's mercy. He wouldn't like being vulnerable, wouldn't like appearing weak.

"It will help if you hold them upright," she said, rolling the remaining canvas packs into another pillow which she positioned on his abdomen. "There, rest your arms against that. When some of the blood drains out of your hands, they won't throb quite so much."

She crept from beneath the covers, startled by the sheer iciness of the air. "I'll put more wood on the fire, and then I'm going to give you some laudanum to help you sleep. Do you want anything to eat or drink?"

He shook his head wearily, his eyes following her as she hastily stoked up the fire and added the last of the bigger chunks of wood. When she returned to bed, she brought her medical bag with her.

"I can only give you a small amount of this," she warned, uncorking the bottle of laudanum. "It's dangerous . . . and besides, we may need it more later."

Rhys obediently swallowed the bitter medicine, making a face but saying nothing. Alexandria put her satchel aside and slid down beside him in the bed. "Are you cold?" she asked.

"Not with you beside me."

"Believe me, I'm not going anywhere else."

"It must be hellishly cold outside," Rhys observed. "Too cold to snow anymore."

Gazing out past the overhanging boughs of pine,

they could see the glow of the fire, with the night sky behind it looking like polished onyx. There were no discernible stars, no moon. Even the wind had died, leaving only an eerie silence.

"Rhys, I feel so guilty about all this," Alex whispered, her breath a tiny cloud of steam. "Is there anything I can do for you?"

"Talk to me until I fall asleep again." He turned his face on the pillow and looked at her. "Will you do that?"

"Of course. What would you like me to talk about?"

One corner of his mouth tilted upward. "Anything you think I'd like to hear."

Alex smiled, moving closer and resting her head on his shoulder. "Well, there is one thing I probably ought to mention. . . ."

His response was wary. "Is this something I want to hear?"

"I don't know, really. But I think it could divert your mind from the pain."

"Then, please . . . tell me."

"Remember when you arrived at Talking Elk's camp? Remember what you said to me?"

"How could I forget?" he growled. "I was so furious I intended to turn you over my knee. Instead, I started . . . well, you know the rest."

"You said you loved me," Alex shyly reminded him. "Did you mean it?"

"I wouldn't have said it if I didn't mean it. You ought to know me well enough by now to realize that."

"Yes, I think I do. And I'm so very glad you

meant it because . . . well, because I love you. I should have told you right then and there, but I couldn't seem to find the words." She nuzzled his ear. "Now I see that they're really quite simple. I love you, Rhys."

He turned his face, letting his lips meet and cling to hers. "You're right," he said huskily, "you've definitely taken my mind off my hands."

Alex stretched her body along the length of his, letting one hand creep beneath the pillow to caress his chest. "I've loved you for a long time," she admitted.

"Then why the hell didn't you act like it?" he demanded in exasperation. "Why did you let me go off with Talking Elk's daughter and never say a word?"

"Would it have done any good? You were rather angry with me at that moment."

"I've spent a lot of time being angry with you, woman. It seemed to me that if you'd cared anything at all about me, you'd have made some sort of protest."

"I couldn't do what I wanted to do," she stated. "I couldn't pull her hair out by its beautiful roots — and I certainly couldn't have forced you into my wigwam."

"You should have tried, damn it. That's all I was waiting for — some sign that you cared. But you just stood there calmly, as though it didn't bother you in the least to see me go off to spend the night in another woman's arms. Hell, I was so mad I was nearly breathing fire."

"Rhys, I realized that I had done a great many

stupid things, and that you were constantly having to rescue me from some trouble or another. At that moment, I thought it best to keep my mouth shut and not cause you any more distress. Besides, I know how things stand between the Indian women and the men of the wilderness. It wasn't my place to interfere."

"You thought I wanted to go with her?"

"Why wouldn't you? Why wouldn't any man?"

"I can't speak for anyone else, but I really wanted nothing more than to be with you."

"Yet you walked away . . . and shared a bed with her."

"I thought I had lost face once too often." His chuckle was interrupted by a yawn. "Besides, I didn't share her bed."

Alex's breath caught. "You didn't?" she asked, hopefully.

"Of course not. I wanted you—and everyone else—to think I had, but in reality, I explained the situation to the chief's daughter, then slipped away to spend the night with Killing Sky." His eyelids fluttered downward, shielding his dark eyes.

"Then what were you talking to her about today?" Alex couldn't resist asking.

"She merely wondered whether or not you had decided to be my woman."

"And you said?"

"That I still hadn't convinced you."

"Oh."

"By the way," he said, through another yawn, "she tells me Killing Sky thinks the white man's courtship is very strange."

Alex's face was wreathed in a sudden smile as she pressed her cheek against Rhys's neck. "Court-ship?"

"Mmmm . . . remind me to ask you to marry me," Rhys mumbled drowsily. "Sometime when . . . I'm not so tired."

"I'll remind you," she promised.

Rhys's only answer was a muffled sigh and a faint, masculine snore. Leaning over him, Alex brushed a strand of hair from his forehead, letting her eyes roam lovingly over his handsome face, now relaxed and peaceful. She brushed a soft kiss across his mouth, then settled down within the pungent pine bed and gave herself up to sleep.

With morning came a renewal of the snow and wind, and unable to keep the cold drafts from creeping into the shelter, Rhys and Alex donned all the extra clothing from the packs. Alex piled the last of the wood on the campfire, then made tea, and they breakfasted on bread and venison.

After the meal, she chopped another hole in the ice and drew a bucket of water before setting off to find more firewood. Rhys insisted on going with her, worried that she would injure herself.

They found only a few hardwood trees small enough for Alex to cut down, and mostly collected dead stumps and branches, which would make a hot fire but one that burned quickly. Using his feet, Rhys rolled the larger logs over the side of the embankment to be cut up later. He found that by holding out his arms and keeping his palms upraised, he could carry small loads of wood back to the shelter without too much pain. Alex fussed and scolded, but filled his arms with the wood because she understood his desire to help . . . and the truth was, they needed as large a supply as they could manage. As it was, it took most of the morning to accumulate a woodpile sufficient to last for more than one day.

As soon as they stopped moving about, the insidious cold closed around them, so they brewed fresh mugs of tea and returned to the relative warmth of the shelter. Later, Alex got out her medical case and announced her intention to rebandage Rhys's hands. When the old bandages were removed, she winced to see the charred, blistered condition of his palms and fingers. No doubt he would carry the scars for the rest of his life.

Alex sighed and reached for the salve. Circumstances had placed them in a very real struggle against nature, and it was a useless waste of time to try to place the blame for this or that on either of them. Whose fault it was that they were here no longer mattered. What did matter was their survival — and the fact that they were waging this battle together.

Rhys dozed off in the afternoon, and while he slept, Alex made a stew of potatoes and the remaining venison. When he awoke to the enticing aroma of a hot meal, his pleased smile made her efforts worthwhile. She had to feed him again, as his hands were still too tender for him to make use of a fork or spoon, but he seemed less agitated by his helplessness. He no longer even fretted about those times Alex had to accompany him to the stand of brush they were using as a privy. He seemed to accept, for the time being, that it was her turn to take care of him.

While the darkness of a snowy night settled around them, Alex heated a pan of water for sponge baths. Using a clean strip of petticoat material, she bathed Rhys's face, and dried it. Then, because it was too cold to undress him, she merely opened his shirt and washed his chest and upper arms.

"My grandmother used to say that no matter what's wrong with a person, he'll always feel better after a good bath." She pulled off Rhys's moccasins and wool socks to bathe his feet.

"Are you saying that while we may freeze to death, we'll at least be clean?" There were amused glints in Rhys's eyes.

"Don't talk about freezing to death," she cried. "That's not going to happen to us."

"No," he said more seriously, "I don't think it is. You're taking good care of us, sweetheart."

She replaced the socks and the knee-high moccasins, lacing them up. "Thank you, Rhys. It cheers me to know you're not worried about our situation."

He watched as she busied herself with her own bath. She stripped off the heavy coat she wore and began unbuttoning the men's shirts underneath. His breathing sounded harsh even to his own ears as he saw her draw the wet cloth along her slender neck and onto the creamy skin showing above her cotton chemise.

"There is only one thing that worries me," he said in a slightly strained voice.

Alex turned to look at him, brows arched questioningly. "What's that?"

"How on earth can I make love to you with my hands like this?"

Alex's blush was apparent even in the dimness of the pine shelter. She lowered her head. "Perhaps I could help you?" she suggested in a small voice.

"Well, you have shown a knack for . . . taking me in hand, so to speak." His white teeth gleamed behind his moustache.

Alex went onto her knees and, being careful not to jostle his hands, leaned forward to cover his mouth with a warm kiss. "Just tell me what to do, Rhys, and I'm sure we'll manage just fine."

He bent his head to brush his lips along the tops of her breasts. "Will you be too cold if you open the front of your chemise?" he asked.

With a shake of her head, she pushed the shirts aside and untied the ribbon closings of her undergarment.

"My Lord, but you are lovely," he breathed, tracing a line of kisses along the rounded sides of her breasts. Carefully, he slid his arms about her waist and pulled her to him.

"Don't hurt yourself," she whispered. "Let me do everything."

Gently, she disentangled herself from him, then pushed him back onto the blankets. Timid and brazen at the same time, she unfastened his buckskin pants and tugged them downward. "What a shame that it's too cold to completely undress," she said, untying her own belt and letting the too-large trousers drop to her ankles.

"When we get back home," Rhys promised, and then his voice caught in delighted surprise as she lowered her body over his, taking him inside her. "Oh, God, Alex—oh, love . . . !"

Alex leaned over his chest, her breasts warm against his bared flesh. As her hips shifted against his, her hands were busily stroking his shoulders, cupping his head and lifting his face for her fervent kisses. He murmured her name over and over against her lips, until his voice was only a harsh, passion-roughened sound in the still night.

Her movements became almost frantic, less rhythmic and more erratic, driving them both to trembling heights until a startling, soul-shaking explosion overtook them, tumbling them through empty space before hurling them back to more earthly planes. Sobbing and gasping, Alex lay upon Rhys's heaving chest.

"I love you," he whispered, brushing her hair with one clumsy, bandaged hand.

"And I love you," she said, when her breathing had calmed.

They lay quietly for some time before Alex attempted to move away.

"No," he gently protested, "stay here—I'd like to sleep this way."

Contented, she pulled the blankets around them, snuggling back against him. She sighed deeply and placed a reverent kiss along Rhys's square jaw.

Somehow, their lovemaking had put to rest her vague fear that they would never make it back to Sabaskong Falls. Now some sure, sturdy inner voice told her they would be safe. With such a strong and perfect love at stake, nothing could defeat them. They were invincible.

As she drifted into dreamless sleep, even the distant, bloodcurdling howls of a pack of timber wolves failed to disturb the happy smile that hovered about her lips. All she could hear was the steady, reassuring heartbeat of the beloved man within whose arms she slept.

Chapter Nineteen

For breakfast, Alex roasted the last potatoes in the glowing coals of the campfire and made weak tea with the rapidly diminishing tea leaves. Afterward, she checked Rhys's hands, applying more medicine and fresh bandages, and then they made a foray for firewood.

Though the activity helped warm them, Rhys's strength seemed to wane quickly. Alex knew that was partly due to the scanty meals they had been eating. Another was his body's reaction to the severe burns he had suffered. At times she saw him shudder, as though racked by chills, and at other times, he seemed flushed and restless with fever. She knew the pain was unrelenting, for his features were drawn and tense, although each time he saw her gazing at him with a worried expression, he would force a smile and make some teasing remark. But occasionally she did convince him to take a swallow of the laudanum, which permitted him an hour or two of oblivion.

That afternoon, as he slept, Alex acted on an idea that had come to her as they worked. She had found a length of twine and a fishing barb carved from caribou bone among the supplies and was determined to try catching a fish for their supper. Not only would it taste delicious, it would supplement their cache of food, delaying the moment when all they had left to eat was the pemmican she so disliked.

Cautiously, she edged out onto the ice, testing it with the toe of her boot before taking each step. About three yards from the shoreline, she used the axe to chop through the frozen surface, which was now several inches thick. She dropped the barb, baited with a piece of bread and weighted with a notched stone, into the opaque water. Because it was too cold for her to remain on the ice, Alex tied the end of the twine to a sturdy stick she laid across the top of the hole. She then retreated to the warmth of the fire to watch and wait. Twenty minutes later, the stick laying atop the frozen lake began to wiggle, then turn, and she knew she had caught a fish. With glee, she pulled a good-sized pike from the frigid waters, and when Rhys awakened, she was busily cleaning her catch with surgical precision.

Rhys told her how to make a roasting spit from green wood, and soon they were dining on crisp fish and bread. The unexpected and tasty meal lifted their spirits considerably, and they spent the late afternoon in lively conversation. They discussed their childhoods, Alex becoming nostalgic as she recalled the happy years she had spent with her grandparents. Rhys, on the other hand, grew somber until he began to relate stories about his arrival at Lake of the Woods. Though he owned several properties in Montreal, he vowed he had no desire ever to live in the city again. This rugged land of pine and granite and merciless weather was his home. Alex nodded in understanding. Even perilously close to life-threatening dangers, she was under the spell of the northland. She looked into the familiar face of the man sitting beside her in the darkened shelter and knew it had not been a mistake for her to abandon civilization, as she had known it, and trek into the wilderness. Indeed, it had been the wisest decision of her life.

As dusk crept silently over the islands, Alex chopped the re-forming ice from the fishing hole and dropped the line into it a second time. Huddled beside Rhys in the shelter, she anticipated another meal of fish, but when the stick moved, indicating one had taken the bait, she went to pull in her catch and was horrified to find the weight of the pike had broken the twine. Not only were they left without their dinner, they had lost the barb and, with it, the opportunity for catching other fish. Gloomily, they finished the last of the bread, and though Alex declined, Rhys ate two or three strips of pemmican, washing it down with more of the weak tea.

That night they made love with a passion that sprang from the knowledge that their situation was growing more desperate by the hour. In the morning, Rhys had promised, they would test the ice.

With their food supply now so low and no game on the island, it was going to be necessary for them to make an attempt to get back to the Falls. Time was running out. . . .

"Alex, look!"

Rhys's graveled whisper cut through Alex's troubled dreams, waking her with a start. Seeing his form crouched by the entrance to their shelter, she tossed away the blankets and crawled to his side.

He greeted her with a smile and an exuberant kiss. "Look out there," he said.

Dawn had tinged the snow-covered lake a pale pink, leaving the jagged pines, a deep, greenish black color, silhouetted against the sky. Alex followed Rhys's gaze, and her breath caught at the sight of a massive bull moose slowly ambling across the frozen stretch of lake between theirs and the nearest island.

"Do you know what that means?" he asked, his laughter warm against her ear.

"Breakfast?"

"No, you greedy little wretch! It means, if the ice is solid enough to support his great weight, it's surely safe for us to start out." He touched her mouth with a swift kiss. "We're going home, Alex — today!"

There were, as she soon discovered, several things that had to be done before they could be on their way. First, Rhys insisted, it was important that they have something to eat. Alex nibbled at the pemmican, reminding herself she would need to keep up her strength, and, surprisingly, the dried buffalo meat and berry mixture was more palatable than she'd expected. They finished the meal with the last of the herbal tea, grateful for the warmth it provided.

Then, following Rhys's instructions, Alex cut a straight spruce pole about eight feet in length. This would be used to prod and test the ice as they traveled along, and in the event she accidentally stumbled onto weak ice and fell through, the pole could be laid across the edges of the hold and used to haul her to safety.

Alex packed the remaining supplies into the two canvas packs they would tie onto their backs with rope. The damaged canoe and anything not vital to their survival would be left behind, to be collected in the spring. Alex used the knife to cut the scorched remains of her dress into strips, which they then wound around their feet for added protection from the cold. Even though the strips of wool made their boots fit almost too tightly, Rhys was adamant that they take every precaution against frostbite. She cut the sleeves away from the gown, and these they used to cover the lower halves of their faces, protecting their skin from the slicing arctic wind. For additional warmth, they wore the blankets like cloaks, tying them at the throat with short pieces of rope.

After dousing the campfire, Alex settled the larger pack on Rhys's broad shoulders and handed him the musket, which he carried by crossing his arms over his chest. She then shouldered the second pack, and giving their crude shelter one final look, they set off in the direction of Sabaskong Falls.

Hours later, Alex was so tired she didn't think she could go on much longer. Her arms ached from stabbing at the ice with the long stave she carried, her muscles clenched in agony from the heavy pack on her back. Glancing behind them, she saw that Rhys was leaving footprints in the snow covering the lake, but her own tracks were just shallow grooves made by her dragging feet. An exhausted sob tore at her throat, tears froze on her lashes. She wanted to simply give up, but she knew if she stopped, Rhys would—and she couldn't stand the thought of him dying so needlessly. Each time she came close to utter exhaustion, Rhys would notice and call a halt for a few minutes. But they dared not linger too long, for the cold was a constant danger.

"Come on, Alex," Rhys urged, "it's not much farther now. Doesn't that grove of aspen on the hill look familiar to you?"

She nodded, but in reality couldn't tell whether she'd ever seen the trees before or not. The landscape all looked the same to her—bleak, never-ending forest and rugged, snow-hazed hills. And lake . . . miles and miles of treacherous, frozen lake . . .

"Don't give up now, sweetheart," Rhys coaxed, though there was a cautious lilt to his words. "I think I see . . . yes, by God, there's smoke! Smoke, Alex—we're home!"

Nearly swaying with exhaustion, Alex followed his pointing hand and, after a breathless moment, made out the white curl of smoke against the winter sky. Her eyes began to glow above the cloth masking her face.

Her voice quavered as she said, "I'll make it now."

"Yes, it's not far. . . ."

Thirty long minutes passed before they rounded a bend and saw the boat dock in front of Rhys's cabin. His hoarse shouts soon brought Pierre, his hired man, running to greet them.

"I thought you would come today," Pierre exclaimed, lifting the pack from Alex's back. "The ice is solid now."

The short, bulky figure of Jacquetta appeared on the path, and she waved a frantic hello before disappearing into Rhys's cabin. A fresh spurt of white smoke from the chimney told them she was building up the fire in preparation for their arrival, and by the time they stumbled through the front door, she was putting a hot meal on the table.

The plump French-Canadian woman fussed over them as they ate hot soup and dried-apple pie, and then she led Alexandria away for a long, soaking bath. Pierre scurried off to take news of their return to the village before dark, and Rhys fell asleep at the pine table, his head resting on his arms.

Jacquetta woke him and shepherded him into the bathtub, despite his embarrassed protests.

"I am an old woman, and you possess nothing I have not seen before, *monsieur*," she assured him. "If it will make you happier, I will turn my back until you get into the water, but then I am going to scrub you because you are not to get your hands wet."

After his bath, Rhys thanked Jacquetta and shooed her away, telling her he wanted nothing more than to sleep for a week. Alex, looking pale and peaceful in a borrowed nightgown, lay asleep on the big feather bed. Rhys climbed in beside her, carefully slipping an arm beneath her shoulders. She didn't stir as he brushed a kiss against her temple, nor did she hear when he whispered, "You've made me proud of you, Alex . . . proud of the way you've succeeded in becoming a real wilderness woman."

Daylight found Aberdeen and Waldo Anderson tramping the path to Rhys's cabin. Waldo carried a bag containing clothes for Alex, and Aberdeen clutched Nasturtium beneath her cloak.

The Scotswoman paused at the front door just long enough to call out "Ya-hoo!" before entering the cabin and heading unerringly for the bedroom. Waldo followed obediently.

"She's been that restless," Aberdeen said without preamble, marching to the foot of the bed and releasing the gray tiger-striped cat onto the quilts. "I think she has missed you."

Surprised by the unexpected intrusion, Rhys shot into a sitting position and muttered, "What the hell . . . ?"

Then, seeing the cat and remembering her disdain for him in the past, he quickly crossed his arms over his bare chest to protect himself from her claws. But instead of showing her usual hissing impertinence, the cat merely brushed against his arms, purring loudly.

"Ain't it the damnedest . . . er, strangest thing?" queried Waldo, beaming. "Ever since that feline took up with the Pattersons' tomcat, she's been gentle as a lamb."

"T'would appear she has even taken a liking to ye, Mr. Morgan," Aberdeen observed. "Which, from the looks of it, is just as well—since her mistress seems to have done the same thing. Funny how love makes fools of us all."

With a groan, Alex opened her eyes. "Deenie, is that you?"

She sat up, then blushed furiously as she realized she had been discovered in bed with Rhys, certainly a most compromising situation.

"Aye, 'tis me, lass. I've brought you some clothes. Why don't ye put them on while I brew up some tea?" Her black eyes darted to Rhys. "Herbal tea."

Rhys couldn't hold back a roguish grin. "God, Aberdeen, couldn't I have coffee for a change? It seems I've drunk nothing but herbal tea for a week."

Aberdeen sniffed loudly. "Well, I suppose it won't matter what ye drink."

As she turned to leave the room, Rhys spoke again. "Oh, by the way, Aberdeen, while we have our breakfast perhaps you could help us plan a wedding. . . ."

The dour face broke into a merry smile. "Aye." She nodded. "Perhaps I could."

It wasn't until Alex actually heard Rhys discussing the matter with Aberdeen and Waldo that she began to think things could be worked out to the satisfaction of everyone involved.

"If Alex agrees," he said, "I want us to live in my cabin. But I'll bring her to the Falls each morning to open the doctor's office."

"What if there is an emergency durin' the night?" Waldo asked.

"Scotty has a big brass bell at the trading post that could be rung as a signal. It wouldn't take us long to get to the settlement from my place."

"And if Waldo and I live in the doctor's cabin, we can keep eye on patients in the hospital for ye, Aberdeen offered, turning to Alex. "Or ye could even stay the night, if necessary."

"It can be worked out, Alex," Rhys said, laying a bandaged hand over hers. "I promise."

"The only thing . . ." Aberdeen's black eyes fell to her cup of tea. "What if there are bairns?"

"It's not going to be a problem," Rhys stated firmly. "I think I'll be a capable enough father to manage."

"But what if you're busy with your own work?" Alex asked. "Or the baby is fussy? Or ill?"

"If you think it will work better, sweetheart, I'll make an Indian cradleboard, and the baby can go with you."

"Aye . . . and in the meantime, there's always herbal tea." Aberdeen smiled crookedly, a deep blush starting at the collar of her black dress and spreading rapidly to the roots of her severe hairdo. "And perhaps I should . . . ahem, join ye in some right now. I could use a strong cup this morning."

Waldo, too, blushed and had just started to speak when the cabin door was flung open.

"What on earth?" muttered Aberdeen, dropping the china cup she was holding. It hit the planked wooden floor and shattered.

Lily staggered across the threshold, looking like a pale witch with her golden hair tangled wildly about her shoulders, her eyes wide and staring in her colorless face. She had gone out without a cloak, and the plain cotton dress she wore was torn and bloodstained. "Help me! Oh, my God, somebody please help me!"

"Lily, what has happened to you?" Alex leaped to her feet and hurried to the girl's side.

"It's not me," Lily gasped, her breath coming in short, panic-stricken gasps. "It's Pacer. Oh, dear God, I think they've killed him!"

Chapter Twenty

"Waldo, get the others," Rhys commanded, as Alex put her arms around Lily, who was now sobbing hysterically.

"Lily, where is Pacer?" Rhys questioned. "You'll have to calm down long enough to tell us what happened."

"He-he's at our cabin. Oh, Rhys, he was so still! And there was blood everywhere. . . ."

"How did he get injured?"

"That man, Bacconne, he stabbed him over and over. And then he ran off into the woods and left Pacer to die." Lily stared down at her bloodstained hands. "He was too heavy . . . I couldn't lift him."

"The men will go for him," Alex soothed. "You'll see, he'll be all right." She felt a pang of guilt at telling what was probably a blatant lie, but she couldn't let Lily suspect that she doubted Pacer could have survived such an attack.

The men who had been working in the new

community building were the first to arrive, with Waldo in the lead. As they crowded through the door, Rhys said, "It's Pacer. Bacconne tried to kill him. He's been stabbed several times."

"Where is he?"

"At their cabin."

"We'll bring him here."

"I'll go with you," Rhys stated, throwing on his buckskin jacket.

"I'd better go, too," Alex began.

"No . . . please don't leave me," Lily cried, clutching Alex's arm.

"It might be best if you stayed with Lily," Rhys agreed. "Scotty can see to him until we get him to the hospital."

To his surprise, she didn't argue. "I'll have things ready for him," she said. "And in the meantime, I'll try to calm Lily."

They had torn the door from Pacer's cabin to use as a stretcher to carry him back to the settlement. As soon as Lily saw his unmoving form, she screamed and flung herself upon him.

"He's dead," she shrieked.

"No, he's not," Alex said sternly. "I can see his eyelids fluttering. Now, Lily, you'll need to stay out of our way, or Aberdeen will have to take you into the other room. We can't help Pacer with you acting like this."

Reluctantly, the girl backed away, hands over her mouth. "Please don't let him die," she pleaded in a stricken whisper.

"We'll do everything we can for him," Alex promised, indicating the cot where she wanted the men to place Pacer's unconscious body.

"Would someone help me undress him?" she asked quietly, and Scotty moved to her side to begin stripping off the buckskin coat, shirt, and pants. Rhys stood by helplessly, his bandaged hands hanging at his sides.

Paying little attention to him or to the others in the room, Alex began a thorough examination of the young Indian man. Two deep stab wounds scored his chest, while other, less serious gashes covered his arms and thighs. One long, slashing gouge—Bacconne had clearly meant it to disembowel Pacer—had fortunately not been fatal because it had sliced into the hard surface of the hip bone.

"There's another bad wound on his back," Scotty said. "Probably the first Bacconne inflicted, if I know that man's method of attack."

"There were two of them," Rhys explained to her in a low voice. "While Pacer was struggling with the other trapper, Bacconne must have struck from behind. Then, when Pacer turned, the bastard slashed at him like a madman."

"What happened to the other man?" queried Alex, gently probing the bruised edges of one of the chest wounds with her fingertips.

"Pacer killed him. Malachi, Waldo, and John Hay are bringing his body in."

"And Bacconne?"

"He was gone." Rhys cast a glance at Lily, who

stood within the circle of Aberdeen's arm, looking very much as though she could swoon. "But Pacer must have injured him, because he left a trail of blood in the snow. Hardesty and Joe are tracking him."

Alex was unaware of her worried sigh. None of Pacer's injuries were bleeding freely now; most had only slow, sullen blood oozing from them. She shook her head. How many times had she heard her grandfather say that that was a bad sign?

"A puncture wound needs to bleed to cleanse itself," he'd said. "Otherwise, it's filled with poisons that cause high fevers and oftentimes death."

Praying for the best, Alex accepted the basin of soapy water Scotty handed her and began cleansing the lacerations.

It took over an hour to clean the stab wounds, stitch up the worst of them, then apply poultices and bandage the rest. By the time she finished, Alex was literally swaying on her feet, but she refused to rest until she saw Pacer settled as comfortably as possible in one of the narrow hospital beds. Lily sat beside him, a haunted expression still etched on her delicate features.

When Alex was certain she had done all she could for the time being, she allowed Aberdeen to convince her to take a brief nap.

Rhys stood, watching her go, his eyes shadowed and unreadable.

Alex leaned close to Pacer, dismayed by his rapid, shallow breathing. Except for the rise and fall of his chest, he did not move.

"How is he?" Rhys asked, walking into the room to stand at the foot of the bed. "Any change?"

"No, he just lies there." Alex brushed her hair back off her forehead. "At least Aberdeen convinced Lily to eat something and rest for a while. She's worried sick about Pacer."

"Did she tell you what happened out there this morning?"

Alex sighed wearily and sank into the straight-backed chair at the bedside. "Most of it." She plucked idly at the apron she wore over her gray wool gown. "Lily said that Pacer had gone out to check his traps, as usual, and while he was out, Bacconne and the other man broke into the cabin. It seems the two of them had been living in an old deserted shack over on Lecuyer Creek, just waiting for an opportunity for revenge."

"Damn Bacconne to hell," Rhys cursed. "I should have killed him when I had the chance. I've regretted it more than once."

"You couldn't have known he was crazy enough to stay in the area, not after the beating you gave him. Thank God, his other two companions probably went back to Rainy Lake. Pacer would never have stood a chance against four of them."

"They've probably been watching the settlement for weeks," Rhys muttered. "Waiting until they thought we'd forgotten about them."

414

Alex shuddered. "I remember how Bacconne stared at Lily that night. . . ."

"Did he hurt her?" Rhys's sharp question jolted her out of her unpleasant meditation.

"No, thank heavens. He slapped her and tore her clothes, but before . . . before anything could happen, her screams brought Pacer. The other man was standing guard at the door, and that's why Pacer fought with him first. He killed him with a hunting knife, but Bacconne came at him from behind, just as Scotty thought."

"Yes, that would be his way."

"Pacer told Lily to go for help, but she only hid outside the cabin until Bacconne was gone," Alex said. "Otherwise, he might have killed her, too."

A low, keening moan issued from Pacer's lips as he turned his head on the pillow. Despite the movement, his eyes remained closed.

"Do you think he is going to make it, Alex?"

"I simply don't know. He's hurt so badly."

"Well, he's in good hands," Rhys stated firmly.

Surprised, Alex glanced up into his face. After a moment, she said, "Thank you."

With a nod and a promise to remain close by, Rhys slipped out of the room.

Sometime after midnight, Alex, dozing in the chair at Pacer's bedside, was startled awake by a savage cry.

"Don't touch my wife, you bastard! Get your hands off her!"

Pacer was sitting up in the bed, his handsome face distorted by a look of stark hatred. His glazed eyes stared into the darkness at the end of the bed. "I'll kill you," he shouted, starting to rise.

"No," breathed Alex, leaping to her feet and placing her hands on his shoulders. "Pacer, you mustn't get out of bed." She turned her head and yelled for help.

"Aaaeeiii!" Pacer screamed. "You'll die for that!"

The young half-Indian trapper was filled with an inhuman strength. He shoved aside the blankets and swung his legs over the side of the bed. Frantically, Alex threw herself across his naked body, pushing him back onto the mattress.

"No, Pacer. You've got to stay quiet. You don't know what you're doing."

He shook her off like a pesky insect, knocking her against the wall, where she slid weakly to the floor. Growling curses, Pacer got unsteadily to his feet. Just as Alex picked herself up, Rhys and Waldo burst into the room.

"What in the hell is happenin'?" Waldo cried.

"He's delirious," Alex replied. "We'll need to restrain him."

It took both men to get Pacer back into the bed, and then Rhys had to continue holding him down while Alex administered laudanum and checked the bandages.

Lily, looking fragile in one of Aberdeen's long white nightgowns, appeared at the door, her frightened eyes going swiftly to her husband's face.

"What's wrong?" she whispered.

416

"Pacer's out of his mind with fever, Lily," Alex said. "He wants to get out of bed."

"He'll listen to me," the small woman said with assurance. She lay down beside Pacer and began stroking his forehead, murmuring soothing endearments into his ear. Though he never roused from his delirium, Lily's presence seemed to calm and reassure him.

But sleep, when it came, was far from peaceful. Pacer trembled and moaned beneath the onslaught of terrifying dreams.

"He's burning up with fever," Alex murmured.

"What can we do?" asked Rhys.

"Wait it out," she said quietly. "Look, you've hurt yourself." She reached for one of his hands, indicating the blood that had seeped through the cloth.

"It's nothing," Rhys insisted, but when he would have pulled away, she retained her grip on his wrist.

"Let me see it, please. I know you must be hurting."

Wryly, Rhys reflected that in one way or another he had been hurting since the first day he'd met Alexandria MacKenzie. Of course, that hurt had been all mixed up with the purest joys of his life.

Fatigue, as well as a number of unnamed emotions, curled through Rhys's body, rendering him vulnerable to her soothing touch. He allowed her to lead him into the kitchen, where she pushed him down on the high-backed bench and began unwinding his bandages.

"They seem better," she said brightly, but the

compassion that shone in her eyes told him she wasn't pleased by what she saw.

"Maybe so, but they hurt like hell." He let his mouth curve upward into a slight smile. "How long before I'm going to be able to do anything with these hands? The others are getting tired of me just supervising the work on the community hall."

"Let's leave them bandaged for a few more days—then we'll see."

"Whatever you say."

Alex went into her office for gauze, and when she returned, she sat down beside Rhys and drew his hands onto her lap. Carefully, she began applying thick, soft yellow salve to his burns, and again, her touch pacified and heartened him. He would have given everything he owned to be able to carry her away to bed at that moment. They both needed twelve hours of uninterrupted sleep, and after that, he needed to tell her what was in his mind and, more importantly, his heart. He needed to love her, needed to know she returned his love.

But it was impossible. In the next room a good man and close friend battled death. Whatever their private dilemmas, these were of no significance compared to that fact. There would be time for them later. Right now it was essential to secure time for Pacer and Lily.

When Alex was finished, Rhys put his newly bandaged hands on either side of her face and tilted it up to receive the soft kiss he brushed across her lips.

"Promise me you'll get some sleep now?"

She nodded. "I'll try. What about you?"

He indicated a blanket spread near the hearth. "This is where I'll be sleeping. I'll hear Lily if she calls."

Alex's gray eyes regarded him soberly, but she didn't say any of the things he knew must be on her mind. She, too, realized the time wasn't right.

"Good night, Rhys," she said quietly.

Pacer's fever didn't abate by morning and, if anything, grew worse as the day went on. Alex and Lily took turns bathing him with cool water and dribbling small amounts of a tisane down his throat, in an effort to cool his burning body.

Pacer thrashed and mumbled and fought imaginary demons. But he didn't get better. He didn't recognize any of those who hovered over his bed, not even his distraught young wife. By nightfall, worry and despair had driven Lily into a stuporous state, and Alex had no choice but to administer sleeping drops and send her off to rest, despite her pitiful protests.

"It won't do you or Pacer any good if you collapse," she'd said, with more conviction than she really felt. "Aberdeen and I will sit with him tonight, then you'll be ready to take over in the morning."

Waldo and Aberdeen took the first watch, sharing the duty of sponging Pacer's heated flesh—all they could do for him at that point. At midnight, Alex sent the older couple off to bed and began her own determined vigil. She was holding on to the last threads of hope with every bit of strength in her soul.

A wooden rocking chair had been placed next to the hospital bed, and now Alex sat in it, head back, eyes closed. It was that time of night she hated most—the long, lonely hours after midnight when dawn was still just a wishful thought. In moments like these the human spirit was most frail and defenseless, she suspected, most unable to keep morbid fears at bay.

Pacer stirred and groaned, mumbling Lily's name in his sleep, and Alex leaned forward to look at him, laying a hand across his burning forehead. Damn the fever! Would it never let up?

She poured fresh water into the basin at the bedside and, wringing out a cloth, began to gently bathe his face. His handsome features, the result of his French-Canadian and Indian heritage, were striking framed by the straight ebony hair against the pillow. Though he looked as if he might have been hewn from the native granite, Alex knew all too well how mortal he really was—and how quickly flesh and blood could be conquered by the dark powers of death.

Folding back the bedcovers, she stroked the cool cloth across his wide shoulders and down the sinewy arms lying so impotently at his sides. There was so much passion and gentleness contained within the inert body before her—how could anything happen to someone as vitally alive as Pacer had always been?

Alex remembered that first night at Fort Kaministiquia, when he had come forward to claim his bride. His black eyes had glowed with a mixture of awe and possessive pride as he'd touched Lily's bright hair. And on the journey to Sabaskong, he'd barely let her out of his sight, carrying her over the portages, singing to her in French as their canoe glided along the waterways. Though their marriage had seemed like the mating of an eagle with a small, golden finch, Pacer and Lily had found a secure aerie in their love for each other.

And now, their happiness being threatened this way was more than Alex could bear. What could she do? How could she give them back all they were in danger of losing? She dropped the cloth into the basin and pulled the quilts over Pacer again. If only she were more experienced . . . if only there was something she could do besides simply sit and wait.

With a soft, anguished cry, she buried her face in her hands. She hated being so helpless!

Rhys had stood in the doorway, silently watching Alex as she worked over her patient. She was dressed in her nightgown and a dark green flannel wrapper, the candlelight making her unbound hair a vivid halo around her head. She was lovely but fragile-looking—and very, very tired.

When she sank back into the chair, her face in her hands, he could stand it no longer. He strode into the room, her name a harsh murmur on his lips. At the sound, she sprang to her feet, her eyes wide and frightened. Her shadow danced erratically across the log-beamed ceiling.

"Sweetheart, I didn't mean to scare you," he said, his hands resting on her shoulders. She immediately clutched at the sleeves of his buckskin shirt.

"I don't know what to do, Rhys," she cried softly. "Pacer's just going to lie there and die—and I don't know what to do!"

"You've done everything you could," he assured her.

"No, there must be something else. Why can't I think? Why don't I know more about medicine?"

"Alex . . ."

"I'm ignorant!" A sob caught in her throat. "God, I'm not fit to be a doctor."

Oblivious to the pain it caused his hands, Rhys seized her and pulled her hard against his chest. Deep, wrenching sobs shook her body as he held her, one hand stroking her fiery hair.

"Shh, Alex," he soothed. "You don't know what you're saying . . . you're just tired and upset. Shh, now."

He rested his cheek against the top of her head and when he spoke again, his breath was warm and comforting as it fluttered over her. "Don't tell me you're not a doctor," he lovingly scolded. "I know better. I've been watching you for the past two days, sweetheart. I've seen how you've neglected yourself to care for a friend. How you've gone without food or enough sleep so you could stay by his side. I've seen your skills, love, and more importantly, I've seen your fears. No, don't expect me to believe you're not one damned fine doctor, Alexandria MacKenzie, because you are."

She raised a tear-stained face. "Do you honestly mean that?"

"I honestly do." He kissed her damp eyelids. "Hell, I've seen doctors with more years of experience than your lifetime totals, but without the gifts of compassion and love, experience doesn't matter a bit. You may have reached the end of your practical knowledge, Alex, but you haven't given up—you've just resorted to the more womanly devices of hope and prayer. And it occurs to me those are the very attributes that set a truly dedicated physician apart from an ordinary one."

"Thank you," she whispered, resting her face against the steady beat of his heart. "But, Rhys, I won't be able to stand it if Pacer dies."

"Yes, you will. You'll have to. That's another part of being a doctor. But don't give up too easily. Pacer's young and strong, and he's had good care. Let's have a little faith, shall we?"

She gave him a watery smile and a brief nod. "I'm just tired, that's all."

"And why wouldn't you be? Come here. . . ." He lowered himself into the rocking chair and drew her down onto his lap, wrapping the quilt about her. "Now, you just lean on me and rest. I'll wake you if Pacer needs anything."

423

With a grateful sigh, Alex snuggled close to his big, warm body and accepted the solace he offered. As always, it felt good to simply relax and let Rhys take care of her.

Some time later, Alex shifted positions in her sleep, and with her face against his throat, mumbled, "I love you, Rhys."

Something cold and unyielding that had been within him since he was a boy, slowly melted and disappeared, leaving him with a breathtaking feeling of freedom. Freedom to love — freedom to live as man is supposed to live.

"That's all I needed to know, sweetheart," he whispered, tucking the quilt more securely about her slender shoulders. "And now that I know it for certain, I'll never let you go."

Tenderly, he kissed her temple. "Never."

Lily woke them the next morning when she came to sit with her husband. She looked pale but refreshed. A grave smile came to her lips at finding the two of them sleeping peacefully together in the chair.

"Pacer isn't so feverish today," she announced, brushing the dark hair back from his forehead. "Perhaps he is going to start getting better now."

"Aye, that's what we'll pray for," said Aberdeen from the doorway. "Rhys, Alex, I've got some breakfast for the two of ye. Come along and eat."

"I'll call if I need you," Lily promised.

For the first time in several days, Alex ate a

hearty meal, surprised at how good fried ham and oat porridge could taste. She and Rhys were just finishing a last cup of coffee when Waldo came out of the back bedroom. His face was still pink from its morning shave.

"Damn . . . er, Lord, but it smells good out here," he said, pausing to give Aberdeen a smacking kiss on one thin cheek. "How's my little wifie today?"

Aberdeen blushed, but did not push him away. "Och, go on with ye, man. Ye're becomin' as sweet as a clootie dumpling. Ye don't act like yerself at all!"

Waldo winked at Rhys and Alex. Then, giving Aberdeen a surreptitious pinch on the bottom, he poured himself a mug of coffee and sat down at the table.

"How's Pacer this morning?" he asked. "Any change?"

"Not much," Alex answered. "However, we're . . . hopeful."

He nodded as Aberdeen placed a steaming bowl of porridge in front of him. "That's good." He spooned maple sugar over the cereal, then reached for the pitcher of milk.

There was a knock on the door, and Aberdeen opened it to admit Joseph Patterson and Hardesty Ames. Obviously cold and tired, the men were immediately drawn to the fireplace.

"We just got back," Hardesty said, rubbing a hand over his haggard features. "That bastard Bacconne won't be causing any more trouble. Pardon my language, ladies."

"No need to polish up your language on our accounts," snapped Aberdeen. "The man was a bastard."

"What happened to him?" Alex questioned.

"He's dead," Patterson said in clipped tones as he reached for the mug of coffee Aberdeen handed him.

"How?" Rhys quietly asked.

"It was the dangdest thing," Patterson continued. "Hardesty and I tracked him from Pacer's cabin—he was cut up some, leavin' a pretty good trail of blood. Anyway, we caught up with him about two miles down Lecuyer Creek. Seems Pacer had been trackin' a big black bear that'd been snoopin' around his place—he'd set a trap, and damned if ol' Bacconne didn't step right into it. Don't know how long he laid there before the bear got wind of him, but sometime or other, that animal went after him. Tore him to pieces."

"Oh, Lord." Alex's voice was faint.

Bacconne was one of the most evil men she had ever met, but she wondered if anyone deserved to die in such a horrible way.

"And between the bear mauling him and hungry timber wolves, there wasn't much left to recognize," Hardesty explained, digging into his pocket and tossing an object onto the table. "Only this."

Alex stared at the gaudy, beaded hoop Bacconne had worn in his ear. With a shudder, she remembered it dragging across her face and tangling in her hair the night he had attacked her.

426

"Not much left to bury, either," Joe commented. "We just put his body in that old shack and burned it."

Waldo took a huge bite of ham. "Better'n he deserved."

Aberdeen tapped him on the shoulder. "Don't talk with yer mouth full, ye great gowk."

"I beg yer pardon, dovie." Waldo beamed at her before turning back to Rhys and Alex. "I don't reckon anyone is sorry to see the last of Robber Bacconne. He caused more than his share of trouble around here."

"That he did," Rhys agreed.

"I only hope—" Alex's words were interrupted by Lily's high scream.

"Alex! Oh, my God, Alex, come quickly!"

"Pacer," Alex breathed, a stricken look on her face.

"Easy, love," Rhys cautioned, following her toward the hospital room. She stopped abruptly in the doorway, and he bumped softly against her rigid back.

Looking past her shoulder, Rhys started to grin, then chuckle, and in a moment was laughing aloud.

Pacer, still unhealthily pale for a man of mixed blood, was sitting upright, propped against the metal headboard of the bed. One arm was looped around his wife's waist as he held her across his chest for a kiss that should have sapped what strength he had left.

Blushing, laughing, and crying all at one time,

Lily disentangled herself from Pacer's grip and stood, her face transformed by joy. "Just a minute ago," she told them, breathlessly, "Pacer woke up and said my name. His fever's gone, and he says he feels fine."

"Thank God," Alex cried. "Oh, thank God!"

"Welcome back to the land of the living, man," Rhys said, his mouth quirking in a relieved smile.

"Good to be here," Pacer said.

"Are ye hungry, laddie?" asked Aberdeen, leaning around Rhys's shoulder.

Pacer grinned, then reached for Lily's hand. "Starved," he said.

Crawling carefully onto the bed beside him, Lily draped her arms around Pacer and lifted a tear-streaked face for his fervent kiss.

Alex cleared her throat. "Come along," she said to the others, "let's leave them alone. I think our patient is going to live."

Alex awoke slowly, feeling better than she had in days. She yawned and stretched languorously. The rosy sky outside the window told her that the day was nearly gone—no wonder she felt so rested.

The moment she had declared Pacer out of danger, Rhys had swept her into his arms and carried her away to his cabin. He had, he insisted, spent his last night alone.

Alex smiled as she recalled how feverishly they had made love. Then, pleasantly exhausted, they had fallen asleep, awakening later to make love

428

again, that time with a slow, deliberate tenderness. She turned her head to look at Rhys's empty pillow, wondering where he had gone.

Just as she sat up in bed, preparing to toss aside the covers, the bedroom door was flung open to bang noisily against the wall. A tall figure stood there, outlined by the fire from the other room.

"Rhys?" she murmured uncertainly.

"No, *mademoiselle* . . . it is me."

He came closer and her heart jolted in terror as she gazed up at the man clad in bloodstained buckskins. Bacconne!

"Ah, you did not expect to see me again, eh?"

"I . . . I thought you were dead," Alex whispered. "We all did."

Never had she seen anything as frightening as this man's face, his features etched with evil, his eyes glowing with the deep, flickering fires of madness.

"That is what I wanted you to think." He came a step closer to the bed, and she shrank back.

"But whose body . . . ?"

He laughed. "A former companion, shall we say? He chose not to return to Rainy Lake, but when we decided to take the wife of the half-breed trapper, he lost his nerve. I killed him and left his body for the wild animals. If the trapper hadn't discovered him and realized something was wrong, we could have seized the golden-haired Lily and been on our way. It was unfortunate that he chose to return too soon, eh?"

Alex's fascinated gaze moved over Bacconne's

horribly scarred face, coming to rest on a jagged tear down the earlobe once adorned by the dangling earring. Bacconne chuckled as he gently touched the swollen ear.

"My friend—he tore off the earring just before I cut out his heart. I left the trinket in the snow beside his body, hoping he would be mistaken for me. The smell of his blood drew the animals, and in the end, my plan worked well enough, did it not?"

"Why did you come here?" Alex asked abruptly. "Why aren't you fleeing for your life?"

"Oh, I intend to do that, *mademoiselle*, but first I have a score to settle with your man. It is a pity he is not here. . . ." He reached out to run a filthy, blood-caked finger down the sleeve of her nightgown. "Of course, his absence gives me the chance to deal with you while I wait to kill him."

Alex jerked her arm away and slid to the far side of the bed. "I will not submit to you, Bacconne, no matter what."

"Oh, come now, little one. I have been hiding in the forest for two days, I'm hungry and tired, my arm burns like fire where the trapper slashed me. Surely you cannot think I am interested in your body?"

"Then . . . what do you want?"

"I have to kill you, *mademoiselle*. I do not have the strength to enjoy you now, nor can I take you with me." His fingers began their habitual caress of the hilt of the hunting knife at his hip. "But I do not forget the insults you have given Bacconne in

430

the past. And I do not forget the way Morgan humiliated me." Slowly, he drew the knife from its leather sheath. "I am going to cut your pretty throat and leave you for your lover to find. Then, as he kneels over you in grief, I will strike."

Alex closed her eyes and fought off the nausea envisioning Bacconne stabbing Rhys in the back had brought on. She struggled to stay calm, knowing it was the only way she could outwit this man. When she opened her eyes again, they were filled with determination. Somehow, she had to get past Bacconne and out of the bedroom. She had to warn Rhys.

Unexpectedly, Bacconne lunged, and with a cry, Alex leaped from the bed and ran. She heard his mad laughter, and fear rippled up and down her spine. Just as she reached the kitchen, Bacconne seized a handful of hair and spun her around, pressing her back against the log wall. Alex gasped in pain, and lifted her chin to ease his hold on her hair. Instantly, she felt the sharp point of the knife pricking the flesh below her ear. Her heart all but stopped as she waited for him to end her life then and there. Rather than overpowering fear, a thousand memories of Rhys filled her mind.

After a long moment, Bacconne spoke, his breath foul against her face. "Ah, but you make it too easy, *mademoiselle*. Bacconne, he likes a challenge. You cannot expect me to enjoy killing you without a little fight, eh?"

He lowered the knife and stepped away from her, loosening his hold on her hair. Alex leaned against

431

the wall breathing heavily.

"I deeply regret having to kill someone as beautiful as you, Alexandria. Sacrebleu! What a picture you make standing there in your nightgown, your hair so fiery about your perfect face. Ah, you should have been my woman. . . ."

Regaining her composure, Alex began sidling away from him. Bacconne let her go, his undamaged eye glittering with excitement, his mouth twisting in a sly smile.

"That's right, little one, you must try to escape me. Let me enjoy the terror in your eyes just a while longer."

Alex judged the distance to the door, but he sensed her purpose and stepped in front of it. Forcing back panic, she glanced around the room, seeking a weapon. Bacconne was not foolish enough to allow her to leave the cabin; she would simply have to stand her ground. Rhys's musket hung over the mantel, but even if she could get it down, she knew nothing about loading or firing it. She thought of the kettle of steaming water hanging from the fireplace crane, wondering if she could possibly snatch it up and fling it into Bacconne's face. Her hands clenched and unclenched as she imagined his howls of pain and fury, but there was no other choice. Stealthily, she began to step backward, closer to the fire, and Bacconne followed, stalking her like woodland prey.

"It pleases me that you are frightened," he said, brandishing the knife in a wide arc. "You are like a doe, poised for flight . . . and yet, *mademoiselle,*

432

you know there is no place for you to run, eh?"

As Alex whirled toward the fire, her hand reaching for the teakettle, Bacconne snarled a curse and, grabbing her shoulder, flung her away from the fireplace. She fell across the table and before she could move, he was there, bending over her, his chest pressing into her back. With one hand, he grasped her chin and pulled her head up, exposing her throat. He uttered a sinister growl as he placed the edge of the knife blade against her thrumming pulse.

"Do you think I am so stupid," he hissed, "that I didn't know what you were going to try?"

"I-I don't know what you mean. . . ."

Cruelly, he forced her head higher, and through the dizzying pain, Alex thought her neck would surely break. She was scarcely aware of the sound of the door opening.

"Alex!" Rhys's voice was tinged with horror. "What the hell . . . ?"

When Bacconne released her, Alex slumped upon the table, fighting for breath. Weak relief flowed through her. Rhys had come in time.

She heard the shock in Rhys's voice as Bacconne turned to face him. "You! I should have known you weren't dead. You're too goddamned mean to die easily."

"You will wish you could say the same for yourself, *monsieur*," Bacconne sneered. "I am going to carve you into pieces with this knife."

"Not if I kill you first," Rhys vowed.

Bacconne's harsh laughter rang through the

cabin. "And how will you kill me, Morgan? A gun . . . a knife? Perhaps you will strangle me? Tell me, how does a man with bandages on his hands go about slaying someone?"

Alex's low moan echoed in her own ears. My God, she had forgotten about Rhys's hands—he couldn't defend himself! She pushed away from the table and met Rhys's gaze. The realization of his helplessness haunted his dark eyes.

Before she could devise any plan, Bacconne threw himself at Rhys, the hunting knife raised high in the air. Using his arms to protect his face, Rhys kicked out, his foot catching Bacconne in the groin.

"Aagh," the French Canadian groaned, going down on one knee. "You . . . you will die like a pig for that."

"Alex, get out of here," Rhys cried. "Run to safety!"

Cursing and moaning, Bacconne staggered to his feet, his black eyes gleaming with hatred and blood lust. He lurched toward Rhys, the knife slashing through the air with lethal precision. Rhys backed away, trying to get into position to kick out with his foot again, but Bacconne was attacking so swiftly he could do little more than try to stay out of range of the deadly blade.

Enjoying the chance to toy with his intended victim, Bacconne made short, stabbing motions toward Rhys's chest. Instinctively, Rhys threw up his hands to shield himself, and, with an evil laugh, Bacconne turned the blade and used the flat side to strike Rhys's bandaged palms. With a cry, Rhys sank to the floor, his body hunched over his now-bleeding hands. Behind them, Alex screamed, and cursing, Rhys tried to get to his feet.

Frozen in terror, Alex watched Bacconne raise the knife in order to plunge it into Rhys's unguarded neck.

"No!" she whispered, and felt her body surge with energy—and with a renewed desire for life. Not for herself but for Rhys.

Almost without realizing what she was doing, her hand closed around the heavy iron poker leaning against the stones of the fireplace. For a brief moment, she looked down at it. As a doctor, she had taken an oath to save lives, not take them. Never had she foreseen this moment. She wondered if she possessed whatever it took to kill a man.

She lifted the poker and swung it with every ounce of strength she had, striking the back of Bacconne's head. He pitched forward, taking Rhys down with him.

Alex stared at his bleeding head a few seconds, then took a deep breath.

"You bitch," Bacconne screamed, suddenly lumbering to his feet. "I should have killed you when I had the chance." His palsied hands grasped at her throat.

She raised the poker again, and this time, it smashed into the handsome, unscarred side of his face, sending him reeling against the fireplace. She knew she would have swung the poker over and over, had it been necessary, but thankfully, Bac-

435

conne's head had struck the hearth with a sickening impact, and he lay unmoving and still.

Alex let the poker clatter to the floor. Rhys had struggled to his feet and now took her into his arms, resting his head against the top of her tangled hair.

"It's all over," he soothed. "Thanks to your courage, it's over at last."

Several hours later, as Rhys and Alex stood at the bedroom window gazing out at the moon-silvered snow, the peacefulness of the winter night flowed over them like a soothing balm.

Rhys slipped an arm about her shoulders, and she turned to cling to him for a long moment. When she finally stirred, she looked up at him and murmured, "The past few days have taught me something very important, Rhys."

He brushed her mouth with his own. "What is that, sweetheart?"

"It isn't weak to need someone." She tilted her head and gave him a slow smile. "For so long, I thought I had to be independent to be happy. Now I see that needing someone, loving someone — well, that's what makes a person strong and . . . and brave."

"I think we've both learned something about giving and taking," Rhys said quietly. "And though we've had to discover it the hard way, we each know there'll be times when you or I will be the strong one . . . times when one of us will simply have to trust in the other's care."

"I like the sound of that," Alex whispered, standing on tiptoe to press a kiss at each corner of his mouth.

"Enough to put up with it for a lifetime?"

"More than enough."

Rhys bent his head to thoroughly kiss her, but just before their lips met, he murmured, "Then, Alexandria Mackenzie . . . Morgan, welcome to the wilderness forever."

Epilogue

Rhys Morgan stood just inside the door of the new Sabaskong Falls community building and felt a sense of undeniable pride that Alex had been instrumental in its creation. Decorated with flowers and streamers, it was filled to overflowing with residents of the settlement, for the Reverend Isaac Johnstone had arrived the night before, and today there would be three weddings and a christening.

Smiling complacently, Rhys let his eyes roam around the room. Birdie and Cordelia were supervising the arrangement of food for the supper that would follow the ceremonies, issuing good-natured orders to their husbands, John Hay and Malachi Harper. Mellicent Braunswager was serving the tall, raw-boned minister a cup of tea, while a jovial Albert amused the man with one of his renowned stories.

At the opposite end of the room, Toby and Annie Marsh were proudly showing their mother and stepfather some of their school papers, which had been tacked to the wall by their teacher. Claire and Gideon, holding hands, smiled indulgently at each other over the children's heads. Nearby, Lily had taken a primer from the bookshelves and was demonstrating her new skill to Pacer, who beamed at her as though she had invented reading. Through the long winter months, the trapper's wounds had healed, and under Lily's devoted care—or in spite of it, Rhys thought, his grin widening—he had regained his strength.

Hardesty and Judith Ames were seated on one of the benches lining the wall, Hardesty looking on with interest while Judith knitted a small garment. Each time Rhys saw her, he was startled anew at the astonishing prettiness that had settled upon Judith's rather homely features in the last few months. The heavier with child she became, the more graceful and feminine she appeared, and the prospect of becoming a father had mellowed Hardesty, as had his wife's obvious contentment.

In fact, Rhys reflected, not one of the brides had shown any desire to return to Montreal, even after five months of winter, when snow had drifted to the windowsills, discouraging socializing. And now throughout the north country it was Rendezvous time, but the men of Sabaskong Falls and their wives had been content to remain at Lake of the Woods, hiring a group of unmarried trappers to travel to the fort for supplies.

A strange wailing cry caught his attention, and Rhys whirled about with the inborn caution of a woodsman. He had to hide a smile as he realized the noise was issuing from the mouth of two-week-old Andrew Robert McPherson III, the child who would be baptized that day. As Rhys watched, Scotty leaned forward to twine a finger in his son's red-gold curls and plant a fond kiss on his wife's glowing cheek. Christiana had amazed them all by growing stronger through each month of her pregnancy, delivering her child with an ease that left Alexandria speechless.

But then, Alex's continued determination to be a doctor had provided her with another major surprise. Following Pacer's recovery, the men of Sabaskong had slowly, but surely, turned to her for medical care and advice. Just recently, even Albert Braunswager had sauntered into her office, a sheepish smile on his face. He'd been forced to ask her to lance a particularly troublesome carbuncle on his left buttock, and before the day was out, the big German had spread word of her remarkable skill from one end of the settlement to the other.

"Where's your little redhead, Rhys?" Waldo asked, as he and Aberdeen strolled up. "Me and Scotty are anxious to get this wedding business underway."

"Aye, so am I," agreed Aberdeen, appearing much younger in a pale blue gown. "But come to think of it, I haven't seen Alex since yesterday when I visited her office to tell her I was thinking of giving up herbal tea for the rest of the summer." She smiled coyly at the scrawny trapper by her side, and he nearly choked.

"Giving up yer tea?" he gasped. "Woman, can you mean it?"

"Indeed I do, ye great gowk. I'm no' gettin' any younger, ye know."

"I'll go fetch Alex," Rhys interjected, realizing they weren't hearing a word he said. "She told me she needed something from the doctor's office."

As he stepped out into the sunshine, Rhys took in the view of majestic pines and glittering lake. He'd come to appreciate the beauties of the wilderness even more this past year. That, like all the other good things in his life, could be attributed directly to Alex.

As he strode down the path toward the doctor's cabin, he recalled awakening with her in his arms that morning. Rosy with sleep, she had turned to kiss him.

"It looks like a beautiful day for a wedding," he had murmured against her mouth. She had sat upright in the bed.

"Oh, my goodness, I've got to get busy! There are still a dozen things to be done."

"Can't they wait?" he'd asked, letting his fingers trail along the side of her neck, hesitating and then deliberately unfastening the row of tiny buttons down the front of her nightgown.

"Rhys," she had laughingly protested.

But his hand had slipped inside the garment to cup and fondle one warm breast, teasing her into ardent willingness. With a delighted sigh, she drew his head down for a lingering kiss.

"They'll wait," she'd said.

By the time Rhys found her outside the doctor's cabin, he was bemused and more than a little anxious to get through the wedding ceremony and hurry his wife back home.

"They're waiting on us, sweetheart," he said in his graveled voice. "What are you doing?"

"Picking flowers for my wedding bouquet," she replied, indicating the armful of deep purple, lavender, and yellow pansies she had just gathered from the overflowing window boxes. "Heart's ease." With a smile, she sniffed them. "Remember when I told you this place was going to bring me heart's ease?" she asked softly. "I want you to know that it truly has."

"I'm glad. Because that's what you have brought me, too."

For a long moment, Rhys gazed at his bride. She was achingly lovely in an ivory satin gown that seemed to set fire to her glorious hair and turn her skin to fine silk. When he leaned down to kiss her, he could see the purple of the flowers reflected in her eyes, along with all the heartfelt love any man had a right to expect. He curved one hand along her jaw, and she turned her face to kiss his scarred hand.

"We've been through so much together, haven't we?" she asked.

"Yes, all of it good. Even the bad." He grinned broadly. "And now, let's go get married."

Taking her arm, he led her off the porch, just in time to witness the solemn and stately procession Nasturtium, the Pattersons' yellow tom, and their brood of multicolored kittens made as they pranced by, tails straight in the air.

Rhys laughed and shook his head. "There must be something in the water around this place."

"Oh, that reminds me," Alex murmured. "After all these months, don't you suppose your hands are well enough for you to start work on one of those cradleboards?"

Abruptly, Rhys stopped walking.

Alex moved on down the path a few steps before turning to give him a slow, teasing smile.

"Come along, Mr. Morgan, or we'll be late for our wedding."

"Good God, Alex," he growled. "When will I ever learn what to expect from you?"

Even as he said the words, he knew it was something he really didn't want to learn. His life with Alexandria would be filled with sweet love, easy laughter and delightful surprises. And that was something he had waited a long time for.

It had, his heart told him, been worth the wait.

FIERY ROMANCE

CALIFORNIA CARESS   (2771, $3.75)
by Rebecca Sinclair

Hope Bennett was determined to save her brother's life. And if that meant paying notorious gunslinger Drake Frazier to take his place in a fight, she'd barter her last gold nugget. But Hope soon discovered she'd have to give the handsome rattlesnake more than riches if she wanted his help. His improper demands infuriated her; even as she luxuriated in the tantalizing heat of his embrace, she refused to yield to her desires.

ARIZONA CAPTIVE   (2718, $3.75)
by Laree Bryant

Logan Powers had always taken his role as a lady-killer very seriously and no woman was going to change that. Not even the breathtakingly beautiful Callie Nolan with her luxuriant black hair and startling blue eyes. Logan might have considered a lusty romp with her but it was apparent she was a lady, through and through. Hard as he tried, Logan couldn't resist wanting to take her warm slender body in his arms and hold her close to his heart forever.

DECEPTION'S EMBRACE   (2720, $3.75)
by Jeanne Hansen

Terrified heiress Katrina Montgomery fled Memphis with what little she could carry and headed west, hiding in a freight car. By the time she reached Kansas City, she was feeling almost safe . . . until the handsomest man she'd ever seen entered the car and swept her into his embrace. She didn't know who he was or why he refused to let her go, but when she gazed into his eyes, she somehow knew she could trust him with her life . . . and her heart.

Available wherever paperbacks are sold, or order direct from the Publisher. Send cover price plus 50¢ per copy for mailing and handling to Zebra Books, Dept. 3175, 475 Park Avenue South, New York, N.Y. 10016. Residents of New York, New Jersey and Pennsylvania must include sales tax. DO NOT SEND CASH.

HISTORICAL ROMANCES BY VICTORIA THOMPSON

BOLD TEXAS EMBRACE   (2835, $4.50)
Art teacher Catherine Eaton could hardly believe how stubborn
Sam Connors was! Even though the rancher's young stepbrother
was an exceptionally talented painter, Sam forbade Catherine to
instruct him, fearing that art would make a sissy out of him.
Spunky and determined, the blond schoolmarm confronted the
muleheaded cowboy . . . only to find that he was as handsome as
he was hard-headed and as desirable as he was dictatorial. Before
long she had nearly forgotten what she'd come for, as Sam's
brash, breathless embrace drove from her mind all thought of
anything save wanting him . . .

TEXAS BLONDE   (2183, $3.95)
When dashing Josh Logan resuced her from death by exposure,
petite Felicity Morrow realized she'd never survive rugged frontier
life without a man by her side. And when she gazed at the Texas
rancher's lean hard frame and strong rippling muscles, the determined beauty decided he was the one for her. To reach her goal,
feisty Felicity pretended to be meek and mild: the only kind of gal
Josh proclaimed he'd wed. But after she'd won his hand, the blue-
eyed temptress swore she'd quit playing his game — and still win
his heart!

ANGEL HEART   (2426, $3.95)
Ever since Angelica's father died, Harlan Snyder had been an-
gling to get his hands on her ranch, the Diamond R. And now,
just when she had an important government contract to fulfill,
she couldn't find a single cowhand to hire on — all because of Snyder's threats. It was only a matter of time before she lost the
ranch. . . . That is, until the legendary gunfighter Kid Collins
turned up on her doorstep, badly wounded. Angelica assessed his
firmly muscled physique and stared into his startling blue eyes.
Beneath all that blood and dirt he was the handsomest man she
had ever seen, and the one person who could help her beat Snyder
at his own game — if the price were not too high. . . .

*Available wherever paperbacks are sold, or order direct from the
Publisher. Send cover price plus 50¢ per copy for mailing and
handling to Zebra Books, Dept. 3175, 475 Park Avenue South,
New York, N.Y. 10016. Residents of New York, New Jersey and
Pennsylvania must include sales tax. DO NOT SEND CASH.*

SUMMER LOVE WITH SYLVIE SOMMERFIELD

FIRES OF SURRENDER   (3034, $4.95)
Kathryn Mcleod's beloved Scotland had just succumbed to the despised James IV. The auburn-haired beauty braced herself for the worst as the conquering forces rode in her town, but *nothing* could have prepared her for Donovan McAdam. The handsome knight triumphed over her city and her heart as well! She vowed to resist him forever, but her traitorous heart and flesh had other ideas.

AUTUMN DOVE   (2547, $3.95)
Tara Montgomery had no choice but to reunite with her soldier brother after their parents died. The independent beauty never dreamed of the journey's perils, or the handsome halfbreed wagonmaster Zach Windwalker. He despised women who traveled alone; she found him rude and arrogant. They should have hated each other forever, yet their hunger was too strong to deny. With only the hills and vast plains as witnesses, Zach and Tara discover a love hotter than the summer sun.

PASSION'S RAGING STORM   (2754, $4.50)
Flame-haired Gillian Kendricks was known to the Underground Railroad only as "the Guardian Angel." In reality she was a young Philadelphia beauty with useful connections which she doesn't hesitate to use to further her secret cause. But when she tries to take advantage of her acquaintance with the very handsome Lt. Shane Greyson who carries vital papers to Washington, her plan backfires. For the dark-haired lieutenant doesn't miss much. And the price of deceit is passion!